D1256099

Valhalla

ALAN ROBERT CLARK

Fairlight Books

First published by Fairlight Books 2020

Fairlight Books
Summertown Pavilion, 18–24 Middle Way, Oxford, OX2 7LG

A CIP catalogue record for this book is available from the British
Library

1 2 3 4 5 6 7 8 9 10

ISBN 978-1-912054-16-9

www.fairlightbooks.com

Printed and bound in Great Britain by TJ International Ltd

Cover designed by Emma Rogers

MIX
Paper from
responsible sources
FSC® C013056

In memory of Isabel and Robbie Clark and of Stephen Speed, pupil of the Royal Ballet School, White Lodge.

Principal Characters

May, *Born as Her Serene Highness, Princess Victoria Mary of Teck. Later Duchess of York, Princess of Wales and eventually Her Majesty Queen Mary.*

The Duchess of Teck, *May's mother. Her Royal Highness, Princess Mary Adelaide of Cambridge. Granddaughter of King George III, first cousin of Queen Victoria.*

The Duke of Teck, *May's father. His Serene Highness, Prince Franz of Teck, from the German royal house of Württemberg.*

Georgie, *May's husband. His Royal Highness, Prince George of Wales. Grandson of Queen Victoria, younger son of Bertie, Prince of Wales, and Princess Alexandra of Denmark. Later King George V.*

Aunt Queen, *Queen Victoria, May's second cousin, but known to her from childhood by this name.*

Madame Bricka, *May's tutor, friend and confidante. Later tutor to May's own children.*

Harry Thaddeus Jones, *An Irish-born portrait painter.*

Liko, *His Serene Highness, Prince Henry of Battenberg, scion of a minor German royal house. Married to Beatrice, youngest daughter of Queen Victoria, thus an uncle by marriage of May's husband, Georgie.*

Eddy, *May's first fiancé. His Royal Highness, Prince Albert Victor of Wales, Duke of Clarence. Elder son of Bertie, Prince of Wales and Princess Alexandra of Denmark.*

Bertie, *His Royal Highness, Prince Albert Edward of Wales. Eldest son of Queen Victoria and Prince Albert. Later King Edward VII.*

Alix, *Her Royal Highness, Princess Alexandra of Wales, wife of Bertie. Daughter of King Christian IX of Denmark. Later, Queen Alexandra.*

The Little Prince, *His Royal Highness, Prince Edward of Wales. Eldest son of May and Georgie and later King Edward VIII. After a reign of less than a year, he abdicated in December 1936 to marry the American divorcee Wallis Simpson, thereafter becoming Duke of Windsor.*

I

Winter, 1952

The old woman, mummified in mourning black, stands in the vestibule of her great mansion. The thuggish wind that shoulders its way through the half-opened doors does its best to ruffle her hair, but the golden curls of her evening wig cling like barnacles to her skull. Her coiffure has rarely been out of place in eighty-five years and, like her, it will not behave differently now. She hates the wind. She always has. The damnable disorder of it. If anything gets her in a temper, it is the wind.

A little blizzard of leaves has blown in through the doors and drifted up against a wall. She looks down at them; shrivelled, dry as dust, like ancient artefacts in some botanical museum. How odd that nobody has brushed them up, but nobody in Marlborough House is quite themselves today. Strange too there should be dead leaves anywhere in February, the branches long since bare. What do her gardeners think they are doing? Heaven help them if her husband had still been master here. Or perhaps, she thinks, there is some defiant tree which has clung to the last vestiges of autumn glory and refused to bow to the natural order of things. And now, on this bleakest of days, it has abandoned the struggle and let the wind do its worst. The old woman knows how it feels. Tonight she is the tree. Tonight is the closest she has ever come to giving up.

The car is waiting, the engine already purring, its sharp black lines smudging into the darkness of this God-forsaken night. Beside it, a figure stands to attention, a cashmere rug draped over an arm, gilt buttons flashing beneath the long pendant lamp in the porch.

'I can still see Papa up there in the gallery,' he says suddenly, 'shouting at us to wipe our feet and not to run indoors.'

It is said without levity or nostalgia for some golden childhood. The tone is not lost on her.

'Papa never meant to be unkind,' she replies.

'Oh well,' he says. 'No more running for my poor brother now.'

'No indeed.'

'You shouldn't have come downstairs, Mama. We don't want you catching cold.'

'People complain that this house is a refrigerator,' she replies, 'but I never feel it myself. Isn't that rather rum? Don't they say that those close to the grave feel the chill of it approaching? But I am always perfectly warm.'

'Perhaps you're going to hell instead, Mama.'

She knows it is a careless joke. He is not trying to hurt her. The shock of sixteen years ago, when he abdicated from all that she believed in, is long since passed; only empty echoes of it now remain. But still the joke nips her. She wants to say that, thanks to him, she has been to hell already but, as is her way, she pretends not to hear.

'I always come down to see people off,' she says. 'A hostess must take proper leave of her guests.'

Now it is she who has said the wrong thing. She realises it as soon as the words have left her lips. Her guest, not her child. She catches the look on his face, the silent sigh in his eyes. She has seen that sigh so many times before. Once again he is wishing she were not as she is. Today has hardly been a social occasion, after all. They have just buried his younger brother. His poor, exhausted brother. Three of her five boys have gone now and the one standing beside her exists in her mind in a kind of limbo; a ghost-son, neither dead nor yet quite alive. These past days she has been asking God if it is her punishment to lose so many children. What has she done that He should take them from her? God has not yet replied.

She insists on going right outside to the purring car. Her woman comes and fusses, drapes a coat across her shoulders. He offers his arm again as they shuffle forward into the winter night.

It is the stoop she hates the most. She was prepared for the wrinkles and the lines, the bags below the eyes, the melting of the jaw-line, but she didn't reckon on the stoop. One morning, when they were dressing her, she noticed it in the cheval mirror and felt it like a punch. All her days, she had been straight as an infantryman. Had it not been said that no queen ever possessed such majesty? But now she is aware that she no longer looks at people with a level eye. Now her gaze falls on their chests or even, on a bad day, their bellies. Now she has to raise her head and peer upwards at their faces, like some hideous old tortoise. God, how she hates the bloody stoop.

Under the porch light, he kisses her on both cheeks. She feels a prick of irritation. Since the nursery, the 'little prince' has always needed to be different from the rest of them. A simple, no nonsense English kiss on one cheek would have been quite sufficient. But no, not him. Always trying to be so chic, so cosmopolitan, so different from his dull as ditchwater family.

'Well goodbye,' she says. 'Please give my regards to your wife.'

She sees him swallow, choking on what he no doubt considers her hypocrisy. Yet, to the old woman, it is no more than the proper thing to do, to send a polite greeting to the person who is married to her son. Legally married and in the eyes of God, though heaven only knows what, sixteen years ago, He made of that cut-price spectacle. That this person had shaken her life like a terrier with a rag-doll is immaterial. There are ways to behave. Let others transgress them in this strange modern age, but she will not.

'Wallis will be delighted, Mama.'

The name, she finds, still grates on her, even after all this time. It is a name for a butler, not for a woman. Not that the witch-wife looks much like a woman. All straight lines and sharp angles like a geometry set. All calculation.

At the open door of the car, they are not alone. Not just the chauffeur, the footmen and the fussy creature who brought the coat, but those other faces who jostle their way into her mind's eye. The witch-wife of course, who waits now in New York, high in a glittering tower above Park Avenue. Her husband and his father, the long-gone ruler of both their lives. But today, above all, the brother taken years too soon. The second-best king will always loom between them now, fragile as a butterfly but brave as a lion, the one who sacrificed himself when the 'little prince' would not.

'Like your Papa, I've never meant to be unkind either,' she hears herself whisper. 'But I'm too old to change now.'

He looks hard into her eyes, as if searching for something, then swiftly turns away, curling himself into the cushioned womb of the car.

She refuses to go inside till the tail lights disappear into Pall Mall, taking him to the airport, back to the glittering tower of the Waldorf Astoria. For a moment, she stares at the empty space where the car has been. A black cat appears out of the darkness, stops in the beam of the porch light and stares back at her before scooting away again into the shrubbery. Oh look, she thinks, the witch-wife has come to see how they've been getting along. Suddenly the sciatica shoots down to her ankle. Bugger this leg. Can't it leave her alone even today? Does it have no finer feelings?

Her woman guides her to the foot of the staircase. This was the great general's house once, its painted walls trumpeting his triumphs at Blenheim, Ramillies and Malplaquet. When her body began to disobey her, this staircase became her battleground too. She would damn well climb those black marble steps as she had always done, no matter how long it took. But in the end it vanquished her.

The first time she travelled in the tiny lift she found herself with tears in her eyes. They tried to make it nice with a rose-red carpet and a little seat covered in matching brocade, but she hates that lift like she hates the stoop. And it is now, in the blasted lift, she forces herself to face the truth that she has denied for these sixteen years. As if it has pushed itself into the tiny space and is pressing her against the wall. Despite the face she gives to the world, she is no stranger to strong emotion. Joy, sorrow, hope, fear, rage, even desire, she has known all of these in her time, although she has learned to keep them to herself, like a group of unsuitable acquaintances. But she has never encountered the feeling that invades her now and quite takes her breath away.

Her woman waits on the first floor, ready to push open the folding grille.

'Goodness Ma'am, you look quite worn out.'

She does not answer, does not argue, lets herself be helped along the corridor to her apartment. In the sitting room, the door that leads through to the bedroom is open. As always, her dresser is waiting. The bed is turned down, the pillows puffed and inviting, her lawn nightgown with its pale-blue bows splayed out across the moss-green quilt, as if it has retired before her. How pretty it looks, she thinks. All her life, she has sought the consolation of pretty things. If there is prettiness around then, no matter how life seems, it is possible to convince oneself that all is fine and dandy.

She feels hungry. She ate next to nothing at supper. They sat mostly in silence; the only sounds the ticking of the ormolu clock and the spongy footfalls of the servants. When they spoke it was of trivialities; how long it would take to fly back to New York, the difficulty of finding a chef in the Waldorf Astoria able to cook a decent Yorkshire pudding. Now she orders more coal for the fire, a ham sandwich and coffee.

'But Ma'am, you'll never sleep.'

'Oh my dear, how could I sleep tonight?'

The dresser means well, though she is a little Hitler; there is even a hint of the moustache. How they all bully her now, in a way they once would not have dared, but tonight she will not be bullied. She allows her wig to be removed and put on its wooden stand but surely, she says, she can take off her own clothes just this once? It won't kill her. She's not quite helpless yet. Don't make a fuss, there's a good girl, she tells Hitler.

The feeling that came in the lift stays with her, only it has moved south now and settled in the pit of her stomach. But, she wonders, is the thing not a presence but an absence? Is that why she feels hungry? Is something needed to fill the void? She wonders too if it is a portent. Are we forced to face up to ourselves only at the end, as the scythe is being sharpened?

She eases herself down at the writing desk that stands in the middle of the room. As the world has closed in on her, the desk has become the centre of her orbit. A great slab of satinwood, topped in scarlet leather. The housemaid whose job is to dust it told her wearily there are exactly ninety-six items upon it. Yet there is no disorder, no confusion. The old woman knows precisely where even the smallest object lies: her books, her papers, her letters and the catalogues she loves to compile of all those pretty things she has collected. In gilt frames are photographs of almost everyone who has mattered to her. How could her children think she does not care for them, when she looks into their faces twenty times a day? How could her eldest son believe, as she is quite sure he does, that there is ice in her veins? But how pointless, she reflects, to ask yourself a question when you already know the answer. She has never been able to tell them that she loved them; she who was once so full of love. Now she could no more do so than fly through the air.

The coal for the fire comes, the ham sandwich and the coffee pot. She orders the lamps switched off, except the one on the desk. They leave her alone with the crackling of the flames and the feeling that has settled in her stomach.

It occurs to her that, in truth, her children know so little of her. As children grow, they are focused on their own emergence into the world; they have scant curiosity about how their parents did the same, way back in the dreary mists, in a time so very different from their own. How can she blame the ghost-son for not understanding her, if she has never made any attempt to explain herself, to tell him her story? It may well be too late to change now, but could she not at least make him understand how she came to be as she is and that she was not always so? But how on earth could she do that? Across all these years, across an ocean, across a gulf of empathy surely impossible to bridge?

She ignores the ham sandwich and lights a cigarette. To hell with the doctors; surely she can have at least one on a day such as this? Her glance falls, as it so often does, on the watercolour that hangs over the chimney piece. She is just seventeen, sitting in a garden in Italy, in a dress of creamy muslin and a Tuscan straw hat with two long red ribbons dancing down her back. A tumble of violets lies in her lap. She remembers how she had instinctively bunched the flowers together, but the artist had demanded that they must be loose, disordered. She remembers too how handsome he was, how he made her heart race. She can still see him as clearly as if they had met last week. Dead now of course. They are all dead. All the ones who mattered most. Well almost.

In the portrait, she is smiling slightly, her lips apart. Her eyes, china-blue, pierce through the canvas, wide open, ready for life. Georgie had never liked it.

'It's just not *you*, May,' he had said, in that manner which brooked no discussion. 'Just not you at all.'

In the forty-two years of their marriage, that had always been the way of it. No discussion. Words spoken aloud had always frightened Georgie. Such dangerous things, words. Far better to employ them sparingly or, if possible, to avoid them altogether. For forty-two years, so little had ever been said.

But soon after Georgie had gone, she rescued the watercolour from its distant cupboard and put it where she could see it every day. A comforting reminder that she had not always been an ugly old tortoise. Tonight though, it suddenly becomes a darker object. Tonight, it becomes a reproach.

She sips the coffee and nibbles at the ham sandwich. Her gaze stays latched onto the portrait, remembering the people, the places and the dreams that once existed, just outside its frame, in the springtime of her days. Would any of the hazy, long-lost faces who had strolled in the garden by the Arno recognise her now?

After a while, the old woman is conscious of rain spattering against the window where she sat this morning to watch her dead child's funeral procession pass by. She had not been able to face the Abbey. Rarely in her life had she shirked any duty, but she had shirked this. Surely, they could not expect it of her? Surely, every mother would understand? She pulls herself across the room and peers out into the night. It is pelting down. The light of the street lamps diffuses the rainwater into hundreds of droplets, like handfuls of tiny diamonds thrown against the glass. She can just make out the regiment of black banners hanging from the lampposts. This morning they flapped noisily in the wind; his last applause; a compensation for the respectful silence of the crowds. But now the breeze has suddenly dropped and, motionless, the banners droop in the downpour, as weary as herself.

The pain shoots down her leg again. The scythe is being sharpened and no mistake. She thinks of her first child, the 'little prince', soon to be flying through the darkness above the unseen ocean, returning to the exile from which she refused to release him. How she wishes he might come to know the girl in the Tuscan straw hat and of the things that befell her. He would learn how she had sinned against herself, sinned against the light that had once been within her. Then perhaps they might forgive each other before it is too late.

She eases herself back into her chair. The feeling in her guts is still there; the truth, denied for sixteen years, that she has made him what he is.

'It was my fault, wasn't it?' she whispers to the portrait above the chimney piece. 'All my fault.'

Desperately now, she wants her bed. It is tricky enough to remove her wig, but undressing herself is a frightful business. It is years since she attempted it and it is far harder than she imagined, in fact quite impossible. She curses the buttons and the clasps, the hooks and the eyes. In the end, she only succeeds in slipping off her shoes and falls, exhausted, under the quilt still dressed, the ropes of pearls still fastened around her neck. She will be in such trouble in the morning. Hitler will be furious, unbearable for days. Oh God.

As she reaches to turn out the lamp, she sees the wig on its stand, the golden curls shining in the soft light. Throughout this dreadful day she has, with her usual fortitude, managed to contain herself. But the sight of those curls, once no artifice but real and rich beneath the glow of an Italian sun, is too much. On the satin pillow, the old grey head trembles and weeps.

II

Summer, 1875

She is at the back of the line. In front of her, seven other little girls, porcelain-perfect in their bridesmaids' frocks, clamber up the wide stone steps behind the bride. She is nervous, more so than she has ever been in her eight years of life.

At the last minute, she is a replacement for someone who has caught the measles. All the others are well rehearsed for this splendid moment when every eye in Windsor will be upon them and every throat will feel a lump rise at the sight of their playful innocence. They have been drilled and practised till baby tears washed their tired eyes, tiny feet were stamped and tantrums thrown.

But May of Teck has had no such opportunity. By the grace of God, the dress of the stricken bridesmaid just about fits her, though her mother's seamstress was up all night making the necessary alterations. Yet still it is a bit too tight and the peach-coloured satin strains against her ribs and, though she is the calmest of children as a rule, her heart pounds and her breath comes and goes too fast, like the bellows used to rouse the fire back home. Above all, she is most afraid of fainting. Why only last week, daft Daisy, one of the kitchen maids, passed out and cracked her head on a lavatory bowl. May is now quite scared of lavatory bowls. And on that subject, whatever happens today, she must hold in her wee-wee for as long as she possibly can. She can hardly raise her hand and ask to be excused halfway down the aisle. Just think of the shame. On an occasion like this, when it feels like half the world is watching.

But now, as she reaches the top of the steps and passes through the great portal, something happens inside the little fair-haired head framed in its wreath of jasmine and orange blossom. In an instant, every fear deserts her and she is suffused with a sensation she has never known before. She gasps out loud, she cannot help herself. It is the most beautiful place she has ever seen.

She is not unused to churches. Every Sunday she is taken to the one beyond the gates of their park or to that beside her grandmother's house at Kew. She has been marched for a history lesson to the big old abbey in the middle of the city. But these are dark, gloomy caverns where she is bored and even a little frightened as some old man, with a red face and bushy side-whiskers, thunders down at her with words she does not understand. Yet this place seems hardly like a church at all. It is something from a picture book, a fairyland no less. The sun pours honey-coloured light through windows so finely wrought it seems they are scarcely there at all. Pillars like pale white arms reach towards the roof, fanning out into stony fingers as if to hold it up for the glory of God. At only eight years old, May Teck has only the vaguest notion of this God person, but she has never yet felt a stronger certainty that He exists. The Chapel of St George is nothing less than a heaven on earth. This moment, she decides, is the greatest she has ever known.

This is a belief supported by the fuss her mother has been making for the past two days. When the telegram arrived, Mary Adelaide, Duchess of Teck, near melted with excitement. She read it once again, rocking to and fro in her chair, gurgling with pleasure.

'What an honour for us Francis!' she said to her husband. 'At last, a recognition of our rightful place in the family.'

The Duke grunted and aimed another spoonful of his breakfast egg towards his mouth, though much of it landed in his moustache. His wife sighed, wiping up the yellowy mess with her napkin.

'Oh Francis, Francis. What am I to do with you? You look like one of the dogs at his bowl.'

The arrival of the telegram was like a swarm of bees flying in through the window. The household at White Lodge went into a flap, running upstairs and down, this way and that. Young May's hair must be washed, her fingernails trimmed, her ears examined for wax. When exactly is the bridesmaid's dress coming? The seamstress should be fetched at once. Their carriages must be polished, the horses brushed till their coats shine like coal, the grooms and footmen ordered to have baths the night before so they will not smell on the day. Oh, the thrill of it all.

But poor Duchess. Her exhilaration was cruelly short. Just a few hours later, as the second-hand dress was finally delivered, so too was a second telegram. She slumped down onto the ottoman, her fingers splaying out across her vast bosom as if to stop her heart from breaking.

'What's wrong *now*, Mary Adelaide?' her husband asked, glancing up from his newspaper. 'Is it from the stables? Has one of the horses developed a squint?'

'We are asked to give up our seats in the choir stalls. The Maharajah of some God-forsaken state now comes after all. Her Majesty would be most grateful, it says. Can you believe it?'

'The Lord giveth and the Lord taketh away,' said the Duke.

His wife struggled to her feet; the tears streaming down flushed cheeks, like the morning dew on two ripe nectarines.

'But we are asked to sit out in the nave, away from the family. In the nave with all the rest!' she cried. 'I am the granddaughter of a king. Don't you *care*?'

In a minute, he thought, he would hear the weeping from the bedroom above.

But indeed the Duke did care. In fact, he cared so much that he could not express it. He *dared* not express it. Already, he knew, he flung too many flower vases across too many rooms. He kicked too many dogs, or even servants, when the rages rolled over him like a November mist from across the park. Instead, he breathed deeply, drummed his fingers on his thigh and stared blindly at the pages of *The Times*. What was yet another insult, another slight, he tried to tell himself? What mattered yet another reminder that his branch of the family was tolerated but never fully embraced? But, in the tumult of his mind, he still pictured himself sitting there in his chintzy armchair, the newspaper on his knee, his body pierced by arrows from the top of his head to the tips of his toes. The Saint Sebastian of poor relations.

Even at her tiny age, his only daughter is already aware of a pall that hangs over her parents, though not of why it exists. May Teck is a quiet child and, as such children always are, she is an acute observer of her own small world, saying little, seeing everything.

Today, as she enters the great chapel, her sense of wonder does not obliterate the awareness of her parents' humiliation. She has been told to look straight ahead at all times, yet she cannot help but search for them from the corner of her eye. Ah, there they are, in the front row of those condemned to the nave; her mother's girth requiring her to be accommodated with not one but two gilded chairs. As always, the comedy of the sight embarrasses her. That shard of sadness to which she is accustomed lances through her once again, though followed as ever by a rush of love for this bizarre creature who has given life to her. Nothing, she vows, is more important than that Mama and Papa should be proud of her today. So May straightens her spine, tilts her chin higher. She may be at the back of the line but she will be the bridesmaid people will remember.

'Who's that little lady bringing up the rear?' they will whisper to each other.

'No idea. Never seen her before.'

'Well whoever she is, isn't she splendid?'

May, observing, doubts that anyone will think it about the

gaggle of girls in front of her. Despite all their practising, they are scarcely behaving well. One has dropped her bouquet twice already. Another is sucking her thumb and picking her nose at the same time. The three Wales sisters keep whispering to one another. May does not care for the Wales girls. She doesn't much like their two brothers either. A few times, they have been brought to play with her at White Lodge, but they are rough and noisy children, little savages who break train-sets and decapitate dolls. May and her own brothers have learned to hide their best toys when the Wales gang invades their nursery. Today, they have hardly bothered to speak to her.

'Are you here because poor Amelia has the measles?' said the first sister eventually. 'Poor, poor Amelia. Is she going to die?' asked the second.

'I expect so,' replied the third. 'Oh I do wish she were here instead of May.'

The bride herself was scarcely more welcoming. She bears a long, foreign name that May cannot remember. In the robing room, she bleated about the weight of her train of Venetian lace. May wonders why she seemed so unhappy. Is what the Duchess teaches her daughter not true? That a good marriage is the goal of every woman, high or low? Should this gloomy bride not be aglow with joy at the prospect of being joined forever to her lord and master? Instead, her eyes are still red and puffy. May is confused.

But when May passes through the screen that separates the nave from the choir, all this disappears from her mind. The organ is playing, the trumpets sounding, the choir singing. The music seems all the more magical because she cannot quite see whence it comes. It whirls around her in the air, her tiny self somehow at the vortex. Might God himself be making it? Now, after the virginal purity of the nave, she finds herself in a sudden spasm of colour. The banners of the knights hang down above her, threaded through with rainbows of red, yellow, green, turquoise and cobalt blue. Above the stalls, their coronets, swords and shields flash out against the wood, rich and shiny as the darkest chocolate. In the distance, the altar shimmers in silver and cloth of gold beneath a reredos of pink and cream marble. Bathed in the febrile light of a thousand candles, its outline is blurred as if it is not quite of this earth. Surely, May Teck thinks again, this place must indeed be paradise. If so, she is glad to be looking her best. She is even wearing new knickers. Not that anyone here will know that of course, but still it is a comfort.

High up above the choir, a little balcony of finely carved wood juts out from the wall, like a box at the opera. Here stands Aunt Queen, at once part of the proceedings and yet above it all. This is little May's reward for the too-tight dress, the painful removal of her earwax, the worry about holding in her wee-wee.

'This is the day you will see Aunt Queen,' said her mother this morning, almost in a whisper as if it was a secret. 'A day you will never forget.'

It is certainly odd, May thinks, that she cannot remember having seen Aunt Queen in person before. Her presence looms so large under their roof, it often feels like she is someone who lives with them but never leaves her room. But Aunt Queen is not what May expected. She wears no crown and carries no orb and sceptre. May wonders where these are. Mightn't she have troubled to put them on? It is a wedding after all. But no, she is all in black with only a mantilla of fine white muslin that spumes down across her shoulders. How small and round she is. And old too. This queen is not a Guinevere, a Cleopatra or even the first Elizabeth. In truth, May decides, she looks more like Mrs McCready, the Irishwoman who does the laundry at home.

And yet there is something. Even an eight-year-old sees that at once. Something that seems to exist in the ether around the dumpy body. How strange that it should just be a vacant space, a distance between her and any other being. It is in the way the old woman holds herself too, the way she bows her head in acknowledgement of the bride's curtsey, not extravagantly like some actress, just the slightest lowering of her fat, dimpled chin. It is, May presumes, what her Mama calls majesty.

But she knows this is more than mere majesty, it is divinity. May Teck's mother has taught her emphatically that the monarch is chosen by God. No ifs, no buts. It is as simple and pure as that. And was that not proven by the vast West Window under which she entered this heavenly space? In images of coloured glass, the saints and monarchs are mixed together on equal terms, gazing down benignly on all lesser mortals. Why, even the Virgin Mary herself is content to be in their company. Deities and monarchs, monarchs and deities. They are indivisible. They are the same thing. May Teck has no doubt of it. For the rest of her long life, it is a certainty she will not relinquish for a single second.

While the other girls fidget around her, May stands straight as a sapling, holding her little bouquet. If Aunt Queen's eye happens to fall on her, she must not be found wanting. She looks straight ahead, her gaze fixed on the altar. She listens to every word the archbishop speaks. He says the bride is being 'given' to the groom. What does that mean, May wonders? Is the bride some sort of present, like you get on a birthday? Has the groom done something quite splendid for which he must be rewarded? Won a battle perhaps or even slain a dragon? May's head, inside its wreath of jasmine and orange blossom, whirls with all this as she stands stock still beneath the banners of the knights. Above all, she wonders again why the young woman at the altar with the strange foreign name looks so sad. As if something has been lost to her rather than found.

When the thing is done, the waves of music swell to carry the procession back the way it has come. Again, she is the last in line and now sees something she has not noticed before. Her head has been so far in the clouds, she has not thought to look down at the floor. But surely they are walking on a place they should not; where even angels would fear to tread? The train of Venetian lace, the groom's shiny boots and the slippered feet of thumb-sucking bridesmaids have trampled across the great vault itself, the resting-place of kings and queens. The names stare up at her from the stone: the eighth Henry, his poor lost Jane, the first Charles who had his head chopped off. She is shocked that such sacrilege can be so casually performed. What right do any of them, herself included, new knickers or not, have to trespass on the tombs of these divinities? At once, she decides she will not, cannot, do it. She stops abruptly, as if she found herself on the edge of a cliff, and goes no further.

In the choir, she is now the object of general notice. What is that little girl up to? Aunt Queen herself must be looking down on her, but it does not matter. Then she knows what she must do. To the occupants of the vault, she performs the deep curtsey her mother has taught her for use on this special day. She sinks as low as she can go without falling over, then slowly rises again. All around, hard old faces break open and smile down upon her. She is indeed the little bridesmaid they will remember.

Outside, at the foot of the wide stone steps, as the onlookers cheer and stir the dozy summer air with tiny flags, the bride and groom's landau moves off towards the castle for the wedding breakfast. From some hidden corner, a flock of white doves is released into the sky of cerulean blue. It is unfortunate that the possible consequences of this have not been considered. The moment of May Teck's tiny triumph is destined to be brief. One nervous dove, perhaps an apprentice at public occasions, chooses her as its target. The wreath of jasmine and orange blossom, not to mention her straw-blonde curls, are defiled in one terrible, unforgettable instant. The stuff runs down her face. The mess is indescribable.

The Duchess cries out and hurries to her with a handkerchief, only succeeding in making it worse. The Duke fumes, scarlet-faced. The three Wales sisters begin to giggle as, despite her best efforts, May's tears start to flow.

'My flowers, my pretty flowers,' she sobs.

Up at the castle, photographs are taken of the happy couple and their eight angelic bridesmaids. Furthest from the lens, at the back of the line, is May Teck. She alone boasts no wreath of summer glories. Her hair, quickly rinsed out by a maid in a kitchen basin, is plastered against her skull. When a copy of the photograph is sent to White Lodge, the Duchess tears it up and flees to her bedroom. The Duke looks around for something to throw. Another arrow pierces his heart.

III

Autumn, 1883

'There go our coffins,' he says.

Porters are loading their trunks onto the boat train. Over thirty of them, great black sepulchral things.

'Hush Papa. Do cheer up or you'll make yourself ill again,' she replies.

'Well this *is* a kind of funeral, isn't it Pussycat?'

Oh dear. His mood is drooping like his moustache. She has to keep a constant vigil on him now. Good days and bad days, sunshine and storms. Only sixteen years old, May Teck has already appointed herself as her father's keeper. Nobody else seemed to want the position, least of all her mother.

It is a nippy evening for early autumn and they are swaddled tight in their travelling capes. But the family of the Duke of Teck need not fear the spectre of an English winter. They will be far distant, feeling the chill in quite a different way.

On the platform at Victoria Station, a small knot of people is gathered. The casual passers-by, hurrying in search of their compartment, would assume them all to be together, but in truth they are two tribes, the vanquished and the victors. In the first group are her mother and father, her three brothers, the necessary servants and of course herself. In the second, her mother's family; her uncle, her aunt and, *in absentia*, the great Aunt Queen herself, whose authority hovers over everyone and the need for whose approbation runs through all their lives like the very blood in their veins. It is all of them who have tried May's mother for her spendthrift ways, judged her shockingly guilty and sentenced her to an indefinite period of detention in a hopefully inexpensive corner of the Continent. The two tribes stand slightly apart, pain and embarrassment hanging in the air like the silvery steam from the hissing engine.

In this strange *tableau*, the Duchess of Teck takes centre-stage as she always does. Those casual observers, however flustered and late for the train, would easily identify the leading lady. Even if they have no idea who she is, they would recognise at once that she is *someone*. The figure of Mary Adelaide draws every eye, though it is not merely a matter of bulk. Somehow, the air around her quakes as she sucks it in, as if it doubts it can possibly sustain such a spirit, such a force of nature.

Yet the Duchess is no actress. The ability to dissemble is not among her many gifts. As a rule, her face shows exactly what she is feeling; the words that gush out of her express exactly what she thinks. But this evening, for once, on the dank station platform, she is giving a performance worthy of Bernhardt or even Mrs Langtry. Her judges have come expecting tears and protestations, a scene of penny-dreadful melodrama. Might Mary Adelaide have to be literally bundled onto the train like a sack of mail, the doors slammed and locked behind her? But they need not have worried. She gives orders to the porters as if she is merely going to Eastbourne for a fortnight. She refuses to let her family see that they have trampled on her heart.

The stationmaster, dressed in his best, bows low and tells her it is time to board. She stretches out a lilac-gloved hand for him to kiss with the same grace she would extend to a bishop or the emissary of some foreign potentate.

'Oh my good man, a thousand thanks for your kind attendance. And how spick and span you keep your most impressive railway station.'

It is an absurd remark; they are entombed in a blackened cathedral of soot, sweat and pigeon shit. But when the man stands up straight again, his eyes are shining. He will never forget the kissing of the lilac glove. Gorged on her love of life, the Duchess has the blessed knack of reaching out to everyone without effort or condescension. It is why the people love her. God bless Fat Mary, they say. She's a game old girl and no mistake. Always got a smile and a wave for us. Not like her gloomy cousin in Windsor, with her widow's weeds and a face like a slapped arse. You could almost imagine having a beer with her down the pub, though she might not fit in the snug.

And yet she never lowers herself, never lets anyone forget she is a royal princess, granddaughter of poor mad George no less. The only time she ever diminished herself, in the eyes of some at least, was in her marriage. It came late in life, when the family had almost given up hope and a permanent place on the shelf was being made ready for her. But Mary Adelaide's road to the altar was long and strewn with withered bouquets.

'I don't believe I wish to embark on such a *vast* undertaking,' one potential candidate had said with a smirk, before fleeing back to his *Schloss* above the Rhine.

So when a minor German princeling was finally sniffed out, hunted down and indicated a willingness, everyone breathed a sigh of relief. Franz Teck was good-natured and notably handsome. In the uniform of the Austrian Hussars, he had fluttered hearts of both sexes across the ballrooms of Europe. In Vienna, he had waltzed with the Empress Elisabeth herself. He had even shown valour in battle. What more could any maiden have desired? Unfortunately, as the vulgar expression goes, the paragon was also flat stony broke. Worse yet, his royal blood was forever tainted by the morganatic marriage of his lovesick father to an unsuitable woman. But who cared about all that? At last, somebody was game for taking Mary Adelaide off the shelf and off their hands. The Lord be praised.

They came to care soon enough. Like a snowball rolling down a hill, the small drawbacks of the handsome Hussar swiftly loomed larger than was at first apparent. However much her closest relations originally smiled on the alliance, her husband's shadowed blood made his wife a little less royal than before. The huge family of Aunt Queen functioned as an infinitely long dinner-table; everyone precisely seated according to rank. From now on, Mary Adelaide would always be below the salt.

But it was Franz Teck's stony broke-ness that would eventually lead them to the boat train at Victoria Station. The new Duchess no more understood money than she understood Swahili. Faced with running her own establishment, she was utterly lost. What a shame she rarely read a book; the advice of Mr Micawber might have been invaluable: never spend a farthing more than you possess. But the necessary funds had always come from somewhere, had they not? It really was *too* bad to be troubled by such common considerations. And was she not economising all the time? Saving string from parcels and writing on both sides of the notepaper?

'What *more* can I do?' she had bleated in answer to her brother and sister's constant pleas to, as it were, tighten her belt. 'Must I be reduced to just *one* carriage?'

But even Mary Adelaide was troubled by the sight that greeted her one morning as she glanced out of her bedroom window at White Lodge. How pretty the deer looked as always, moving with that delicate precision through the green-gold swathe of the park. Then she noticed other brown-clad creatures, weaving their way among the antlers and heading straight in her direction. A more terrifying species entirely. Oh my God. It was a deputation no less and when it reached the doors of White Lodge, a letter to the Duke and Duchess of Teck was, respectfully but very firmly, presented by the shopkeepers of Richmond, Kingston and Sheen. Eighteen thousand pounds was collectively owed to them and if payment was not made at once, the debtors would go to court and sue for the removal of the sofas on which the Tecks sat, the beds in which they slept, the shirts on their backs and the bonnets on their heads.

As soon as the deputation had withdrawn, a panicked telegram was sent and within the hour, Mary Adelaide's brother, head of their branch of the family, came hurtling across the greensward in his pony trap, face like a bursting tomato, riding crop thwacking against his thigh. Within a minute, the walls of White Lodge were scarce able to contain him.

'Eighteen thousand pounds! Good grief Mary Adelaide, how have you managed that? Are you feeding your scullery maids on grouse and *foie gras*?'

Uncle George was commander-in-chief of the British Army. In forty years of military service, there had never been an insubordinate soldier he could not whip into line, but his damn spendthrift sister had always been quite beyond him. A defeat he much resented and was now determined to reverse.

'Well this is it, you know,' he shouted. 'This is your Balaclava, Mary Adelaide. The family will take no more. You've refused to change your ways and now you expose us to public shame. Something must be done, once and for all.'

May listened outside in the hall, hidden among the palms in the shadow of the staircase. She had long since discovered that the adoption of such tactics was the only way to know what was happening in this crazy house.

'Not all the sheep in Surrey are white,' Uncle George ranted on. 'There are two very black ones sitting in this room who've had their hooves clamped tightly over their ears for far too long. Well now, at last, they must listen.'

Uncle George came charging out of the drawing room. He flung the door wide so it ricocheted against the wall. On the threshold, he turned and threw one last grenade back into enemy lines.

'I am now going directly to Her Majesty. She will decide what must be done.'

He stopped when he spotted his niece among the foliage.

'Tell me, young May,' he snapped, 'which one of your parents do you take after? For your sake, I hope to God it is neither.'

Through the open door of the drawing room, she saw her father with his head in his hands. Her mother sat with her palms pressed together, as if in prayer, her bosom heaving like the sails of a galleon in a following wind. For May Teck, it was the moment which must come to everyone sooner or later; when one's mother and father, those gods of childhood, first wobble dangerously on their pedestals, revealed for what they truly are. All too human, all too frail, all too childlike in themselves.

So Aunt Queen deliberated, then passed sentence. Their beloved home, occupied only by her grace and favour, was to be shut up. Most of the servants were paid off, some of who May had known since the nursery. A public auction was held of the best furniture and pictures; a disgrace from which the Duchess fled in her carriage till the horror was over, sitting by the river and sobbing all day long. Dust sheets were draped over what remained. The same fate, May thought, was befalling the landscape of her childhood: the rolling, rumpled carpet of the park, the distant view of St Paul's from King Henry's Mound, fishing with her brothers in Pen Ponds, the topiary pyramids beneath her window, the creaky old swing. All of it was to be suddenly, shockingly, snatched away. For how long, young May did not know.

Now, on the station platform, the Duchess turns to her brother and sister, those chief justices of her downfall, and embraces them warmly.

'Rush home now, my dears. You mustn't delay your dinner on our account. We shall all be perfectly fine.'

Oddly, it is her sister who begins to cry, perhaps realising at last what is being lost to her.

'Tsh tsh, my angel. No cause for tears,' says the Duchess. 'What a grand adventure we embark upon.'

May shivers inside her travelling cape. She wants to go home. She wants to sleep tonight in her dear little bedroom, in her own little bed. Then she remembers that, apart from a watchman or two, her home no longer exists. It is shrouded, shuttered, silent.

Of course, she says nothing about how she feels. She certainly doesn't make a fuss. Already she loathes and detests fuss. Sometimes she thinks she is drowning in the fuss all around her, clinging for dear life to her own good sense as a whirlpool of inconsequence tries to pull her under. No, fuss is not her way, though even if it had been, nobody would have paid much attention. It is her mother and father whose wishes and needs create the climate of her life, in fair or foul weather. Trying to compete, to make herself heard above the tumult, would be a waste of time. Besides, it is her brothers who will carry the name of Teck into the future. A girl hardly signifies. She learned that long ago.

When the boat train lurches away from the platform, all waving and blowing of kisses done, her mother sighs and sits right down on top of her. The girth of the Duchess means that looking round to see what might be behind her is no easy business and one which she often abandons altogether.

'Goodness chick, how *did* you get there? Heavens, do I not have enough to cope with today?'

The train roars towards Dover with indecent haste as if it can hardly wait to be rid of them. Mary Adelaide dozes off, exhausted by the effort of her performance. The Duke too sits with his eyes closed. Yet the fingers drumming on his knee tell his daughter he is far from resting, but trying to calm himself, to stop his poor nerves getting the better of him as they so often do, when he explodes at those he loves for no reason at all. She reaches out and encloses the drumming fingers with her own.

'Who are we now, May?' he whispers, without opening his eyes. 'Where do we fit in?'

Poor Papa. He has never fitted in at the level to which he believes himself entitled. That tainted blood means he can never reign over the small Germanic state which should have been his birthright. In his dreams, in his very heart and soul, he will always be King Franz of Württemberg. But instead of being a king in his own little country, he has become something of a joke in somebody else's; Fat Mary's downtrodden husband, walking a few paces behind her, diminished in her bustling shadow, passing the time with trivialities. Scarcely a man at all. Marriage to an English princess did not exactly bring him the *entrée* he imagined. Nor indeed the small fortune for which he had hoped; a misunderstanding, a concealment even, for which he resents Uncle George to this day.

'I could have married some North Country heiress you know,' May heard him shout at Uncle George on the day of the crisis, 'and lived in clover for the rest of my days.'

But he didn't. And all of it preys on his mind and his nerves. So often in his dreams, he is still dancing with the Empress Elisabeth round and round the ballrooms of Vienna. She is slim as a reed and light as thistledown, pearls threaded through the chestnut hair that cascades down her back. And then he wakes and sees Mary Adelaide snoring gently beside him.

Now on the boat train May, the only one who understands him, strokes his hand and murmurs soft words of consolation.

When the ship pulls away from the harbour, she goes out onto the upper deck alone. It is dark now, the moon almost full. The great white cliffs, faded to a ghostly grey, tower above the sea like a long high bastion shutting her out. Her father's words lurch in her head. Where *do* they fit in now? And who is May Teck? A shy girl, not very pretty, who hardly speaks unless she is spoken to. Consigned to the shadows, she has learned to be comfortable there. Increasingly though, she wonders how it might feel to step into some sort of light.

The sea is disgruntled tonight. She watches as the swell rises, falls and spumes behind the ship. She dislikes the sea as she dislikes the wind and always will; its unpredictability and disorder. She has already learned to hate disorder in anything. Has it not now brought them to this pretty pass?

Below her on the poop deck, by the swinging light of the navigation lamps, May sees a lone figure walking towards the stern. Her mother still clutches the bouquet of white roses presented by an official in the port. Despite her size, she is famously light and graceful on her feet and now she performs a little *pas de deux* with the heaving sea. As the deck tilts this way and that, never putting a foot wrong, never overbalancing, she reaches the railing. For a while, she stands looking at the last lights of England as they pull back from her and mingle with the stars. Then, one by one, Mary Adelaide casts the roses out over the waves. For a split second, each bloom catches the moonlight as it arcs through the air till it falls from grace and is lost in the heartless wake. High above, May has the urge to shout 'bravo'. Despite everything, she loves her mother.

IV

Autumn/Winter, 1883

'I think, chick,' her mother whispers to May so that the menfolk cannot hear, 'you and I might have to purchase thinner knickers. I fear we may roast in the ones we're wearing now.'

All the way down through France and Switzerland, the Duchess keeps up her performance. How lucky they are to be heading to warmer climes as the nights grow longer.

'It will be sunshine for the Tecks from now on,' she declares, embracing the metaphor, as the train bursts from the mouth of the St Gothard tunnel. 'I know it. I just know it. Francis dear, do look at this beautiful scenery.'

Still May's father sits with his eyes closed, fingers drumming on his knee.

To be sure, the landscape is glorious as they travel further south, sitting out on the open balcony of their compartment. Chestnut, mulberry and walnut trees; villages scattered carelessly like corn seed across the valleys; peasant farms of sun-baked stone; tiny churches perched on lonely hillocks. But to May Teck, however beautiful, it is alien. How she longs for the view from her bedroom out over the park, where she knows every time-blasted oak, every copse of wildflowers, every herd of fallow deer. Now she is uprooted from the soil of her memory and cast into the four winds.

Nor does Florence, their destination, turn out to be quite the shimmering Camelot that the Duchess has advertised so effusively all the way from Calais. They arrive on a cool, drizzly evening. On the frantic platform, porters shout in a language May does not understand. How dirty and uncouth they look and, when she is jostled, she can smell their garlic breath. She has never been jostled before. Is this, she wonders, what happens to those of little consequence? Is she now to be jostled forever?

But the English consul has come to meet them and May clings to his shadow as he guides them through the maelstrom of the station out into the night. Yet the silence that envelops them now is almost more discomfiting. Their carriage is soon swallowed up in a skein of dark streets lined with ancient palazzos grim as fortresses, their vast doors firmly closed, their windows barred and shuttered. It is as if a plague has struck. There is no sign of life at all, except when another carriage tries to pass in the narrow lanes and a fracas erupts between the coachmen; yelling in a way no English coachman would ever do, certainly not with ladies on board.

'What is the man saying?' says the Duchess to the English consul who is escorting them to the private hotel where they are to lodge at first.

'Well, your Highness...' he replies, suddenly engrossed in his cufflinks.

'Pray sir, tell me.'

'He's saying that the other fellow's mother is a whore and that she is known as such to most of the Italian army.'

'Gracious! Please sir, don't say such things in front of my dear girl.'

'You *did* ask, Ma'am.'

May's brothers splutter with laughter which earns them a whack from the Duke's umbrella. They are sweet boys and she will miss them when, after a while, they must return home to school. Even Aunt Queen is not prepared to interfere with the education of three young English gentlemen, however far beneath the salt they may sit.

Already May is sure she cannot like this place. How can she ever settle amidst such chaos? It is a relief when the carriage breaks out from the labyrinth onto the banks of the Arno, but even this is a disappointment. The river is still almost dry after the hot months, the water sluggish and fetid. The Duchess holds her kerchief against her nose.

The carriage halts again. Now a funeral procession must cross its path. In a moment they are hemmed in, front and rear, by a herd of mourners. But these seem a far cry from the good folk of Richmond or Kew when paying their respects to the dear departed. Those who process along the Lungarno on this gloomy evening wear long white robes and conical hoods which entirely cover their faces; only the eyes are visible through tiny holes slashed into the fabric. Every mourner carries a blazing torch to illuminate his way to the graveyard; their conical shadows flickering against the rusty ochre walls of the palazzos.

And then May sees the body. There is no casket, just a bier quite unprotected from the elements. It passes close enough for her to see the old man, arms folded across his chest, a rosary in his hands. The drizzle runs like tears down his sunken cheeks and the breeze from the river blows through the wisps of dead white hair. May is frozen at the sight, half expecting a gnarled hand to rise and brush it back. She has never seen a corpse before. She grasps her mother's arm and turns to her in terror.

She sees the Duchess try to contain herself, but the performance of the past few days is suddenly, spectacularly, over. Mary Adelaide stares at the dirty trickle of the river, at the facades of the shuttered palaces, at the colourless eyes peering at them through the slits in the hoods.

'How far we are from home,' she sobs, the big body trembling. 'Oh, how very far we are from home.'

*

'Did you have the dream again, Papa?'

She sits beside the bed, watching over him and doing her embroidery. The nice American doctor has declared that there is no great cause for alarm. It is nothing more than a touch of sunstroke, though it may take quite some time to recover.

One morning, the Duke woke up in their rooms at the Hotel Paoli with his left arm paralysed, his left leg useless and his mouth crooked on the same side. Can the sun really do all that, May wondered? The day before, her father had no more of it than the rest of them as they took their daily carriage ride. So why were they not all similarly afflicted? May had wanted to ask the nice American doctor, but of course it would not have been right for a young girl to question a distinguished man.

She does not care for doctors because she does not care for ill health. It unsettles her and she will always shrink from the mess that it brings, as she shrinks now from the sight of the handsome face slightly twisted and the fine figure, that once waltzed with the Empress Elisabeth, lying here like some broken puppet. But it is her duty as a daughter to stand watch in this darkened bedroom, quietly mopping the sweat from his brow. So that is what she does.

'Was it the dream again, Papa?' she asks once more.

A sound comes from the crooked mouth but it is not quite intelligible. Only the eyes give the answer.

'Oh Papa,' says May.

She knows too well the significance of the dream. It only rises up when his spirits are down and the weight on his shoulders feels insupportable.

It is the dream that tells of the disastrous marriage of his parents, at least the tragic end of it. His mother, the morganatic wife, the carrier of commonplace blood into the pure royal line of Württemberg, attended a military review. Her horse, frightened by the noise, bolted and carried her straight into the path of a cavalry regiment at full gallop. A hundred hooves had trampled on the beautiful face that had so bewitched his father and so blighted them all. It was muttered by some that a woman of untainted blood would have known how to handle her horse. Breeding, they said, or the lack of it, will out.

Little Franz Teck was only four years old when his mother died. He scarcely remembers her, rarely speaks of her. But there came an evening back in White Lodge when he took a little too much port. My mother should have known her place, he told May. If she had, his silly father would have married someone else and his son and heir would have come into that which had rightfully belonged to him and of which she had deprived him.

Till the day he dies, whenever the void in his heart seems unbearable, he will hear the sound of the hundred hooves bearing down on her presumption and crushing it into the ground.

V

Winter/Spring, 1884

It is to be the place and time that is forever perfect. It is where and when she is purely happy. In the future, when she is sad or hopeless, she will always flee to it in her imagination. When her husband dismisses her opinion as being of no consequence. When she stands beside a burial mound of dead young men in the desolation of the Somme. When she hears the news from Ekaterinburg. When three of her children die before her and her eldest betrays everything she holds dear. All her life it will never fail her.

Eden is not too strong a word, she thinks at first sight of it. A garden in Tuscany. A garden to steal the soul.

It is quite unlike an English garden, where trees, plants and flowers must struggle against the elements. In the garden of the Villa I Cedri, the different aspects of nature work in harmony. Cossetted by the Italian sun, nature has no care in the world except to stretch herself out and ravish the eye like some spoilt, pretty woman. It is an easy life and that's a fact. Only the attentions of the gardeners who come to primp and preen intrude on her wild serenity. The English people who own the garden, and those of their race invited to admire it, seem to demand at least a semblance of neatness. Perhaps all that abandoned beauty discomfits them a little. Is it not just a little *de trop*, she hears them murmur from beneath their parasols, even a little bit vulgar?

But May Teck, the girl who recoils from disorder, never finds it so. In the space of a moment, she falls in love with every cypress tree and holly oak, with the great cedars that give the villa its name and bless the midday lawns with welcome rays of shadow. She befriends every white and pink magnolia, every bed of daffodils, violets and hyacinths, every crusty old urn bursting over with jonquils, heartsease or aconite. Nothing pleases her more than to sit by the edge of the pond and watch the frogs meander from beneath one lily pad to another.

On the other side of the garden wall, fields of olive trees roll down to the banks of the Arno. Here a rash of poppies tangles among the long grasses and a weir forces the sluggish water to wake up and shake itself into a frenzy of froth and spray. On the far bank, a tumbledown mill-house is half buried in a shroud of vines. From the terrace of the Villa I Cedri, the only sounds are of goat bells among the olives and the distant music of the water spilling over the weir. It is in this sleepy place that May Teck begins to open her eyes to the vibrancy of the world. It is here, in a landscape of light, that some sort of switch is pulled in her soul. And here too where she wins her very first compliment.

'You know May Flower,' Harry Thaddeus Jones says one day, 'I'm thinking you'll be quite an attractive young woman.'

At first she wonders if she has misheard. He says it without looking at her, his eyes cast down at his palette, his brush stabbing at a mess of watercolour splodges. He says it as if it is a simple, unremarkable fact then carries on with his work. It is as well she is required to sit perfectly still, otherwise she might run away into the sanctuary of the villa, where nobody has ever said a remotely similar thing, or down to the riverbank to sit among the poppies with cheeks as red as their petals. Instead, duty demands that she goes on sitting there, her expression unchanged, in her dress of creamy muslin and her Tuscan straw hat with two red ribbons falling down her back.

She notes of course that he has not said beautiful or even pretty, but then she never expected that.

'Oh chick, you've got Queen Charlotte's nostrils,' her mother declared when she was only six or seven. 'Let us pray they diminish with time.'

So now May wonders exactly what attractive means. Is it just a compensatory word for the absence of beauty or might it incorporate something else, something more meaningful? She dares to let herself hope.

As if reading her mind, Harry Thaddeus Jones looks up from his easel.

'Sure, I know you don't think that, May Flower,' he says. 'I watch you shrinking back from everything as if it'll bite you, but it is true. An attractive young woman. And when I finally allow you to look at this painting, you'll maybe be seeing it too.'

He always calls her May Flower. By rights, he should address her as Your Serene Highness, but he can get away with any impertinence in this house, because the Duke and Duchess adore him. Both have always been susceptible to a handsome young man. In their eyes, 'Mr Thaddy' can do no wrong. Harry Thaddeus Jones from the city of Cork, the up and coming artist, is their latest pet; frolicking round Mary Adelaide's skirts, coming whenever she calls; going for long walks with her convalescent husband and speaking of the things men talk about when alone. They were quite taken aback when, after dutifully capturing them both on canvas, he humbly asked to paint their daughter. No fee would be required, he said quickly.

'Oh chick, I believe you have a gentleman admirer,' the Duchess gushed from behind her fan.

But today in the garden, he calls her May Flower in quite a different way. No longer does it seem just a silly name for a young girl; there is something else too. She is sure of that, though she will not allow herself to put a name to it, not even tonight in the secrecy of her room.

He is no more than a few years older than she is, with dark, dancing eyes and an Irish voice that swoops and soars as he tells his funny stories and shows his card tricks. May, observing, at first thought Mr Thaddy as empty a vessel as most of those who now make up their acquaintance, but the impression soon changed. She saw there was a purpose and a weight to him, shining out of those dark eyes and lighting his way forward. She had never met anyone quite like him and, in her silent way, she is soon quite smitten.

When she examines her parents, as she does even more often these days, she can see little purpose there. Her poor Papa, recovering slowly from his seizure in the Hotel Paoli, still squanders his days looking for subtle slights and imaginary insults. He is not the same as he was; aged before his time, his infant tantrums are now worse than before. He is sliding away from her, she thinks, down an endless hill towards the edge of some precipice and, no matter how fast she runs, she cannot catch him up and pull him back. From this prospect, her Mama runs away, losing herself in a maze of trivialities; her gossip, her musical evenings and her charity bazaars. Why, May asks herself, do they seem to want nothing more?

Their first, bleak opinion of Florence did not last. In those first October weeks, they viewed it through the prism of shame at their exile and their yearning for home. But it was soon apparent to the Duchess that behind the facades of the shuttered palazzos hid a society that was highly congenial, at times even dazzling, especially in winter when half the aristocracy of Europe fled over the Alps towards less punitive climes. As the cousin of the great queen, all doors were flung wide open to her. Calling cards and invitations piled up around her feet like the autumn leaves, not just from the expatriate British, but from the oldest Florentine families and the glittering Russian nobility, rich beyond the bounds of decency. If Florence, or the part of it that mattered, had heard whisper of the deputation of the shopkeepers or the auction of the furniture, it chose to turn a deaf ear. It bowed low before Mary Adelaide and pulled her into the dance. In no time, she was comporting herself as a queen across the water and the news of it trickled back to the real monarch in her castle above the Thames.

'I *much* regret to hear that you have chosen Florence in which to settle,' she wrote. 'A town full of attractions and temptations to expense. Some quieter and more retired spot would surely have been better!'

But the slapping of the wrist came too late. The wrist in question was far too busy waving graciously from the royal box at the opera or from the carriage pulled by two white horses which she had hired to display herself, at the fashionable hour, along the bosky avenues of the Parco delle Cascine. At the soirées, she sat in splendour, bedecked in her tiara and the family diamonds which, even in the darkest hours of her disgrace, she had flatly refused to sell or even to pawn. Draped across her great bosoms, they shone like the badges of her triumph over adversity.

Week by week, their heartache for home eased, then a piece of luck came their way. An English lady humbly offered the use of her country house, a few miles from the heart of the city. The Duchess rushed to inspect it and declared it a fitting setting for someone of her station; a decision reached all the faster as no payment would be necessary. Miss Light was honoured to do this small service; all she asked in return was the great pleasure of inclusion into the Duchess's circle of friendship. Mary Adelaide was jubilant. What a saving would thus be made! And so much more spectacular than the hoarding of string, the economic use of writing paper or the use of second-rate horses to pull the carriage. Surely even Uncle George would be impressed.

With its roof of warm ochre tiles and walls washed in a shy yellow, the Villa I Cedri had stood on its bend of the Arno for five hundred years. Inside it was not without elegance, some magnificence even; the Galleried Hall quite outshone the drawing room at White Lodge. Yet its true benefit was not that it was free of rent, but that it was a happy house, suffused with sunlight and cheerful spirits. The Villa I Cedri embraced them inside its yellow walls, treated their wounds with its beauty and bade them be of good heart.

And so, on a hot spring afternoon just before her seventeenth birthday, young May Teck finds herself sitting in the garden, wild violets scattered in her lap, being painted by a young Irishman called Harry Thaddeus Jones.

'Mr Thaddy, since I came to Florence, I have realised that I know nothing,' she hears herself say in the direction of the easel.

Such an outpouring is quite unlike her but, since it seems she is on the way to being attractive, she is suddenly bold as well. 'At least nothing of importance.'

'And what exactly is it you'd be wanting to know?' he asks, his eyes not leaving the canvas.

'Everything. Absolutely everything. I should like to be an educated woman, you see. I should like to be of use in the world.'

'I'm aware of that, right enough,' he replies.

'How are you aware?'

'I'm a painter.' He smiles. 'I spend my days staring at faces. Do you imagine that I only see the flesh and bone? Do you think I can't read what is underneath?'

Inside the dress of creamy muslin, May's heart races and she prays to the Lord that is not true. She would never be able to look Mr Thaddy in the face again. These days, she is aware of feelings she has not felt before. She tells herself it is the heat.

'And what do you read in *me*?' she asks, the boldness vanquishing all else.

'That you're surely a changeling because you're not like the rest of your family and those who flutter round them.'

'But *you* flutter round them, do you not?'

Harry Thaddeus Jones throws back his handsome head and laughs.

'Ah yes May Flower, but I've got a living to earn and a reputation to make. I wasn't born a prince or a duke like your Papa. I'm having to bow and scrape a little. I must get my hands dirty and my clothes splashed with paint. But in truth that's a blessing. We need to get our hands dirty in this life. You'll never have to, which is a sad thing indeed.'

'You mean I won't ever really know the world.'

'Oh a few dainty corners of it sure, but not in the way you should.'

'But I'd so much like to,' she replies. 'My learning has been a paltry thing so far. They think it wasted on a girl.'

He puts down his brush. She is speaking with such animation that the pose is lost. Besides, it is hot now, too hot for this work. He mops his broad brow with a bright blue handkerchief and gazes hard at her until she has to look away, out over the fat magnolias towards the river. There has been a heavy shower of spring rain in the night and the weir is almost roaring.

'Well May Flower, if you're really wanting to know the world, you'll never start in a better place than this old town. The essence of life is here. Its pulse beats strong. But it's far beyond the confines of your mother's carriage. You'd have to stand down on the grubby earth with the rest of us.'

May rises from the chair. She gathers up the violets strewn across her lap and walks towards him.

'Would you guide me?' she asks, a bit more eagerly than she intends.

'Well, be warned, I would show you everything. Perhaps even things you'll not care to see.'

'I'm not afraid to dirty my hands,' she says.

Harry Thaddeus Jones folds his arms and studies the girl before him till she must look away again.

'You're a changeling right enough, are you not?' he says. 'Well then May Flower, we have an agreement.'

From the terrace, the Duchess calls them in for cool drinks and a little cake. Miss Light has arrived and brought her guitar. We might have a few songs, she calls. Wouldn't that be delightful?

'Jesus Christ,' says Harry Thaddeus Jones under his breath. Miss Light's voice is not as good as she believes it to be.

He folds his easel and stows it under one arm; his box of paints and brushes under the other. He strides off towards the terrace, then stops and looks back over his broad shoulder.

'I do believe,' he says, 'that you have all the makings of the *maitresse femme*.'

May Teck knows what both words mean, but has no idea of their combination, except to sense that it may not be entirely decent. Mr Thaddy smiles.

'No cause for blushing, May Flower,' he says. 'All it means is that you'll be quite a girl.'

She unfurls her parasol against the afternoon sun and follows him back across the garden. By now, she would follow him anywhere.

VI

Spring, 1884

It is after one in the morning, an hour at which most respectable young English ladies of not quite seventeen would be tucked up in bed, having said their prayers and begged forgiveness for their innocent sins. But that would be England and this is Italy. Thus, at such an ungodly time, May Teck is standing by a marble pillar in the salon of Lady Orford with Harry Thaddeus Jones by her side. Young Italian men with the coal black curls and silk-smooth faces of Botticelli angels crowd the room, but she would not swap her Irish cavalier for the lot of them.

For May Teck, this glittering chamber is not what it seems. It is not a pleasure palace but a classroom. Mr Thaddy is taking his promise most seriously. Not just in the palazzos of the *beau monde* or in the galleries and museums, but in the streets and in the marketplace, he is opening her eyes to the way of the world. Not the one she has known, hemmed in by the borders of Richmond Park and the trifling demands of her mother, but a world without boundaries. He does it of course with a degree of discretion. He is the Duchess's little pet after all. He cannot afford to incur her wrath and be thrown from her carriage to fend for himself. Not just yet anyway. The education of May Teck must be done by stealth and subterfuge, by nods and winks or, as now, whispered in her ear by a marble pillar in the small hours of a starlit Tuscan morning.

'See now over there,' he whispers, 'the woman playing whist.'

'With the three gentlemen?'

'One is her husband, another is her lover.'

May gulps and colours. She cannot think what to say.

'Why?' is the best she can manage.

'Because life, and in particular marriage, is a complicated business. Like the Arno, it doesn't always flow smoothly. Sometimes it is turbulent, sometimes it is arid and perhaps even ugly. But, in time, the calm of the surface can usually be restored. A civilised solution will be found. In this case, it is called a *menage a trois*.'

'And who is the third gentleman?' she asks.

'He's an earlier husband from whom she is now divorced.'

'Divorced? And she is still admitted to society?' says May. She has never heard of such a thing. Certainly not in Richmond or Sheen.

Mr Thaddy makes no reply, just looks down at her with that smile of which she dreams in her hot little bedroom at the Villa I Cedri.

For the rest of the night May can hardly take her eyes off the whist players. They are like strange creatures in a zoo, the like of which she has never seen before. How on earth do they make such an arrangement work? Who instigated it? And who is in control? Could it possibly be the woman? Surely not. Her own mother keeps her Papa firmly under her thumb, though that is largely a matter of domestic convenience; a comedy of manners like a cartoon in *Punch* of the big fat woman and the henpecked husband. But can an ordinary woman ever be the one who decides the important things, who lays down the rules by which her existence is lived?

She wonders if the Duchess knows in what company they find themselves tonight. If so, does it bother her? Or does she embrace it as exotic and even exciting? She wonders too if her mother might have another set of beliefs and values, kept tightly corseted inside her public self, of which her daughter knows nothing. Is that what all grown-ups do? Has young May been taken for a fool?

'I was right, wasn't I?' she says again to Harry Thaddeus Jones. 'I know nothing. Nothing at all.'

On the far side of the room, the Duchess is enthroned on a sofa beside old Lady Orford, fluttering her fan against the heat and the black cigar of her hostess. Lady Orford is a self-appointed head of the English in Florence; once a week she holds a salon from ten at night till four in the morning, puffing away without pause. It is this *grande dame* who offers May her first cigarette.

'But she is rather young, don't you think?' says the Duchess.

'Nonsense,' croaks the old lady. 'Most women are improved upon by being viewed through a slight film of smoke. It gives a haze of mystery they would not otherwise possess.'

Of course May chokes and coughs and feels a little sick. But the second is better than the first and the third better than the second. And how much she would like to possess an air of mystery, to be a woman of the world.

On the other nights of the week, the Duchess tests the springs of countless other noble couches. By day, she is visiting a church, a convent, an orphanage or a hospital for sick children. Or lunching in one of the gracious villas scattered in the hills around the city. Or playing hostess herself in the garden of the Villa I Cedri.

Mary Adelaide has found herself a whole new audience to captivate. She is, more than she ever imagined she could be in her exile, perfectly happy.

So hectic has her social life become that she scarcely notices much else. Without difficulty, Mr Thaddy persuades her to employ tutors for her daughter in Italian, French and music. He creates a reading list and presents it for Mary Adelaide's perusal. Since the Duchess never opens a book other than her own diary, she gives it no more than a glance. Had it contained *Lady Audley's Secret* or any other unsuitable work, she would have been none the wiser. But it does not. There is nothing scandalous or sensational here. The books are respectable literature, both English and, in translation, foreign; their laudable object to pull a sheltered mind into a whirlwind of new thought and feeling. Whenever she can get away from her mother, May sits in the garden or by the river among the tall grass and poppies, drinking in the paragraphs like someone who has just crossed a desert.

Yet after a while, even the Duchess notices the amount of time her daughter is spending in the company of Harry Thaddeus Jones. Dead Italian artists are safe, but a living Irish one, young and finely made, is a different thing altogether. Besides, when she feels in need of a compliment and looks around for Mr Thaddy to provide it, she is put out to be informed that he is otherwise engaged. And after all, the granddaughter of a king must observe certain proprieties. With perfect timing, the required chaperone appears off the train from London. A genteel lady of their acquaintance from Twickenham, named Mrs Monson. Wan and fluttery, like a nervous butterfly, she is no match for the Duchess in full sail. Poor Mrs Monson abandons whatever private plans and pleasures she may have envisaged and spends her time in Italy traipsing around in the tiring wake of Harry Thaddeus Jones and his eager pupil.

Dutifully, they tour the Duomo and the Baptistery, the Palazzo Vecchio, the monastery of La Certosa. They examine the frescoes in the churches of Santa Croce, Santo Spirito and Santo this, that and the other. They climb to the highest tower of Castello Vincigliata and up to Bellosguardo to admire the panorama of the city. They visit the houses of Michelangelo and Dante. They walk in the Boboli Gardens and around the Parco delle Cascine. Above all, they haunt the echoing chambers of the Uffizi and the Palazzo Pitti to make at least the passing acquaintance of Titian, Raphael, Leonardo, Fra Angelico, Andrea del Sarto and a score of others whom May struggles valiantly to remember. It is, she thinks, like going to some house party where there are just too many people. Yet she craves an introduction to them all, to find out how knowing them might help her know herself.

Now and then, from a distance, she sees a whispered exchange between her teacher and her chaperone. It is always the same; Mrs Monson fluttering, Mr Thaddy gritting his teeth. Oh what now?

'It seems I'm not to be taking you into that particular room, May Flower,' he says crossly. 'It seems you must not visit, as it were, the private parts of the gallery.'

Mrs Monson blushes and fans herself.

'There are things it is not fitting for a young lady of quality to see.'

'Nonsense,' snaps Mr Thaddy.

'Why not?' asks May.

'That is just the way it is,' replies Mrs Monson. 'And the way it will always be.'

'Christ preserve us,' says Mr Thaddy.

May herself is angry now. Though she rarely dares to show it, she has inherited a slice of her father's temper.

'But dear Mrs Monson, I often walk through the Piazza della Signoria,' she says. 'I am quite familiar with the statue of David.'

'Yes, well *that* is most unfortunate,' says Mrs Monson, fanning herself with even more vigour. 'I always raise my parasol against the sight of it and you, my dear, should do likewise.'

The same problem arises at the theatre. They see the great Salvini perform the Scottish play. When Lady Macbeth declares that she has 'given suck', a sharp intake of breath comes from May's chaperone. Nevertheless they return the next week to see him give *Othello*. Strangely, Mrs Monson appears to have no previous knowledge of its content and is even more upset. A white woman in a marriage with a black man is bad enough, but the suspicion of infidelity therein is even worse. Good grief. Such things do not happen in Twickenham. As Desdemona expires, Mrs Monson reaches for May and tries to coax her from their box. But May will not budge, gripping like a leech onto the arms of her chair. She is entranced. She wonders if she might ever induce such a violent passion in someone. How marvellous if she did.

By now, Mrs Monson's exhausted feet are covered in blisters. One morning, faced with the Uffizi yet again, she flops down at a pavement café and declares she can go no further. No my dears, not so much as an inch. Distracted by her own discomfort, she agrees that, on this occasion, the young people may enter the gallery without her. She will sit here for an hour or two and take a coffee in the sunshine. Perhaps with just a little brandy for her poor feet. Mrs Monson is fond of brandy.

Harry Thaddeus Jones seizes his chance. He leads May into the Uffizi through the front door and straight out of another at the rear.

'What are you doing?' she asks.

'I want to show you another painting,' he says. 'Quite unlike the ones you'll find in there.'

He hails a cab and hustles her into it, bearing her away from the elegant town with which she has become familiar. Up behind the basilica of Santa Croce, the streets soon get narrower, the houses smaller and humbler. The people passing by seem smaller also, smaller and more pinched, as if they find existence a harder thing. There are few pretty parasols to be seen here. Mr Thaddy stops the cab and jumps down.

'We're walking from here,' he says, reaching out his hand for her.

May finds herself in a scruffy street, the windows of the houses no more than ten feet apart. There is scarcely a glimpse of sky. Between the windows, washing hangs limp from fraying ropes. Women shout to each other across the chasm. Children in tattered clothes charge around May's skirts, chasing balls, bumping into her without fear or apology. Mr Thaddy strides out ahead, leading her off the street and into a small piazza. In one corner stands a tiny church with a dwarfish campanile, a far cry from the glory of Santa Croce. The church door is open. An organist, not very good, is practising and fills the little square with indifferent Bach. An old priest sweeps the steps, a cigarette drooping from his lips. He kicks away a dog relieving itself against the door.

'*Bastardo!*' The dog bares its teeth and flees.

At the opposite corner, men drink and smoke outside a tavern. Children charge and yell here too, earning a clout or a curse from the drinkers. Women stroll slowly around the piazza. They have rouge on their faces and cheap flashy bangles at their wrists. They try to win the attention of the men. Insults are thrown at them which are hurled right back on gobs of spit. One of the women spots Mr Thaddy.

'*Buongiorno* Harry,' she cries. '*Come stai, mio tesoro?*'

'*Buongiorno* Livia,' Mr Thaddy waves, but hurries on.

'You know that woman?' asks May.

'I do indeed,' he replies. 'I'd introduce you but we haven't got time.'

'But, isn't she...?'

'A woman of the streets?' he replies. 'She is, right enough. A fine model too.'

'You've *painted* her?' asks May, breathless as she tries to keep up. Mr Thaddy stops and turns.

'As I've painted your parents and yourself?' he laughs. 'Do you not care to be in her company?'

May blushes and does not reply. In the garden of the Villa I Cedri, Mr Thaddy spoke the truth when he said he could read her face.

'I've merely sketched the poor woman. I only use paint on those who can afford to pay me for it.'

A horrid thought strikes young May Teck.

'Did she pay you for the sketch? With the money that she...?'

'That she earns on the street?' he replies. 'No, I paid her, so you needn't be worrying about that.'

Mr Thaddy stops laughing and looks straight into her eyes.

'Welcome to the grubby earth, May Flower,' he says.

He puts a key in the door of a tattered building beside the church.

'What is this place?'

'My studio,' he replies. 'Come and see.'

It is not the first time that May Teck has visited the studio of an artist. With her Mama, Miss Light and Mrs Monson, she has been received into the ateliers of several of the city's most notable painters and sculptors to watch them at work and, it is devoutly hoped by their hosts, to make a purchase. But such places have never been more than a stone's throw from the safety of the Piazza della Signoria. Workshops or not, they have been acceptably neat and tidy. There has always been a well-upholstered sofa to sit on while they drink the tea and eat the cake offered by a uniformed servant. No lady required to avail herself of the facilities in such an establishment need ever be anxious about their cleanliness and comfort.

But this is different. May has never seen such a mess except perhaps in the bedrooms of her brothers in White Lodge. To be sure, there is a sofa, but it is ripped and sprouts horse-hair, its ancient damask faded by the sun and stained with God knows what. The smell in the room is unlike anything her young nose has yet encountered; paint and turpentine, the glue that binds canvas onto frame, old tobacco and the aroma of cooking that has lodged in the cracks of the fissured, peeling walls.

A door leading to another room lies half-open. She glances through it and wishes she had not done so. An old iron bedstead, sheets rumpled, clothes draped across a chair or dropped onto the rough wood floor. Just like the smelly bedrooms of her siblings, except there is some other scent too. An odour she does not recognise. Harry Thaddeus Jones follows her gaze and quickly closes the door.

'I'm not sure I should be here,' she says.

For the first time ever in his company, May feels just a little afraid, though she knows that is ridiculous and that she is only afraid of herself.

'You surely shouldn't,' he replies. 'But don't worry, this is purely a cultural excursion. I've only brought you here to show you a painting.'

She turns to look at the drawings pinned carelessly on the walls and the canvases propped up against the old sofa. She sees uncompleted sketches of faces she knows; her mother and father, old Lady Orford, Miss Light posed with her guitar.

'No not these,' says Mr Thaddy. 'These are bread and butter, nothing more. Here's the thing I want to show you.'

He goes into the closed bedroom, returning with a canvas wrapped in a piece of rough cloth. He swings it up onto an easel and pulls away the veil.

'This is the piece of which I am most proud.'

In the dark interior of a peasant's cottage, a young woman attends a wounded man. A shotgun, a hat and two poached rabbits have been cast down on the floor. The young man's jacket hangs on the back of his chair. His torso is naked; a wound visible on his shoulder. As the woman cradles his head and tends the injury he leans into her body for comfort. It is clear she knows every inch of him and he of her. Into his pain, she brings balm. Intimacy exudes from the picture so strongly that it feels like an intrusion to breathe the same air. May feels her cheeks begin to burn.

Despite the best efforts of Mrs Monson, she has not been entirely shielded from the acres of bare celestial flesh on the walls of the Uffizi and the Palazzo Pitti. She has been up to her eyes in breasts, buttocks and the comical appendages of the male. But she has never seen anything like this before. There is nothing celestial in the hovel of the peasants, she thinks, but realises at once that judgement is quite wrong. As much as any female from the brush of Michelangelo or Titian, the peasant's wife is an angel. An angel who stands on grimy earth, but an angel for all that. May Teck wonders if she will ever cradle a man's head just like that. Will anyone ever turn his face into her breast to seek shelter there?

Unlike in the Uffizi, Mr Thaddy does not provide his usual little lecture about the canvas before them. He does not speak of its inspiration, its brushwork or its play of light and shade. For several minutes, he says nothing at all. He merely watches her as she vanishes into his picture and waits till she begins to re-emerge.

'I'm not sure I'm ready for this,' she says, so softly he can hardly hear the words.

'Oh, I'm thinking you are,' he replies, 'or I'd not have shown it to you. Do you like it?'

'That's not the right question.'

'No indeed. Will you remember it then?'

'Oh yes. Always.'

'Do you understand why I wanted you to see it?'

'Oh yes.'

In the doorway, May pauses.

'And where is the sketch of your friend Livia?' she asks.

'Ah well... Livia.' He smiles. 'Perhaps you're not quite ready for Livia yet.'

VII

Spring/Summer, 1884

On her seventeenth birthday, God is kind and gives her a perfect day. One of those Tuscan mornings when it feels like He lives not on some distant cloud but in this very city, in some grand but discreet palazzo, keeping Himself to Himself and getting on with the many jobs he has in hand.

The sky is the soft blue of a baby's bonnet. In the clear air of late spring, the distant dome of the Duomo and the tower of the Palazzo Vecchio are etched needle-sharp against the Apennines. And before the torrid summer comes, the waters of the Arno are still a pretty yellow-green as it navigates between the arches of the Ponte Santa Trinita. But visitors must now queue for the best tables at the cafés in the Piazza della Repubblica. The hotels are fast filling up and in the expensive shops the tills are ringing like carillons. Even the vain carriage-horses seem to tilt their chins a little higher and shake their plumed heads more than strictly necessary.

In one such conveyance, May Teck is being driven to the Cascine. This is no novelty as they go at least thrice a week so that the Duchess may be seen by her public, but today is special. Today is not just May's birthday but also the day of the great flower *Corso*. Today, the fashionable ladies of Florence are to be worshipped by the fashionable gentlemen. In pony traps brimming over with flowers, the gentlemen will career at high speed between the avenues of trees pelting the ladies' carriages with blossom and adoration. By the end of the morning, a woman of even passable looks should have gathered an armful at least; while a beauty can expect, like a diva at the opera, to be ankle deep in petals and stems. Venus herself could hardly ask for more.

May does not especially want to go. Parades are for her mother, she thinks, not for her. But of course, there is no escape. The Duchess can hardly wait to get there. She has spent twice as long at her toilette as usual. Surely it is not just an event for young girls; can the more mature woman not expect to be admired also? After all, is there not still beauty in the fullest of blooms? Are the Italians not noted for their appreciation of the larger figure? Nobody is likely to shout 'Fat Mary!' at her here. Anyway, Mary Adelaide does not consider that her petals have even begun to crinkle.

Yet, on the birthday of her daughter, she is not entirely self-centred. Yesterday, in the greatest secrecy, she offered Harry Thaddeus Jones a sum of money to distribute among some young bucks of his acquaintance. Since it is to be her chick's special day, might they kindly aim some of their missiles in her direction? The Duchess would be most grateful. She was surprised when her lapdog, for the first time in their acquaintance, growled fiercely back at her.

'Fie Duchess, I don't think that will be remotely necessary,' he snapped at his mistress and turned on his heel. Well, well.

And the lapdog is proved correct. No bribes are required to ensure that tributes land safely in their carriage. And not merely from those whose acquaintance they have already made in the palazzos. Unknown young gentlemen, those of the Botticelli skin, hurl copious blossoms towards May Teck.

'*Buongiorno bellissima. Come ti chiami?*'

She flushes of course, but no longer does she look away as she would have done so recently. Nor does she giggle or gush or throw up her hands with girlish glee. Instead she simply smiles and inclines her head. The young bucks pretend to swoon. They shout across that their hearts are breaking, that they will dream tonight of her beauty.

But now she breaks her own spell and begins to laugh. Harry Thaddeus Jones realises he has never heard May Teck laugh before. And what a laugh it is; deep, gurgling and unstoppable as the water cascading over the weir at the Villa I Cedri. Christ, it is almost that of a man.

'Oh chick,' says the Duchess. 'You really mustn't laugh out loud. You have such a *vulgar* laugh.'

May raises her fan to cover her face but still the laughter goes on. Mr Thaddy starts too and soon all dignity is gone from the carriage of the Tecks. The Duchess seems a little put out and orders the horses turn towards home. Too much excitement before luncheon, she declares, bodes ill for the rest of the day. All along the Lungarno, people smile and wave at the carriage with the young English girl set like a pearl in a bower of blossom.

May finds herself waving back, not in the refined way she has been taught by her mother, but as if she has known them all her life. It amazes her that she could ever have found the Italians unappealing, needing a wash and stinking of garlic. Now she thinks them the most wonderful people in the world, overflowing with the joy of God's creation. Now she thinks of this city as the unexpected destination of her soul. May, observing herself as well as others, sees quite clearly that something inside her has shifted. While the Duchess shelters in the shade of her parasol, May stays in the full spring sunlight. For the first time in her life, she no longer feels like the smallest person in the carriage. There has never been, she thinks, a day like this.

In the Galleried Hall of the Villa I Cedri, her presents are displayed on a table, all ready to be opened. A golden bracelet, an embroidered cushion, a book of songs, an album for photographs, a sheaf of writing paper, a *bonbonnière* of sugared almonds, a brooch, a sapphire horseshoe pin. From her grandmother in England come two pounds only, perhaps feeling that no larger sum could be safely entrusted to any child of Mary Adelaide in case extravagance might be a curse that runs in the blood.

Mr Thaddy gives her a fan on which he has painted apple blossoms. There is a shyness in the giving, quite unlike him, that touches her far more than the gift itself. This sudden modesty must mean something, no? But the fan is a mere *bagatelle*, he says. She will have his real present tonight.

In Tuscan twilight, the gardens of the Villa I Cedri fill up with the acquaintances of their exile. Chinese lanterns are strung between the cedars but they are scarcely needed; the moon is floating upwards and the sky is pocked with stars. Miss Light brings her guitar but thankfully is not required to play it as the Duchess has hired a small orchestra. No expense must be spared on her chick's birthday and honestly, she tells the Duke, it is hardly more than a band.

A wooden surface has been laid for dancing. May waltzes and polkas with her Papa, her brothers, the elderly gentlemen of her parents' new court, even one or two of the Botticelli bucks. Over every shoulder, she searches the throng for Mr Thaddy, but he is nowhere to be seen. As the darkness deepens, the fireflies come to join in the waltzes and the polkas. May watches them flutter and flicker through the air. How beautiful they are, but oh how brief their time. And with no other purpose, no other relevance, beyond the parading of their prettiness. May looks at the other young women, the girls of her tribe, dancing round the garden, happily wrapped inside manly arms which will protect them from falling, but also steer them in whatever direction those arms decide they should go. Are they content with that? Can it be enough for them? And what will they feel one day when the mirror shows them that their fire is beginning to fade? Like her own mother, many will refuse to countenance that idea and will flutter on too long. But, May wonders, would the fading matter so much if there was something more they had to offer?

At seventeen, perched like a diver on the cliff edge of life, young May Teck is exhilarated, but uneasy too. What might *she* donate to the sum of humanity? And what if there is nothing at all to donate? What if she is merely ordinary? If her pretty dress and her diamond earrings were to vanish in a flash, would she be of any more significance than the maid who cleans her room or the peasant who washes her laundry?

These past few months, as Mr Thaddy has led her through the galleries, museums and churches, she has at least shaken hands with greatness. The acquaintance of Signori Titian, da Vinci, Michelangelo and the rest, has not left her unmarked and she is grateful for it. But that of course is the greatness of men. Where is the glory of her own sex? They cannot all be dancing in moonlit gardens, riding in the Cascine or even suckling children. Or can they? Aunt Queen is the only woman she knows of much true import in this world. But even she, the deity in lace and bombazine, is hemmed in and tied down by the men in the black frock coats. It is hardly encouraging. Yet, she thinks as she lies awake in the Florentine night, there must surely be some way to make herself of some consequence. Above all, she fears what her French tutor, a melancholic would-be poet, calls *la petitesse de la vie*. May Teck will not, she vows to herself, ever settle for the smallness of life.

She is often awake in the early hours now. Listening to the cicadas and the distant tumble of the weir, she frets about other matters too. The things that worry any girl who stands on the cliff edge fearful of, yet yearning for, the moment of the dive. Once, when she dreamed, she saw the painting of the wounded poacher, his head cradled by his ministering angel. But now it was the tousled Irish head of Harry Thaddeus Jones and the comforting arms were her own. When she woke and remembered, her hand drifted down between her thighs as it had learned to do of late. There was wetness there too, though not the kind she had come to like. Oh no. Damn and blast. She pulled herself out of the stained sheets, the rage rising up in her. Why must only women bleed?

Tonight, after supper is served, the highlight is to be the unveiling of her portrait by Harry Thaddeus Jones. Nobody has been allowed a previous glimpse of it, not even its subject. Only now does the artist appear among them, carrying his offering under his arm, wrapped in a cloth of deep green silk. The guests gather in the Galleried Hall as Mr Thaddy pulls the cloth away. Everyone applauds and mutters the right words, but they do not trouble to really look. It is just another portrait after all and most of them already possess at least one such of their own. They drift quickly back to the gardens and the dancing. Only artist and subject remain.

May stares at herself in the Tuscan straw hat with the red ribbons down the back. He has not flattered her, she thinks. Queen Charlotte's nostrils are quite evident, but it hardly matters; he has, as they say, caught her. Not as others see her, the quiet girl in the shadows, nor the way she used to see herself, but as she now recognises herself to be. A girl who no longer knows nothing. The twinkle in the china-blue eyes. The faint smile on the lips. The possibility. The woman to come.

'Well?' asks Harry Thaddeus Jones.

'So that is me?' she says.

'It's how I find you,' he replies, 'which is all the artist can do. Does it please you?'

'Yes.'

'And do you see it May Flower?'

'Yes. I see it.'

'I told you, didn't I?' he says. 'Behold the *maitresse femme*.'

'I'm still not sure what that means,' she replies.

'It means you have the strength to steer by your own star,' he says, 'if that's what you're wanting to do.'

'It is,' she says. 'If only I am brave.'

Through the doors from the terrace her mother returns, trailing the notes of the polka behind her. For once, the Duchess does not bustle or rush, but walks slowly towards them across the Galleried Hall. She had applauded with the rest of them yet said not a word. Mr Thaddy is a little anxious now. Does Mary Adelaide not like it? His funds are getting low and he needs a new commission from one of her gilded friends.

The Duchess stops before the painting on the easel. Instead of the usual gush and gabble, there is only silence. Several times, she looks from the picture to her daughter then back again. It is a look of curiosity. In the light of the candles, May sees that her mother's eyes are glazed, but then a smile breaks out on the nectarine cheeks. She takes her daughter's hand and kisses it.

'Oh May,' she says. 'Oh May.'

VIII

1885-1891

When the Duchess descends from the boat train at Victoria Station, May thinks her mother might fall to her knees and kiss the platform.

The stationmaster whose devotion Mary Adelaide had won on her departure eighteen months before, is waiting in his best uniform, a bunch of roses in his sweating palm.

'My good man,' she exclaims, gazing all about her. 'Everything as lovely as ever.'

The sentence on the Tecks was now judged to have been served and Uncle George, with the sanction of Aunt Queen, has permitted them to return home in the faint hope that lessons have been learned. But the Duchess is still regarded as a delinquent and remains on probation. A comptroller installed by Aunt Queen is now to run the errant household at White Lodge. On first acquaintance, he seems a pleasant, meek man, but his meekness is deceptive and at last Mary Adelaide meets her match.

'Does your Highness really require a barouche, a landau, a brougham, a phaeton, a waggonette *and* a dog-cart?'

'Yes!' she replies, perplexed, as if it is the stupidest question she has ever heard.

They exist together like fencing partners. Now and again, the Duchess will inflict a flesh wound or two on his endless proposals for financial restraint but most of the time, he has her right up against the wall with the tip of the foil at her throat. Next week, or perhaps even tomorrow, they will duel again and so it goes on.

At first, May Teck was deeply happy to be back in White Lodge. Once just a simple hunting-box from which the first Hanoverians had sallied forth to chase the deer, it has grown with the years; now two curving corridors link the *corps de logis* to a matching pair of smaller wings. May always fancies the curving corridors look like arms thrown wide to welcome you home. And how pleased she was to return to her dear little bedroom high above the park, to see the familiar faces of the servants and take the well-worn walks along the river to Ham or Marble Hill. The dust sheets of her old life were thrown back and folded away as if they had never been employed at all.

Yet the climate soon oppresses her. She does not mind the bright winter cold, it is the dirty grey umbrella of an English sky that crushes the spirit. It never bothered her before, but now she has tasted a life in the light and her heart still yearns for its radiance. As she lies awake in the early morning of yet another doleful day, it seems as if the old yellow walls of the Villa I Cedri are now no more substantial than the gossamer palaces of her dreams. She fights to keep them solid, to keep the memory of Florence at the very core of her being, but it is hard. Dear Lord, how hard. She is now daughter, secretary and lady-in-waiting rolled into one; the very personification of the comptroller's enforced economies. The barouche and the landau may not be sacrificed but it seems that the happiness of a child is carelessly expendable. She is '*May-do-this, May-do-that*'.

Once more, she is imprisoned in the shadow of her mother, once more she is the smallest person in the carriage. As it drives through Richmond Park or Kew Gardens, no young men throw flowers or shout that they might die of love. In Italy, her days were filled with the excitement of expectation and discovery. Now instead, they have become indistinguishable, each following the other like sheep through a gate. Good works. Worthy causes. Well-meaning people. A visit to a factory in Finsbury, to the Barnardo's Home in Bethnal Green. Above all, the damned Needlework Guild; her mother's favourite charity, the one which Mary Adelaide is sure will guarantee not just her admission at the Pearly Gates, but that St Peter himself will be there to offer his arm and escort her inside.

But poor May Teck is blessed with a saving grace. Soon after their return to England, she corners her parents and demands politely, but with more stubbornness than she has ever shown, that she be allowed to continue the studies she began in Florence. The comptroller is consulted. He will permit the hiring of a live-in tutor in exchange for the removal of the phaeton, two horses and a groom. May frets about the groom and strives to find him a new place, but does not back down and soon a little woman from Alsace sweeps into White Lodge. She is middle-aged, thick-waisted and far from pretty with a mottled complexion that knows neither powder nor rouge. But, like the comptroller, appearances are deceptive. A bracing breeze, Madame Helene Bricka brings with her the cool perspective of someone who has never lived in a lilac-scented cocoon. Not used to royal personages, she does not bow and scrape. Mary Adelaide meets yet another match.

'Who is the mistress of this house now?' the Duchess snaps one day. 'Not me any more, that's quite certain.'

At once, Madame Bricka becomes May Teck's best friend in the world. Her comfort and joy. Her only hope of salvation. She and Madame Bricka hide themselves away in a small white sitting room at the far end of one of the curving corridors, as distant as possible from the Duchess and her demands. Here there is stillness. Here hangs her portrait from the garden of the Villa I Cedri. Here is where the books live. As the months and years pass, the white sitting room becomes the heartbeat of May Teck's existence. Here is home.

Madame Bricka's designated task is to teach French and German, but she leads her pupil into far wider landscapes. They read history, ancient and modern, and the lives of great personages. They read journals and treatises on the industrial and social conditions in Aunt Queen's realm. They read modern literature. Sitting in her favourite small chair, its back carved into the shape of an open fan, May makes the acquaintance of Dorothea Brooke, Maggie Tulliver and Gwendolen Harleth and is amazed to discover that Mr George Eliot was not male. She is even more surprised to learn of the author's scandalous life; living in sin with a married man, unabashed at her exclusion from polite society.

'And such a plain creature, ugly even,' Madame Bricka laughs. Despite all her cleverness, she is a giggler too. 'Perhaps there is hope for me yet. Perhaps I could tempt your Uncle George.'

'Oh Bricka,' says May. 'You *are* wicked. Have you tempted many gentlemen?'

'Certainly not.'

'But you must once have tempted Monsieur Bricka, surely?'

At once, May regrets her impertinence. The tutor never speaks of her past life. The mildest enquiry is met with the briefest answer as if the question is a pointless distraction. But Bricka, with a sigh, fixes May in her gaze.

'Monsieur Bricka does not exist, *Princesse*. He never has. I am not Madame, I am Mademoiselle.'

'I don't understand.'

'When graciously offering me this position, your Mama decreed that it would be best if I were given the status of a married lady. Especially a woman of my age. To win me respect in the eyes of the other servants. In your eyes too of course. It seems this is common practice in all the best houses.'

'But my respect for you would never depend on such a thing,' says May.

'Then you're the exception, *ma chere*,' replies Bricka. 'In this world, the unmarried woman is often to be pitied and dismissed as being of no value. After all, she's a failure, is she not? She has failed to win the protection of a man. She has failed to bear children and contribute to the future of humanity. What is the point of her? A question asked not only by men but by other women, too, perhaps even more fiercely.'

Madame Bricka feeds a corner of chocolate biscuit to May's little dog and sighs again.

'Whatever her achievements, the single woman counts for little in their eyes. It scarcely matters that she might, as I do, speak four languages or be as well-read as any professor of literature at Oxford or the Sorbonne. Or be able to debate with any man, should she dare such impertinence.'

'Or even to argue with my Mama?'

'I'm not as brave as you think. If I were, I should have refused to have your mother's small deception imposed upon me. It is my shame and I regret it. But I suppose I must now go on being Madame. Oh well, *tant pis*.'

'Then dear Bricka, let's promise each other that inside this room, we shall always speak the truth and be concerned only with the things which really matter.'

'Indeed we will, *Princesse* and let us be very grateful for this place. We are privileged. So many women, most perhaps, have no such room to call their own. No sanctuary from the responsibilities and expectations laid upon them in this world.'

But their hours in the white sitting room are often hard-won. The Duchess does not relinquish her grip that easily. Every year, the principal rooms of White Lodge are turned into a draper's shop as the new-made clothing from the good ladies of the Needlework Guild is gathered on trestle tables to be sorted and distributed to the poor. Everyone in the house, even Madame Bricka, is sucked into the merciless vortex.

'I've had the most peculiar dream,' May says one morning at breakfast, six summers after they have returned from Florence. 'I was walking across the inner hall past all those tables laden with the clothes. Suddenly, the arm of a jacket came to life. Truly. It reached out for me and slipped itself through mine. Then pairs of trousers wrapped themselves around my legs. Scarves around my neck. What can it mean, Bricka?'

'It is perfectly obvious, *Princesse*,' replies Madame Bricka, crunching into her buttered toast with more force than quite necessary. 'It does not require a great detective to work it out.'

'I struggled against them, like poor Laocoon wrestling the serpents,' says May. 'But they were dragging me down into some dark, awful place when I woke up with the most frightful start.'

'I know exactly where they were dragging you,' says Madame Bricka. 'To that miserable cell which you so correctly call *la petitesse de la vie*. A destination from which it is my role in this house to protect you.'

Madame Bricka dabs her lips with her napkin to remove crumbs of toast or smears of butter, pushes back her chair and heads to the door.

'Wait here,' she says.

In a few minutes, May hears raised voices coming from her mother's room. Her old habit has not died; again she hides herself among the potted palms at the foot of the staircase.

'The Princess must have sufficient time to devote to her studies.'

'Yes of course, Bricka. I do so agree.'

'But how can she have time when you require her to assist you in so many of your charitable works?'

'May has plenty of opportunities for reading her books. Goodness me, her nose is never out of one.'

'It may seem so to you Duchess, but I assure you it is not the case. We have a strenuous programme of work to accomplish this winter.'

Mary Adelaide has a busy day ahead, her mind already racing with the things she has to do, all those good folk she wants to please. Wherever she goes, she is Lady Bountiful and wishes to remain so. But she is older now and her energy is not what it has been. She eats ever more sugar plums to sustain her. And worse, with every year, her husband becomes more vexatious, more unpredictable. The illness he had suffered in Florence, the attack so swiftly dismissed as sunstroke, was clearly something more. Yesterday he threw a teapot straight at her. He missed her head but struck at her heart. She wonders what the future holds and she is frightened.

So the tutor chooses the wrong moment at which to confront the Duchess. When she gets no reply, she repeats herself.

'A really strenuous programme,' she says. 'And the Princess's education is surely more important than the Needlework Guild.'

'Why?' shouts Mary Adelaide, driven beyond endurance. 'Answer me that, Bricka. Why? Education for a girl is no more than a *divertissement*. What good will it do her in the real world? Do you wish to make her too clever to get a husband?'

May abandons her hiding place among the palms, flees up to her room and locks the door. From the window, she watches her mother's carriage head off into town.

'*Why?*' she calls aloud in its wake. 'Why Mama? Because what else is there going to be for me? What else Mama?'

On her next birthday, May Teck will be twenty-five. In the eyes of the world, or at least of the one she must inhabit, the bloom is even now beginning to fade. At the balls in Park Lane and the country house weekends, she is gently manoeuvred into the path of potential suitors but, with a smile, a bow and a few crumbs of polite conversation, they skirt around her and go on their way. The young princes who go hunting in the salons of Europe search for dazzling beauty or, failing that, for obvious, easy charms. May Teck has neither. Even more to the point, they seek unblemished blood and unlimited fortune. Nor does May Teck possess those advantages. They have looked her up in the *Almanach de Gotha* and found her wanting. That comfy place on the shelf, which her own mother only avoided at the very last minute, now looms large in the imagination of her daughter. History is repeating itself most cruelly. *May-do-this, May-do-that.*

Of course, none of this is spoken of. But from time to time, once or twice a year perhaps, a strange atmosphere enters the house. Her parents, both so noisy as a rule, become suddenly quieter. For a week or two, it is almost as if they are avoiding her, sneaking into the Duke's study for private conversation. Sometimes Uncle George scampers across the park in his pony trap and disappears into the study too. On these occasions, May returns to the potted palms and listens to the voices beyond the door.

'Well, this one won't have her either,' she hears the Duke sigh one day. 'The letter has come from his father in Germany. Most gracious of course. The boy was charmed to meet her etcetera, but...'

'Oh poor May,' says the Duchess. 'Poor May.'

'Your daughter falls between two stools, sister,' replies Uncle George. 'That's the nub of it. Too noble for the average British aristocrat, not noble enough for the Protestant royal houses of Europe.'

'My blood you mean,' says the Duke. May can almost hear his fingers drumming on his knee.

'Sorry Franz, but that's about the size of it. You know what sticklers they are for such things. The Germans especially.'

'I know it all too well.'

'But perhaps that might not signify if the right young man appears,' says the Duchess. 'Cupid's arrow may strike. Love can conquer all.'

'May is a good, sensible girl,' replies Uncle George. 'But I doubt, sister, that she will ever inspire great passion in anyone.'

'Oh brother, how cruel,' says the Duchess, a sob cracking in her throat.

So that is the judgement? A good, sensible girl. She forces herself to remember that is not what Harry Thaddeus Jones had recognised and painted. The *maitresse femme*. The girl who could steer by her own star. She remembers too that other painting, of the wounded poacher and his wife. Still, she dreams of someone who will rest his head on her breasts and look to her for comfort and solace. Someone who will hold her in his arms and seek no greater joy from his time on this earth. How she would repay such devotion.

But now, she thinks, the words of her uncle may stay with her forever.

IX

The stag is at bay. The lady is not. Across a few yards of fern, moss and limp autumnal bracken, they stare at one another. The stag seems discomfited; he is not accustomed to formidable women. He is the leader of his herd, used to deference and obedience. He cannot understand why this female stands her ground.

'Jesus, will you be careful there, Madame Bricka,' calls Harry Thaddeus Jones. 'Stay well back now. It's the rutting season, remember?'

'All the more reason to face him down, *monsieur*,' the lady answers over her shoulder, not shifting her gaze from the monarch of the heath.

'It is the stag and the lioness,' whispers May Teck. 'Bricka knows no fear.'

'Well I bloody well do,' he says, 'and I'm not wanting those feckin' antlers in my arse one bit.'

He pulls May towards the partial shelter of the old oaks that fringe the pond. She is glad of it. Ever since childhood, she has been a little afraid of the deer of Richmond Park. She prefers to appreciate their beauty from her bedroom window or the safety of a fast-moving carriage. Up close, where she can see the ticks on their coats, smell their dung and look into their eyes, is infinitely less appealing. Like her Papa, they are docile one minute and aggressive the next. Like her Papa, they can be wild, even frightening creatures.

The stag is stamping and pawing the ground. He starts to pace round in tight little circles. He seems at a loss for what to do.

'Christ, he's going to charge,' says Harry Thaddeus Jones.

'What are you going to do?' asks May.

'*Me*? You're expecting me to wrestle it to the ground? You overestimate me sadly, May Flower.'

It is a calm day without the faintest whisper of a wind. The reds, golds and yellows still cling to the branches of the oaks and elms. The leaves hang motionless, as if by doing so they might escape the attention of the first great gale of autumn which will rip them from their perch and pulverise them into the sodden earth. On the two little lakes called Pen Ponds, the mandarin ducks cackle in panic as the swans lose their temper and flap them out of the way.

As Harry Thaddeus Jones wonders if he must try to be a hero, the stag stops pacing, throws back his head and gives a roar that echoes across the blue-black water and deep into the wilting October woods. He gives the woman in the brown serge cape one last contemptuous glare then bolts off into the undergrowth.

Madame Bricka turns to her companions. There is no smile of triumph on her face, just the prim satisfaction of a task accomplished.

'Bricka, you nearly made my heart stop,' says May.

'Fear not, *Princesse*,' she replies. 'I have no intention of leaving this world while your grip on the French subjunctive remains as shaky as it is.'

Their walk is resumed. Mr Thaddy carries a bag with sketch pads and pencils in case they find an interesting composition. Now though, he has lost interest for today. Nothing, he claims, is going to top *Woman With Stag At Bay*. He must get back to his studio in Kensington to start sketching it. Who knows, he might become the new Landseer.

May sees so much less of him these days. Since he too returned from Italy, the coming man has well and truly arrived. By now his august sitters include Mr Gladstone, the great Franz Liszt and Pope Leo himself no less.

'The first Irishman to paint the Holy Father,' he wrote to her. 'Sure is that not something May Flower? If they carve that on my tomb, I'll die happy.'

Still, whenever he can, he drives out to White Lodge to visit his old patrons whose beneficence in Florence and whose connections across the courts of Europe have been the springboard for his current elevation. He remains the pet of the Duchess, though now he is allowed a considerably longer leash. And still May's heart lifts at the sight of him. For the last few years it has been something for her heart to do. It has been otherwise quite unoccupied.

Now, in the desolate aftermath of her uncle's words, it was Harry Thaddeus Jones she wanted to see more than anyone else in the wide world. He didn't need to say or do anything of consequence. Just a look would have sufficed, just one of his smiles, to remind her that she once had possibility.

A telegram had been sent inviting him to tea, but he replied that he was off to Paris in the morning. An important new commission. He would return within the month and promises to call at once. He looks forward to seeing his May Flower. For the next few weeks, she read that telegram again and again.

But her poor mind was given little peace. In those same weeks, as she waited for Mr Thaddy, the strange atmosphere descended on the house once again. And this time, her parents were behaving even more oddly than before. Yet she was confused. Since the most recent candidate took flight, there had been no more balls, no more dinner tables at which to be marooned beside some young gentleman, both clutching for the lifebelt of some topic which might rescue them from silence. But there was something afoot, she was quite sure of it. By now, she could smell it. It was quite unmistakeable. The smell of her own fear.

But at last Harry Thaddeus Jones returned from Paris and has finally come to tea. And now, with Madame Bricka, they walk around Pen Ponds with the sketch pads and the pencils. Years ago, when her two friends had first met, May had worried that they would not be compatible: the academic from Alsace and the Irishman who painted the prostitutes of Santa Croce. But the anxiety was unfounded. In their different ways, they had travelled the same hard road from nothing to something; brother and sister under the skin.

'Something's going on,' May blurts out suddenly. She half-fancies she has said it in her head, then realises she has not.

'*Princesse?*'

For a moment, May hesitates. But she wants, she needs, to confide.

'Something's going on,' she says again. 'Have you not felt it, Bricka?'

'There is certainly some kind of agitation in the house.'

'Mama says hardly a word to me, but she is sitting on something like a goose on a golden egg. I think she might soon burst with the effort.'

Mr Thaddy stands at a distance, looking out over the ponds as if, suddenly, he is no longer of their party. Madame Bricka makes no reply.

'Do you know anything, dear Bricka?'

'I know nothing, *Princesse*.'

'But you suspect something don't you?'

'Have I ever lied to you?'

'I'm sure you haven't.'

'So I repeat. I know nothing, but yes, yes I do suspect.'

Nothing more need be said. Madame Bricka does not lower her eyes, does not flinch from May's frightened gaze, any more than she flinches from anything else. Instead, she holds it firm and returns it with reassurance and an unspoken promise. Whatever happens now, Bricka will stand by her side.

'Dear God,' says May.

She looks towards the figure gazing out over the pond. 'Mr Thaddy, do you hear?'

He turns, smiles, nods. But in the nod is the veiled weariness of a reader at the ending of a tale whose inevitable denouement he has long ago foreseen.

An autumn shower begins to spit across the surface of the water. The mandarin ducks paddle to the shelter of the reeds. The trio hurries back towards the house, Mr Thaddy striding ahead, as he always does, the bag of sketch pads under his arm. May's mind flits to the garden of the Villa I Cedri, following in his wake across the soft Tuscan lawns as she follows him now through the harsh English bracken. But it is not the same in the rain. The sunlight has gone out of it.

When White Lodge veers into view, she knows at once that the incipient fever inside its walls has finally taken hold. The house is disorientated, flustered. There are lights at windows never lit this early in the day. From the stables, horses whinny and grooms shout. Figures bustle around the garden gates. A footman, bearing umbrellas, runs down the slope towards them. She sees her mother calling her, gesturing her home. Yet instead of hurrying, May stops dead in her tracks. The fever reaches out for her. Her stomach tightens, a sweat breaks out on her brow and is lost among the raindrops that already glisten there.

The footman holds the umbrella above her head. Madame Bricka slips her arm through May's and gently guides her forward.

'*Courage, Princesse. Je suis ici.*'

The Duchess waits. With one hand she clings onto the iron gate, as if in need of its support. With the other, she holds a piece of brownish telegraph paper, waving it like a handkerchief. When Mary Adelaide speaks, it is not in her usual voice. It is almost in a whisper, as if she hardly dares to utter the words.

'May, oh dear chick. Look May. Oh do look. A telegram from Aunt Queen.'

'Is Her Majesty ill?'

'No my dear. She is in robust health and long may God grant her such,' says her mother. 'She is in Scotland and commands you to go to her at once. At once, mark you.'

'Goodness, when must we leave?'

'Not *us*, chick, much to my chagrin, only you. Only you, my dear. You know what this means, do you not?'

May cannot reply. She feels Madame Bricka's fingernails tighten on her arm. At this moment, and she will always remember it, it suddenly seems as if her skin has been flayed off and all her senses laid bare. The water dripping from the brim of Mr Thaddy's floppy hat. Her brother's gramophone music through a half-open window. Her mother's rapid breathing as the big bosom rises and falls. The October odours of the earth beneath her feet as the ground tilts under the life she has known up to today.

The Duchess abandons the support of the gate and gently brushes the rain from her daughter's cheeks. Mary Adelaide's eyes are saucer-wide as she contemplates the world now opening before them all.

'We are made, chick,' she gasps. 'We are made.'

X

Autumn, 1891

As if she were a sack of mail, she is rushed to Euston Station and bundled onto the night train. Her parents say farewell with febrile kisses. If it were possible, May thinks, her Mama would climb into the driver's cab and shovel the coal all the way to Aberdeen. Yet nothing of moment is said, nothing is acknowledged. A little trip to the Highlands. How delightful, even in November. And what an honour for the family.

She does not travel alone after all; her oldest brother is invited to accompany her, though he is a mere formality and will be largely ignored. In the carriage, he snores or buries his nose in the comic papers. It would never occur to him to enquire what she is thinking. It wouldn't occur to anyone. Except of course Madame Bricka and Harry Thaddeus Jones, but they are far away. They cannot help her now.

May stares out through the sooty square of the window. It is a clear night; a full moon spills freezing white light across the moors of the north. There is beauty in the landscape, but a terrible bleakness too; the world stripped back, its harsh, unforgiving contours laid bare. She feels very small against it and pulls down the blind to shut it out. The gaslight flickers and wobbles inside the pretty shades of misted glass; the red damask tassels on the curtain pelmet quiver with the motion of the train. May Teck is quivering too. A sudden anger floods through her. What *am* I thinking, she asks herself? And why does nobody want to know? Why is her acquiescence taken for granted? Does it not occur to them that she might resist? It is her life after all, her happiness. Dear God, it will even be her body. Taken from her home and everything she knows, given to a stranger to do with as he pleases. To surrender to his possession. Part of his goods and chattels. Not a person, but an arrangement. Do none of them think of that?

Her eye falls on the cord hanging from the wall. She could pull it right this minute, stop the train and jump to the ground. She could melt away into the wild moonlit moors. Spend the hours till morning in some shepherd's hut, then stride out towards some other future. Like Jane Eyre, she might meet some St John Rivers who would take her in from the cold and offer her a different life entirely. A quiet life of no fuss, of reading books and of growing more like herself with every day that passes. And if not a vicar, then perhaps a teacher, a musician, a painter like Mr Thaddy or some other cultured man. A man who will respect what is in her soul.

Oh you stupid, stupid girl. Why deny that the quivering inside her is not just fear but excitement too? No need to worry about '*la petitesse de la vie*'. Nor about another deputation of the shopkeepers marching to the gates of White Lodge. The comptroller can pack his bags. Her Mama and Papa will never again be humiliated. Never again will the Tecks be placed below the salt.

With a violent snore, her brother wakes himself up then falls asleep again. The comic papers have tumbled from his lap onto the floor. May picks them up, restores the scattered pages to their rightful order, folds them neatly and places them on the seat beside him. God, she has been fetching and carrying for them all as long as she can remember. *May-do-this, May-do-that.* How nice it would be to escape from all that.

And there is another thing too. The thing that cannot be spoken of, not even to Bricka. The head on her breast. The scent that wafted out of Mr Thaddy's bedroom door in the scruffy studio behind Santa Croce. She wants all that and she knows it.

As the train powers north under the moonlight and moors give way to lakes, then lakes to hills, then hills to mountains, May Teck's mind spins as fast as the great iron wheels.

*

The little Scottish castle of Aunt Queen is perishing cold. The old lady is a disciple of the cult of fresh air. Even in November, the windows of Balmoral are thrown open and flaccid fires of beech logs are only lit in the evenings. Her ladies shiver, the servants shiver, May fancies even the hideous tartan walls shiver too. But the spell Aunt Queen cast that day in the chapel on the little substitute bridesmaid does not diminish. Close to, it is only greater. The childish observation that Aunt Queen resembled Mrs McCready their Irish laundrywoman, now seems sacrilegious.

All over again, May is dazzled. Entranced by her proximity to the living deity. Yet when they go out for their daily drive along the banks of the Dee, the feeling that first came to her on the day of her seventeenth birthday comes again. She is not the smallest person in the carriage. She is not overshadowed. Yet how does that make sense, she asks herself? By rights, she should feel like a speck of dust in the trail of Aunt Queen's glory. It occurs to her that perhaps, till now, she has simply been travelling in the wrong carriage and that she is now where she belongs. That thought suffuses young May Teck. It will never leave her. Her doubts and fears about what may be in store for her evaporate on the grey wind that cuts through the valley like a butter-knife.

'You are an excellent and clever girl,' says Aunt Queen as May adjusts the tartan rugs around the old woman's knees for the bumpy ride to Loch Muich. 'There is a frightful shortage of young women like you.'

The comment, kindly meant, is a little unfortunate for it is all too near the truth. In the Protestant palaces of Europe, there is a serious dearth of girls of marriageable age who are not dog-ugly, mentally deficient or congenitally suspect. Buck teeth, hair-lips and squints are all the rage. Aunt Queen has spent long wet afternoons poring over the *Almanach de Gotha* till she swept it off the table in despair. But this is an emergency. Dear sweet Eddy, naughty boy that he is, must be married off at once before his name is attached to any more scandals; scandals of such a nature that they cannot be spoken of. Eddy's father imagines that she knows nothing, but she knows everything. Though she will give her name to an age of spotless middle-class propriety, she is the aristocratic child of a far more lurid epoch. Nothing that humans may do lies outside her ken.

So when the Teck girl arrived for inspection, it was not so much a case of scraping the barrel as that she was the only fish therein. The tainted blood was unfortunate but, in this situation, Aunt Queen was prepared to overlook it. And the girl, to her delight, is a real find. A pearl right under their noses all this time. A good, sensible girl. Just what dear Eddy needs. Strong hips too, so hopefully no problems in that direction. Already Aunt Queen hears the patter of the tiny feet of a third generation. What monarch could ever bequeath such stability to her peoples?

On the last evening of May's visit, in the tartan drawing room with the tartan carpets, they have an extra glass of sherry. Aunt Queen catches May's eye and drags it across to a framed photograph of Eddy on the chimney piece. The old woman smiles softly. Still nothing is said, nothing is acknowledged.

The next day, the train bears May Teck back south across the mountains, the lakes and the moors. Now, a life that is used to moving slowly, if at all, suddenly gathers speed. It is just a few weeks from the chill of the granite castle to the boudoir of an overheated mansion to the north of London. A country house party at Luton Hoo. Eddy and May are both to be invited. Shooting and dancing.

Games of charades and bezique. Young people in all their finery, the air filled with the scent of tuberoses and romantic yearnings. A perfect opportunity for the doing of duty. Everything is arranged.

Since the far distant days when the wild Wales children laid waste to the Teck nursery, May and Eddy have rarely met. But, on the night of the ball at Luton Hoo when, in the sweltering boudoir of their complicit hostess, he proposes and she naturally accepts, she cannot help but notice how very handsome he is. Quite different to her adored Mr Thaddy, he is tall, slim as a reed, his features as perfect as those of his famously beautiful mother. His clothes are immaculate; his moustache waxed to turn upwards like a smile. He is shy and sweet and infinitely vulnerable. She likes him much more than she ever expects to.

'Might we make a go of it?' he says. 'I would be so honoured.'

And when they sit close together on the little sofa, flushed with the heat of the room and the significance of the occasion, she sees something else in him. Her figure has filled out nicely now, all gangling girlishness gone. His eyes are going back and forth to her breasts. The tiny tip of his pink tongue peeks out from between his full red lips. She sees desire blossom out from duty and her heart begins to race even faster.

When they return to the ballroom, the good news written on their faces, all hell breaks loose in the sumptuous house at Luton Hoo. Though it is the opposite of a surprise, the Duchess still passes out cold on the floor. She has to be lifted up and beached across a *chaise*, a task requiring four strong footmen. To the embarrassment of the gentlemen present, the Duke begins to weep; but he is a foreigner after all.

Later that evening, in the room she is sharing with two other young ladies, May's reserve deserts her entirely and she twirls around the room, lifting her skirts to show her pretty ankles. The others laugh and curtsey in mock obedience.

'Oh don't be silly,' says May.

But silliness has nothing to do with it. They are already wondering how this acquaintanceship with dull, bookish May Teck might benefit them in the future. Anyway, May no longer seems so dull. A light from heaven now shines down upon on her. It will never go out till the day she dies.

And when she returns to London the day after, there are crowds to greet her at the station, waving and cheering. In her mother's shadow, they have hardly noticed her before.

'God save Princess May!'

For a month or more, she dances through her days. She and Eddy waltz around ballrooms to the music of *Cavalleria Rusticana*, whose pretty strains are all the rage as Christmas comes. They go to the theatre. Eddy loves the theatre as much as she does. In an exhibition at Olympia, they glide in a gondola through an artificial Venice. As they sail under the Rialto Bridge, he plants a quick kiss on her cheek. Again, the people clap and implore God to save the happy couple; the coarser elements shouting ribald remarks. May Teck blushes of course, but all the time Eddy goes on smiling sweetly and glancing down at her breasts.

*

'Do you really think I can take this on, Mama?' she asks.

They sit together in the little conservatory, their laps awash with linen, serge and cotton, with needles, scissors and thread, stitching yet more garments for the Needlework Guild. Surely, May thinks, they must have clothed an army by now. Out on the lawn of White Lodge, dusted with hoar frost, the Duke is throwing a rubber ball to May's little spaniel. Her father is all smiles, as if it is midsummer in the garden which, in a sense, it is. No sun, even at the very zenith of the year, could possibly outshine the dazzling good fortune now beaming down on the House of Teck.

'Take it on?' repeats the Duchess. 'Take it on? You make it sound like a burden. My child, you have won the greatest prize there is. I never thought to see such a day. Never in a hundred lifetimes.'

'I'm not ungrateful, Mama. Truly I'm not. Just afraid that I'm not up to it.'

'If anyone is up to it, you are. Besides, Eddy is so kind and gentle and good. Everyone says so, don't they?'

'Yes Mama, but...'

'But?'

'They say other things too, Mama.'

'Who do?'

'The girls I meet at the houses we visit. They whisper. They gossip. They repeat stories,' she says.

'What stories?'

May does not know how to reply. She darts a glance at her mother; Mary Adelaide's eyes are firmly fixed on the seam she is stitching.

'He seems to have something of a reputation.'

'Many young men have a reputation *before* they are married. Marriage is the cure for reputation. Few men possess one afterwards. And you do like Eddy don't you?'

'Oh yes Mama. He is very kind and polite to me.'

'Then you must not worry, chick. I won't pretend that marriage does not bring challenges. Heavens, I took on your dear Papa, didn't I?' She laughs. 'As both you and the good Lord know, that has not always been a bed of roses. But we are really quite devoted. Don't judge things by the occasional teapot flying through the air.'

Mary Adelaide leans across and pats her daughter's knee.

'It will all be quite splendid,' she says. 'Ignore silly gossip from silly girls. I have never heard anything at all against our dear Eddy.'

But still the Duchess does not raise her eyes from her seam. On the rare occasions when her mother is lying, May can always tell.

By now, the house in Richmond Park is permanently *en fete*, pulsating with the expectation of momentous change. The door to the wine cellar is never shut for long. Lights blaze in unoccupied rooms at all hours of the wintry days and nights. The comptroller protests but nobody is listening. Damn the expense. What does all that matter now? May is aware that everyone, from the parlour maids to the stable boys, is looking at her quite differently.

Only Madame Bricka seems unaffected by all the to-do. She says the right things and is helpful when asked to be, but otherwise stays detached, alone in the white sitting room at the far end of the curving corridor.

'I do hope you're happy for me, dear Bricka,' May asks one day.

'*Mais bien sur, Princesse*, if you are happy for yourself.'

May and Eddy are to be given apartments in the old palace of St James's. It is a forbidding warren of a place, the rooms dark and dusty, but a man from Maples comes with a book of cheery wallpaper samples. There is no garden, just a barren courtyard, but May already plans which plants and flowers might prosper. Hanging baskets, trellises of jasmine and honeysuckle, tubs of lavender. A bench of white-painted wood, where she can sit and read. An aviary perhaps.

'Oh Eddy, it's not perfect,' she says to him. 'But we will make the best of it.'

'Of course we will,' he says, and smiles his sleepy smile.

Just before Christmas, all the Tecks are summoned to Aunt Queen's other castle; the far greater edifice that looms above the river at Windsor. If anything, it is even colder than the Scottish one. The weather outside is vile; filthy clouds brush the very tops of the towers. They are imprisoned inside, swaddled in woollen shawls. Worse, her parents, still half-drunk with exhilaration, are being embarrassing. The Duchess flutters around, even more majestic than Aunt Queen. The Duke gazes out the window at the pelting rain and makes up doggerel in an attempt to amuse the inmates.

'It glowers round the towers,' he recites. 'It glowers. Round the towers. For hours and hours. There is small chance of picking flowers.'

'Indeed dear,' says Mary Adelaide. 'Thank you dear.'

May flees, as always, towards the books. In the library, Eddy hunts her down huddled over the fire, her shawl wrapped tight around her. It is the first time they have been alone since the boudoir at Luton Hoo. He offers one of his exotic Turkish cigarettes. When she coughs and splutters, he laughs and gently rubs her back. A gesture which would be innocent in the company of others is something else entirely in the flickering gloom of the library.

'God, they're strong,' she gasps.

'Wonderful though, aren't they?'

'Oh yes.'

They smoke beside the flames and strive to find one another a little. But Eddy has been sad for days; the sleepy smile rarely seen. She takes her courage in both hands and asks why. His tutor at Cambridge, a young man little older than Eddy himself, is very ill and confined to a special hospital. A sickness of the mind. Eddy went to visit him, though his Papa had cautioned against it. It would not do, Bertie said, to be associated with a lunatic.

'But I had to go,' says Eddy, 'though it nearly broke my heart. He believed in me, you see. When nobody else did. Slow, sleepy Eddy. Not quite up to the mark. But dear old Jem saw something there. Bless him.'

He lights another cigarette and stares into the firelight.

'But now he's lost. Lost to himself and to everyone. And to me.'

'And is that rather frightening?' she asks.

'Oh yes. I can't begin to tell you. With everything that lies ahead for me.'

He is looking straight into her eyes now, in a way he has not done before.

'For *us*, I suppose.'

'I'm sure you will be up to it, Eddy.'

'But I'm not up to it,' he says, throwing the cigarette into the flames. 'Didn't they tell you that?'

The strangest feeling comes over her now. An anger perhaps, a passion certainly, infuses the good, sensible girl. She reaches out and seizes his hand. She pulls him to his feet and half-drags him from the library. She does not loosen her grip as they cross arctic galleries and shuttered rooms till they reach the chamber that houses the great chair. Eddy stops at the door, digs in his heels like her stubborn spaniel often does.

'Goodness May, what are you doing? I don't want to go in there.'

'No Eddy, you *shall* come.'

She throws open one of the shutters. A shard of feeble winter light falls on the ivory throne of Travancore, given to Aunt Queen by her peoples in India. She pushes Eddy down onto the green velvet cushions.

'Eddy, the support of your friend may be gone and I am sorry for it. But I am here.'

May Teck takes a step backwards and, the woolly shawl round her shoulders, falls into a deep curtsey. She bows her head and does not rise.

'I will dedicate myself to you in everything. I will stand by your side and never leave you.'

There is no answer. When at last she looks up, he is still sitting on the ivory throne of Travancore, staring at her, the tears spilling down his cheeks.

Love may come, she tells herself. She is quite sure of it.

XI

Winter, 1892

She has never watched anyone die before and it is a terrible thing.

She has seen the dead of course. She can never forget those open coffins twisting through the alleys of Florence, the mourners in the conical hoods with the flaming torches. Still less, the corpse of a servant's child, struck down by a fever of the brain on a warm spring morning and who was cold by the following dawn. But those, at least by the time she saw them, were *tableaux* of resignation to the will of God, of the calm after the storm. Until now, in the little bedroom of the ugly house on the flatlands of Norfolk, she has never been caught up in the storm itself, never witnessed the rage, the fear, the struggle against the fading of the light.

From time to time, someone or other persuades her to leave the room and she complies, secretly ashamed of her eagerness to do so. How good it is to take the harsh, cutting air of the January garden into her lungs. The lungs of the young man dying are full of fluid now as he slowly drowns from inside himself. But even the sharpest air cannot eradicate the odours of Eddy's little bedroom. They seem to cling to her nostrils, her skin, her hair, her clothes. She shudders and walks faster across the frozen parterre. Perhaps if she strides more quickly, she might flush the odours away and somehow forget, even for half an hour, the catastrophe that has befallen them.

She comes to the lake where, in normal times, there would be skating. On such afternoons, lanterns were hung from the trees and bushes so they need not be chased indoors by the twilight. A trestle table was set up with jugs of hot negus, kept warm on burners. The skaters whirled around, the young men showing off to the girls. The older folk, cossetted in furs, were pushed around the ice on sledge-chairs. Eddy, no sportsman as a rule, was surprisingly good at skating. He circled the lake with grace and elegance, almost like a dancer, as his mother sighed at the beauty of it.

'Look,' she said to anyone who would listen, 'isn't my Eddy just like a gazelle?'

Today the edges of the lake are blurred, half-lost in the freezing fog which creeps in from the east across the German Ocean. The skating parties seem almost like a chimera, something she has imagined. Like the last six extraordinary weeks of her life. A fresh flutter of fine snow has obliterated the twirling patterns of their blades. There are no pretty lanterns at Sandringham now. No nothing. As if they had never been there at all.

But she must not stay out for long. Her place is at his bedside. She is his betrothed after all. They are to be married at the end of February. The preparations are well underway. In government offices, plans are being worked out. Choirs are practising and guardsmen drilling. The guests are deciding which gown and tiara, which uniform and medals will be worn. The country is waiting to be cheered up. The wedding of Eddy of Wales and May of Teck will be the first sign of spring after this ghastly winter.

The germ comes from China this time, they say. Thousands have already died. An eminent preacher thunders that the Angel of Death has spread its wings over the land. This upsets Aunt Queen. In eternity, the preacher must answer to God, but in his earthly stipend he answers to her. A reprimand is delivered. He will think twice the next time. But nobody had expected the Angel to wrap its wings around dear Eddy. His constitution has always been delicate, but he is young and the young are resilient. It was only a bad cold after all, they had thought at first. Everybody has one this damn winter: his mother, his sisters, half the servants too.

'By God, we'll soon be making our own beds and peeling potatoes in the kitchens,' Eddy's father had joked, a man with only the vaguest notion of where his kitchens actually were.

The ugly house, like some red-brick galleon, is becalmed in the fog. Within though, it has been crammed to the rafters. It was Eddy's birthday. On the day itself, in his sweet, shy way, he had struggled down to view his presents, but it was not long before he went back upstairs. Nobody imagined he would never come down them again.

'Eddy has influenza,' his mother telegraphed to Aunt Queen. 'Cannot dine. So tiresome.'

The birthday party went on without him. It was ridiculous but that was the way things were done. Somehow the guests battled through to reach the house. As did the ventriloquist and the banjo player hired to entertain. It fell to May's father to propose a toast to his future son-in-law. When the Duke rose to speak, many fingers were crossed under the table. May saw him trembling, but all went well. And why would it not have? No father had ever contemplated gaining a son with such enthusiasm. Never had a toast been more sincerely raised. At home in White Lodge, no door had been slammed or dog kicked for six whole weeks. And no more dreams about a woman, risen above her station, trampled to death beneath the hooves of a thundering regiment.

But a thousand toasts to the health of the groom would be of no use against the germ from China. Still, for a day or two more, nobody worried much. And then they did. The expensive doctors came. It was no longer influenza, it was pneumonia. Like the fog from the sea, horror enveloped the house.

Back in the tiny bedroom on the east front, May thinks it is a quite ludicrous space for the boy who will be king. Had he the strength to do it, Eddy could reach out from his plain, iron bedstead and touch the chimney piece. Into this space, into the heat of the fire and the blast of the fever, come over a dozen people. There are not enough chairs; May has to share a seat, buttock to buttock, with one of the awful Wales girls. As the hours pass into days, the air becomes rank, not just with the voiding of bowel and bladder but with the words which come from Eddy's mouth. In his delirium, he spews out things from the life he has lived; the things men say which should never be heard by women. As the light pulls back from him, he clings to the names and the memories he will take into the darkness. The name of May Teck, so soon to be his wife, is not among them. At these moments, as Eddy's shouts pummel the walls of the tiny room, his father takes her arm and guides her firmly away.

But Eddy's mother will not budge from the bedside. Alix dabs his brow with a cool flannel, hardly taking her eyes from his face, except to turn them pleadingly towards the doctors.

'Is there nothing you can do to save him?' she asks. 'Nothing at all?'

When they shake their heads, Alix's hand flies to her mouth. Eddy's father strokes her shaking shoulder, before he edges back from the abyss and goes outside for a cigar.

'This cannot be happening,' he says to his younger son.

'I wish God would take me instead,' says Georgie, his face paler by the hour as the spectre of what this means rises before him.

His three sisters huddle together at the head of the staircase. One cuddles her favourite doll. Young women now, they have, like their mother, never quite grown up. May watches them from a distance. They must, she thinks, grow up quickly now.

Down in the drawing room, her own mother drinks endless pots of tea and, unlike almost everyone else, eats voraciously. Buttered toast, scones with cream and jam, teacakes, marzipan and fudge, the carpet at her feet snowed in crumbs. It is how the Duchess handles disaster. But it is her father May watches most. Like everyone else, the Duke is numb with disbelief, but God knows what he might say or do when that wears off.

By the fetid, restless bedside, they watch and wait. It cannot be long now. Outside, the fog still rolls off the German Ocean, over the moribund fields and through the woods, into the park and across the gardens, slumping against the windows of the ugly house, sealing them off from the world beyond. May stares out through the misted glass, longing for even a breath of wind to blow away the fog and let some light break through. For the past six weeks, she has basked in her great and unexpected expectations, the first she has ever known. Now she wonders if she will ever feel the light again.

After battling the Angel of Death for nearly a week, Eddy can fight no longer. But it takes seven more long hours for the great wings to close around him and carry him into the darkness. They are dreadful hours for everyone who sees and hears them. His mother, beyond exhaustion, goes on mopping his face as the fever soars, consuming what little is left of her child: the naughty boy, the cause of so much worry and heartache, but no less beloved for all that, indeed maybe more so. Just before the Angel takes him, he calls out again and again, each time weaker than the last.

'Who is that? Who is that? Who is that?'

May wonders what presence it is that comes to him in his final moments. She hopes and prays it is only a loving one, perhaps even his Maker. She cannot bear to think that he is frightened.

In among the weeping and the wailing, she sees people's eyes drift to her, sees pity peep out from their devastation. A widow before she is a bride. Poor May.

At the funeral, Eddy's father places a wreath of orange blossom on the coffin; the flowers May Teck was to carry at her wedding. But the act is too much for Bertie. The tears pour down his face like the wintry rain streaming down the windows of the great chapel at Windsor. Poor May, he says aloud. Poor May, says everyone in the chapel under their breath. Poor May, says everyone across the whole damn empire.

'God is so loving and merciful,' writes the Duchess to Aunt Queen's daughter, the Dowager Empress in Berlin. 'One feels there must be a silver lining to the dark cloud, albeit our tear-dimmed eyes cannot distinguish it.'

But Mary Adelaide is disingenuous. Everyone from Aunt Queen and the Dowager Empress to the humblest housemaid in the land can see perfectly well what it is. It is as clear as the gentle dew of a spring morning.

XII

1892

She sits in another sunny garden beneath the warm stone walls of another villa. But this garden is different from that of the Villa I Cedri, so wild and free, so careless of its own charms. This demi-paradise is a place for show; self-conscious and perfectly manicured. It tumbles down the hillside in terraces sculpted out of the slope. There are statues of Carrara marble and fountains with sparkling water spouting from the mouths of cherubs. Fat urns are pregnant with spring flowers. Early roses climb up walls and trellises; trees stoop, round-shouldered with oranges and lemons. From the terraces, she can see the bay of Cannes far below, bold and blue, stretching out towards the pink-hued peaks of the Esterel. It is quite entrancing, yet she is not entranced. An anger blazes through her, which the breeze from the Mediterranean does nothing to cool.

A servant pads towards the bench under the palm tree where May Teck sits, a book lolling unopened in her lap. Is there anything she requires? She shakes her head but, as he retreats, she aches to scream in his wake.

'I require peace. I require being left alone. I require not to be treated like this. I cannot bear it any more. Do any of you understand how this feels?'

How ironic that the purpose of her being here, the version touted in newspapers across Europe, is to find that peace. To staunch the red raw wounds of her tragedy, to heal herself with the beauty of the world after having been so cruelly exposed to its horror. No one with a heart grudges 'poor' May Teck this little holiday. Not even the ragged urchin in the slums of St Giles, the wretched prisoner in Pentonville Gaol nor the prostitute who walks the streets of Whitechapel. While May's wreath of orange blossom wilts on Eddy's tomb, in the music-halls of Leicester Square, sentimental ballads are sung as woozy patrons blink back their tears. The Angel Of Death. Noble Prince Eddy. Fair Princess May.

Even here, when her parents drag her out for a walk in the flower market, three black beetles in deepest mourning, creeping through the bower of blazing colour, a crowd soon gathers round them. The market women curtsey and make the sign of the cross. Elderly gentlemen raise their hats and ask permission to present her with a bunch of violets. Soon the Duke can hardly see his way ahead for the bouquets piled high in his arms. Everyone is so very kind and she is not ungrateful, yet all this benevolence is tainted. The kindness, the sunshine, the sea breezes, the terraced garden with the palms and the lemon trees; it is a trick, a disgrace, an abomination even. Above all, it is an insult to her intelligence. Do her parents really think she is so stupid as not to know what is going on?

'Oh chick, such splendid news,' said the Duchess at breakfast. 'Dear Georgie and his Papa come over tomorrow from Menton. Won't that be just lovely?'

'Well, what a nice surprise,' said the Duke to May, as if it were indeed such. 'I do think Georgie such a fine young man. Don't you Pussycat?'

Dear God, can they not be subtle? She flushed, excused herself and sought the sanctuary of the garden.

Again and again she sees, in her mind's eye, her father's face eight weeks earlier as, like the rest of them, he staggered from the small reeking bedroom in that cold Norfolk house to roam aimlessly along its sepulchral corridors. They were all quite used to the Duke mumbling to himself, chattering away about nothing as he read a newspaper or petted the dogs. Few bothered to listen as a rule, yet they could not help but hear the single sentence he repeated endlessly on that January morning.

'It must be a Tsarevitch,' he said. 'It must be a Tsarevitch.'

Nobody had needed a translation. For once, this was not a jumble of inconsequence, but a statement of crystalline logic. Eddy's own aunt, the sister of his mother Alix, had been engaged to the heir of Russia. But that poor boy too had died suddenly before he reached the altar. Instead, after a decent interval, she was passed to his younger brother. The marriage was successful, six children were born and now she was an empress. Such were the benefits of pragmatism.

'Hush Francis, hush my dear,' the Duchess said, gently tugging him towards a quiet corner of the drawing room where, like an embarrassing child, he might be seen but not heard. But still he muttered the same sentence.

'It must be a Tsarevitch.'

*

Across the landscapes of a desolate country, through towns and villages trapped in the icy aspic of winter where little moved except the tolling bells, the Tecks had made their dazed way back to the house in Richmond Park. The servants lined up in the entrance hall tried not to catch their eye. Even Madame Bricka, never at a loss for words in any language, simply wrapped her arms around them. What on earth could one say? Everything had been given, only to be snatched away almost at once.

It seemed to May as if she had never been gone. In the white sitting room, with Bricka's help, she tried to deal with the battalions of black-edged letters that invaded White Lodge, but each fresh word of condolence was another dagger in the wound. Heavens, she could not even read a book. Madame Bricka tried to tempt her with the pleasures of Barsetshire, a place they had not yet explored, but they made only the briefest acquaintance with Septimus Harding and Mrs Proudie before giving up. May wandered down to Pen Ponds and back again. She threw the ball for the spaniel then wondered why the dog brought it back to her. She could settle to nothing.

As best she could, she avoided her mother and father. But raised voices began to come from the drawing room with increasing volume.

'The trousseau,' whined Mary Adelaide. 'Have you thought about the trousseau, Francis? Who is to pay for that now?'

'God knows, my dear, for I certainly don't.'

'And all the other expenses we have incurred against the expectations which lay before us. Dear God, shall we be ruined a second time? Shall we have to auction the pots and pans once again? Where might we be banished this time? St Helena perhaps, like Napoleon? We must plan, Francis, we must plan.'

Only the next day, as she approached her father's study, she heard some more.

'They are going to the Riviera!'

'How very nice for them' replied the Duke.

'I said, they are going to the Riviera. To Menton.'

'I heard you, Mary Adelaide. I'm not deaf yet.'

'You heard, but you did not listen. They are going to the south of France and therefore so must we.'

'And how pray are we to find the money for that?'

'I don't know. Not yet. But, as God is my witness, I will find a way.'

Within the week, a shard of sunshine broke through the pall of hopelessness that had hung above Richmond Park. The Duchess bustled into breakfast waving a telegram, a smile blazing on the nectarine cheeks.

'Dear Lady Wolverton is taking a villa on the Riviera almost at once and we are all invited to be her guests. Is that not excellent?

Just the tonic we need. Come chick, we must prepare for our journey. So much to do. So much to do.'

May knew at once that Lady Wolverton had no previous intention of a trip to the south of France. The thought had been gently planted into her mind, then carefully nurtured into blossom. But she was a woman of great wealth, one of that precious band always ready to help out their impecunious friend the Duchess who, they reminded themselves as they wrote the cheque, was the granddaughter of a king. May could imagine the conversation only too well.

'Oh how wonderful it would be to feel the sun on our faces. What a lot of good it would do poor May.'

'Yes indeed. An excellent notion,' Lady Wolverton would have replied.

'Ah my dear... if only...' The Duchess shrugged and sighed and waited. It only took half a minute.

'Well why don't I take a place for a few weeks? You could all join me there. As my guests of course.'

'What a splendid idea. They tell me Menton is particularly lovely at this time of year.'

And so it went. The plan was executed, but not without a bump in the road. When, through Uncle George, it reached the ears of Bertie, he put his foot down with a stomp that echoed from Norfolk all the way to Richmond Park. No more than his sainted mother, was he averse to the continuing role of young May Teck as his prospective daughter-in-law yet, for a man who had conducted his life with notorious impropriety, he could be oddly sensitive to appearances. Uncle George was dispatched to tell his sister, most politely, that it would be preferable if the Tecks were, in the present sad circumstances, to reside at a greater distance from their grieving cousins at Menton. A little more delicacy might be helpful in bringing the ship into safe harbour. Though fond of his cousin Mary Adelaide, he considered that a little of her went a very long way. And oh there was such a lot of the Duchess.

So Mary Adelaide was compelled to hint to Lady Wolverton that Cannes might in fact be more congenial. And now, May Teck finds herself sitting beneath a palm tree looking out across the azure sheet of the bay. But her lips are pursed, her brow creased, her spirit under siege by forces beyond her control. Mr Thaddy, she thinks, would not want to paint her now. Not like this. Would he even recognise the girl he knew in Florence?

'You are strong enough to steer by your own star,' he had said on the night of her seventeenth birthday.

What he would say if he could see her today? Shrinking back once more from the light. The nervous child who, enthralled by the beauty of the hummingbird, had finally summoned the courage to stick her finger in its cage. But life has bitten May Teck now, so she tends her wounds and retreats from it again. She does not go on the excursions to the Ile Sainte Marguerite or to the luncheons on Cap d'Antibes. She hides under the palm tree, the book unread in her lap.

'I fear I am getting more reserved than ever,' she writes home to Madame Bricka. 'But what can I do to prevent it?'

In her bedroom, on a rosewood *escritoire* by the window, she has placed a framed photograph of Eddy. In the nights when she cannot sleep, she turns on the lamp beside the picture and thinks of him. Odd images come. The patterns of the wallpapers she had chosen for their first home. The barren courtyard she would have transformed into a haven of flowers and shrubs where children might one day play. Eddy sitting on the great ivory throne, herself in a curtsey before him. The awful *tableau* of the little bedroom on the east front.

She had promised she would never leave him, that she would support him and she had meant it. What joys there might have been. Why does nobody around her seem to think of that? To understand that she is truly grieving, not just in her mourning weeds, but in her heart and soul?

'They only expect me to regret the loss of good fortune, not of the man himself,' she writes to Bricka. 'Is that not quite dreadful? But when I am alone with my thoughts, I do miss him so.'

She does not tell Bricka of the other feelings though. The ones that come in the night, when she sees Eddy's face up close to hers, handsome and hazy through the smoke from his Turkish cigarettes or when she remembers the warm closeness of his body on the little sofa, the pink tip of his tongue when he looked at her breasts. Dear Lord, she is almost twenty-five years old now. She was lying to herself when she laughingly contemplated her place on the shelf, straight-backed and unconcerned. All the time these feelings grow stronger. Sometimes her own fingers assuage her for a while. But how long is she to wait for this fulfilment? How she wishes she could talk about it to someone but, my God, that would not be the done thing at all; certainly not to her mother, not even to Bricka.

This apart, it is the correspondence with her tutor that is her lifeline and gives her connection to the white sitting room.

'*Bien Chere Amie*, do write me one of your clever letters,' May pleads, 'and tell me of anything interesting happening in the *thinking* world. Here there is too much gossip. Here I see nothing but women, women, women. And oh how silly so many of them are. Do they not see it?'

In this though she is partly wrong and she knows it. The machinations going on around her may be unfeeling but they are hardly silly. Far too much rides upon them for that. Georgie and his Papa will come to lunch tomorrow and there is nothing she can do to stop it. Alix and the awful Wales girls will remain at Menton; there is little reason for them to come too. This is man's work after all. This is a business trip.

And so May Teck sits alone in a far corner of the terraced gardens, trying to hide from what is being done in her name.

XIII

1892

In the night she prays for a thunderstorm that might put them off or a landslide that would block the road. But no, it is another beautiful day, with just a few balls of cumulus daubed onto a luminous sky. As usual, her dresser pulls her corsets tight and buttons her up inside her very best black gown. For once, May is glad of the constriction, of the bonds that encompass her. She will never get through this otherwise.

Poor Georgie, she thinks. What little she knows of him, she likes well enough, but she cannot bear the thought of seeing him. What will they say to one another? How can she look him in the eye?

At the sight of Bertie heaving himself out of the landau, her heart begins to pump. Though he has always been kind to her, she is a little afraid of him. Those hooded Hanoverian eyes that see everything. But today he embraces her gently and the eyes grow moist at the sight of her.

Georgie comes forward, kisses her hand and smiles a flaccid smile. How wan and drained he still looks, his cheeks sunken against the bones. Poor Georgie, she thinks again.

'Dear Miss May,' he says. The name for her which he always uses. 'How very nice.'

After that Georgie says nothing at all. The guests are shown round the gardens before luncheon. The Duchess takes Bertie by the arm and pulls him ahead along the paths; the Duke does the same with Lady Wolverton. They never look back. The ploy is obvious, excruciating. May and Georgie must bring up the rear. In places the way is narrow and they have to walk shoulder to shoulder. She begins to tremble a little and drops her cream silk parasol, the breeze wafting it into a flowerbed. Georgie runs to retrieve it. How funny he looks in his smart linen suit, standing in a bed of aconites holding a lady's parasol. She almost smiles and he sees it. For the first time, a little colour comes into his face.

'Thank you, Georgie.'

'Um, I'm afraid it's landed right on a spot where your dog has done its business. So it's now somewhat... um... soiled.'

'Well let's just leave it there, shall we?' she replies. 'One of the gardeners can dispose of it.'

For the first time in nearly three months, May Teck laughs her vulgar laugh. And now he looks at her properly. Now, just for a moment, a grin inflates his sunken cheeks.

Luncheon is laid on the upper terrace. May and Georgie scuttle back into silence. Not that there is any need for them to speak. The Duchess prattles on about Lord This and Lady That while Bertie eases the pain with a fine Côtes de Provence, wolfs his way through six courses and burps discreetly into the clear sea air. After coffee, the Duchess suggests that he might like to see the aviary up behind the villa. Though perhaps, she says, that might be rather boring for the young people; perhaps they should remain here and play a game of bezique. What Bertie really wants after six courses is a little nap. He looks at her as if she is mad until the penny drops, then drags himself dutifully in her wake towards the bluebirds and the parakeets.

May has always hated bezique. Yet she is compelled to learn it as a necessary accomplishment. Ridiculous. An accomplishment which accomplishes nothing. She does not recall the heroines of *Middlemarch* or *The Mill On The Floss* playing bezique. But now she and Georgie sit obediently at the card table in the library, like two ill-behaved children kept in after school. They play in near silence, their eyes fixed on the cards. Only now and then, when she is sure he is concentrating, does she allow herself a glance.

As it was with Eddy, she hardly knows him. And the brothers were chalk and cheese; Georgie much shorter, scarcely taller than herself, though broad and fit. The bulldog to Eddy's greyhound. Nor is he anywhere near as handsome as his swan-like sibling. Though the features are good enough, they are hidden behind a sailor's bushy beard from out of which peek two garishly red lips. And the quality that Eddy had, the one that stirred something within her, is not there.

She has been told he can be spirited and merry, though she has not yet encountered it. Like her own, his eyes are bright blue, but she has never yet seen joy in them. He was already sick with the typhoid fever when she and Eddy became engaged and the aura of it hangs round him still. In the little bedroom of the house in Norfolk he was just one more in a sea of faces drowning in shock and disbelief, clutching at any shred of hope till the last breath rattled in the throat. Caught up then in her own grief, she had no energy left to recognise that of the brother. But now, suddenly, as she peruses her cards, he lets her see it.

'It is eleven weeks,' he says without looking up, as he scribbles their scores on the back of an envelope.

'Yes,' she replies. 'I know.'

'Do you really?' he asks.

'Of course I do. And twelve next Thursday.'

Georgie glances at her now, surprise on his face.

'You cared for him then? A little?'

'More than a little,' she replies. 'And it would have become a lot.'

The blue eyes glaze over. He swallows hard.

'I'm so pleased to hear that,' he says. 'One never knows... um... in such arrangements.'

Georgie reaches out across the card table. For a moment she thinks he will take her hand in his, but he simply pats the back of it as if she were a puppy before pulling away again.

'Thank you, Miss May,' he says.

They play on for a while. She feels something more should be said, but knows not what. Then she is emboldened.

'You must feel the loss, Georgie.'

'Yes.'

The word is no more than a strangled whisper escaping, as if by accident, from the bright red lips but getting somehow lost in the beard. He holds up the pen he is using to keep the scores.

'This was his. I shall use it till the day I die.'

The game is over. She quite forgets to let him win as she intended. Voices are heard from outside; the expedition to the aviary is returning.

'Well Georgie, and when do you return to sea?' she asks, gathering up the cards.

'To sea?' he replies, as if it is the silliest question he has ever heard. 'The sea is over for me now. So much is over for me now. Everything has changed. Surely you must understand that?'

For a moment, she sees the fear in his eyes. How very like it is to the fear she saw in his brother on the day she had made him sit on the ivory throne of Travancore.

Out on the terrace, May feels her mother's gaze bore into them, like a gypsy trying to read a palm. And how are our two young people getting along, she asks? May cringes, sees Georgie cringe too. If she had the strength to lift her mother up and fling her over the terrace wall into the flowerbeds below, she would do it this instant. Bury her where she falls, rip up a few spring flowers, throw them on top and walk away. Of all the blushes her mother has caused her in her young life, this is perhaps the worst. The anger blazes through her again. How dare they do this to her? And to poor Georgie?

The visit is done. The landau is sent for. Bows and curtseys and kisses. Bertie screws up his eyes as he bestows one on the Duchess. But when it is May's turn, he takes her chin gently in his podgy hand as if trying to ascertain how well she fares.

'We've seen such trials together, have we not dear girl?' he says. 'But the sight of you today does me good.'

Georgie hangs back a little, examining the bridles on the horses. As their hooves paw the gravel, anxious to be off, he does the same with his foot.

'Well goodbye, Georgie,' she says, going across to him. The red lips kiss her quickly on the cheek. The blue eyes return to the gravel. His foot paws the ground again. He is struggling to speak. How hard, she thinks, do words come from him. Like blood from a stone.

'Just eleven weeks,' he says, as if making some sort of apology.

'Twelve on Thursday,' she replies.

'Twelve on Thursday. Still so soon, don't you think? So very soon.'

He makes to climb into the landau, then turns back to her.

'You would have made him a fine wife, Miss May,' he says quietly. 'As I'm sure you will for somebody else one day.'

And then he is gone. Before the landau is out of sight down the hill, her parents have her pinned against the wall. Like dentists with pliers, they try to extract every word, every intonation, every expression. They anaesthetise her with compliments on how well she has conducted herself today, but it is extraction nonetheless. Isn't Georgie such a fine boy? Wasn't it sweet of him to dash into the flowerbed for your parasol? What did you talk about? Did he comment on how much better you're looking? And what was it he whispered as he climbed into the landau? Oh, do tell us May.

And she does tell them. The Duchess's smile wobbles and falters.

'As I'm sure you will for somebody else one day?' she repeats. 'What a singular thing to say. What on earth does *that* mean? To whom he might be referring? Oh, he's an odd fish, dear Georgie. Always was.'

What May does not tell is that, as she studied her cards at the bezique table, she had caught Georgie looking at her breasts. The tip of a pink tongue had appeared between the bright red lips.

May is exhausted now. The day is hot. She goes up to her room for a nap. From the window, she sees her parents pacing the gardens, heads close together. The Duke throws his arms up in the air, slumps onto a bench and puts his head in his hands. The Duchess rubs his back as if he is a baby with wind. Calm yourself Francis or you will make yourself ill again. Patience my dear, patience.

The next morning, on the little balconies of the hotels and villas that look out across the bay towards the Esterel, a neatly folded local newspaper lies in wait beside the orange juice, the coffee pot and the *pain au chocolat*. Eagerly, it records the visit of the Prince of Wales and his son to their cousins the Duke and Duchess of Teck, currently residing at a villa in the hills. The tragic families reunite, they report, still searching together for a way through their grief. But might there not be a glimmer of sunshine on the horizon? A happy ending to a sad tale? The newspaper undertakes to keep its readers informed of all developments. Indeed its readers will be the very first to know, it promises, far in advance of those misguided enough to take a competitive journal.

It is not just the newspapers of the Riviera, but also those of the United Kingdom of Great Britain and Ireland. Madame Bricka writes to tell her so. The tradesmen of Richmond and Sheen are keeping their fingers crossed. Hope rises in the hearts of the couturiers of Bond Street; will the trousseau soon be paid for after all? From John O'Groats to Land's End, at the breakfast tables of the great and good, the clever and the stupid, the ardent monarchist and the sour-faced republican, it is soon known that Prince George has played bezique with Princess May of Teck. The spy is found to be a discontented parlour maid. She is dismissed on the spot without a reference.

It is not long before Lady Wolverton's lease is up and they must think of England. But when May Teck thinks of it, she flinches. She pictures the platform at Victoria Station, that very same one from which they had headed into exile so long ago. The panting tribe of newspapermen at the barrier; the crowds of people eager to catch a glimpse of her. All those strangers who know so much of her, although she knows nothing of them. All those eyes trying to discern what she is thinking, feeling. How dare they? With every day, she withdraws a little more.

Her trunks are retrieved from the cellar and deposited in her bedroom ready for her dresser to start packing. She stares at the great things, their mouths agape, waiting to swallow the corsets and the petticoats, the shoes and the hose, the hats and all the black gowns. Suddenly she feels sick. Her hands grip the cool sides of the marble basin as the sweat breaks out on her brow and her stomach retches. Nothing comes, though she wishes it might. When the spasm passes, she sits on the bed and trembles. Then the good, sensible girl becomes someone else entirely. The rage in her belly rushes to her head. Now, she thinks. Now, something must be said, something acknowledged. At last. Right this damn minute.

It is early in the evening, just before dinner. Her parents are on the upper terrace with a decanter of Lady Wolverton's sherry. The sun sinks lower over the pink-hued mountains, turning them to a bold reddish-black. Pleasure boats steam back into harbour from the Ile Sainte Marguerite. The lights from the town begin to spread up the hillside, a *riviere* of tiny diamonds on bottle-green velvet. May grips the back of a small bamboo garden chair.

'Mama, Papa. I'm not going home,' she says.

'We don't want to go home either, chick,' the Duchess sighs. 'Do we, Francis? Oh, how I'll miss this view. It is forever printed on my heart.'

'I'm not in jest, Mama,' she says. 'I refuse to return to England for the time being. All this talk. I simply can't bear it.'

'And what talk is that, chick?'

'You know perfectly well, Mama. The talk of which we do not speak. Or rather of which you both speak all the time, but behind closed doors, never to me. Never to the person most directly affected. Well we must speak of it now. Dear heaven, I'm far from a child.'

The Duchess is a fox caught in a beam of light. Without waiting for the nearest footman, she helps herself to another sherry, but does not reply. The Duke drums his fingers on his knee. The cicadas sing in the cypress trees. Some plate smashes in the distant kitchen, followed by a curse. May tightens her grip on the bamboo chair.

'Then I will speak of it alone and you must listen. The talk of Georgie and me. Poor dear Eddy hardly cold in his grave.'

'But it is what Aunt Queen wishes,' replies her mother, 'what Eddy and Georgie's parents wish. It is what your own loving parents wish. Goodness, what the whole country, even the whole of Europe, longs for.'

'And what of Georgie and me? What of us? Georgie still grieves. I still grieve. It is horrible, indecent, unfeeling.'

'You will both do your duty!' The Duke leaps up and sweeps the decanter off the table. The crystal shatters into a hundred pieces, the sherry streaking like amber blood across the marble of the terrace.

A footman comes running. The Duke screams at him to leave. The sickness returns to May Teck's stomach, but she holds it down. Enough is enough.

'I've always done my duty, Papa. *May-do-this, May-do-that.* Have you ever found me wanting? Have I ever let you down?'

'Then do not do so now. Not now,' her father shouts. 'We must have this marriage. Do you hear me May? We must have it. It must be a Tsarevitch!'

The Duchess rises from her seat. She stumbles and must catch the edge of the table. Instinctively May reaches out to help her then, for once, pulls herself back. Suddenly she sees Madame Bricka and the stag in Richmond Park. She will not back down. For the first time in her life, she will keep her parents at bay.

'But this thing that is happening. It's wrong, Mama.'

May Teck is quite used to the tantrums of her father. But now, for a moment, she glimpses a mother she has not seen before. It is as if Mary Adelaide, the flighty Fat Mary, adored by the people and with a heart as big as a barn, has suddenly suspended its loving beat. She becomes cold and hard as the glass-strewn marble beneath her feet.

'Never forget that we are members of the greatest family in the empire, perhaps in the world,' the Duchess says, in a rasping whisper that somehow frightens May more than any sherry decanter flying through the air. 'We must always put our private needs aside so that we can serve it. I always thought you believed that too. The family, the institution it represents. It is what we do. It is who we are.'

'Well maybe it isn't me, Mama. I used to think that it was, but now I don't know. But I know for sure that it's not all of me. And that other part of me revolts against this… this obscenity.'

'But it is the greatest position there is,' shrieks her father. 'The blessed Lord gave it to you but then, in His infinite wisdom, took it away again. For a reason we cannot understand. Now it may be that He is offering it once again. A second chance. Will you throw it back in His face? In *our* faces too?'

'I cannot believe your blessed Lord approves of this, Papa. Not in a million summers.'

Her tears are coming now, but she will not let them see her weep. As she turns her back on them, she feels a wetness in her palms and imagines it is from the flying sherry. But when she looks it is blood. In her passion, she has gripped the chair too tightly; a sliver of bamboo has gone under her fingernail. She had not even felt the pain, but now she does. The sickness rises yet again, stronger than before. She stands in the doorway, the bloody hands upturned.

'I'm not going home,' she repeats. 'I'm not going home until all of this stops.'

She rushes towards her bedroom, staunching the blood with her kerchief. Even through her distress, she notices an acrid smell on the landing. Opening the door to her room, she finds an inferno. The breeze from the half-open window has blown the muslin curtain against the oil lamp on the rosewood *escritoire*. The flames are clawing their way up the curtain. The *escritoire*, and everything upon it, is ablaze. She shouts for help. Maids scream and footmen race with buckets of water. The curtain is ripped down, stamped upon. Blankets suffocate the flames. The damage is contained. It looks far worse than it is. Still of course, the Duchess faints and the Duke shouts some more.

But nothing on the *escritoire* is saved. May sees the charred pile of her precious letters from Madame Bricka. And, in the smouldering ashes, her picture of Eddy. The gilded frame now blackened metal, twisted out of shape like arthritic fingers. The photograph itself no more than dust. She has never felt more alone. How she misses him. Oh Eddy, where are you?

XIV

Spring, 1893

But of course she does go back in the end. From Cannes. She does go home. Yet, after their trunks leave the villa above the bay, it is to be three more months before she will agree to brave the boat train platform at Victoria Station.

After the night of the flying decanter, the Duke and Duchess retreat a little and rethink their strategy. Their good, sensible daughter is now considered to be their good, sensible yet difficult daughter. They treat her with a wariness which has not been there before. She notices it. Regrets it in part, but is glad of it too. After all these years, it is no longer *May-do-this*, but *May-might-you-possibly?*

So they board a different train; to Germany, to Stuttgart, where various Württemberg relations permit themselves to be used as a hotel. Spring gives way to summer. Madame Bricka sends regular reports on the stories in the British newspapers. Like curious hounds, they grow bored of sniffing at the story of May and Georgie and move on to other lampposts. Nor do her Mama and Papa once mention his name in her presence after they have crossed the Alps. It is as if, like his poor brother, he has ceased to exist.

'Very well, Mama,' she says to the Duchess as June becomes July.' I am willing to go home now.'

In the event, Victoria Station is not the ordeal she expects and the sight of White Lodge rising up from the midsummer park makes her heart flip over. And there, at the front door, is

Madame Bricka with her arms flung wide, almost jumping up and down.

'*Ma chere Princesse*, how I have missed you.'

A kiss is planted directly on May's lips. Goodness. Nobody since Eddy, on the sofa at Luton Hoo, has done that. She is taken by surprise and takes half a step back. Madame Bricka's mottled cheeks flush a little; a liberty has been taken that should not have been. But within the hour they are back in the white sitting room.

'Oh Bricka, I've been travelling too long. Now I want no other world but that of this room. It's a small room to be sure, so why does it never seem so?'

'Because *Princesse*, this room has no walls, no horizons. From here, as if on a magic carpet, you can go anywhere you wish. Right up until your very last breath. That is the wonder of such a room as this.'

'Then where shall we two go, dear Bricka? What shall we read next?'

So, with joy, May Teck returns herself to the thinking world in order to avoid thinking about anything else. The summer passes, as so many of her summers have before. Shopping in Richmond and Sheen. Walks with Madame Bricka to King Henry's Mound or around Pen Ponds to feed the ducks and watch her Papa try to catch the carp, roach or bream. When Mr Thaddy comes to tea, if he can spare the time from his fashionable world, there will be a little sketching and tales of his latest grand commission. How he would love to paint Her Majesty, he says. Does May Flower think the Duchess might drop a word in the right ear?

Over these months, she and Georgie meet a few times, especially after his oldest sister and her geriatric husband come to live at Sheen, within walking distance of White Lodge. They take tea together, eat crumpets and play more damn bezique. Now though, she remembers to let him win.

'Ha! I triumph again, Miss May,' he says, barking that doggy laugh of his.

'Oh you *are* clever, Georgie,' she sighs, as if crestfallen.

But it sticks in her craw. Georgie is not clever. Not remotely.

'Why do I permit him to win?' she bleats to Madame Bricka later. 'It's ridiculous. I could have vanquished him ten times over. Why?'

'Because you instinctively know, as all women do, that men do not have the strength to be defeated,' sniffs Madame Bricka. 'They're all the same. Think of it as an act of charity.'

So she tries that, but every time her craw seems narrower.

As the months ease the first shock of loss, Georgie unbends a little. He even tells jokes. Some of them are quite risqué, the legacy of the quarterdeck. His sister slaps him down; not in my drawing room you bad boy, she says. But May laughs her great laugh and, forgetting herself for a moment, tells an even better joke, learned from the most dissolute of her brothers. Georgie slaps his knee, then slaps her on the back. He is staring at her breasts again. It is nothing at all really, yet perhaps it might be something.

They have exchanged little notes too. He sends a greeting on her birthday and she on his. In reply, he writes a few lines, no more. He hopes she is well and that her parents are well. He even hopes her spaniel is well too. Not even, it seems, with Eddy's pen in his hand can fluency come to him, though it is still more than the red lips ever manage. That glimpse of his deepest heart which he had shown her at the card table in Cannes has not been shown again.

Autumn comes, then winter. The Tecks are invited to the house in Norfolk for the first anniversary of her engagement to poor Eddy. It is uncomfortable, embarrassing, but they have to go. On their last afternoon, his mother insists they make a pilgrimage to where the horror happened. May shivers as she crosses the threshold of the little bedroom. At once, the smells of that day return to her nostrils. The room has been made into a shrine. A fire burns in the tiny grate. His clothes still hang in the wardrobe.

The bristles of his brushes still carry his hairs. The soap, half-used, lingers in its dish. Now though, a large Union Jack covers the bed, triumphantly almost, as if death had somehow been defeated; a battle won not lost. It is not long before both his parents break down, as they still so often do. For them, time has not yet begun to heal. Georgie stands close to the doorway, not quite in the room, as if he longs to run. Run fast and never look back.

As they go down the staircase, she touches his arm.

'Are you all right, Georgie?'

'Yes thanks, Miss May. And how are you today?'

It is as if they have bumped into each other at the horse races on a perfect summer's day.

When Christmas comes, he sends her a simple little bracelet. What it means, nobody knows. Does it mean anything at all? The Duke and Duchess examine the tea leaves. If she could, Mary Adelaide would hire Mr Sherlock Holmes himself to investigate how many other bracelets Georgie may have sent this Christmas and to whom. The Duchess begins to wonder how much more of this she can take. Her head aches constantly. She even loses a pound or two.

As the year turns, the Tecks are summoned again. This time to the great fortress at Windsor. Aunt Queen decrees it would comfort her to have dear May by her side on the next awful anniversary, the actual date when, as the old woman puts it, their dear one went to sleep. On the dreaded fourteenth, she and Aunt Queen go alone together to the small chapel that nestles behind the grander one of St George. Though beautiful, it is much darker than its parent. For some reason, the sun declines to flood it with any hope of resurrection. Here no vibrant banners hang, no trumpets sound nor heavenly choirs give voice, though perhaps that is as it should be, for this is a chamber in remembrance of lost possibility. Here Eddy now lies beside his uncle Leo, youngest son of Aunt Queen, the cleverest of them all, who carried the fatal defect that is never spoken of, where the blood does not clot, where the smallest cut or bruise can mean disaster. Leo had stumbled on a garden path and banged his head. Gone within a day, dead at thirty.

'I'm glad that they rest here together,' May says and means it. It helps to see Eddy at peace now, far removed from the thrashing agonies of the fetid little bedroom in Norfolk. Despite herself, her eyes are wet.

'Poor May,' says Aunt Queen, slipping an arm through hers. 'I see how much you feel it, my dear. It is the waste that breaks the heart, is it not?'

'Who knows what great things each might have done?' May replies.

'A stumble on a step, a little germ from China,' says Aunt Queen. 'We can never know what may come crashing around the corner towards us, like bolting horses. Gracious, nobody understands that better than me. We must make the most of every moment that the good Lord decides to grant.'

The old woman squeezes May's hand. 'And sometimes, in His mercy, He even gives us second chances.'

Today, Eddy's catafalque is encircled by wreaths of winter flowers. Small white cards carry messages of love and respect from his parents, his brother and sisters, his friends in the army and from his Cambridge days. Yet one message is missing; a message never sent, from the tutor whom Eddy had loved but who had lost his reason. At the news of Eddy's passing, the man had starved himself and had followed him into the darkness within the month. Tongues have wagged. Were those stories about Eddy, the ones May's mother dismissed so airily, true after all?

May helps Aunt Queen to place her wreath. The old woman's knees no longer follow her command. For a while, they stand in silent prayer. Then Aunt Queen pulls her thick tweed cape around her and heads back towards the pale January light. In the doorway, she turns.

'Dear sweet May, I've often said what a good and *sensible* girl you are,' she says. 'But you are more than that. You too are someone who could do great things.'

In the brougham going back up the hill to the castle, Aunt Queen fixes May Teck with that gaze of hers which makes you feel she sees everything.

'I say again child,' she says. 'It is always the waste that breaks the heart.'

A lunch is given in the octagonal dining room, an eyrie in the north-east tower, perched high above the river. A gloomy affair, not least because it is parsimonious. Aunt Queen slurps gently at chicken broth and nibbles on bread without butter. A little lean ham is served, garnished with a few stunted potatoes. The Duchess fears her stomach might think her throat is cut. A fearsome rumble echoes round the octagon which everyone affects not to hear.

In the afternoon, May asks permission to show Madame Bricka around the great chapel of St George. May's dresser is sick and Bricka has come as *femme de toutes choses*, though protesting that it is beneath her dignity. An educational excursion might improve her mood. So it is into the brougham and back down the hill.

Even on a dark day, its windows splattered with rain, the chapel takes May's breath away, as it always does. She watches Madame Bricka try not to be dazzled. Heavens, the woman questions everything, doubts everything, even the existence of God; something May would never tell her mother lest her precious tutor be taken from her. But Madame Bricka does believe in beauty, worships it even and, in the face of so much of it, it is as if her plain Alsatian features absorb it and reflect it back from her shining eyes.

Standing in the choir, beneath the banners of the knights, May tells of the day when she was the unwelcome child bridesmaid, the unkindness of the Wales girls, the sad eyes of the foreign bride.

'I sometimes wonder what happened to her.'

'She will either be very happy or very miserable,' comes the reply. 'Whichever it is, those who arranged the match are unlikely to be concerned.'

Madame Bricka pauses before the vault in the floor where little May Teck had stopped and curtsied so long ago.

'Or of course, like Queen Jane here, the poor thing might be dead.'

'What makes you think that?' asks May.

'Well no doubt she was a brood mare like all the rest. Isn't that the main business of your tribe? Then, now, always. If you imagine it is much more then you're mistaken. To be young with good strong hips is the only accomplishment worth having.'

'Did you never wish for children, Bricka?'

'Children only get in the way of oneself,' she replies. 'All that mess and noise and constant need. How could one ever concentrate on anything finer? Perhaps there is some lack in me, some terrible abyss but, if so, I've never felt it.'

'Yet you spend your life with the young.'

'Only in the hope of making sure they pass as soon as possible to adulthood. No more mewling and puking.' Madame Bricka smiles. 'Besides, my young ladies have always been my children. The cliché of the teacher, but it is true enough. *Et toi Princesse, tu seras toujours ma fille.*'

May moves forward and stands before the high altar. The spot where she would have stood with Eddy. But now handsome Eddy rots in his tomb in the smaller chapel only yards away. Nobody stands beside May Teck now. That space is empty air. It is weeks now since she last had a note from Georgie; a feeble thing as usual, limp as lettuce.

'Is this what you really want, *Princesse*?' asks Madame Bricka from behind her. 'To stand here one day and be, as they aptly put it, given away? From the possession of one to the possession of another? If so, think hard.'

'But Aunt Queen thinks I might achieve wonderful things.'

'No doubt. But will they let you?'

'I want to do something that matters in this life. I thought you would approve of that. Something that makes a difference.'

'And I ask again, will they let you? Or will they keep you in your place?'

'But I'm afraid, Bricka. I realise now that I don't want to be the spinster daughter of White Lodge.'

'Then be aware that you may pay a price. Will lying here throughout eternity in all this splendour really be worth it?'

'I don't know,' May replies. 'Truly I don't. But if I were brave, I'd face down my fears and find out, wouldn't I? Like you, I'd have the heart of a lioness.'

'Yes, I suppose you would.'

'And Bricka, there's something else too,' whispers May, with words she could not speak to any other creature. 'I should so like the chance of love. Just the chance of it.'

The Frenchwoman comes up to the altar now, putting her arm through May's.

'Oh, so would I,' she says.

Helene Bricka takes May Teck's chin in her hand and fixes her with the saddest gaze May has ever seen.

'On the day you go down the aisle,' she says, 'it will not be your Papa giving you away. It will be me.'

XV

Spring/Summer, 1893

Like a kite stuck in a tree, she can neither fly nor float down to earth.

It is one whole year now since they played bezique in the villa high above the bay of Cannes. For twelve long months, she has had no clear idea of what might happen to her, how the story of her life is to be written.

But the confusion that has kept May Teck awake at night has hardly signified to the plotters and schemers around her, from Aunt Queen down. Georgie had to be married and soon. The typhoid of last year could have killed him as easily as the flu vanquished Eddy. Aunt Queen is getting old. Bertie, fatter than ever and ravaged by the pleasures of the table and the brothel, will surely never make old bones. If Georgie were to die before he sired an heir, the eldest of his sisters, drippy, droopy Louise, not quite connected to reality, would have to sit on the ivory throne. It was not to be contemplated, Aunt Queen declared. The men in the dark suits who ruled over her agreed. Georgie must be married. He must do his duty with his vows and with his loins. There was no time to waste.

Yet the plotters and schemers have been flummoxed. They discovered that their leading actor had stage fright. Hesitant and highly strung, he must be calmed down and encouraged to believe he will be perfect in the role of husband and father.

But finally, on a fine spring afternoon, the curtain goes up to reveal the garden in Sheen of drippy, droopy Louise. The French windows are all open. The tulips are in bloom. The birds are singing in the hedgerows. From somewhere, a gramophone is playing Schubert. Good heavens, if not now, when?

'Now Georgie,' his sister says, when the teapot is drained to the dregs and the last cucumber sandwich has vanished from the cake stand, 'don't you think you ought to take May to look at the frogs in the pond?'

May sees the fear glint in Georgie's eyes, the same look she first saw over the card table in Cannes when, for a second, he steeled himself to gaze into his future. Again, she feels sorry for him.

'No need, Georgie, if you'd rather not,' she hears herself say. 'I saw them when I was here last week.'

Drippy, droopy Louise sighs and looks up to heaven, an act which, coming from her, passes as energetic.

'In that case May dear, *you* can show them to Georgie,' she replies. 'Point out the one which looks most like someone in the family. Make him guess whom. Such fun.'

Without looking at each other, May and Georgie take the path that leads to the pond. They walk in silence, but she hears him breathing hard. The sun irradiates the yellow-green water of the pond, the patchwork of the lily pads floats as if on air. She herself feels strangely calm. After all, it is a scene she has played before: once on a sofa in an overheated boudoir, now beside a pond in a Surrey garden.

Georgie looks at the frog. The frog looks back at Georgie then scampers for cover under a lily pad.

'Perhaps it can't bear the sight of a handsome prince,' he says. 'Maybe it was hoping you might kiss it and turn it into me. Ha!'

His jokes, when not risqué, are often feeble as this, followed by that barking laugh. What sort of man, she thinks, laughs at his own jokes? Nevertheless she is always sure to smile. Not just because it is polite, but because it is another reason to feel sorry for him. And perhaps, she reflects, feeling sorry might be a way in to love.

Besides he is nervous, far more so than any of the jittery creatures in his sister's garden. The frogs, the squirrels, the blue tits are all much braver than this less than handsome prince. There is sweat on Georgie's brow. How unattractive, she thinks. And there is something nestling in his beard. Some crumb of cake or buttered scone from the tea table or a flake of tobacco from his cigarette. She is not sure what but, for some reason, she cannot take her eyes off it.

Then, with one deep breath, he takes her hand in his.

'Now listen Miss May, I've had a jolly good think about this,' he says. 'In particular, I've asked myself what poor old Eddy would feel about it. And… um… I'm pretty certain the dear boy wouldn't mind a bit. In fact, I'm damn sure he'd say, "Go on Georgie." So…'

But instead of going on, he stops completely and watches several pairs of bulbous eyes peering up at him from just above the surface of the water. At this pivotal moment of her life, the one all Europe has been waiting for, May Teck is aware of a distinct *ennui*.

'Well then Georgie dear. Do go on.'

To the gentle accompaniment of croaks and splashes, the question is asked and the answer given. She kisses the prince, trying to avoid whatever it is that lurks in the beard. Duty is done. The bulbous eyes sink down into the depths. The water is still again, as if nothing at all has happened.

She wonders exactly what she feels at this moment. Does she even like him? She is sorry for him of course, just as she was for his handsome brother. The albatross that hung around poor Eddy's neck now hangs instead around Georgie's. Spoilt by his adoring mother, he is self-centred, lacks imagination and, like the rest of them, never opens a book. But he is not a bad man; she is fairly sure of that. He holds himself in too, just as she does herself. Two peas in a pod then. What could be better? Except that May Teck is clever enough to understand that she is attracted to those qualities which are the opposite of her own. That is what she found in Harry Thaddeus Jones. That is what stimulates her, that is what she needs and that is not what stands beside her now, shyly clasping her hand, beside the lily pond. And suddenly she knows, with a stabbing certainty, that even with a crown upon his head and the holy oil anointed upon his forehead, this will always be the truth of it.

She looks down at their reflection in the water. It wobbles slightly, their outlines blurred. Somehow, she does not look quite like herself. And then she remembers that what May Teck might feel does not matter. It really does not matter at all.

*

It is the zenith of Mary Adelaide's time on this earth, her triumph more than anyone else's. Her wildest dreams made reality and every hope fulfilled; all trials put aside, all humiliations forgotten. In the wedding procession to the old palace of St James's, she rides in a glass coach beside Aunt Queen. As she waves her podgy hand, swollen with every ring and bracelet she possesses, the crowds roar back their approval. God bless Fat Mary. She's a game old girl. She deserves this day.

'I rather think *you* are sovereign on this occasion, dear cousin,' says Aunt Queen, not unkindly. 'But only for today, mind.'

The Duchess clasps the hand of her benefactress and kisses it, trying to say with her eyes what she feels in her heart. She is not unaware of the debt that is owed. As the glass coach breaks out from Constitution Hill into the wide-open circus of Hyde Park Corner, another roar comes from the crowd. Mary Adelaide throws back her head and smiles up at God. It would not have surprised her if the glass coach and its four cream, high-plumed horses had suddenly lifted off the common earth and floated up Piccadilly, several feet in the balmy air.

Aunt Queen had decided that the wedding should be in the city, not in the chapel at Windsor where May would have stood beside Eddy. She is grateful for that delicacy at least.

But dear Lord, all those people with the ravenous eyes. Even more, it will later be said, than on Aunt Queen's Jubilee in 1887. And all of them looking upon her, little May Teck from Richmond Park. Heavens, who would ever have thought it?

And indeed it is all quite sensational. The summer day quite perfect. The clattering of the soldiers riding alongside her landau, the July sun glancing off their swords and the bridles of the horses. The military bands, trumpets and cornets, fifes and drums. Scarlet and gold. Flags and bunting. Rich and poor. Bowler hats and cloth caps waving. Children carried on shoulders or climbing up lampposts garlanded with summer flowers. Tra-la-la.

In May's landau, in her silver and white wedding-gown, the Duke clings tightly to his daughter's hand, his palm soaking into her white glove, his knees trembling. Right to the very altar, she thinks, the child is required to be parent to the father. Whatever nerves she might suffer today, and goodness who would not, they must be suppressed to comfort his own. *May-do-this, May-do-that.* Surely she should now be free of that burden at last. Despite his shaking knees, the Duke is otherwise stiff as a statue, not smiling, not waving.

'Today I am vindicated,' he says above the din. 'Look Pussycat, look how they clap and cheer the child of my blood.'

He presses her hand against his chest.

'Today May, I repossess my dignity. It has been a long time coming. And you have given it back to me.'

'Oh Papa.'

The landau turns onto the downward slope of St James's Street, the old palace and its chapel waiting at its foot. Soaring arches of greenery span the roadway, suspended from Venetian masts, encrusted with blossoms. At the end of this floral tunnel is the rest of her life.

Going down the aisle of the chapel, she gives quick nods to the familiar faces among the herd of noble strangers. Aunts and uncles. Cousins from Germany. Old friends from the days of the Villa I Cedri. Eddy and Georgie's parents smile kindly upon her. But how pale Alix is, how wan her smile. Well, small wonder. No doubt it is her darling Eddy she pictures waiting at the altar. And when May sees Madame Bricka and Harry Thaddeus Jones standing side by side, she averts her eyes, so that they will not see her sudden tears.

Georgie does not turn to greet her, nor do they look at each other as they speak the wooden words in which she gives herself to him. When they walk together back up the aisle, she tries to catch his eye, but still he looks straight ahead. How she longs to know what he is thinking. Is he happy? Is he sad? Is he as afraid as she is?

The wedding breakfast is celebrated at the great mausoleum on The Mall. Aunt Queen dislikes Buckingham Palace and rarely goes there but today an exception is made. She has now made Georgie a duke. The Grand Young Duke of York, he has taken to calling himself. At the meal, May can eat almost nothing. The speeches are interminable and she longs to pee, though her mother had taught her the exercises that make it possible for a woman in the public eye to hold her water. By now, May thinks, the muscles of her pelvic floor could bear the weight of the Victoria Falls.

When she retires to change her wedding dress into something suitable for a railway journey, her mother fusses and flaps, getting in the way. Only when her daughter is once more pretty as a picture, does she send the dresser from the room. All at once the fussing stops. Mary Adelaide sinks down into a chair, shuts her eyes and takes a long sigh. The warrior, victorious but exhausted.

'What will I do without you by my side?' she says. 'What in God's name will your silly old Mama *ever* do without you?'

'You will be fine, Mama. You still have Papa. And the boys,' replies May. 'Besides, I thought this was what you wished.'

'Oh it is. Today, I have been given my heart's desire,' says the Duchess. 'And yet something is lost too, is it not?'

May feels a tightening within herself.

'Well it's too late to worry about that now, Mama.'

May rings for the dresser to return. When the woman arrives, the Duchess heaves herself off the chair. In the same second, mother and daughter realise what has happened in the ringing of that bell. For the first time in her life, May Teck has dismissed her mother. A frisson of surprise hangs in the air between them. How long this moment has been in coming.

In the open doorway, Mary Adelaide embraces her child.

'Thank you, chick,' she says. 'Thank you for this.'

Down in the quadrangle, slippers and rice are thrown. Undaunted by the presence of Aunt Queen, the young ones come off their leash; the august space becomes the playground of some unruly school. May stands up in the carriage to throw her bouquet. Suddenly, she spots Madame Bricka in the throng, stock still as the crowd swirls around her. May Teck, no mean bowler in the cricket matches of her brothers, aims it straight at her. Her companion of the white sitting room could easily have caught it but Bricka's hands stay firmly by her sides. Instead the flowers are caught by Harry Thaddeus Jones. The crowd laughs and boos its disapproval. Mr Thaddy, an artist to his fingertips, executes an elegant arc of the arm and returns the bouquet to its sender. But it is the kiss he also blows that she will hold in her memory.

'You must throw the bouquet again May,' says Georgie.

'No, I think I'll keep it now,' she laughs.

'But that would never do,' he says.

'Oh I'd so like to keep it, Georgie,' she says again. 'A souvenir of the day.'

'No, that's quite impossible. Not how these things are done. You must throw it again, May. At once.'

And so she does. Mr Thaddy's flowers fly through the air into the arms of some squealing young cousin.

As they roll out through the gates into The Mall, May looks back to the balcony high above the forecourt where the families begin to gather. The band is playing 'Auld Lang Syne'. Her Papa is weeping; his hand held by Aunt Queen. Her Mama is singing as if her breast might burst. Her three brothers, arms thrown round each other's shoulders, belt it out like drunkards on New Year's Eve. Again the warm sun glints down on the swords and breastplates of the soldiers who trot beside the carriage. Still the children wave their little flags from the lampposts. The imperial banners fill gratefully with a brief puff of wind, as if taking a quick breath to see them through to the close of this long hard day.

Once more, May glances up at the balcony as it quickly pulled away from her, the figures upon it shrinking into insignificance. And that, she reflects, is now the truth of it. Firmly she turns her head from west to east and to the man sitting beside her.

Georgie raises his hand to the crowd, makes hesitant inclinations of his head as if they are people he vaguely knows, but cannot quite place.

'You must wave more often,' he says without taking his eyes from the pavements. 'Your frequency is not sufficient. Come on May.'

So she waves and waves all the way to Liverpool Street. From the train, she waves at people in tiny suburban gardens. At mayors and their ladies on small town platforms, assembled in chains of office and fat feathered hats, to bow and curtsey as the steam blows in their faces. At scruffy children and dogs running along the railway line. At farmers in cornfields, at cows and sheep. She waves at every last one of them.

It occurs to her now that she will be waving for the rest of her days, to people of whom she knows nothing, but who know all about her. How very singular that is. The dwellers in the suburbs, the mayor and his lady, perhaps even the farmer in his field, know the names of her parents and brothers, that she comes from a house in Richmond Park, that once she lived in Florence, that she is studious and has read many books, indeed from cover to cover. The women may have drooled over the items in her trousseau, not to mention the cost of it all, which their favourite ladies' journal would have carefully calculated. Dear Lord, how will she cope with such invasion?

In the train, Georgie talks mostly to his manservants; smoking with them in the adjacent compartment. Through the open door, she hears them discussing the things which men discuss. How she wished she had brought one of those books that she is famed for reading. It has never occurred to her that such an item might be required as part of a trousseau.

Already she feels an ache in her shoulder from all that waving. She must learn a new way to do that. No doubt Georgie will know the trick of it and will instruct her. No doubt there will now be new ways to do so many things in her life.

'Let Georgie be your guide and compass in all matters,' her father had said in the landau this morning. 'Remember that your husband will always know best.'

XVI

Summer, 1893

Oh no, she thinks, not now, not tonight. The thunder comes out of the east, rolling in off the German Ocean, rushing to meet them at the railway station. It comes in malevolent waves of black cloud, drowning out the limpid blue of a drowsy summer evening. Behind them in the west, in the world that they have left, the sun still hangs low in the sky, its beams dissolving into the flat Norfolk fields.

She hears the first rumble as she shakes the hand of the station master, praying it might be the last of the thousand hands she has shaken today. At once, her heart beats faster. For May Teck is petrified of thunder. Since childhood when she ran for sanctuary to the bed of her nurse, or even to that of her parents, it has always thrown her out of kilter. In its violence and rage, it seems like the wrath of God; Judgement Day for all her childish sins. The lightning, she is quite sure, serves to illuminate her failings for the eyes of the Almighty. The boom that follows is the expression of His disapproval. But tonight, of all nights, she really does not want to hear Him. Tonight, she needs Him to be as quiet as a mouse.

She almost falls into the open carriage. Bride and groom are both exhausted, their conversation reduced to monosyllables. From the tiny station, the road up through the midsummer woods is dry and dusty. The hooves churn it upwards till her 'going away' dress of creamy Irish poplin and her bonnet trimmed with ostrich plumes is filmed in grubby grey and his frockcoat has turned from black to almost white.

'We shall soon be like mummies from some ancient tomb,' says Georgie with the barking laugh.

Then the first spit of rain hits her cheek. By the time the carriage reaches the gates of the park, the dust on their clothes has become a sort of paste. The day has been so hot it has not occurred to anyone to bring umbrellas. Georgie lets rip a string of epithets at the coachmen. Having grown up with three brothers, May is not discomfited by such language, merely by the temper with which it is expressed. How red his face becomes, how his eyes shrivel to pinpoints of unforgiving ferocity.

The first flash comes as the big house at Sandringham lumbers into view. It is shut up, the windows dark, nobody in residence except a few forgotten servants. The lightning throws it into merciless relief, its ugliness even starker in its abandonment. The first clap cracks out as they pass below the little room on the east front. May jumps in her seat. She sees Georgie turn his head away, but she does not. Her hands trembling, her face streaked with rain, she silently begs Eddy for his blessing.

'The young people go to Norfolk after the wedding,' Aunt Queen had written to her daughter the Empress in Berlin, 'which I think rather *unlucky.*'

The Duke and Duchess thought the same, most people did, but Georgie decided he could think of nowhere nicer than the little villa on the edge of the park which his Papa had given to them as their country retreat. Why go to the Riviera, Lake Como or the islands of Greece? Just think of the expense, not to mention the bother. Quite absurd. Surely, everything one might ever want is right here.

So the carriage canters past the shuttered mansion, along a narrow drive lined with rhododendrons, fat and fussy as crinolines, till it opens out again beside a reedy pond. Here stands the small house in which May Teck is to spend almost half a lifetime. As she looks at it, in the very eye of the storm, its walls and windows seem to shake and shudder. But at least the damn windows are lit and people are hurrying out with umbrellas. They enter the hallway like half-drowned sailors reaching a shore.

It is not yet ten o'clock but Georgie tells the servants he will retire at once. Tea should be brought upstairs. May presumes she is included in the decision, though at the word 'retire' her heart misses a beat. She longs for bed, but the marital bed can surely be like no other.

She climbs the narrow staircase to a dressing room, scarce bigger than a linen cupboard, where her maid is waiting. The sodden dress, cape and bonnet are removed. The lawn nightgown of pastel green, which she and her Mama had chosen together, is lowered over her head. How pretty it is, with its tiny pearl buttons and moss-coloured ribbons. The maid takes a gentle comb through her battered hair, restoring the curls to their rightful position. What a day those curls have had; small wonder they are as worn out as she is. May and the maid are careful not to catch each other's eye. They work together in quiet acceptance of what is to come. But when the servant bobs and slips wordlessly away, May longs to call out to her, to follow wherever it is the woman might be going.

Georgie, in a dressing gown of manly grey, waits in the bedroom next door. He is not far off thirty now and, bereft of naval uniform or smart frockcoat, he suddenly looks much smaller. They blush at the sight of one another.

'Tea?' he asks, pouring it without waiting for an answer. They drink in silence, listening to the rain still pelting against the windows. He clears his throat as if he is about to make a speech.

'I should think we're both rather tired, aren't we?'

'Yes indeed Georgie dear. Perhaps a little.'

'Nevertheless…'

He turns down the lamps. He removes his grey velvet slippers and places them neatly side by side at the foot of the bed. He turns his back and removes the dressing gown, which he lays out on a chair, crossing the sleeves carefully across the chest as if it had just passed away. In his serge nightshirt, looking down at the carpet, he takes her hand then tries to plant a kiss on her cheek. But she moves her head at the wrong moment and it lands on her ear.

'Ha!' says Georgie. He pulls back the quilt. 'I'll sleep on the left.'

May thinks her legs will give way if she does not lie down at once. She craves for sleep and for a mind switched off. But Georgie has always done his duty and so has she. After all, this whole thing is about duty, is it not?

The dying fire still gives light to the room, though she wishes fervently it did not. She keeps her eyes closed, except for a split second when she dares to peek up at him only to find that his eyes are tight shut too. His breath smells of cigarettes though he does not attempt to kiss her again. His beard smells too and his body carries the sweat of the long, long day. Then she sees them. Writhing around his forearms. Two tattooed dragons, their teeth bared at her, breathing flame. And now the fear finally strikes her.

Under the weight of the sheets, he has trouble pulling up his nightshirt and curses, his face going red again as it had in the carriage. He pushes up her nightgown and puts the thing between her thighs. So this is it then. She wonders suddenly if he has done it before, then tells herself not to be stupid. Of course he has. She remembers the stories the giggling girls in the country house bedrooms have told her. How Georgie kept a woman in a house in St John's Wood and shared her with Eddy. Good heavens. There are different rules for men and women, her Mama had always said, shaking her head.

Still, May thinks, it is well that he knows what to do, because she most certainly does not. Her mother has told her a little, but not much. Only what sad indignities a woman must suffer for the later joys of motherhood. Now at first, as the dragon arms wrap themselves around her, she tries to imagine that the thing between her legs is nothing more than her own finger, but that deception only lasts a moment. If the bridegroom has experience, he has not yet learned finesse. He pushes it inside her with little more delicacy than a loader cleaning the barrel of a shotgun. Her first terrible cry is muffled by a thunderclap.

Suddenly, God knows from where, she pictures Madame Bricka standing in a corner of the room, looking on and laughing. Be careful what you wish for, she had said.

But at least her trial is over quickly. Soon it is Georgie's time to cry out into the storm, his face locked in grimace as if some kind of agony has come upon him. At the same moment, she feels fast pulses of intrusion deep inside herself and a viscous wetness running down her thighs. He rolls off her and lies panting. Under the sheets, he pats her hand.

'Well, there it is, Miss May. Excellent. Jolly well done.'

He turns away and soon his snores rumble in tandem with the thunderclaps.

When sure he is asleep, she slides from the room, tiptoes in the darkness across the little landing to the bathroom. It is now to her horror, she catches the bitter-sweet scent of her own blood mixed in with residue of his fluids that still seep out of her. She starts to shiver then finds she cannot stop. She sits on the lavatory and shakes from head to toe. She sits there for endless minutes, then finds a flannel, draws some water and does her best to clean herself. The water is ice cold which makes her tremble all the more. She hides the bloody flannel behind some towels inside a cupboard. She will retrieve it in the morning, though God knows how she will dispose of it even then.

She creeps to the bed and to the cold, hard back of her husband. Still the storm rages outside. Will it never roll away and leave her in peace as he has now done? In the hated wind, the topmost branches of a big laurel bush rap against the window. In the lightning flashes, she sees their silhouette through the blind, waving and writhing like the arms of drowning people. Help us, they cry, we cannot survive this. May Teck turns her face away and smothers it in the pillow. But, she reminds herself, she is May Teck no longer. Now she has a different name. Now she carries the name of the snoring back in the serge nightshirt. Now she is someone else altogether.

How odd it is to sleep beside a stranger. The smell of him is still in her nostrils, on her skin and, despite her trip to the bathroom, still coming from between her thighs. She wonders if she will ever be used to that. Somehow his odour on her body is more intrusive than the thing he pushed inside her. It is as if he will permeate her now. And why did he roll away from her when he had finished his business? Why did he not wrap her in his arms and allow her to permeate him in return? It might have been all right then. The two of them. In this together. Is it some inadequacy in her? Is she a dreadful disappointment?

Those numbing words of Uncle George crash back into her mind. 'I doubt, sister, that she will ever inspire great passion in anyone.'

She thinks of her bedroom back at home. Her own comfy bed. Her pretty things all around her. The windows half open to the warm summer night. The lowing of the deer in the park. The lark song at dawn. The first sounds from the kitchens and the stable yard as the house stirs below. But soon the maids at White Lodge will have stripped her old bed. The windows will be firmly closed. Dust sheets will shroud her dressing table, the cabinet with her Venetian glass ornaments, her blue velvet chair. The door will be shut tight and the key turned. It will be as if she never existed there.

Though the storm from the German Ocean still crashes on towards the Fens, sleep at last envelopes May Teck, though it is fitful, grabbed in grateful snatches between the bangs and flashes. But her mind refuses to join her body in its rest. She dreams she is in the garden of the Villa I Cedri, that place to which she still flees whenever flight is necessary. It is hot as always but a light breeze comes off the Arno. With a basket of fresh peaches on her arm, she goes through the garden gate and across the field of olive trees down towards the river. She can already hear the water tumbling over the weir. Harry Thaddeus Jones is waiting for her. Among the poppies on the riverbank, the easel and the stool are already in position, facing the old crumbling mill on the far side. In the background, the towers and domes of the city quiver in the sunlight and behind them the mountains. She has sketched this view often before but, as Mr Thaddy says, there is always something fresh to discover, some trick of the light perhaps, or something in the wind, which makes it worth trying again. And he is right. In this life, he says, there is rarely anything which cannot be improved upon.

And when the new sketch is done and the afternoon pulls them into drowsiness, they lie together hidden in the long grass, eating peaches. His skin carries the smell of the sunlight; his breath the scent of the fruit. He brushes her cheek with the back of his hand, as softly as if she was made of thistledown. Now he kisses the cheek he has just caressed then moves his mouth to her lips. And when, after a time, he enters her, it is so gently that she scarcely feels it until the sensation of melding into him suffuses her and brings her a joy she has never imagined, not even in the small hours of the Italian night. His eyes look down on her with some kind of wonderment and, as sleep overcomes them, he smiles and rests his head upon her breasts.

Such is the stuff that fantasies are made of. But when May Teck opens her eyes, she is beside a serge nightshirt on a Norfolk morning, the rain and wind still pounding against the window panes. She has made her bed, she thinks. And now, she lies upon it.

Georgie snores and wakes, stretches and yawns, swings his feet onto the floor.

'Good morning, Miss May,' he says, then barks his laugh. 'I suppose I must stop calling you that. It's hardly appropriate now is it? Ha!'

Without looking at her, he reaches round, pats her hand and disappears towards the bathroom, where the bloodied flannel hides its pain in the cupboard meant for towels.

XVII

Summer, 1893

It is a ship she lives in now. A ship, not a house. It takes a few days to realise the fact, but this is how she will always think of it. The analogy is inescapable.

'I love small rooms like these,' he says. 'They remind me of my cabins at sea. So cosy and *gemütlich*, don't you think?'

May Teck would choose other, less flattering adjectives but she does not articulate them. There is scarcely a chamber in this glum little villa in which to swing the ship's cat. The staircase, the hallway, the passages are barely wide enough for two people to pass. Maids and footmen must plaster themselves against the walls to avoid inappropriate intimacy with their betters. Three times a day, the smell of cooking drifts upwards even into the nostrils of those on the topmost floor. But soon she realises he will never be happier than when he is here.

Perhaps, she imagines, little Georgie feels bigger in these Lilliputian spaces than he ever does in the vast rooms of his parents and his grandmother. Beneath the sumptuous ceilings of Wren, Nash and Wyattville, he is lost, unnoticed even. It is all a matter of proportion. But here, magically, he grows taller and broader. Everyone must jump at his command. Here he is captain of the vessel.

On that very first morning of her married life, when Georgie disappears into the bathroom, May listens as he empties his bowels and clears his lungs from the vestiges of yesterday's tobacco. God, will he do this every morning? She prays he will at least open a window, rain or not. She prays too that, last night in the darkness, she rinsed away every last drop of her blood from the basin. Now though, the relief of being alone in the bed is immeasurable; a feeling she notes and of which she is ashamed.

In a while, she rises to be bathed and dressed in the manner to which she is accustomed. Out on the landing, there is a strong aroma of frying bacon, which is oddly comforting. She creeps towards it down the absurdly narrow, curving stairs; hardly the *grand escalier* in the house of a prince. She asks herself why she creeps. This is her home now, after all. She straightens her back.

In the little hallway, a young maid near crashes into her. The girl looks as nervous as May herself; perhaps she is new here too. Breakfast will be served in fifteen minutes, the girl splutters and scuttles away. May wonders where this will happen. She has absolutely no idea.

Yet she has been in this house once or twice before. It was usually employed as a billet for bachelor guests when the big house was bursting at the seams. And Eddy brought her here the very day before he fell ill. This was where he had been exiled with his tutor in preparation for going up to Cambridge. How hard he had worked in this sitting room, he'd groaned, determined to show the world he wasn't as stupid as they thought.

It is this room May enters now. She hardly recognises it; it is quite transformed. The dusty bookishness and scent of old pipe smoke is gone. It smells of fresh paint and polish. The furniture, the carpets, the curtains; everything is palpably new. It might be a setting for an exhibition at Olympia devoted to domestic felicity.

'So what do you think? Are you pleased?' he says.

Georgie stands at her shoulder with a grin like a Cheshire cat. He is dressed for outdoors; his coat is soaked through, his hair plastered to his forehead.

'Isn't it splendid?' he says. 'My mother and the girls arranged absolutely everything. There's nothing at all for you to do.'

May's throat closes up and refuses to deliver a reply. To give herself time, she walks around the room, pretending to examine things. She keeps her face turned away from him. She knows she must smile and speak in a moment, but right now both are quite beyond her.

'Some chap came up from Maples with books of samples. Like bloody great tombstones. My Mama and the girls chose all the patterns. They've done out all the rooms on this floor. All for you. Do say you like it.'

May looks out of the French windows as the rains pummels the flowerbeds. She takes a long deep breath and turns to face him.

'It is charming, Georgie,' she says. 'Quite charming. How kind of your mother and the girls to go to such trouble for me.'

She is shown the dining room, the morning room and the other rabbit holes which have so thoughtfully been arranged for her. Each room smells exactly the same; the odd scent of new fabric and carpet glue.

Conversation at the breakfast table is as sticky as the thick-cut marmalade and the yolk of their boiled eggs. As if the coupling of last night has cut them off from each other, rather than the opposite.

'What made you go out in such weather?' she asks at last.

'I wanted to say hello to the chaps in the stables,' he replies. 'Old chums. Known some of them since Eddy and I were boys. I'll take you across later if you'd like.'

'Well perhaps, if the rain stops.'

'If the rain stops?' he says. 'Good God May, we don't bother about a spit of rain in Norfolk. You're far too much of a town bird. But I'll soon make you into a country girl.'

'I *do* come from Richmond Park, Georgie,' she says.

'Richmond Park? That's a pansy's notion of the country. This is the real England. Don't worry. Within a year, you'll be watching the vet shove his fist up a cow's arse without flinching.'

May makes a mental vow that, when the splendid day comes, she will not be seen to flinch, though she flinches at this moment. A girl brought up with three brothers is not unused to schoolboy crudity, so she is not offended. She merely yearns for something better.

Georgie is right though. She is indeed a town bird. Here, when she glances outside, she sees nothing but anodyne fields. At the ground floor windows, blowsy bushes of laurel and rhododendron have been allowed to grow unchecked, blocking out light and air, slumped against the glass like drunkards. This is a ship without horizons, floating in some eternal nowhere.

In the sitting room, he settles down to read the Norfolk newspaper. Fascinating stuff, he says. He reads some of it out aloud. A gentleman has lost an eye in a shooting accident. Damn fool, snorts Georgie; probably a grocer with ideas above his station. A real gentleman would have known how to use his guns. And there is an outbreak of poaching on a nearby estate. The culprits are let off with a fine. Six months in Norwich prison would be more like it, he says. Oh splendid. There is a cattle market in King's Lynn next week. They should definitely go to that, he says. A chance for the locals to get a good look at her, though he'll not allow them to examine her rump or the size of her udder. Ha!

It is chilly in the room but a fire has been laid to offset the unseasonal weather. May rolls a small armchair on its castors a few feet closer to the warmth. Georgie looks up and frowns.

'Why did you do that?'

'Do what?'

'Move the chair.'

'Why not? It's far better nearer the fire.'

'But my Mama spent ages arranging everything in the best possible position. When she visits, she may be hurt to see that you've shifted it.'

'I'm sure she won't even notice, Georgie.'

'I'm perfectly sure she will. She really did go to so much trouble, you know. Getting everything just so. And all for you.'

The red lower lip is slightly pushed forward, in that way he has. Like a boy denied an ice cream.

'You'd prefer me to move it back then?'

'There's a good girl,' he replies.

And so she does. But she sends for a shawl and wraps it tightly around her shoulders as if she is about to embark on a trek across the Arctic. She knows he is watching her, but does not meet his eye. He turns the pages of his newspaper with the noisiest possible rustling.

They sit in silence for an hour or more. May pretends to read a ladies' journal, but the words glaze over. This time yesterday, she was clattering along Piccadilly in the sunshine, the focus of tens of thousands of those ravenous eyes. Today, as the rain keeps falling, nobody is looking at her at all. Not a living soul. A small flutter of panic catches in her throat.

Georgie folds his newspaper and places it neatly on a side table. He declares that the rain has eased and that they can go for a walk now.

In truth, it has eased hardly at all. Umbrellas braced against the wind, they walk around the grounds. As promised, he takes her to meet his friends in the stable yard. They bow and doff their caps; the oldest groom tells tales of the brothers as boys and how naughty they were, especially Georgie. Foul-mouthed by the age of ten, Ma'am, he tells her, and the navy only made it worse. The accused is delighted and slaps him on the back. The men move to discussing matters of horseflesh; a favourite old mare may need to be put down and a new foal seems to have a deformed leg. Damn bad luck. They will have to shoot him. They turn their backs on May Teck and she is left to stand alone, with the stink of horse in her nostrils and the hem of her skirt soiled by the muddy floor.

They do a circuit of the park, skirting around the big house, past the lake where everyone had skated that last winter, Eddy outshining them all. Georgie stops by the lakeside and looks out across the water. She wonders if he is seeing the same picture in his mind. Suddenly, she longs to ask him, to draw him to her in the bleak comradeship of grief, as she had once done over the game of bezique above the bay of Cannes.

'Happy memories here, are there not?' she says.

He does not answer, tilting his umbrella so that she can no longer see his face.

'Georgie?'

'Yes indeed. Long gone now.'

The umbrella turns away and strides off along the path. She wants to run after him and slide her arm through his. On this first day of a honeymoon, what could be more natural, more loving? Yet she does not. Somehow she knows it would not be welcome. The certainty of that stabs her like a rapier.

At the far end of the path, the glum little villa comes back into sight. Heavens, how ugly it is; as unappealing as the big house, but at least that building has a certain grandeur. York Cottage, as it is now to be called in celebration of Georgie's new dukedom, might as well be in Surbiton or Sydenham, owned by a solicitor, doctor or some prosperous tradesman. It is a strange edifice, a bizarre amalgamation of Tudor and Gothic, a jumble of little turrets and gables, clad in workaday pebbledash; chaotic and malformed, as if its architect had been drunk as a lord. What a contrast, she thinks, to the elegant lines of White Lodge, so graceful and pure, the pearl of Richmond Park.

Yet, in mimicry of its grander neighbour, the little house too has been given its own lake, though 'pond' would be more accurate. Wild ducks cower among the reeds; a leaden pelican sadly contemplates the ruffled water, wondering what happened to summer. A hump-backed wooden bridge leads to a tiny island, smothered in dripping purple rhododendrons. A rowing boat, half-rotted, is tethered to a post on the bank. On this miserable morning, as May and her umbrella follow Georgie's marching back, the stygian pond reminds her of a scene from one of Madame Bricka's works of literature. Wherein the desolate heroine, having fallen from grace in one way or another, decides to end it all and wades into the welcoming waves.

XVIII

1893

She floats up towards consciousness. The distant voices which trickled down into her dream still gurgle in her ears. In a second, she realises they are real and coming from downstairs. The clock on the bureau says it has only just gone eight. Who on earth can it be at this hour?

She bathes and dresses quickly. When she reaches the dining room door, her hand freezes on the knob. She raises her eyes to an unmerciful God. Oh please, not again. Not this early. The damn woman was here only yesterday afternoon, not to mention the day before and the one before that. A sing-song voice is telling Georgie he is spreading too much butter on his toast. Soon, it bleats, he will be as fat as his Papa and one great roly-poly bear in the family is quite enough thank you. Other voices let fly a stream of high-pitched giggles. May Teck's spirits sink even further. All three of them at once. Again she remembers the vulgar ditty from the music-halls that one of her brothers used to hum. About a bride whose mother-in-law went along on the honeymoon. What a funny song it was. May no longer finds it amusing.

'Ah poor May, at long last,' says the sing-song voice as she braves the room. 'We were starting to wonder if you'd passed away in the night.'

'We rise early in Norfolk,' says the first giggler.

'That's right,' says the second. 'You'll have to buck your ideas up, dear.'

'A wife should always be there to make sure her husband gets a good breakfast,' adds the sing-song voice.

Less than a fortnight after the wedding, the shutters of the big house were thrown back, the rooms aired and the bedrooms made ready. The kitchens were opened up, the vegetable garden stripped of its bounty and the larders filled to the rafters. The gardeners raked and mowed from dawn till dusk; their sculpted flowerbeds laid waste to fill the vases of Meissen and Sevres. Everything must be perfect; anything less would be incomprehensible. And all this for three of the silliest creatures on God's earth.

Her mother-in-law Alix, she of the sing-song Danish voice, sits at the breakfast table in the bay window, eating scrambled egg with such delicacy it might be *pâté de foie gras*. The morning light haloes round her, as if in obeisance. Half of Europe is in love with Eddy and Georgie's mother; with her beauty and elegance, her charm and sweetness. *'The Sea-King's daughter from across the sea'*, the great Tennyson rhapsodised when, thirty years ago, she had crossed the German Ocean to marry Bertie. Even now, at nearly fifty, she looks scarcely older than the two grown-up daughters who sit on either side of her.

And, in truth, she is not. Inside that gracious head is a mind which, for some reason, failed to grow much past childhood. She retains the simple verities of the fairy tales which Hans Christian Andersen himself read aloud to her in the nursery in Copenhagen. A world of heroes and villains, of black and white, of happy endings and virtue triumphant. Yet her own fairy tale has not ended so well. The curse of the deafness in her family has been handed down to her. With every year that passes, she is locked away inside it more and more. Yet that is not her worst affliction. For all her attributes, she could not keep her husband faithful to her for long. Bertie likes clever, smart people and Alix is not that. He exists, in a fog of cigar smoke, boredom and pointlessness, in the watering-holes of London and the Continent. For more than twenty years, he has lived in a parallel universe, among a second family of cronies and mistresses.

'But am I not far more beautiful than any of them?' she will pout to anyone who will listen.

And it is true. But it is not enough. And that is the cross she bears; though she shoulders it with dignity, as if it weighs almost nothing, though that would not be true. With the loss of her husband's attention, Alix clings to her children, trapping them beside her in her nursery mind. Only death had been able to prise Eddy from her grasp. Now the four who remain must be held even closer to her bosom. Reluctantly she has allowed the eldest girl, drippy, droopy Louise, to marry and now, under even more pressure, her precious little Georgie-boy. But why should that change much in Alix's tiny world? May Teck is such a sensible girl. She will be no trouble.

The two remaining daughters are no more than dim satellites around Alix's sun. No trace of her beauty can be discerned in their heavy, Hanoverian faces. Whenever May looks at them, she thinks how cruel God can sometimes be, giving them the features of their father instead. Little Maudie, the youngest, small and sharp-beaked as a sparrow, is amiable enough, but Toria is not. Lumpen and lugubrious, an old maid before her time. Already she has turned in on herself and, from that lonely place, she strikes out with mockery and sarcasm. Yet May is sorry for her. She knows too well what it is like to wither in somebody else's shadow. She knows how close she might have come to being Toria.

'I hope you're pleased with everything we did to welcome you to your new home,' says Alix feeding marmalade from her fingertips to the yapping creature on her lap.

'I'm really most grateful. You've all been so very kind,' replies May.

'We didn't want you to have to bother with anything at all,' says little Maudie, 'except with being in love.'

The sisters break out in more giggles.

'Hush now. What naughty girls I have,' says Alix. 'Look, you've made my darling boy blush.'

'Of course, we're going to need some bookshelves,' says May quickly.

'What do you want with bookshelves?' asks Toria.

'What would you imagine, dear?' replies May.

'My Georgie-boy hardly reads anything but the Kings Lynn paper and the Admiralty reports,' says his mother.

'Perhaps not, but I do.'

'Oh poor May, I forgot you're such a swot,' says Toria.

A change has occurred to her appellation. Before the wedding, she was always 'sweet May' but now, she notes, she has become 'poor'. It is the same with their pets, their servants and the dolls which still litter their pretty pink bedrooms. As if everyone who is not themselves should be pitied and comforted for that calamity. Poor Rover. Poor Tiddles. Poor May.

'When Bertie built the big house, he ordered the books just as he ordered the carpets and the curtains. By the yard!' says Alix. 'Really it's true. By the yard. Too amusing. I doubt more than three have been read in thirty years.'

Everybody laughs. May wonders why. Why is it amusing to admit to ignorance? Indeed to celebrate it. Or is it perhaps that they are laughing at *her*?

'Poor May thinks we're an uneducated crew,' says Toria. 'Don't you May?'

The glint comes into Toria's bulbous eyes. The one that comes when she wants to make mischief.

'If I did Toria dear, I wouldn't be so impertinent as to say it,' she replies. 'Such is the civilising benefit of education.'

'Oooh bravo, May,' says Toria, crunching into her toast. 'But whatever use is an education to the likes of us? Our path is laid out. What on earth would it change? We might as well go on being as dumb as the leg of this table.'

More giggles dance around the teacups.

'Might it perhaps make the path more bearable?' says May.

Toria stops laughing. She glares across at her new sister, stands up and whistles for her dog.

'We need to do poo-poo,' she snaps and leaves the room. Georgie's lower lip juts out.

*

That night they are bidden to dinner at the big house. May dreads it. It will be Bertie's smart set from London. The women overdressed; brittle and knowing. The men, rancid with entitlement, little in their heads beyond the potential advantages of connection to a future deity. How they will all laugh at Bertie's jokes and tell him he is wonderful; bejewelled substitutes for his mother who never did. But when the old girl drops off the twig and he sits in her place on the ivory throne of Travancore, it will be worth all the bowing and the scraping and the laughing at the jokes. Their entitlement will be gloriously verified.

As they move from the drawing room towards the dining table, May overhears Toria mutter to a stout gentleman, shiny with sweat and rather feminine, who looks, she thinks, a little like Nellie Melba.

'Now do try to talk to May at dinner, though one knows she is deadly dull.'

At dinner, the conversation is of the going at Newmarket, the latest gun from Purdey, the new French milliner who has opened in Bond Street. It is of the cost of servants, the price of borrowing money and how to gamble it away. The women polish little darts of wit or malevolence, or both combined, and throw them at one another across the table. The stout, sweaty man beside her drinks too much, nudges her elbow and asks the new Duchess of York how she is enjoying married life.

Along the length and breadth of the room, no topic is discussed that carries any more weight than the wings of the butterflies she can see still fluttering among the flowerpots out on the terrace as sunset falls over the gardens. If only she could melt away through the big plate glass window and wander among them in the hazy evening.

So she says little more than courtesy demands. She is indeed deadly dull. It is hot and, so that Alix can hear, it is loud. Inside herself, May Teck screams to get out of here. Back to White Lodge. To Madame Bricka and the white sitting room and the books. Even just back to her bedroom in the glum little villa.

She glances at Georgie at the far end of the table; a *placement*, May is sure, decided by Toria in order to isolate her among the worst of the hearties and force her to sink or swim, in the hope and expectation of the former. Mind you, Georgie is no more at home with this crowd than she is. In conversation about the Purdey gun, he is fine, but with millinery or the joys of the casino at Deauville, he is quite hopeless. She watches the woman beside him, a fading temptress all satin and feathers, try to engage him, flirt with him even, then give up in despair. It strikes her now that whatever else may come her way, her husband will not be a *roué*. He will never, unlike his father, leave behind him the fetid whiff of scandal and dishonour. She will not have to tread the same lonely path as Alix. Well, that's something.

Then May, observing, is struck by a second truth. She has escaped from one playpen only to enter another. Her new family, her husband himself, is no more grown, no less demanding and capricious, than her own mother and father. Still she is surrounded by infants in white ties and tails, in diamond tiaras and *rivieres* of emeralds. Is this to be her fate in life? Toria was quite right at breakfast. What May Teck has to give is not needed here. Nor wanted either. And Bricka was right too, that day in the great chapel. Good strong hips, she had opined, were the only accomplishments worth possessing.

After dinner, the infants are coaxed towards another game. The old conservatory has lately been converted into a bowling alley. The women sit along the edges while the men play. It is even hotter in here; fans flutter and jackets are even permitted to be removed. But neither the perfumes of Monsieur Worth nor the fog of Havana cigars can quite defeat the smell of sweat and brandy breath. Inside her tightest corsets, May begins to feel a little sick.

After a while, Georgie's mother demands that the ladies should be allowed to play too. Throwing the ball along the alley, she fails to hit a single skittle, overbalances and falls flat on her backside. Tinkling with the laughter which enslaved the great Tennyson, Alix is helped up by Georgie and has another go. But the result is no better, nor do any of the other women manage to topple more than a couple of their targets. May hangs back, trying to shrink into the walls.

'Poor May hasn't had a try,' Toria calls out, the glint in her eye.

'No thank you dear. I should be quite useless.'

'We're all useless. Come on, don't be such a stick in the mud.'

'Go on May,' says Georgie.

'I really don't want...'

'Go on May,' says Georgie again, the lip jutting out.

Her face flushed, May takes the ball. She can hardly bear the thought of landing on her arse and Toria's ugly face brimming with delight. She knows she would be quite incapable of dusting herself down and laughing merrily as her mother-in-law did. She would want to push through the throng, run away along the corridors and out in the darkness of the night. And that of course would never do. God in heaven. But now it strikes her that this game is not that different from bowling cricket balls to her brothers. Back then she had always bowled underhand, so surely she need only bend her knees and aim the ball low. So that is what she does. The ball roars along the alley like a bat out of hell and topples every single pin with a smash that echoes the length of the alley. Nobody else tonight, not even a man, has done that.

There are cheers, bravos, applause, though not of course from all. In victory, May Teck does not whoop or clap her hands. She does not laugh or even smile. She merely inclines her head to the crowd, then returns to her chair to hide behind the fan painted with apple blossom that Mr Thaddy had given her on her seventeenth birthday.

'Goodness Miss May,' says Georgie. It is the first time he has smiled for the past three hours.

At the close of the evening, Alix walks with them out to the porch. She kisses her Georgie-boy then, when he has turned towards the homeward path, she touches May on the arm.

'You won't take him from me entirely,' she says. The sing-song inflections of the voice make it difficult to judge if this is a question or even a plea. Then, in the beautiful face, May sees quite clearly what it is. It is a declaration.

'There is nothing quite like the love of a mother for a son,' says Alix. 'Nothing in this world. Poor May, you will discover that for yourself one day.'

XIX

Autumn, 1893

It is a room on the first floor. Small of course, but that does not matter. Once a bedroom for some diminutive guest, it no longer contains a bed or indeed much else. Old pictures are stacked against the wall. A roll of unwanted carpet. Georgie's battered chest from his years at sea. It seems to be a place of little purpose now. But it has a pretty little chimney piece, a tolerable view across the pancake-flat fields and May Teck sees its purpose in an instant. Oh yes indeed. It is to be her boudoir, her *sanctum sanctorum*, the recreation of the white sitting room from home.

She must ask Georgie of course, but he scarcely bothers to look up from the King's Lynn paper. Footmen are instructed to clear it out and maids to clean it up. A painter is called to sweep his brush over the faded woodwork. A carpenter puts up bookshelves, which shrink the room even more but she does not care about that. She has brought only her clothes and most necessary possessions to Norfolk, but now she telegraphs to Madame Bricka and summons her books, her favourite chair with the fan-shaped back, more framed photographs of her nearest and dearest, of Pen Ponds, of Florence and the Villa I Cedri. She summons too the portrait Harry Thaddeus Jones painted for her seventeenth birthday. The day on which, at first sight of it, she believes she became a woman. Hurry please, do hurry, she says in the telegram.

When everything arrives and whenever Georgie is out in the coverts, she spends hours sorting it all out. The new young servant, the nervous one, helps her. Pilgrim is a quiet girl, easy on the spirit and, like her mistress, far from home. Every day, May becomes more glad of her.

'Oh Ma'am,' says Pilgrim, as the portrait is hung above the fireplace.

'Do you like it?' asks May.

'You look so lovely, Ma'am,' the girl says. 'If you don't mind my saying so, Ma'am.'

'Well perhaps someone will paint you one day.'

'Me, Ma'am? Heavens, who'd want to paint the likes of me?'

'Don't be so certain. We can never know what life might bring us.'

'Oh no Ma'am,' the girl replies. 'A photograph on the sands at Cromer is the best I can hope for.'

Georgie steers well clear of the comings and goings in the creation of the boudoir. Though it is only yards from their bedroom, he does not even cross the threshold till, when all is arranged, she invites him to visit.

'So this is it,' he says, coming no more than a single pace inside the room. 'Though what you need it for defeats me, with these splendid rooms downstairs all newly done out for you.'

'You have your study Georgie,' she replies. 'So it's nice for me to have a little one of my own.'

'Never heard of a woman wanting a study before,' he says. 'Except Grandmama of course, but that's quite different.'

'Is it? Why?'

Georgie's eyes rake around the room. It is, she thinks, as if he is cataloguing every object, estimating its value and finding nothing of the slightest worth. His gaze lands on the portrait above the fireplace.

'What's that?'

'It's me of course. When we lived in Italy. Didn't you recognise me?'

'Hardly. It's just not you, is it? Not you at all.'

'Well I was only seventeen,' she says. 'Don't you like it?'

'No,' he says and turns on his heel.

Summer beaches are deserted. Church fetes are postponed. The visit to the cattle show in King's Lynn is cancelled. In the pelting rain, they are trapped together inside the ship of pebbledash. But the slightest hole in the shroud of grey-black cumulus takes Georgie outside to shoot at something, anything at all, foolish enough to poke its head above the sodden bracken. How she despises the culture of the guns, will despise it till the day she dies, though she is wise enough not to let it show. Any attempt at discussion of the ethics of slaughtering God's creatures would be greeted with incomprehension, derision and even concern about her mental state.

So May Teck says nothing and, as he marches off towards the woods, she retreats to her boudoir, takes a book from the shelf and settles into her fan chair in front of the fire. It doesn't much matter if she has read it before, perhaps even dissected it with Madame Bricka. It is her way back into the thinking world. But on a day when her mind will not settle, when there has been some new little rub at the breakfast table, she might choose a book of pictures instead; her favourite an album of sketches of Florence which Mr Thaddy had once given her. Again, she finds herself in the Piazza della Repubblica, in the Boboli Gardens or riding down the avenues of the Cascine where the young bucks once threw flowers at her carriage. On the newly painted bookshelves of May Teck's boudoir, every occupant is an old friend. Every one of them speaks to her, reminding her of who she is. And there she sits, until, from below, she hears the crunch of boots on gravel. The book is put back on the shelf. The past is sacrificed to the present. Georgie is back and she must go down. That is the way of it now.

On one of those mornings when the clouds part for a little, she goes to visit the cottage of a labourer whose child is mortally sick.

It is Georgie's idea. She must show herself to the people of the estate as soon as possible. No shirking, he says. How little he understands her. May Teck has never shirked in her life. Such visiting is as natural to her as the breath she takes. On the coat-tails of Mary Adelaide, there is no invalid she has not tried to comfort, no poverty or deprivation she has not witnessed.

She takes Pilgrim with her in the pony trap, bearing fruit and vegetables from the kitchen garden. It is hard to see the dying child in his cot. She senses that the poor mother would like her to touch the boy, but she cannot. That urge to retreat from the chaos of sickness invades her again, as it did when her father was afflicted in Italy and when Eddy was drowning from inside himself. It shames her, but she cannot overcome it. Instead she says the right things, promises whatever help might be needed, knowing the child is well beyond its reach. Going back in the pony trap, Pilgrim begins to weep.

'Hush now, the poor child will soon be safe,' May says.

'I suppose so Ma'am but oh the waste of it Ma'am.'

The words of Aunt Queen come back to her, uttered as they stood together beside Eddy's tomb.

'It is the waste that breaks the heart,' she had said.

Those words, May thinks, will never leave her.

By the time they get back to the glum little villa, the rain has started again and her head is splitting. She yearns to lie down for a little. But there is some small thing she wants from her boudoir. Only when she picks it up from a table does she notice what has happened. Surely the table is not quite where it stood this morning. Nor indeed is anything else. The *escritoire* no longer sits beneath the window to catch the best of the light. The Sheraton cabinet is against a different wall. The framed photographs of her family smile out from alien positions. Mr Thaddy's portrait now rests in a corner, on the floor, its face turned to the wall as if not good enough for display; its place above the fireplace usurped by a tepid watercolour of Norwich Cathedral. Her beautiful fan chair is nowhere to be seen; instead a fat chintz object of remarkable mundanity now squats beside the hearth. It feels like a punch to the pit of her stomach. She can hardly breathe. She goes and splashes her face with ice cold water in the hope that it might calm her. The stratagem works, but does more than that. It also wipes the cobwebs from her eyes. She looks hard at herself in the mirror, slows her breathing and goes downstairs.

He is in his study, hunched over his stamp albums with a magnifying glass. When she enters, he does not look up.

'Georgie, what has happened in my room?'

'Your room?' he replies.

'Everything has been moved around. Some of my things have even vanished.'

'Ah yes, Mama and the girls came over. When they heard you were out, they thought I might be lonely.'

He is still peering through the glass.

'You must come and look at this Mauritian Red. It's quite exquisite.'

'My things, Georgie?'

'What? Oh yes, Mama asked to see your new retreat. She thought it might be even nicer for you if she altered things just a little. So sweet of her, don't you think? To go to the bother?'

'Where is my little chair with the fan-shaped back? The chair I always sit in to read.'

'I haven't the faintest notion. No doubt, one of the footmen has put it somewhere out of the way. Does it matter?'

May turns on her heel, closing the door behind her. She summons both the footmen. The fan chair is in an outbuilding now, along with some of the old furniture removed to make way for the new stuff from Maples. She asks for it to be brought to her and does not move from her position in the hallway until it arrives. She stands stock still, as straight and tall as she has ever stood in her life.

When the chair arrives, the wood is moist to the touch and a large watermark stains the upholstery. The roof of the outbuilding leaks a little, the footman explains, not meeting her eye. She orders it dried and cleaned and returned to its previous home before they undertake any other task.

At dinner, she is almost silent. She makes none of her usual efforts at conversation, declining to lob tennis balls in the hope of a decent return that never comes. He hardly seems to notice. Between mouthfuls, he mentions that one of the old dogs at the big house must be put down tomorrow. Dear old Brutus. Damn shame. And little Maudie has got a verruca on her foot and can hardly walk. Poor darling. May sees a piece of potato stuck in his beard. Normally she would gently tell him. Tonight she does not. The piece of potato can nest there till hell freezes over.

She goes to bed early. When he comes up later, she pretends to be asleep. Still he rolls himself up against her as usual. She does not move a muscle, she hardly even breathes.

'May?' he whispers.

She pretends not to hear, but the question comes again and then once more.

'Georgie, I am tired.'

He rolls away onto his back. He sighs the sigh of a man sorely tried and put-upon. She can picture the redness in his face.

'You took a vow did you not?' he says.

'And I will honour it,' she replies. 'But not tonight.'

'I'd remind you that you have a duty to perform. I always thought you to be a dutiful girl. We all did. That is why you're where you are now.'

'I'll not fail in my duty Georgie. But, you must excuse me, not tonight.'

There is another silence in the dark bedroom overlooking the pond. She hears the faint quacking of the wild duck in the reeds. The long sigh comes again.

'Well I'm sorry, but I believe that I'm within my rights to insist.'

For a split second she resists, crosses her thighs and locks her arms across her breasts.

'May!'

She takes a long breath, lets it out and makes her body limp as a broken puppet. In her mind, she travels to the garden by the Arno. Let him do as he wants with her. She will not be there. And anyway, it will all be over in less than three minutes. No more remarkable than the boiling of an egg.

When she wakes in the morning, he has already left the house. Gone fishing they tell her, with his chums from the stables. She breakfasts in blessed isolation. Though she tries to ignore it, there is some pain between her legs. Last night, in his irritation, he was not gentle.

She goes up to the boudoir. The seat of the fan chair is still damp, so perching on a stool, she writes letter after letter. To her mother and father, to her brothers, to Madame Bricka, to Mr Thaddy, to anyone she thinks might care to hear her voice. On the pages, she says nothing they would not want to hear, not even between the lines. Everything is fine. She is happy. How kind and considerate dear Georgie is. His stamp albums really are most interesting.

Then she puts her portrait back above the fireplace. As she stretches up to hang it on the hook, she feels the pain between her legs again. In the space of a moment, the pain shifts from there into her heart and soul, growing in intensity as it does so, from a mild discomfort to a consuming rage. But it is not like any rage she has felt before; those hot intemperate flames of anger inherited from her father, which fade as quickly as they flare. This is an ice-cold thing, as if the needle of a barometer inside her had lurched in another direction altogether.

She rings for Pilgrim. Fetch the footmen here at once. She orders the furniture restored to exactly the way it was. When that is done, she leads them all downstairs. In the sitting room, the dining room, the morning room, even in Georgie's study, they are made to move every chair, sofa, table and cabinet to a position of her choice. Every picture, mirror, plant pot and what-not is reassessed for both beauty and practicality beneath her merciless eye. If it fails to please her, it is dispatched to the outbuilding with the leaky roof. She cares not a jot if it has only just left the factory of Mr Maple.

She can see that the footmen are nervous, hesitant even.

'Are you quite sure Ma'am?' one says.

'Who is the mistress here?' she replies.

The man's eyes swivel to and fro, like a rabbit facing the barrel of a shotgun. He pauses a second too long.

'If you're not sure of that answer, perhaps you'd be better suited to employment elsewhere.'

When the work is done, May surveys each room then turns on her heel. She goes upstairs to the boudoir and slams the door with a noise that reaches down into the kitchens and up into the servants' attics. She falls onto the fan chair, damp or not. Now the coldness that had come into her melts away. How she longs for an arm to wrap itself around her. The arm of her Mama, of Bricka, of anyone at all.

There is a knock at the door; soft as a whisper.

'I brought you some tea, Ma'am,' says Pilgrim. 'And a bit of cake. There's nothing like good strong tea is there?'

And so, when May Teck breaks apart and buries her head in her hands, it is the thin, white arm of a parlour maid from Cromer, scarcely more than a child, which encircles her shoulders and, without saying a single word, brings her comfort.

XX

Autumn, 1893

'Jesus Christ!'

From downstairs, there is another slamming of another door. It is loud enough to shiver the petals of the roses atop her Sheraton cabinet. It shivers May Teck too and she steels herself for the marching feet along the landing. But they do not come. There are no more blasphemies. After the slam, there is silence in the house. The usual sounds of pots and pans crashing in the kitchen, of a footman whistling as he polishes in the boot room, even of the horses in the stables, are gone. The captain of the ship is in a temper and the crew creep around him on tiptoe.

She does not go down to luncheon. Pilgrim offers to serve something light in her room, perhaps just a little cold chicken. Do eat something, Ma'am, the girl entreats her, but she cannot. She lights one cigarette after another. All afternoon, she sits staring out at the drizzle, dozing a little or trying to read the latest book Madame Bricka has sent her. A new novel by Mr Gissing about two sisters made impecunious by the death of their father. One of them, wanting to find independence in a cold hard world, takes genteel but hateful employment, while the other, terrified of any such thing, flees into the security of marriage with an uncongenial man. May almost smiles. Oh dear, how unsubtle the clever-clogs Bricka can be sometimes. But try as she might, she cannot advance past the first few chapters.

Towards evening, the drizzle stops and she flings open the window. The weakening sun appears from beneath the skirts of the cumulus, spreading a tawny light across sodden grass of the garden and the flat fields beyond the fence. She inhales the smell of the earth as it dries out, the same smell she knows from her bedroom window at home. She closes her eyes and tries to pretend she is back there. When she opens them, she prays she will see the view straight down Queen's Ride into the very heart of the park and glimpse the sheath of Pen Ponds through the trees. She will see her brothers striding off with their fishing rods. She will see the familiar pathways through the ferns and the bracken, on which she could find her way even on a moonless night.

A knock on the door compels her to open her eyes to her new reality. A note is delivered on a silver salver.

'I shall expect you at dinner,' it says.

And so she bathes and changes and goes down the narrow staircase. To her surprise, the dining room is exactly as she left it. If she catches his eye, he looks away. They eat without a single word until the arrival of the peaches and cream. Good simple food, that's what he likes. Nothing fancy. Like he and Eddy used to get on the ship that took them round the world for three whole years. To this day, he likes to make his mother and sisters laugh by tapping biscuits against the table to check for weevils. How odd, May thinks, that his travels seem to have taught him nothing; left him so incurious about the wider world, perfectly happy with the narrowest of horizons.

'They've all gone now,' he says at last, toying with the peaches. 'Back to London. The big house is shut up again.'

'I see,' she says.

'Mama asked to say goodbye to you. I told her you were indisposed.'

She does not reply. When the meal is over she goes up to bed. She waits in dread for the rolling towards her, the breath on her face, the tugging at her nightgown. But it does not come. They lie together side by side, flat on their backs, rigid as two effigies on a tomb. Is that what their marriage is to be now, she wonders? Dead before it ever came alive? In the night, there is no snoring so she can tell he is awake. Their hands lie on top of the quilt inches apart but do not touch.

Breakfast is as silent as dinner had been, but agitation hangs in the air like dust in a shard of sunshine. When she flicks a glance at him, he is gnawing on his kippers, stripping the last of the flesh from the bone. He slurps at his tea like a man half dead from thirst. Though it never comes to rest on her, his gaze roves around the room, from floor to ceiling, corner to corner as if he has heard a rat behind the wainscoting.

'You will excuse me,' he says rising, the morning paper stuffed under his arm. The door closes behind him. May sighs as the footsteps fade along the hallway. But almost at once they return.

'I'd be grateful if you would put on your shawl and come outside with me at once. I'll wait for you at the front door.'

'I don't wish to go for a walk this early in the day,' she replies.

'It's not a walk. It's something else. Please come.'

It is a better morning. For the first time in weeks, there is a flush of warmth in the air. He walks a pace or two ahead of her, hands behind his back, his gaze bolted to the rhododendron path leading up to the big house. With his mother's departure, the shutters are folded over and the curtains drawn. Servants come and go around the kitchen court; horse-drawn vans are loaded with unwanted food for the people on the estate or the poor of the villages around. In the drawing rooms, maids throw dust sheets over the furniture and carry away the wilting flowers. There is laughing and joking and the singing of tunes; the loosening of stays and the shaking-off of deference, all of which dies at the sight of Georgie and May coming through the front door. Without looking behind him to see if she is still there, Georgie heads to the bottom of the staircase.

'Where are we going, Georgie?'

'Just follow me please.'

Even now, eighteen months on, she still baulks at the sight of this staircase. It is haunted not just by the dead but by the ghosts of those still living; by frightened faces disfigured by shock and disbelief, by the sound of helpless weeping and by cries to heaven to spare them from calamity.

Past maids bearing sheets to the laundry, Georgie marches upwards and she follows. But when he turns down the sepulchral corridor to the east front, she calls after him.

'Georgie, where are you going? I don't like it here as you can surely imagine.'

He turns and looks her in the eye for the first time that day. He stretches out his arm and seizes her wrist.

'No, you *must* come.'

At the door to Eddy's bedroom he stops at last, panting heavily, though not, she realises, from any exertion.

'Georgie please, I really don't want to go in there,' she says softly.

'Neither do I,' he says. 'Christ, neither do I.'

'So why?'

'Because now it is desirable. Necessary even,' he says, staring at the door as if something monstrous waits on the other side. 'If I am to make you understand.'

Still he makes no move to open the door.

'Help me,' he whispers.

May turns the handle and enters. The room is pitch dark. She opens the shutters to let in the sharp morning light. She herself had vowed never to return here, however much pressure was put upon her. Georgie still hovers on the threshold. His eyes take in the fire laid ready in the grate, the clothes in the wardrobe, the hairbrushes, the shaving things, the soap in its marble dish.

'Dear God,' he says.

He creeps into the room and stares down at the mundane little bed, glorified by the Union Jack draped across it. He slumps onto a chair. May takes another. Nothing is said.

How strange, she thinks. There is bustle below them; she should be able to hear the whinnying of the tradesmen's horses, the crunch of feet on gravel, the servants calling out to each other as they work. But she can hear nothing, nothing at all. In Eddy's little room, as if by some warping of time, the laws of nature are altered. It is a shrine indeed, suspended in sorrow, cut off from the very heartbeat of life.

'You'll have realised by now Miss May that I am not a man who is easy with words,' he says. 'I've never quite got the hang of how to use them, so I suppose I shy away from them.'

He glances across at her, but she does not speak, waiting, her back straight in the chair, her hands clasped tidily in her lap.

'But I see that I must make a bit of an effort with you now,' he says, 'or we're entering choppy waters.'

'I rather think we're in them already,' she says.

'Quite.'

Georgie rises from the chair and paces the cramped space around the bed, as if the sentences caged inside him are struggling for release.

'Two people died in this room, not one,' he says. 'That's why I can hardly bear to come in here. I don't want to be reminded of that fact, but it's the truth. When Eddy took his last breath and his destiny transferred itself to me, I swear to God that, in that moment, a bit of me died too. The person that I am was lost.'

She sees the red lips quiver.

'Not a very interesting person perhaps,' he says, 'though no doubt you've worked that out for yourself. Just a rough sailor, who cusses and curses and who's happiest on the quarterdeck. And when I'd got too old for the sea, I'd have spent the rest of my days on an estate like this one, among the grooms and the farmers and the smell of horse dung. Worrying about little beyond there being enough pheasants and partridges waiting for me in the woods. A dull country gent whose life wouldn't leave much of a mark on anyone. But now...'

'Now Georgie?'

'Now I must be this other man. No, that's the wrong word. Sorry. This other thing. That's it, this other thing. *This* damn thing.'

He snatches at the Union Jack on the bed and hurls it across the room to lie crumpled in a corner. May is shocked. She springs to her feet. She picks it up, smooths it down, holds it tightly against her body as if to protect it against him.

'And I thought you would support me and help me. Like you promised Eddy you'd support him. Never leave him, you said. I know because he told me. He was so happy in his last weeks. He believed he'd found the woman to bring out the best in him. And I believed the same of you. Not some silly little princess like my dear sisters, but a woman of substance. Hell, just look at you standing there, draped in that bloody flag. You are Britannia to the life.'

'I believe in this flag,' she replies. 'I believe in this family and that God has chosen it to make a difference in this world. For reasons known only to Him, He took Eddy from us and passed the task to you. And as I promised Eddy, I promise you too. I will stand by you, Georgie.'

'Then why do you challenge me?'

'By moving the furniture around in what is supposed to be my home?'

'I don't give a damn about the bloody furniture. It's your attitude. You have this attitude that I don't understand.'

'What attitude is that?'

Georgie sits down again. He rubs his eyes with his fists like some tired little boy.

'I told you. I'm no good with words. Christ, I can't express it, Miss May.'

'Is it perhaps that I wish to be myself?'

He looks up at her in surprise. A faint smile comes to the red lips as if she has just made a joke.

'Yourself?'

Georgie leans back in the chair, puts his hands behind his head and regards her now with curiosity, as if he is meeting her for the first time. The smile broadens almost into laughter.

'But you cannot be yourself now. Any more than I can be. You're such a clever girl, watching us all silently with those bright blue eyes, I'm amazed you've not grasped that. Did it really never cross your mind?'

She cannot think what to reply. Instead she unfolds the Union Jack back across the little bed. He comes to help her. Like two chambermaids, they tuck the edges beneath the mattress and smooth out the creases till it stares up at them, unruffled and assured.

'Do you know the most comfortable bed in the world?' he asks. 'It's a hammock on a ship. Swinging gently and rocking you to sleep. The waves lapping against the hull. And, through the porthole, you can see the stars in the sky.'

They stand together on either side of Eddy's bed.

'To make this damn thing work, we cannot ever be ourselves,' he says almost in a whisper. 'That is the sacrifice required of us. Do you think you can do that Miss May?'

'I don't know,' she says. 'Truly Georgie, I don't know.'

He sighs and turns away from her. He opens the wardrobe, brushing his fingertips across the row of Eddy's suits; empty husks of tweed, linen and worsted.

'Two lives lost in this room,' he says again as he goes out of the door. 'Two lives lost.'

XXI

Autumn, 1893

The ravenous eyes are on her again.

She enters the Red Drawing Room of the old palace of St James's where the man is ready for her. It is only ten in the morning, but she is dressed in a ballgown of amber silk and organdie, a tiara on her head, her mother's pearls draped around her neck. She has been a little sick this morning but the man cannot be kept waiting. That would not be dutiful. And she must, as her husband continues to remind her, at all times be dutiful.

She forgets this one's name. He is at least the third she is required to sit for in the months since her wedding. It seems the painted image of the Duchess of York must now be captured on a regular basis, the image of who and what she has become. The humble photograph will not always suffice; she must be seen as large as life, perhaps even larger, so she may be hung on a high wall and looked up to.

The man tries to make small talk. This room is perfect, he declares. A good, clear northern light. Not surprising, she thinks. Nearly every room in their apartment here faces north. There may not be laurel bushes up against the windows as in Norfolk, but the sun has no greater chance of entry than it does there. The only views are of inner courtyards or out over the public street; the tops of the guardsmen's bearskins marching to and fro. It is here, in the old palace, that she was to have lived with Eddy. She tries to forget that, but it is hard.

Georgie hates the place; a beastly house he calls it. When they are required to be in London, he comes kicking and screaming. Damn waste of good shooting time. On the train, while he sulks, she must mask the exhilaration of the prisoner freed. As the flat fields at last give way to the suburbs, then the suburbs to the spires of the city, her joy increases with every mile. When she glimpses the dome of St Paul's rushing towards her as if in welcome, she thinks she might weep. And oh, the pleasure of the bustling pavements, the clip-clop of the hansom cabs, the shouts of the hawkers and the paperboys. Soon she will see her Mama and Papa, her brothers perhaps if they are in town. And dear Bricka. For a week or, with luck, perhaps two, she will try to pretend that nothing has really changed. The town bird migrates home.

The only drawback is those ravenous eyes. In the country, with her mother-in-law and the sisters, the local gentry and the estate people, it is bad enough. But here it is worse. On her wedding day, she had steeled herself for the hundreds of thousands of faces and it had not been as awful as she had feared. These had been an amorphous mass, a sea of indistinct pinkish blobs and at a tolerable remove, penned in behind barriers and rows of stalwart policemen. What's more, they had approved of her, cheering and wishing her well, their happy hearts completely on her side.

Now it is different. In this old palace, the eyes are much closer and sharp as skewers as they bore into her. How's the girl doing so far? Is she up to the job? A gamble of course, considering that bloodline. The curiosity is not malign, but it is cautious, hedging its bets, biding its time. And it is not just the eyes from below stairs, but from those above too. Here in the city, there must be secretaries, equerries, ladies-in-waiting. There is always a crowd. Tradition even dictates that the most prominent of these people dine with them at every meal. It is, May thinks, what running a boarding house must be like; the guests, however amiable, a necessity rather than a pleasure. Always the need to converse about something; the October weather, the dogs, the sprained ankle of somebody's mother, how wonderfully Aunt Queen is blazing into the autumn of her years. There is no peace, no privacy. From the minute she rises from her bed till she returns to it, somebody is watching her; either to serve her or, for good or ill, to judge her. In the beginning, she tells herself she imagines it but, with time, realises it is perfectly true and that, till the day she dies, it will be like this. The thought of it begins to haunt her, to obsess her even. They are watching her. It will never end.

Now she sits in the chair that the artist has selected. He asks permission to arrange the folds of her gown and blushes as he kneels down to do so, as if it is an intrusion. And it is.

She is asked to look to one side, not directly at him. Yes, if she focuses on that little marble statue of Venus over there, he says, that will do nicely. So May looks at the goddess, in all her brazen, naked womanhood and wonders what Venus thinks of May Teck all trussed up in her finery. She wonders too what the artist sees. The same as Mr Thaddy those ten long summers ago? She doubts it. Probably he is not even trying to see anything at all beyond the tiara, the pearls and the gown of amber silk and organdie.

'Splendid Ma'am,' the man says. 'Splendid.'

She straightens her back and clears her face of all expression, as she is schooling herself to do. And as she stares at the little marble goddess, she prays silently that the spirit which first came to life in that distant garden is still somehow within her. Beneath the tiara and the pearls. Even if it is now no more than a wisp of gossamer on a warm Tuscan breeze.

*

'It's fine,' says Harry Thaddeus Jones in the Red Drawing Room. 'Honest now, it is.'

'I really am so sorry,' she says. 'So very sorry.'

'It's fine, May Flower,' he repeats with a smile. 'Not another word, not a single one.'

The smile still has some power over her. These days it illuminates cheeks which are fuller than before. In truth, all of him is fuller. An impertinent roll of belly pushes against the fancy waistcoat. He is shiny and prosperous, still sought after across Europe. Lately, he divides his time between London and Cairo where he is now official painter to the Khedive of Egypt.

'Sure, Egypt is bigger than England. Would you credit that?' he asks, the brogue of Cork undiminished, though she suspects it is consciously preserved.

The point of the comment is not lost on her. If the royalty of Egypt welcomes him with open arms, why should he care if that of Britain no longer does? But of course he cares. They both know that.

When the invitation came, a personal note was enclosed.

Well well, who'd have thought it May Flower? You and I both lambs to the slaughter.

She had stared at it for minutes on end. Harry Thaddeus Jones to marry, just a few months after herself. And indeed why should he not? Did she want him to become a cobwebbed old bachelor still faithful, in some ludicrous way, to the childish fantasies she has of him? Yes of course she did. The child in her wanted precisely that, expected it even.

As she had been taught to do, she passed the invitation to Georgie's secretary. A few days later, he asked to see her. A tall scarecrow of a man in a black tailcoat.

'I'm afraid it won't be possible for you to attend this wedding, Ma'am,' the scarecrow said. 'We have made the necessary enquiries and it seems that Mr Jones is marrying a divorced lady. What's more a lady who has deserted her husband, and indeed her children, in favour of Mr Jones. In short, something of a *scandale*. So you must see, Ma'am, quite impossible.'

She went to Georgie.

'Don't be silly,' he said, hardly looking up from the stamps.

'But he is an old and dear friend from our time in Italy,' she replied, 'and now an artist of considerable reputation. Heavens, he has painted the Pope.'

'I don't care if he's painted the Virgin Mary herself,' said Georgie. 'He's buggered his reputation now and no mistake. We can't go and that's that.'

But it did not stop there. The scarecrow soon returned to tell her that the name of Harry Thaddeus Jones has been removed from the list of those artists who may be considered for a royal portrait. A letter had been sent informing Mr Jones, with sincere regret, of this decision.

Now in the Red Drawing Room, as she takes tea with him and Madame Bricka, they are trying to pretend that it doesn't matter, that it changes nothing between them. A mere *bagatelle*. But Madame Bricka is not having that.

'It is quite absurd, *Princesse*,' she says. 'Two people have fallen in love. *C'est tout*. Why must the world be so unkind?'

May does not answer, because she does not have one to give. Instead she takes another cucumber sandwich, sliced thin as a finger.

'It's all about the eyes of Almighty God, Madame Bricka,' says Harry Thaddeus Jones. 'And what the world believes He would wish to see.'

'Well, I do not believe in your God,' she replies, 'but I thought He was supposed to be a merciful one. A God to teach us how to love. I see little of that in this situation.'

May stares down at the rug. The dogs are stretched out before the fire, snoring and breaking wind.

'Hush Madame, it's not May's fault,' says Mr Thaddy. 'No no, not at all.'

'No indeed,' replies Bricka. 'Poor *Princesse*.'

That damn adjective again. The one the Wales sisters throw at her.

How painful to hear it come from Madame Bricka. Can the two friends who have always offered her the gift of possibility, now only give her pity? In their judgement, is possibility now dried up? May looks around the cloying richness of the Red Drawing Room. Here she sits now; after Aunt Queen and her mother-in-law, the third lady in the land. And a plain-faced spinster tutor sees her as some tragic heroine. It is scarcely to be borne. She takes another cucumber sandwich.

'Perhaps we should all be getting back to Florence,' says Mr Thaddy. 'Things would be different there. Not to mention a hell of a lot more fun. Do you remember, May Flower, that evening in Lady Orford's salon?'

'Which evening was that?'

'The four card players. The wife, the husband, the lover and indeed the previous husband from whom she'd been divorced. Playing whist together, without a care. And the next morning, they'd all be in Santo Spirito, confessing trivialities, but never even thinking to mention the mortal sins which had led them to that card table.'

'And without hypocrisy too,' says Madame Bricka. 'That is the English disease. I applaud you Mr Thaddy, and your charming fiancée, for refusing to cower before it. And for facing the price you are paying.'

'I think our princess was a bit shocked that night,' says Mr Thaddy.

'Probably.' May smiles. 'I had little knowledge of such things then.'

Harry Thaddeus Jones touches Madame Bricka's arm and lowers his voice, as if to share some shocking secret.

'May and I made a little agreement, one day long ago in Italy,' he says. 'She declared she wanted to see the world beyond those horizons which she knew. I told her that she'd have to get down on the grubby earth with the rest of us.'

'And did she?'

'She tried right enough,' he sighs. 'Bless her, she tried very hard. She just wasn't able to stand there long enough.'

'Well I did my best to keep her there,' says Madame Bricka, 'if only between the pages of books. It was better than nothing.'

They both turn to contemplate her now, as if she is a promising pupil who has not lived up to expectations.

He excuses himself for a moment. Too many cups of tea, he pleads. How do you women hold it in? A question May doubts has been asked before in the Red Drawing Room.

'You would like Eva,' says Madame Bricka once they are alone. 'I'm sure you would.'

'You've met her?'

'Oh yes, I took tea with them in Fortnums last week. A most interesting woman. No Queen of The Nile, but very cultured. She draws and paints and plays the piano. One gets a sense of great inner strength.'

'She's certainly going to need that,' says May. 'I'd so like to meet her, but a divorced woman with a former husband now living...'

'Well Fortnums is only a ten-minute walk. Perhaps if you wore a large hat with a veil. Perhaps if you just happened to be shopping and bumped into us...'

Madame Bricka is gazing at her again, head cocked to one side.

'Actually *Princesse*, it strikes me now. She is rather like you.'

Mr Thaddy returns, only to take his leave. A sitting with a duchess who shall be nameless. A terrifying harpy who must not be kept waiting. May and Madame Bricka play a guessing game. Which duchess?

'I have it!' cries Bricka. 'The Duchess of Teck.'

May releases that vulgar laugh. What a while it is, she realises, since the last time she laughed so easily. The dogs on the rug wake up, bark and then doze off again. Suddenly, Georgie is in the doorway. He had gone to open a boys' club in Twickenham, but is back earlier than expected.

'Goodness, what a row,' he says.

It is the pricking of a balloon.

'Georgie, you know dear Bricka of course. And this is Harry Thaddeus Jones, our friend from Italy. I'm sure you recall that he came to our wedding and caught my bridal bouquet.'

'Ah yes,' says Georgie, without the faintest flicker of recognition.

'He painted that picture of me too. The one in my little room in Norfolk.'

'Ah yes. *That* picture.'

Silence falls in the Red Drawing Room. One of the dogs breaks wind again. Mr Thaddy clears his throat.

'Forgive me, May Flower, but I really must go. The harpy awaits.'

'What was that you called my wife, Mr Jones?' asks Georgie, not looking at him, but at some far corner of the ceiling.

'We all had daft nicknames back in Florence sir, when we were so much younger.' He smiles. 'I was Mr Thaddy and my pupil was May Flower.'

'We're not in Florence now, Mr Jones. We're all older and times have changed. My wife is now the Duchess of York, so I must ask you to address her in a manner appropriate to her rank.'

'Oh Georgie, we're such old chums, I really think…'

'That is my word on the subject,' says Georgie. 'Good afternoon to you.'

He turns to leave, then stops.

'May, you should rest now,' he says. 'We have important guests this evening.'

'I have important guests now, Georgie,' she replies.

As her husband turns his back on them, he calls over his shoulder.

'Rest now, May. And I think that tonight your dark green gown would be appropriate.'

Harry Thaddeus Jones lifts her hand to his lips. She wants to escape his gaze but cannot avert her eyes.

'Oh May Flower,' he whispers.

*

In her dark green gown, she sits at her dressing table. The dress was one of the mistakes in her *trousseau*. It does not become her. The bodice is cut very high and does not show her figure to best advantage. Odd, she thinks, how Georgie's appreciation of her fine breasts does not extend to letting her display them to others. Odder still that he, scion of the quarterdeck, has begun to take an interest in ladies' fashions and to propose what she should or should not wear.

The bedroom door is thrown open. Her maid and her lady-in-waiting are dismissed.

'What the hell were you thinking of earlier?' he asks. 'You cannot ever receive that man in this house.'

'I can't go to his wedding. I accept that,' she replies. 'But he is my friend and he'll always remain so.'

'You excuse his behaviour and, far worse, that of the woman he is to marry? I'm told she has three young girls by the husband she has deserted. Children she is abandoning for your so-called friend. Did you know that?'

'Yes, I do know that and it must be a terrible thing for her. But yes, I do excuse their behaviour. More than that, I applaud their bravery.'

'In God's name, why?'

'Because they have fallen in love, Georgie.'

'Fallen in *love*?' he repeats. 'What about their duty?'

'To what?'

His mouth opens and closes, trying to reach deep down into himself for the damn words. She feels a shameful prick of pleasure in observing the struggle. Georgie throws his hands up in the air and paces round the room, coming to rest by the mantelpiece to glare into the flames.

'Duty to… um… to the way things are. The way things must be.'

'Bricka tells me that the woman's first husband was most unkind to her.'

'*Unkind*? What the hell does that mean? Did he not buy her enough hats or take her to dine at Romano's? Is that enough reason to walk out on the man who had given her a roof and the protection of his name? Not to mention breaking the vows she made before God?'

In his sudden flash of fluency, Georgie seems unable to stop. 'And as for Bricka, that damn creature. She's the one who fills your head with silly books and stupid notions. She's here far too much. I've a good mind to ban her from this house too.'

'Then I will simply go to see her at White Lodge or in some other place.'

'You will go where *I* permit you! You are answerable in everything to *me*!'

Georgie's hand sweeps across the mantelpiece. A Dresden shepherdess, a small ormolu clock and a framed photograph of Aunt Queen fly through the air and crash to pieces on the marbled hearth.

He sags into a chair, his breath coming in gasps. May stays stock still at her dressing table. They both stare down at the carnage. The fire in the grate crackles and spits.

'So Georgie, it is the woman's duty to stay with the man who abuses her? Even when the prospect of happiness elsewhere is suddenly before her?'

'Yes!' he replies. 'If we fail in our duty we fail in our purpose. In this family above all others. I have told you before. We must be different. We must be better. Otherwise, there's no bloody point to us.'

'So has your own father arranged some sort of exemption with God?'

He glares at her in fury. For a moment she wonders if he will rise and strike her, but the moment passes.

May Teck crosses to the fireplace and kneels down to pick up the myriad pieces of china and glass. He crouches beside her and helps to gather the fragments.

'And if we do our duty without love, how do we cope with that, Georgie?' she says quietly. 'How does our spirit cope with that?'

A nervous knock comes to the door. Her lady-in-waiting appears. The first guests are beginning to arrive. Mr and Mrs Gladstone are already in the hall.

'Good God, we're late,' he says. 'Do you hear that, May? You have made me late. The shame of it.'

He dumps the broken pieces into her hands and hurries from the room.

At dinner, she is placed next to the Grand Old Man. It is not easy. He is eighty-two but energy comes off him like an aura, though he sits as still as a mountain and says very little. Aunt Queen cannot bear Gladstone, complaining that he talks to her as if addressing a public meeting. Mr Merrypebble, she calls him in secret, though merriment is singularly absent from his attributes. Yet May Teck admires what she reads of him. It is even reported that he goes at night into the worst of the slums, into Whitechapel where those poor women were butchered, to try to save such fallen souls and, with God's help, guide them to a better way. How she would love to talk to him of this, but he would surely find her observations banal. No doubt he finds this evening tortuously dull too. I was stuck beside that shy girl, she imagines him telling Mrs Merrypebble in the carriage home.

Instead she tries Ireland. It is only weeks since his latest efforts to let that unhappy island rule itself were so crushingly defeated. She reminds him that, at the time of Eddy's passing, it was being mooted that the young prince should go there as Viceroy, to give parties, shake hands and pour regal oil on troubled waters. How nervous dear Eddy had been, she tells him, but how excited they had both felt at the prospect. The chance of a real purpose to both their lives.

The Grand Old Man shrugs his shoulders.

'I fear it would have been no more than a sticking-plaster,' he sighs into his soup. 'Ireland is a gaping wound that needs a lot more than that.'

Then, as if thinking he may have been discourteous, he allows a social smile to crack the granite face.

'But you, my dear young lady, would have been a veritable ornament to Dublin Castle,' he says. 'Yes indeed. The only word for it. An ornament.'

XXII

Autumn, 1893

'This egg isn't right,' he says. 'What's wrong with my egg?'

They all glance at the egg, as if the problem must be visible. May's father puts on his glasses for a closer look.

'It's too runny,' says Georgie. 'You can't tell me this egg has been boiled for five and a half minutes. It can't possibly be more than four. Perhaps not even that.'

'Bad enough in a hotel,' says May's father, 'but in one's own home...'

The butler is sent for. What's wrong with the kitchen? What sort of galley are they running down there? The man is required to gaze deep into the yolk.

'I'm so sorry, sir. The kitchen is a little tardy this morning. There has been a small upset in the night.'

'What sort of upset?'

'Perhaps I might speak to you privately, sir, once you've finished breakfast?'

'Nonsense. Tell me now.'

'It's one of the maids, sir. She was taken ill in the small hours. A doctor had to be sent for.'

'What's wrong with the girl?' asks Georgie; his interest cooling as quickly as his tea.

'It's rather delicate, sir,' the man replies, his cheeks flushing. 'I hesitate to...'

'Spit it out, man.'

'She has given birth, sir.'

'Given birth? To a child?'

'Indeed sir. A male child. Five pounds and three ounces, the doctor says.'

'I'm quite uninterested in its weight,' snaps Georgie. 'Why were we not told of this situation?'

'It seems the girl herself was not aware of her condition until a very short time before the delivery. The doctor says it is very rare, but not unheard of.'

'How singular.'

'Who is it?' asks May.

'It's young Pilgrim, Ma'am.'

May dabs the corner of her mouth with her napkin and rises from her chair.

'I must go to her.'

'You'll do nothing of the sort,' says Georgie.

'It's my duty to care for the welfare of our servants. That's what you always taught me and the boys, isn't it Papa?

Her father removes his glasses and returns them to his inner pocket, as if this might prevent him from envisaging any sort of scandal.

'Well yes Pussycat, but...'

'But?'

'But this girl has brought shame on my house,' says Georgie. 'What would you like us to do? Take in gifts for the baby?'

'Who is the father?' asks Mary Adelaide of the butler.

'The girl refuses to say, Ma'am,' the butler replies. 'In fact, she claims she doesn't know.'

'An immaculate conception then?' says Georgie.

'I'm going up to her,' says May again.

'But May dear, Georgie doesn't wish it,' says the Duke.

There is silence in the dining room, broken only by the swishing of May's tea-gown as she sweeps from the room.

Mary Adelaide holds up the empty toast rack to the butler.

'A few more slices, I think,' she says. 'Wouldn't that be nice, Georgie? And of course another egg.'

'Five and a half minutes exactly this time,' says Georgie. 'Not a second more or less.'

The butler bows and withdraws, more upset by the crisis of the egg than by anything happening in a distant garret.

On an October morning in the glum little villa, it is cold in the attics where the servants sleep. If the rooms downstairs are small enough, these are hardly more than glorified cupboards, squashed beneath the eaves and inside the turrets. But in the space Pilgrim shares with another servant a fire has been permitted in the meagre grate. The girl lies on an iron bedstead beneath sheets so crisp and white it is obvious that their predecessors, grubby witnesses to the night, have been spirited away to the laundry. The usual ruddy cheeks of the Fens are quite gone; Pilgrim's face is pale as the bed linen. Yet, strangely, May sees a beauty in her that was not there yesterday. Beside the bed, a baby is swaddled in a basket.

The girl tries to rise but falls back onto the pillows, her eyes filling with tears.

'I'm right sorry, Ma'am.'

'Did you really not know you were... in this condition?' May asks.

'No, Ma'am. No, I swear it. I would've told you, Ma'am,' she replies. 'The doctor says it was tucked right up under my ribs, so it didn't show.'

'But how did it happen? Who...?'

'I don't know, Ma'am,' the girl bleats. 'I mean I'm not rightly sure.'

May sits down on a spindly chair beside the bed. She cannot think what to say or do. But that day when she needed it, it had been Pilgrim's arm which had comforted her and now she returns the gesture.

Suddenly, Mary Adelaide bustles into the tiny room, out of breath from the climb. Hardly glancing at the figure in the bed, she goes straight to the basket.

'Oh look how tiny he is,' she says. 'But what a handsome lad. Almost as handsome as my own three darling boys. Oh my dear, you must be so proud.'

The Duchess lifts the child from its crib. It is crying a little.

'This little thing wants his mother,' she declares and places the bundle in the girl's arms. 'That's the only place he needs to be.'

Mary Adelaide smiles down on them.

'Pretty as a picture,' she says.

And something changes in the attic. All sadness flies out through the tiny window and dissolves in the morning mists. Shock and shame, pain and bewilderment all vanish from the girl's pale face. Now she smiles too and some colour comes. She kisses the bundle on the forehead and wraps her arms tighter around him.

May Teck wonders what it would feel like to perform that simple, extraordinary act. She is frightened because she does not know the answer. It is an answer she wants to find. Because, unlike the maid in the iron bedstead, May Teck has no doubt whatsoever that she herself is carrying a child.

*

The Bard is right. When sorrows come, they come not single spies, but in battalions. It is a day destined to ruffle the flat fields of Norfolk. No sooner has May Teck descended from the attics, then the telegram arrives from Georgie's mother.

Bertie has had a terrible fall. Coming alone down the spiral stairs at Waddesdon, Georgie's father slipped and bounced all the way to the foot like a child's ball. They found him lying there, groaning with pain, his leg twisted every which way. Not even the thickness of Baron de Rothschild's carpets saved him from injury, the seriousness of which is not yet clear. Despite the agony, Bertie insisted on being taken back to London, where the best doctors are. Some local quack would hardly suffice.

'That awful house,' Alix says. 'It is cursed.'

Alix hates Waddesdon because she never goes there. Nor would she really be wanted. The mock chateau high above the Aylesbury vale is one of the places where Bertie frolics with his other family; those nursery people, the brittle women and entitled men. Here they wallow in the unrivalled splendours which surround them; the gorgeous fruits of the labours of the Rothschilds, the bankers of Frankfurt who now grease the wheels of half Europe. Yet none of it can protect them from a slip on a stair or a kneecap that breaks. Even such men are not gods after all.

'I must go to London,' says Georgie.

'I shouldn't worry, Georgie,' says Mary Adelaide. 'If dear Bertie is able to return to town himself, surely it can't be that bad?'

'Not worry?' he replies. 'Of course I must worry. Papa is not young, he is not fit, he is much too heavy. Any shock like this... Good God, who knows what might happen? I must leave at once.'

There is a great rushing and flapping in the glum little villa and, long before luncheon, he is gone. At the steps of the carriage, she kisses his cheek.

'Mama is right, Georgie,' she says. 'Try not to get into a state till you see how things stand in town. Your Papa is a tough old bird.'

'It's often the tough old birds who fall swiftest,' he replies.

The carriage is already moving, when he sticks his head out of the window.

'And May, that girl must be gone by the time I return.'

She has been waiting for those words. She has known they would come, as surely as the sand runs through the hourglass.

'Georgie is quite correct,' says her father. 'The girl cannot possibly stay under this roof. Some roofs maybe, but not this one.'

Her dear Papa. Her ill-tempered, not quite right in the head but sweet and loving Papa. It is the first time, May thinks, that she has seen a flash of true cruelty come from him. What strikes her is how casual it is, how instinctive and unashamed. Bred in the bone of the male.

The butler comes into the drawing room. The man seems even more embarrassed than he was at breakfast.

'I've made some investigations, Ma'am,' he says, his gaze cast down on the carpet from Maples. 'As a result of these, the junior footman has admitted to his role in the matter. He maintains the girl was quite, er, agreeable. He has asked me to apologise to you, Ma'am.'

'To me?' she asks. 'He apologises to *me?*'

'Yes, Ma'am. Most profoundly. He's a good lad really. Ambitious and hard-working. I'd not be surprised if he makes a fine butler one day.'

May takes the narrow stairs to the attics again. Pilgrim lies dozing; the baby too. May sits down and waits for the girl to wake. She is glad of the silence. Her mother has not drawn breath since breakfast time; her chatter only increasing as she grows older, as if there is so much still to say before her time is done. May notices an odour in the room which, she realises, can only be the smell of the child. It is an odd aroma; not unpleasant, earthy and warm, but alien to anything she has smelt before.

When Pilgrim wakes and sees May there, such a broad smile floods her face that May feels a catch at her throat. She tells the girl of the footman's confession.

'So that was it then, Ma'am?' says the maid. 'I wondered if it might be. We'd gone for a walk through the bluebell woods on my afternoon off.'

'Didn't you know what he was doing?' May asks.

'It hurt a little at first but then it felt quite nice. Jimmy said he was a bit sweet on me, so I didn't mind really. I just wanted to please him.'

'Did your mother not tell you anything about such matters?'

'My mother died of consumption when I was three, Ma'am,' the girl replies. 'There's just my dad now, back home on the farm. My brother was a soldier, but he was killed in Africa by one of those Zulus.'

'I'm sorry to hear that. It's good to have a brother isn't it?'

'Oh it is, Ma'am. Perhaps that's why Jimmy didn't hurt me much. My brother had often done the same when I was younger, except he just used his finger.'

'Dear God, girl.'

May can find no other words inside herself. She fights to keep her sickness down. She must get out of this little room. As she leaves, the girl on the crisp, white sheets calls after her.

'Ma'am, have I done wrong?'

'In the eyes of some perhaps,' May replies. 'But not in mine.'

'Jimmy said he was sweet on me, Ma'am,' she murmurs. 'He's a lovely lad, Jimmy.'

In her bed alone that night, buffeted between sleeping and waking, May Teck thinks she hears the faint distant crying of a child. She is not sure if it comes from the attics or from her own imagination, from the bastard offspring of a maidservant or from the life now growing inside her.

XXIII

Autumn, 1893

In the morning a telegram comes from Georgie. Bertie is white with pain, but though his knee is broken, he does not appear to have one foot in the grave. He is denied his cigars and curses the doctors, which is a good sign. But Georgie will remain by his bedside until the sawbones are sure there is no danger.

She telegraphs back, sending her dearest love to his Papa and mentioning *en passant* that the footman is the culprit. Georgie replies at once, repeating that the girl must go from under his roof. Unfortunate about the footman though. A good chap. What's more, a fine spare loader out in the coverts. It would be a shame to lose him. Boys will be boys.

May has an idea. She orders the pony trap and goes to the cottage of the labourer on the estate whose young child died not long since. Would they shelter mother and child for a few days, a week or two perhaps, until permanent arrangements can be made? Any expenses will be generously reimbursed. She sees reluctance in the man's face though he tries to conceal it. But the woman does not hesitate. The poor girl will be welcome in their home, she says. Let him who is without sin cast the first stone. Why was their own lost darling not made two whole months before they walked down the aisle of Dersingham church, because somebody was unable to control himself and somebody else could not free herself from his grip because he was half deranged with the whisky? Maybe that was why the Good Lord had taken their darling to live with Him and His angels. The husband blushes and turns his face away.

The girl weeps when May goes back to the attic and explains that she can no longer remain in Georgie's service. She weeps even more at the news that the footman refuses to marry her. He could tell she was not intact, he says now. The girl must be a strumpet. How can he be sure the child is even his?

'Oh Ma'am,' she says, 'what's to become of me?'

'I will make sure that you and the child are cared for,' May replies, with little idea of how this is to be achieved.

The next day at dusk, the pony trap comes round to the servants' entrance. Pilgrim is still a little weak, clinging to the arm of another maid. May and her mother come through the house to the kitchen door. Mary Adelaide cradles the child against her bosom and kisses him before handing him into the pony trap.

'What a handsome boy,' the Duchess says again.

May is trying to think what to say in farewell when Pilgrim reaches for her hand.

'I'm right sorry for the bother I've caused you, Ma'am,' she says.

'What is your name?' asks May suddenly. 'Your Christian name?'

'It's Nora, Ma'am.'

'I'll come to see you in a few days,' she says. 'Goodbye, Nora.'

A wild autumn wind blows in off the German Ocean, ripping the first tired leaves from the trees. The girl coddles her child inside the poor fabric of her coat. As the pony trap draws away, she looks back and waves to the little group by the kitchen door.

It is, May thinks, as if the girl is being taken into some kind of Siberia and asks herself why she is an accomplice to this exile. Why are simple innocence and a yearning for affection being banished from under this roof while cruelty and cant are allowed to remain? Why is Harry Thaddeus Jones to be sent away from her for the same sin of loving? She worships her God, but is this really and truly what He wants? And is this the good which May Teck has so hoped she might do in this world? With whom does the shame really lie?

She watches till the swinging lamp on the pony trap disappears round a bend in the path. She shivers, pulls her shawl around her, hurries through the kitchens up to her boudoir and closes the door. She huddles up to the fire but the shivering will not melt away. In the flaring embers, the face of Mr Thaddy comes to her again.

'Am I standing on the grubby earth yet?' she asks him in her mind. 'Am I soiled enough for you now?'

*

Two mornings later, Georgie returns. He is subdued, tired. For the first time, it is possible to see, etched in his features, both the child that he was and the old man he will become. She notices too how his skin is changing, the callow smoothness already giving way to a blotchy red, the legacy from the quarterdeck of broiling sun and biting wind.

At luncheon, while Mary Adelaide prattles on, he replies in monosyllables to every enquiry about the health of his Papa. Yes, in time Bertie should be able to walk again normally. Yes, he is sitting with his leg up. Yes, cigars are still banned and he is driving everyone mad with his ill-temper. Yes, it was a close shave. Yes, he might have broken his neck and, for God's sake, can we please change the subject now?

In the afternoon, he retires to his stamps and does not come out. While her father dozes, May and her mother work to create a new folding-screen of photographs for the boudoir. From White Lodge, the Duchess has brought a whole valise of yellowing, stony-faced images of grandparents, of half-known aunts, uncles and cousins scattered like seedlings across the map of Europe. They are princes and princesses, electors and electresses, margraves and margravines; the rulers of everything from great kingdoms to trifling principalities and city-states no bigger than pimples on the landscape. May looks at the young girls much like herself, transplanted from their home soil to the alien palaces of Germany and Russia, of Spain, Romania and Greece. At least, she thinks, she has merely been transplanted to Norfolk.

From the gallery spread out across the dining table, Mary Adelaide picks out a photograph of May herself in her cradle, in the christening robe in which Aunt Queen no less had also once been swaddled.

'What a family we are,' the Duchess sighs. 'And just think, *we* are now at the heart of it. The very heart of it.'

In her mother's face May sees a kind of ecstasy and cannot resist the urge that now comes upon her.

'You never let us forget that you're the granddaughter of a king, do you Mama?' she smiles. 'Well you may soon be the grandmother of one too.'

The Duchess shrieks and sinks her teeth into her own bare forearm to silence herself.

'Are you sure?' she whispers after a moment.

'The doctor here believes so, but a specialist is coming from London to be certain. I haven't told Georgie yet, with all this fuss going on.'

'But you must,' says Mary Adelaide. 'You must tell him now, this very minute. It is his right. Besides, the poor thing has been so worried about Bertie, it will cheer him up so.'

'Do you think?'

'Of course! Oh May, a little prince.'

'We must cross our fingers tightly for that.'

'I know it May. God has willed it.'

She goes to the study and knocks, but Georgie is not there. The butler thinks he has gone for a walk, but in which direction the man cannot say. Never mind, there is no hurry. It is only when dusk comes and it is nearly time to dress for dinner that she enquires again. A groom reports that the master was seen heading towards the big house some time ago. Does May wish someone to look for him? No, she will take a breath of air and look herself.

The big house is shut up yet again. It will not be till Christmas that Bertie, Alix, the sisters and all the smart people return in their feathers, furs and furbelows, to sprinkle their glitter and glamour across the frozen, unyielding fields. Once more, the windows will blaze till past midnight. The lake will be festooned with fairy lights and the skaters will pirouette on the ice, warmed by steaming cups of negus. The finest cigars from Havana and perfumes from the Rue St Honore will cock a snook at the pure, uncorrupted Norfolk air. By Epiphany, tens of thousands of birds will have dropped from the sky and be hanging from hooks; regiments slaughtered in a hopeless battle.

Now, on the darkened cliff of the east front, the only light is the lamp in the porch. The watchman comes to the door.

'Yes Ma'am, he has been here these three hours or more. He took a small oil lamp and went off into the house. I can't say exactly where he might be.'

But May believes she does. Another lamp is brought for her. No thank you, she will go alone. It is an act of bravery because, when it is shuttered and dark, this house frightens her. When the rooms do not pulsate with people and light and noise, it is an alienating place. Like a plain woman who sits at her mirror at the end of an evening, removing her jewels, her rouge, her hair-pieces and every other artifice, its fragile charms are instantly lost. But it is more than that. The laughter, the dancing, the bowling and the skating on the lake have a faint air of desperation now. The death of Eddy changed this house forever. However much they try, there is no going back to the way things were.

The wick of the lamp trembles in her hand, casting shivery shadows up the walls of the staircase. She turns into the narrow, sepulchral corridor that still comes to her in dreams. Sure enough, through the half-open doorway at the far end, another flicker of light comes out of the darkness.

The first thing she notices is the smell. The whisky bottle, two-thirds empty, sits on a table beside the lamp. On Eddy's bed, Georgie is curled into a ball on top of the Union Jack. His coat hangs over a chair, his hacking jacket is on the floor along with his cravat and his shirt collar. One of his boots lies on its side; its twin still on his foot. His shirtsleeves are rolled up; the dragons on his forearms writhing in the light of the lamp.

She shakes him gently. Red-rimmed eyes crack open. For a minute or more, he only stares at her. Then, in little dribbles, some words leak out on the whisky breath.

'Papa. Could have broken his neck.'

'But he didn't.'

'And Grandmama. Old now. Can't last forever.'

'Such things are in the hands of God, Georgie,' she replies. 'There's no point dwelling on them.'

The red eyes widen. Terror is there.

'But then it would be me. Don't want it. Can't do it.'

'You can. You can and I will be with you,' she says. 'I promised you that before. We've been through all this, Georgie.'

But Georgie suddenly remembers exactly where he is, on whose bed he lies.

'Eddy, why did you leave me to this?'

He begins to cry, turning his face into the pillow. She allows herself to hope it might be just the whisky. If not, her fear of this dark house would be as nothing compared to what she would have to fear now. That his mother's little Georgie-boy is entirely right, that indeed he cannot do it, simply will not be up to the job. And thus, in compensation, she will not merely have to support him but will have to sacrifice all of herself. Every thought, feeling and fibre, her very essence to be subjugated. Not even a sliver allowed to remain, if the institution is to be preserved and God's will be done.

Trembling now, May Teck clambers onto the small bed behind him, so they lie like two spoons in a drawer. She places her arm around him and gently strokes his hair, trying to calm the panic which now envelops them both.

In Eddy's tiny room, on his very deathbed, half-wrapped in the great Union Jack, she pictures how they must look from above. Far above. In the heavens even. She wonders what God must think of the sight. As she lies there, she prays to Him that Georgie might turn around and, for the very first time, lay his head on her breast to be comforted. But God does not appear to be listening. Perhaps all He can hear is the sobbing which shakes the little shrine on the east front as the October night falls and the shutters rattle in the wind from the sea.

XXIV

Summer, 1894

If she had hoped that the dam, once broken, would never be rebuilt, she was soon disappointed. In the weeks and months to follow, it was merely reconstructed with stronger stone. By the time the sun shone high in the sky again, she had abandoned any illusion that it might ever be breached again.

One morning, he sits on the edge of their bed in the old palace of St James's and holds out the dragon arms.

'From now on, these tattoos must always be covered. Never seen again. Not even within the family. The time for such foolishness is past.'

It is the day they are to open a nursing home for old and infirm sailors. Odd timing, May thinks, to make this decision, when most of the inmates will be similarly illustrated by tigers, snakes and declarations of love to long-forgotten sweethearts. But of course she does not say so. Each day, she learns more and more not to say so.

At the end of the ceremony, they are to be photographed beside the plaque they have unveiled. The tripod is set up; the man is ready and waiting. Georgie looks at him as if he were a dentist with a pair of pliers.

'We should smile now,' she says.

'I've decided I will no longer smile for pictures. I don't now think it fitting for our station.'

'But people like to see us smile, Georgie.'

'No doubt, but it takes something away. There's a word for it. Sounds like gravy.'

'Gravitas?'

'That's it,' he says. 'Anyway, that's my decision. And of course you must do the same.'

In the carriage going home, he clears his throat and addresses her in the tone in which he had delivered his speech to the old sailors.

'I also think it best if, from now on, you address me as George when we're in public and can be overheard by others. I'm sure you agree?'

May does not reply. She turns her head away to stare blankly out of the window. In Bayswater Road, attracted by the escort of glittering Hussars, people on the pavements stop and wave. Behind the rows of faces, secluded in the doorway of a public house, a couple in shabby clothes is canoodling. The young man glances up, raises his cap like the rest of the crowd, then laughs and lifts two rude fingers to the carriage. The girl laughs too. They go back to the kissing and the cuddling. Lost in the small world of the doorway. Needing nothing more. How wonderful, thinks May Teck.

This evening, in support of some other worthy cause, they go to the theatre. She has loved the theatre since she was a little girl, dazzled by that magic when the curtain rises and a beautiful picture comes to life. And then, in Florence, she became aware of a potency far beyond the smoke and mirrors, the powder and the paint. Since that time, with Madame Bricka to guide her, she has witnessed the power of Bernhardt, Duse and Ellen Terry. What women they are. How, in the glare of the footlights, they illuminate our condition; our hopes and dreams, our struggles and shortcomings. On her twentieth birthday, Henry Irving no less presented her with the works of Shakespeare bound in white vellum. She will treasure it all her days.

Tonight though, it is lighter fare. But while the audience roars at the wit of Mr Wilde, Georgie sits in the box without so much as a flicker of amusement.

'It's quite acceptable to smile in the theatre,' she whispers.

'But this is poking fun at our breed, is it not? Am I not being asked to laugh at myself? I may not be a genius, but even I can work that out.'

'Isn't it supposed to be good to laugh at oneself?' she says.

'Maybe for the common man, but not for us. If we start doing that, where will we end up?'

Afterwards, the impresario enquiries if they have enjoyed the performance.

'Your audience seemed to like it, Mr Alexander,' Georgie replies, 'but I can't feel that anyone in our family should have been invited to attend such a play.'

The man looks at him as if he comes from some other planet. May sees the derision in his eyes.

That staircase down which Bertie fell has a lot to answer for. The Grim Reaper lurking in its shadows was cheated that time but now Georgie looks for the spectre in every corner. Until recently, he checked on the health of his Papa almost daily; in person when possible, by telegraph when not, till Bertie, still in great pain, snapped that if he needed a nanny, he would employ one. Even Alix noticed.

'What on earth is the matter with my darling Georgie-boy?' she demanded, feeding sweetmeats to her lapdogs. 'He's so much less fun. Is he liverish? I hope you're looking after him properly May.'

Tonight, when they reach the old palace, he goes before her up the steps.

'What strange shoes you're wearing,' May says. 'They seem to have heels.'

'It's an experiment,' he says.

'But why?' she replies, making the mistake of a smile.

The face flushes, the lower lip juts out.

'When you're wearing one of your bloody great hats, I appear shorter than you. In my position, that cannot be acceptable. Nor indeed for any man.'

'Oh Georgie, does it matter?'

'I will not be laughed at,' he shouts. 'Don't you understand? I must never be laughed at. Never. Not any more.'

*

The brood mare is heavy with the foal.

She hates it. It is disgusting. The sickness is passed now, thank God, though the memory haunts her. She even had to stop smoking for a week or two. But the rest of it, if less horrific, still wears her down. Her back aches all day long. In bed, to lie on her side, cushions must bear the weight of her belly. She is never out of the bathroom; a second cup of tea sends her scurrying. And while her bladder is as nervous as a kitten, her bowels adopt the opposite strategy. She would give her finest pearls for one easy, voluminous shit. Her pretty ankles, that pride and joy, are swollen and tender. Her whole body is in revolt; its customary discipline quite lost, chaos and disorder rampant.

In this matter at least her mother has warned her. Aunt Queen too.

'Nine times I've been through it, May dear,' the old woman says. 'Nine. Each time as tedious as the last. But thank God for the blessed invention of chloroform. They didn't want me to have it, you know. Much tut-tutting from the bishops and their ilk. Not natural. Not God's will. Stuff and nonsense. Let just one of them experience childbirth and they'd soon change their tune. You must demand it if you need it, May dear. Remember now.'

Aunt Queen decrees that the birth of Georgie's heir must be in the city, but it is May's misfortune that the summer is so hot. In their rooms in the old palace of St James's, the air scarcely circulates. Perhaps it is too laden with the dust of history to make that possible. Open windows merely bring in a fetid breeze from the armpits of the sweating city. But if her body cries out against what is happening to it, so too does her spirit. For the ravenous eyes return again, even worse than before.

When the news is broken to the world, the world takes leave of its senses. The newspapers sweep everything else off their pages; the doings of Mr Gladstone and Lord Salisbury are quite forgotten, the explosion which kills hundreds in the harbour at Santander is as nothing compared to what is happening inside her belly. Dull, decorous May Teck is suddenly far more interesting than the naughtiest, half-clad chorus girl at the Gaiety Theatre. The ladies' magazines regurgitate the articles published at the time of the wedding. Once again, her history is told; how clever she is, how she has read even more books than those contained in the London Library. Crowds gather outside the old palace trying to glimpse her whenever she goes out, so she begins to make excuses not to do so. She is immured inside her own four walls.

But even there she finds little sanctuary. Every female visitor who comes to tea requires the most intimate details of her condition. She cannot decide who are the worst; the scarred veterans of motherhood who, like Aunt Queen and her mother-in-law, are eager to warn and perhaps to terrify, or the still virginal girls, terrified already, but nevertheless feverish with wonder at the prospect of it. One afternoon in the Red Drawing Room, over the Madeira cake for which she has developed a sudden, unaccountable passion, she can take no more.

'Heavens, can we please talk of something else?' she says to Georgie's sisters. 'Even just for a quarter-hour. Anything at all.'

'But why?' asks Toria. 'Whatever could be more important?'

'I do hope Georgie is being gentle with you at the moment, my dear,' adds one of his aunts, with lowered eyes. 'If you take my meaning.'

May's cheeks flush to the colour of the Aubusson rug. She cannot believe they are willing to invade her with such forensic indelicacy. She straightens her aching back and does not answer. She offers no more cups of tea and the hint is soon taken.

It is after this tea party that she passes out on the floor of her bathroom and cries out to be taken for her confinement to

Richmond Park. If nothing else, it will be a little cooler there. When White Lodge comes into view, drowsing in the shade of the oaks, she thinks she might weep. At the sight of her mother and Madame Bricka waiting in the portico, she does.

She is treated like the Prodigal.

'Stop fussing, Francis,' Mary Adelaide snaps at her husband ten times a day, as the Duke manoeuvres a stool under his precious girl's legs or tries to put a shawl around her, even though an egg could be fried on the windowsill.

'Thank you, dear Papa,' she always says and kisses him on the cheek.

May kisses him more often now as she likes to see the peace it brings him. With every month that passes, the temper is worse, the mood as unpredictable as a broken barometer. The trajectory of his only daughter, though it has restored his dignity, is no longer quite enough to counteract the fragility of his mind. Like a medicine tried too late, its efficacy lasts but a short while and then is lost.

These days he is master of the house in name only. It only takes half a day for May to realise that this title has passed to Madame Bricka. While Bricka rules the household and takes on May's role as secretary, the Duchess, merry as a grig, continues to rule the ladies of the Needlework Guild and of all her other worthy causes. Mary Adelaide and Madame Bricka are now the old married couple; chalk and cheese, opposites who attract and somehow carve out a life together.

When May had fled to White Lodge, Georgie declared he must therefore come too. It would not look right, he said, if they were seen to be apart at such a time. Since her old bedroom is too small for a couple, there are given a larger room in one of the wings. She is glad of that. At least their bickering is less likely to be overheard there.

'And how is the little prince today?' asks Mary Adelaide every morning at breakfast.

The first time he hears the question, Georgie for a moment thinks she means himself. He considers Mary Adelaide the most irritating woman in the world. The unfailing patience he shows to his own silly mother is extended to the Duchess, but only because courtesy demands it. In the months since the marriage, the Teck carriage has drawn up at the old palace with the regularity of the milk float and the coal merchant's van. When he hears that voice charging into the lobby, Georgie flees to his stamps and locks the door. Only after she departs will he explode.

'She seems to forget you are now married!'

'I know, I'm sorry, Georgie. We were always together, you see. I think she is missing me rather.'

'Then she should have kept you at home as a spinster, like my Mama does with poor Toria. But she seemed happy enough to watch your father give you away to me. To *me*, do you hear?'

Now, at White Lodge, he keeps himself as far away from Mary Adelaide as he can. When May sees the nerve twitch under his left eye, she knows he will be gone in minutes. Out into the park to contemplate the deer and wish he were allowed to shoot them. To the stables to make the acquaintance of the grooms. To the furthest corner of the garden with the Norfolk paper which is forwarded to him every week without fail. He is far better informed about the doings of King's Lynn than many who live there. Most often, however, he takes the carriage back into town pleading urgent business, returning only in time for dinner.

The excuse fools nobody; Georgie has never had urgent business in his life so far. May has often thought how much happier he would be if he had an occupation beyond the slaughter of the birds in the sky. How much more fulfilled, how much more equable his temper. Then it strikes her that of course he does have a job after all. It is not complicated, demands no intelligence and takes no more than five minutes a day. It is therefore well within his capabilities. What is more, half the world is waiting to slap him on the back if he does it efficiently. This occupation is the impregnation of his wife and the world regards it as a permanent position. Dear God spare me, thinks May Teck.

'And how is the little prince today?' asks the Duchess at breakfast as usual.

It is only nine in the morning and too warm already. May Teck trudges off to the bathroom and strains to have a decent shit. Giving up the effort, she cannot summon the energy to pull her knickers up. She sits on the bowl and stares at the wall. How will she ever get through this? Even just this first time, never mind in the years to come? The sash window is raised a few inches to let in some air. In recent mornings, a blue tit has taken to landing on the sill, singing at her while she does her toilette. His beauty and his joyfulness entrance her. Each day he cheers and strengthens her. But today he does not appear and, in the absence of him, May Teck, squatting on the bowl with her knickers at her pretty ankles, begins to cry.

XXV

Summer, 1894

'This room feels quite different somehow,' she says.

'That's because you're no longer in it, *Princesse*,' replies Madame Bricka. 'Now it is just my room, no longer ours. Now it is just an unremarkable place.'

In the old white sitting room, there are unfamiliar chairs and pictures. Side tables are piled high with paperwork. A large elmwood desk is littered with the paraphernalia of the Duchess's frenetic existence: letters, telegrams, invitations to a country house party, to open a school or an exhibition of tapestries.

'It never stops' wails Madame Bricka.

'Poor you,' says May, 'it's all terribly tedious, isn't it?'

'Terribly. Still I admit it is good to see how much pleasure your Mama gives to people. It is only those under her own roof whom she drives to distraction.'

May goes to the bookcase and runs her finger across the volumes.

'Some new ones,' she says.

'On my free afternoon, I still go to see what fresh treasures may have come into Messrs Hatchards. I saw Wilde and Conan Doyle there last week. Such a thrill. How I longed to speak to them but I couldn't find the courage.'

'You Bricka? The woman who faces down the stags in the park?'

'Stags are easy. Genius is a different thing entirely,' she says. 'Then I took tea again in Fortnums with Mr Thaddy's wife.'

'You seem to like her.'

'Eva is the most admirable woman. A stimulating companion. You still haven't joined us there.'

'I'd so like to, but if it were discovered...'

'Oh just be brave, *Princesse*.'

'Whatever bravery I might once have had is deserting me.'

It is the first time she has ever said any such thing to anyone. The first time she has articulated that everything in the garden is not lovely, not a fairy tale come true, a happy ever after.

Madame Bricka puts down her pen and swivels round in her desk-chair.

'Do you want to tell me?' she asks.

'Yes Bricka dear, I do. But I can't. I mustn't.'

May sits down on a little chaise she has not seen before and pretends to look at a volume she has taken off the shelf. Madame Bricka's eyes bore into her.

'I'm just being silly, that's all,' says May. 'My mind is all over the place. Maybe that's normal at a time like this.'

Madame Bricka comes and takes May's hand and gently rubs it. It is enough.

'Oh Bricka, I'm so frightened,' she says.

'Of course *Princesse*, but your own Mama has done it four times and lived to tell the tale. And it will be over in a few hours; at worst, within a day.'

'You don't understand,' May replies. 'Yes, I'm scared of that, but it's not what I mean.'

'What then?'

'I'm frightened because I don't want this child.'

The words shoot out of her like a piece of meat which has been stuck in her gullet, choking her. She gasps and gulps for air.

'But you always knew that was your purpose in their eyes,' says Madame Bricka. 'We spoke of that, you and I, remember?'

'No, you still don't understand,' says May, gripping her arm. 'I don't want this child. His child. I don't want *his* child.'

'Oh *Princesse.*'

At once, May regrets the confession. My goodness, she should not have said that. The days when she could have told anything to Madame Bricka are gone. At all times now, she must remember who she has become or, at least, is on the road to becoming. She may not quite be May Teck any more, but nor has she yet transitioned to being the person she is required to be. She floats in limbo, neither one nor the other, paddling furiously to keep her head above water.

The child gives her a vicious kick of reprisal. She cannot wait for this creature to be out of her. She rises from the chaise and smooths down her dress.

'Forgive me, Bricka dear,' she says. 'Ignore me too. I will go and take a little nap. I think that would be best.'

Madame Bricka looks sadly after her, well aware of what has just taken place, of the intimacy that has, for the first time, just been withdrawn.

'If that is what you wish,' she replies. 'But remember, I am always here.'

As May hurries to leave the white sitting room, this space once so precious to her, she knocks against a side table covered in photographs of Madame Bricka's previous charges, her precious girls she calls them. May catches one picture, larger than the rest, just before it crashes to the floor. It is her own.

'You were the best of them,' says Madame Bricka softly. 'Always the best.'

May goes upstairs to her old bedroom high above the park. It is her habit to come here whenever she can. Here, for while at least, the hands on the clock can be pushed back. A few of her old dolls still live in the dusty corners of the wardrobe. From the open window she can still see the herds of fallow deer grazing on

Queen's Ride; the flock of wildfowl skittering skywards towards Pen Ponds. Her simple, virginal bed is as if she had risen from it yesterday. In the locked drawer of the little dressing table, she has taken to keeping some private things since she took refuge at White Lodge. One of these she takes out now and sits on her bed to read it again; perhaps for the hundredth time. It is the letter Georgie wrote to her after she finally told him she was carrying his child.

'Splendid,' was all he'd said when she'd broken the news at breakfast in Norfolk. 'Splendid. Well done, May. The family will be pleased.'

'It took two of us, Georgie.'

'Ha! Yes indeed. Ha!' he replied.

He blushed to the roots of his beard, avoided her eye and burrowed back into his breakfast. What a conundrum he is. One minute, the coarseness of the quarterdeck; the next, the embarrassed delicacy of a maiden aunt.

'Damn fine egg this. Just right. How about another one to celebrate, what d'you say?'

And that was it until, after he went off shooting one day, the letter was delivered to her.

When I asked you to marry me, I was very fond of you but not very much in love with you. But I have tried to understand you and to know you, with the happy result that I know now that I do love you darling girl with all my heart and am simply devoted to you. I adore you sweet May, I can't say more than that.

Now, in her old bedroom, she folds the letter and returns it to its hiding place. She pulls the bell. Pilgrim comes. She asks for tea to be brought to her here. And if there might be a slice of Madeira cake? Just the one slice, mind.

'Are you all right Ma'am?' the girl asks as she lays down the tray.

'Just a little tired,' May answers. 'And my back hurts. But of course you know all about that.'

'Looking back, Ma'am, yes, though at the time I didn't know what the problem was, if you remember. You'll be fine, I'm sure you will. It's not that bad.'

'And are *you* all right, Pilgrim? Living in this house now?'

'Oh yes Ma'am. The Duchess is very kind to me. She is a sainted lady, Ma'am. I can't thank you both enough for giving me a home.'

The girl has been here for six months now, far away from the scene of her disgrace, sheltering under the forgiving heart of Mary Adelaide. The Duke had grumbled about impropriety, till the Duchess reminded him that he too lived under this roof by the grace and favour of her family, so he would do better to be silent.

'Remember though, you must be very careful while my husband is here,' May orders her. 'He must not see you, Pilgrim. He really *must* not or we'll all be in terrible trouble.'

'I'll bury myself away below stairs, Ma'am. Like a tiny dormouse I'll be.'

Pilgrim pulls back the moss-green quilt and plumps up the pillow.

'Why don't you take a little rest now, Ma'am? Just for half an hour. Do you a power of good.'

Pilgrim unlaces May's shoes and helps her to stretch out on the little bed. She pulls the blind half down against the sun and creeps away.

May longs to doze but sleep will not come. Anyway, after the tea, her bladder won't last long. Instead she lies listening to the sounds from the woodland drifting in on the summer air. A timeless reminder of when, through the rose-hued prism of childhood, everything seemed simpler. How she longs for simplicity again.

I adore you sweet May, I can't say more than that.

In his written words, he is Dr Jekyll. In his spoken words, and sometimes in his deeds, Mr Hyde. Where, she asks herself, is the map for this journey? What is she to think? Or to do? Who would have imagined that she, the good and sensible girl, would ever come to this?

The child gives her another sharp kick. It seems to be having a petulant day. Aunt Queen extols the blessed chloroform. Please, May Teck asks of God, can I have some now, right this very minute? Not for my body, but for my spirit. All is chaos and disorder. Chaos and disorder.

XXVI

Summer, 1894

The indignity will stay livid in her memory. Her pretty ankles in mid-air, her legs wide apart. Her most private place open like a gaping wound for all to see. The blood, the fluids, the odours. The sweat running down her face; her mother dabbing it away. Madame Bricka squeezing her hand.

'Get this out of me!' she shouts more than once.

Even through the pain, she remembers too the flush of embarrassment on her mother's face because the doctor and nurse can hear. Even in this moment of blood, sweat and tears, she is not permitted to be herself. Some level of decorum must be preserved.

'You said I wouldn't need the chloroform,' she wails to her mother. 'You lied to me!'

'Easy now, chick, it will soon be over.'

As the worst of it approaches, Madame Bricka, though still clasping her hand, turns her head away, but not before May glimpses the horror on her friend's face. So, she thinks, this looks as bad as it feels. Sweet Jesus, she swears to herself, I will never ever go through this again. Never. Except of course she knows that she will; that it will not really be her choice.

When the moment comes, late in the summer evening, she cannot tell where her own scream ends and that of the child begins. When the waves of pain start to recede, they bring it to her. Its tiny cheeks are red and puffy; its skin clammy. It is Georgie's to the life.

And it is a son. A little prince. The Duchess, weeping, holds out the swaddled bundle, but May cannot summon the energy to take it. She can only lift a fingertip to brush its cheek before exhaustion overcomes her and she turns her face to the wall. Vaguely, as if from some distant star, she is conscious of a hairy hand patting her own and of a quarterdeck voice telling her she is a good girl.

But there is no rest yet for the other denizens of White Lodge. Through the short midsummer night, telegrams crackle out; west to Windsor, east to Norfolk, north and south to the throne rooms of Europe. In the vast baroque palaces of St Petersburg and in tiny medieval castles perched high above the Thuringian forests, the noble citizens of the *Almanach de Gotha* start their day with the joyful news. Then, like a flock of homing pigeons a thousand strong, telegrams fly back to Richmond Park, borne down with messages, each vying to be the most poetic or portentous expression of congratulation. No adjective is left unturned, especially those of the most revolting sentimentality. Nobody doubts that this child will one day affect the world in the way of the great Alexander, El Cid, Charlemagne or indeed all three rolled into one.

As May Teck sleeps on into the morning, a marquee is erected just beyond the garden walls. On the first day alone, fifteen hundred come to inscribe their names in a book, in the sure expectation that the infant will preserve it to his dying day. A squad of constables is on duty to keep enthusiasm under control and to make sure no loyal zealot, emboldened by beer, tries to scale the palings around the house. When she finally drifts back towards consciousness, she can hear the muted buzz of all the voices. At least, thank God, she cannot see the eyes.

In the days to come, she turns the birth chamber into another womb. It is easy to persuade the doctors that Georgie must continue to sleep in another room for a while longer. She tolerates the windows being half open to allay the heat, but orders the blinds half closed. She does not even glance at the mountain of telegrams waiting for her to read. She takes some tea, but does not want food; the obsession with Madeira cake gone as if by magic. Besides, the thought of pushing out a stool with her aching muscles is too awful to contemplate.

When anyone other than the nurse comes into the room, she pretends to be asleep. She senses her mother and Madame Bricka standing over her; she knows them both by their scent, but does not open her eyes.

'Poor May,' whispers Mary Adelaide to Madame Bricka. 'She's had a worse time than I expected.'

When they leave, the nurse, no fool, dares a reprimand.

'You'd be wise to sit up and take some soup, Ma'am,' she says. 'A slice of toast even. Your muscles will ease up faster if you move them a little.'

But it is three days before she begins to eat. On the third day, she is helped up and into a chair. The nurse washes her gently from a pitcher of warm water laced with lavender. It soothes and calms her, but still she wants no intruders. Georgie of course barges in, but he is answered in monosyllables.

'What on earth is wrong with you?' he asks. 'When Eddy and I were in Asia, we saw women back working in the fields five minutes after giving birth. *You* can't even manage a smile.'

'I'm tired,' she says.

'Well buck up, there's a good girl. Grandmama is coming tomorrow to see the boy. The Russian cousins too. Then my mother and the girls the day after. You really must be up to receive them, even if it's just in a tea-gown.'

She hadn't much cared for the Russians the last time they had met. Nicky the Tsarevitch is an amiable nonentity and Alicky, his betrothed, is a strange, sullen creature, taut as piano wire. She is sure they look down on her blood; Alicky especially, who has a way of excluding her from conversation as if May were somehow beneath her notice. Anyway she will see not them and that's that.

Her mother can take the infant in for inspection. They can all poke and prod the child as much as they like; they will not be allowed to do the same to her. Poor May, how are you? Poor May, was it frightful? Yes it damn well was. The doctors can make up some excuse. She will stay in bed, in the room with the half-drawn blinds.

Now, as the nurse brings in the child, the woman makes to hand him to his father, but Georgie steps back in alarm.

'The boy only cries, sir.' The nurse smiles. 'He doesn't yet have teeth to bite you.'

He looks down at the bundle in his arms. Perhaps, May observes, he thinks the child expects him to make small talk. He has the same strained expression he adopts when he must speak to some official or local worthy but cannot think of a single sentence. She has no clue about what he thinks or feels about being the father of a son. Maybe he will send another note to let her know.

'Excellent,' he finally mutters as he hands the child back. 'Yes, excellent. Well done everyone.'

*

The next day, the carriages from Windsor come crunching over the gravel to the ecstasy of those still queuing to sign the book. Behind the half-drawn blinds, May hears the cheering. She is still trembling from the almighty row of the morning, when Georgie finally understood that she would not come to the drawing room. It was the worst of their rows yet. An eyes-flashing, teeth-baring, fist-pounding row. She had never been called a selfish cunt before. Worse still, the disorder still rampant inside her provoked a strange reaction. For the first time in weeks, she laughed. The laugh he hated so much. And she could not stop. The door to the bedroom slammed so hard that it bounced open again and ricocheted off the wall.

When the carriages have departed and the crowds gone home, May gets up. She raises the blinds and sits smoking by the open window, dressed only in her robe. The park is quiet now, no sound beyond the evening birdsong. For the first time in days, a light breeze carries in the arid scent of parched grass and woodland, softened by the whiff of honeysuckle climbing up the wall. From here, she can look across the forecourt towards the white sitting room in the opposite wing. She pictures Madame Bricka at the big desk, wading through the telegrams that must be answered and cursing the God in whom Bricka does not believe. The space between the wings is no more than thirty yards, but to May it seems like a universe. From the white sitting room and from all that it means to her, she is now exiled forever.

To May's astonishment, Madame Bricka adores the child. The expected disinterest, derision even, is nowhere to be seen.

'Oh do let me hold him again,' she begs, whenever the nurse brings him in.

In amazement, May watches how Bricka's sharp corners are planed away under the inquisitive glance of the mewling, puking thing in the shawl of Honiton lace. Like all the others, she has questions too. But Bricka's questions have a different tinge to them. She searches May's face with a look that May has never seen before. It is a look of desolation.

'Does it feel quite wonderful? That he is yours?' she whispers. 'Does it?'

May cannot produce an answer, at least not the one that the woman wants. Instead she simply shrugs.

'Oh, it *must* feel quite, quite wonderful,' Madame Bricka says again, as the child stretches his rosebud mouth into a yawn.

May feels a sudden fury flood through her. Bricka's words feel almost like betrayal. A betrayal of all the hours in the white sitting room, of the thinking world, of the possibility of escaping from *la petitesse de la vie*.

May wishes the nurse would not bring the child to her so often, though she knows quite well what the woman is doing. May has seen too many litters of puppies and kittens not to understand what is happening to her and yet be unable to resist it. She prays the oppression will lift from her like some huge and seemingly immovable cloud which suddenly slides away on an unexpected blessed breeze. But it does not.

On the fifth morning, a note is brought to her, roughly written, without an envelope. It comes from below stairs. Pilgrim asks most humbly if she might be allowed to see the baby. Just for a minute. Perhaps when the nurse is taking her tea in the kitchen. She will be quiet as a mouse and disturb nobody, certainly not the little man himself. Since Georgie has fled to town once more, permission is given. It is yet another hot day. In the afternoon, May is dozing again on top of her bed when something wakes her. At first she thinks it is the child bleating yet again, but it is a softer sound, muffled and constricted as if it is in hiding. When May opens the door to the nursery, Pilgrim is sitting by the cradle, rocking the little prince in her arms. The girl holds him tightly to her breast as she weeps.

'Oh Pilgrim,' says May.

'I'm right sorry, Ma'am. Truly. But I still miss him. My own boy. Only two weeks of life, Ma'am. Two weeks, no more. And his little grave is so far away from me now, Ma'am.'

At last, May does not think of herself. An idea comes to her.

'Would it help you if we moved him from Norfolk? To somewhere nearby where you might go and be with him?'

'Disturb him at his rest? Would God forgive us?'

'Such things are not unheard of. The Almighty is a loving God, at least sometimes. You have suffered enough, surely. I don't think He will begrudge you that.'

'Oh Ma'am.'

'Then we will arrange it. I will speak to my mother and the arrangements will be made.'

The little prince wakes and reaches up to the girl's face. With his fingertips he traces the tear running down her cheek.

May Teck feels her legs go from under her. She stumbles into a chair and dissolves into some other creature. Like an anaesthetic wearing off, the numbing melancholy of the past five days gives way to searing pain. A pain far worse than the most agonising spasms of the birth itself. Pilgrim rushes to her, the child still in her arms.

'Ma'am, Ma'am, heavens what ails you? Look here's your lovely lad. Take comfort in him for whatever it might be.'

But May cannot answer. She stares emptily in front of her, at some hazy, unseen corner of the room.

'Let's get you back into bed, Ma'am,' says the girl. 'You'll feel safer there.'

The sheets, having been thrown back, are cooler now. Pilgrim pulls them over her and plumps the pillows. The girl brings the child to her, laying him on the bed against his mother. At once he begins to cry. May looks at him with a detachment that, observing it in herself, chills her heart. It is as if she is both deaf and dumb, as if he is nothing to do with her at all.

'All right, Ma'am, all right. I'll take him back to his cradle. You just rest now. Rest now, Ma'am.'

For a while May dozes, then wakens to hear the child again. A sharp piercing wail, like a needle being pushed between her eyes. Why does he do that? What suffering has he yet experienced in this life? Why can't the damn nurse do something to stop it? May pulls the pillow over her ears to blot it out. She curls up into a ball. For the next few days, despite the soft entreaties of her mother and the harsh bafflement of her husband, she will not uncurl. All she wants is to stay inside the womb.

XXVII

Summer, 1894

After May hides for a few days inside the shadowed room, the Duchess takes control in that way of hers in which, like a tidal wave, she sweeps all before her. Even Georgie is flattened. A mother knows better than a husband, she tells him. Childbirth affects some women more than others and their dear, sweet, gentle May is simply one of these. She needs a holiday, a change of scene and that is that.

The little prince is not yet six weeks old when the Duchess and her daughter take the boat train and embark for Switzerland. From a grand hotel in St Moritz, they venture out for short walks along the lake and long drives into the mountains. In the evenings they attend some amateur concert, dine in the villas of the *beau monde* or just go to bed early. And her Mama is right. Dragged from the womb, May breathes in pure, clear air and begins to take some notice of the world again. She lolls in a little boat under a sky-blue parasol and is rowed to and fro across unruffled waters. She sits for ages in a silent corner of the hotel garden, watching the eagles soar around the mountain peaks, wheeling and banking on the thermals. For a few weeks, May Teck has freedom. She had begun to forget the taste and smell of it. How heady it is. How indispensable, surely, to any sort of life worth living.

But the fragile restoration is over too soon. When the boat train is swallowed up by the sooty glass canopies of Victoria Station and the air is once more clogged with filth, it feels as if she has never seen the eagles soar nor felt the balmy breeze off the lake. The old palace of St James is as sunless as ever. Georgie asks almost nothing about her little holiday, does not bother to enquire if it has done her good. The child looks up at her from his cradle and yells anew. Dear Lord, she thinks, it is even louder than before.

*

It is her mother's idea. It is, so to speak, a surprise package. May and the child are summoned from St James's to White Lodge with the promise of a fine tea and a very special treat. No, the Duchess telegraphs, she will not provide the slightest clue in advance or that would spoil the fun. And it might be better if this aspect of the visit is not mentioned to dear Georgie.

The surprise is spread out across a *chaise* in the conservatory.

He is, she notices, even stouter than before. But even if the buttons on his fancy waistcoat are under greater strain these days and the beard does not quite hide a supplementary chin, the rascal has not lost his charm. On either side of Harry Thaddeus Jones, the Duchess and Madame Bricka hang on his every word. Nor does the *scandale* of his private life seem to have impinged on his professional success. In certain quarters, among the free thinkers and such like, it may even be an added attraction. In any case, the Irish eyes still smile and that is all that matters.

How pleased she is to see him and she does not hide it. When he leaps up and bends to kiss her hand, her heart still quickens as it always did. How she would love to throw her arms around him. Such a simple thing to wish for, but how completely impossible. But at least, she thinks, the desire to do it may mean she is not dead yet.

When he looks at her, she feels as if every memory they have ever shared is right there at the front of his mind, intact and unforgotten. Every stroll along the banks of the Arno, every carriage ride in the Cascine, every moment when his easel was turned towards her, his brush held in mid-air as he stared into who she was at the sweet age of seventeen.

'Well now, May Flower,' he says, 'and how is motherhood?'

How can she answer in a way he would be pleased to hear?

'It has been achieved,' she replies.

'Achieved?' says Mr Thaddy. 'Sure, I never heard it put like that before. But look then, here comes your achievement.'

The nurse is on the threshold with the child. Mr Thaddy snatches him from her arms and lifts him high in the air. He lets the tiny fingers explore his beard. The little prince beams and chortles and coos. The infant is more animated than his mother has yet seen him. In truth though, she has only really looked at him when he is asleep in his cradle. As soon as he starts the hellish crying, she abandons him to the nurse. The black cloud that oppresses her has still not entirely shifted. The breeze has not yet come to blow it clean away.

'Enough of this,' says Harry Thaddeus Jones. 'I'm here to work, am I not?'

'May dear, I've asked Mr Thaddy to execute some sketches of you and the darling child,' says her mother. 'Just simple drawings for my bedroom. Only for me and Papa, not to be seen by anyone else. Please say you will do that for your old Mama.'

'Of course Mama. If that is what you want. But I'm hardly dressed for a sitting...'

'Ah, you're fine as you are,' he says. 'In fact, you're overdressed as usual these days, but we can be doing something about that.'

Harry Thaddeus Jones looks at her with that old, unsettling gaze. He tells her to remove her jacket. Leg-of-mutton sleeves, he declares, are an obscene deformity of the female shape, like something from a freak show at the Piccadilly Hall.

'The earrings too please and that brooch at your throat. And undo the first two buttons of your blouse. You've got a good neck, May Flower, you always did. Let's see it.'

'Careful *monsieur*,' says Madame Bricka, 'or you will make my *Princesse* look like a Gaiety Girl.'

'That would be quite impossible, even if I painted her stark naked,' he replies.

'Oh Mr Thaddy!' says the Duchess. 'You're such a naughty boy.'

'Now ladies, away with you, be gone.'

He places May on the *chaise* holding the infant. She is asked to look down at her son, nothing more. What could be simpler? Madonna and Child.

Mr Thaddy sits at a distance on a wicker chair, pad across his knees, charcoal in his hand. He will do some rough sketches today, he says, and progress them in his studio. But it is to be a turbulent sitting. The little prince cries, refusing to lie still and be cherubic. He wriggles around inside his wrappings and makes fists to punch the air. When she tries to calm him, it only agitates him more.

Harry Thaddeus Jones crosses the room and lifts the boy from her grasp. In seconds, the child stops yelling and a beatific smile cools his angry cheeks. Again he gurgles and coos. If only Georgie could do that, May thinks. She has never once seen him pick up his son since the day after the birth. Not once. If only *she* could do it too. There must be a trick to it. Some magic. Some alchemy. How she longs to know what it might be.

'Now young sir, return to your mother and be good,' says Mr Thaddy, crouching down to return the bundle to her arms. 'Your Mama loves you, don't you Mama?'

He does not, as she expects, retreat to his wicker chair, but stays crouched beside her. She realises that he is waiting for an answer or even just for a look that says it instead. It is only when he gets neither that he goes back to his perch.

The little prince quietens a little, though he is still querulous. She tries to find the way to hold him, the words to murmur, which will earn her the smile he gives so gladly to Mr Thaddy. When she sneaks a glance at the artist, the bushy brows are furrowed, the lips pursed. It is not an expression she is used to seeing on that cheerful, open face. At his feet lie two or three screwed-up balls of paper. How she hated it when he called her 'Mama'. How she must have dwindled in his eyes. A mother, nothing more.

After a while, he declares that will be enough for today and soon after takes his leave. It is ten years now since the garden of the Villa I Cedri and the summer night when the fireflies danced the polka.

*

She hears the first rumble when she is dressing to go out. In an instant her heart begins to race. Within minutes, the rain is pounding the windows and the storm slams against the turrets of the old palace of St James's. Damn it. The evening will be ghastly enough without this. They must travel all the way to Greenwich too. At the Royal Naval College, there is to be a charity dinner for impoverished seamen left high and dry by the passage of time. A cause close to Georgie's heart. For once, he does not mind being dragged away from the coverts. Already, he is brushing up tales from his long-ago voyages with Eddy. In the splendour of the Painted Hall, he will show them his trick of tapping the biscuit to check for weevils. How they will all laugh. May will sit and smile and say nothing.

A knock comes to her door. The child is very distressed, her lady-in-waiting says. He is frightened by the storm. His nurse is sick with influenza and he needs a familiar face. Might his mother come? Even for a few minutes?

In the nursery, the little prince writhes in his cot, yelling to high heaven. Her lady scoops him up and plunks him gratefully into May's arms. He stares up at his mother, the tiny eyes wide open. With each crack of thunder, they grow wider still. Cradling him, she sees her own terror reflected in those eyes. Suddenly the gulf is bridged and the connection made; both to the child in her arms and to the child long lost inside May Teck. She murmurs to him the soothing words she always gives to herself. It will not hurt you. It will soon go away. It is full of sound and fury, signifying nothing. The little prince turns his head into her breast, pushing his body against her own. He has never done that before.

The door of the nursery opens. Georgie is bedecked in his admiral's uniform, his hair smeared flat with brilliantine, even his beard neatly combed.

'What are you doing in here?' he says. 'We must go at once. This weather may make us late.'

'The boy is distressed by the storm,' she replies. 'His nurse is not here. I think perhaps I should stay with him.'

'Stay with him? Don't be ridiculous. This lady can do that. Why should you?'

'I'm his mother.'

'You are my wife. Come at once.'

Outside the windows, the eye of the storm settles over the old palace. There is a crack so loud it is as if the earth is splintering. May passes the bundle in the shawl back to her lady. The child starts to scream once more, reaching out his arms towards his mother. He has never done that before either. She looks from the son to the husband and back again.

'With or without you, the carriage leaves in five minutes,' says Georgie, turning on his heel. 'Choose.'

May stands in the middle of the nursery floor. She is shaking now. Still she looks to and fro between the open doorway and the screaming child. Then she puts her hands over her ears and runs from the room. All along the corridor, she can hear the cries of her son. As the horses head out into the raging night, she can hear them still.

In the shadows of the carriage, her hand rests lightly on her breast where the head of the little prince had nestled. At last, she reflects, her yearning had been fulfilled. Someone had lain there to find comfort. She had never imagined it might be a child.

Yet now, with every turn of the carriage wheels, she moves further away from him. Why has she done such a thing, she asks herself? But she well knows the answer. She had to choose and she has chosen. There will not be, there can never be, a turning back.

*

In a week or two, a telegram is received at White Lodge.

'Oh dear,' Mary Adelaide says to her husband. 'Mr Thaddy must suspend work on the sketches of May and the child. He is called urgently to Paris to oversee an exhibition of his paintings. What a disappointment.'

But a parallel message is sent by Harry Thaddeus Jones. This time in a letter marked 'personal and private'. Unlike most missives May receives, prim, proper and considered, the words here, scrawled in huge letters, explode like shrapnel across the paper.

I'm sorry May Flower, but I have failed. I just can't make it work. I'm not finding you now. You have gone from me.

XXVIII

Summer, 1895

As the train pulls her across the fields towards the coast, she sits alone in her compartment, her head resting against the windowpane. When it slows to pass through a station, she pulls back into the shadows. They must not see her like this, not even for a fraction of a second.

She cannot believe it is happening again, then asks herself why it should not? He is on top of her every night, except those on which the slaughter of a thousand birds has overtired him. How she prays for those nights, though she mourns the poor creatures that must be sacrificed to give her some respite. So instead of sleeping unmolested, she lies awake seeing the tiny corpses scattered across the fields and coverts, splashes of feathery red on muddy green, eyes wide open, staring up at the sky in disbelief that they could have fallen so far, so fast.

On the morning when she first retched into the basin, she went down on her knees and prayed to her God that it was no more than a bad boiled egg or a piece of shot left in a partridge. But why would He listen to her? Did she not vow before Him on her wedding day to obey her husband and to worship him with her body? Yet how can she worship when she feels nothing but distaste? With every coupling, she finds him less appealing: the skin coarser, the beard less sanitary, the breath less sweet, the acrid odour of his manhood as it slides inside her ever more revolting. And, when it is over, no terms of endearment will be uttered, the back will be turned and she will be left alone in the darkness.

But on the next morning, she was fine. She blessed that boiled egg. On the third day though, her head was in the basin once more. In an instant, she made a decision. She would tell nobody. Until, like the last time, she can hardly function for the vomiting or until the swollen belly is declaration enough, she will maintain her privacy. She will keep the ravenous eyes, the prying questions, at bay. She will give them nothing to see.

Now, from the window of the train, she catches a first glimpse of the coast; the sea a silvery fingernail beyond the yellowing landscape of yet another glorious summer. Georgie has gone to the island ahead of her. They will all be waiting. The clans are gathered for the yachting; Osborne will be bursting. Ten minutes from now, she will be at the port and then aboard the vessel. Please God, let the sea be calm. In another hour, she will reach the harbour at Cowes. On Trinity Pier, the bunting will flap in the breeze. The brass band will play. Georgie will be there to meet her and the little prince. He will stride up the gangway to awkwardly kiss her cheek and pat the child on the head. She knows how he hates doing such things in public, considers it indecorous but a necessary duty. To the townsfolk, cheering and waving their little flags, they must demonstrate happiness and harmony and show that all is well among their betters. Whatever might be amiss in the lives of ordinary folk, such reassurance will surely be of great comfort.

She keeps the notes in her handbag. She takes them everywhere with her now, clings to them. Tiny life rafts of paper and ink. They do not come often, the notes. Perhaps once every couple of months. In response to something she has done that pleases him, or at least has not displeased him. Still she cannot fathom the notes. Does he even write them himself or requisition them from some secretary of a romantic disposition? The latter possibility makes no sense. He would never be able to handle the embarrassment of making the request. But how else to reconcile the man of the notes and the man in the almost silent dining room or the almost silent bedroom in which the terms of endearment are not uttered? Whatever the truth of it, she still clings to these tiny life rafts. Still, May Teck wants to love.

Her lady-in-waiting comes into the compartment, bearing a quivering bowl of warm water laced with lavender, a flannel and a little towel. May dabs her cheeks and forehead, the back of her neck. The lady brushes down her gown to remove any dust or crinkling from the journey and helps her on with an enormous summer hat. May is slowly circled to make sure nothing is out of place. Between the railway platform and the gangway of the boat, she will be visible for less than five minutes but nothing less than perfection will do.

'You look splendid, Ma'am,' the woman says. 'Quite splendid.'

And it is true. May studies the reflection wobbling on the mirrored wall. She has lived now for twenty-seven summers and whatever might assail her spirit, it does not show on her person. Not for a moment has she ever considered herself a beauty, but she sees now how handsome she has grown. Her skin is flawless, her figure full and fine. This, she thinks, is my prime. The best I am ever going to look, the most fecund my body will ever be. Is this why I am impregnated so easily? Is this the reason the ends of my nerves feel flayed and stripped bare? Is this the time when I am to be most alive, but also when I feel that I am being slowly walled up? Because, despite the furore in her womb, it seems like nothing is truly happening to her. Nothing at all, at least not of any purpose she can bring herself to value.

'You will do great things,' Aunt Queen had said, that day beside Eddy's tomb.

It was clear the old lady did not mean the incubation of a screaming infant, so where are these great things? Essentially, she has no occupation. Neither for that matter has Georgie. He shoots and fishes and collects his damn stamps. Like his father, he waits in the queue for a purpose, even if it is one that terrifies him. Together, he and May traipse from palace to castle to country house to the glum little villa in Norfolk and back again. They change their four walls with the seasons but nothing of note goes on inside any of them, so the journeys are essentially pointless. At every destination, they find the same tribe, the same view of the world and of their place in it. Their presence is much sought, their good opinion treasured, their every word hung onto, but the order is never challenged nor shaken up. It is a life in aspic. She struggles against *la petitesse de la vie* only to sink further into it.

The train snakes its way into the station. She can see the mayor and his lady on the platform, but at least it should be quick. At least there will be no grim, tongue-tied lunch to sit through. She checks her reflection again. The vast hat is in place and so is the expression beneath it. Nothing will be discerned. Nothing will be seen. May Teck takes a long slow breath and draws herself back into the sanctuary of her shell.

*

'Oh come on, May. You can do it. I know you can.'

'No Liko, really. I couldn't possibly.'

'You always say you *love* the theatre.'

'But strictly from the box, not from the stage.'

'But you don't have to say anything,' he says. 'Heavens girl, you don't even have to *move*.'

'I'll still make a spectacle of myself. And in front of Aunt Queen and everyone else too.'

'If you refuse,' he replies, leaning right into her face, 'I shall ask Georgie's permission to put you over my knee and spank you.'

It is the way he says it. May blushes. She knows quite well she is going to agree. Few ladies find it possible to deny Henry of

Battenberg anything. He is, and only the soppiest adjective will do, quite adorable. Liko, as he is called, is wonderfully handsome, kind-hearted and the most outrageous charmer. Opinions are divided over whether or not he might also be something of a cad but, even if he were, he would be instantly forgiven.

And besides. Everyone is sorry for Liko. What a life he leads. When the German princeling asked to marry Georgie's youngest aunt, her mother only agreed on the strict condition that he and his bride would live with her. Dear dumpy Beatrice was quite indispensable to Aunt Queen, at her beck and call from the dawn chorus till the rising of the moon. For ten years now, Liko has known no home but those of his mother-in-law. He has no whim, no wish, no earthly desire that can take precedence over hers. At the age of thirty-seven, his life is as aimless as a puppy-dog with nothing to do but chase its tail.

'Poor Liko,' mutter the men of the family in the billiard room after dinner. 'They've cut his knackers off. Those are his own balls he's whacking round the table.'

The women of the family, at least those on whom Henry of Battenberg's eyes have alighted for more than a moment, doubt that this is entirely true. What a shame, they think to themselves, that such a man should be wasted on Beatrice. A good enough soul but, dear God, how enervating she is. An antidote to romance. A bromide against all passion.

But it is no more true to say that Liko's life is wasted than that his *cojones* have been chopped off. For Liko is a bringer of joy, not just to dumpy Beatrice but also to Aunt Queen herself. There is no heart which Liko wins as entirely as hers. For the first time since the terrible events of 1861, there is fun and laughter within her walls. The marriage she at first resisted, fearing it would lose her a daughter, has gained her a son who brings the sunlight back to her life. Even the patter of tiny feet, when Liko's children arrive in quick succession, has been not just tolerated but embraced far more gladly than was ever the case with her own offspring. Tiny hands tug at the black bombazine skirts, demanding to sit on her lap. Tiny voices scream and shout and giggle. The clouds lift from the towers of the great bastion above the Thames, from the little castle on the Dee and from this mansion on the island in the Solent.

Though she encounters him from time to time, May Teck hardly knows Liko Battenberg. The roving eye has never rested on her for long, their conversations cursory. Perhaps, she thinks, that is because her husband has never bothered to conceal his contempt. A year or two before the mast, snorts Georgie, that would sort him out. When Aunt Queen buys Liko a pleasure yacht, the derision does not lessen. What sort of ship is that, Georgie asks. A plaything no more. Just like Liko himself.

Now, May and Liko stand on the upper terrace looking out across the gardens down towards the sea. She likes it here. Unlike the glum little villa in Norfolk and the old palace in the city, Osborne is a place of light and air, of endless horizons, of some sense of freedom however illusory that might be. The sainted Prince Consort chose this spot for his summer retreat because the view reminded him of the Bay of Naples. And so, above the prosaic little English port of Cowes, arose an unlikely Renaissance palazzo of creamy stone. May likes to close her eyes and pretend that she really is back in Italy. Even on a cloudy day at Osborne, her spirits are brighter.

But there are few clouds today. No more than the faintest haze of cirrus in the highest sky, too timorous to dare spoil the perfection of the picture postcard. Below the terrace where May stands now with Liko, the three Battenberg children are whooping around the fountain, splashing each other with the dancing water.

'Shut up, you little swine!' he shouts down. 'Or I will drown the whole horrible lot of you.'

'No, you won't,' the girl shouts back.

'Well I will in a minute, when I've finished talking with May.'

Liko's eyes shine with pride in his children. May observes and wonders.

Dear Beatrice has another of her summer colds, he says. God knows where she gets them. She cannot possibly take the leading part in tomorrow evening's entertainment. And Aunt Queen has been looking forward to it so much. The *tableaux vivants* have become an addiction in her declining years. No expense is spared on costumes, scenery and props. May, he pleads, is perfect for the role. She has the height and the bearing.

'And there is something else too,' says Liko. 'I cannot quite express what it is. A quality which I confess I hadn't noticed before until I saw it at breakfast this morning. Something has perhaps changed in you, I think.'

At once, she draws herself back.

'Well I can't imagine what that might be.'

Liko throws himself down on one knee and clasps his hands in mock supplication, as if his whole happiness depends on her answer.

'Oh please, May. Do say you will.'

It is impossible not to laugh and so she does. The great deep laugh.

'Heavens May, where did that come from?' he says. 'Why have I not heard it before? That laugh is a wonder of the world. It is the Great Pyramid, the Hanging Gardens of Babylon and the Temple at Ephesus rolled into one.'

'Oh Liko, do shut up,' she says. 'And get up too. You silly, silly man.'

A great rush begins inside the palazzo. The seamstress must alter the dress made for Beatrice. The hem must be let down a little and the waist taken in a lot. It is still not entirely comfortable, but it will suffice. What discomfits her most is its colour. The dress is blazing scarlet. She has never worn such a shade in all her born days. She has never thought she had the right. Certainly her Mama has always discouraged it.

'No May dear,' the Duchess once said in a salon in Bond Street. 'You were born for pastels. A strong colour would only swallow you up.'

The stage is set up in the great chamber recently added onto the main wing. The Durbar Room is designed like the throne room of a maharajah; a sumptuous confection of ivory and marble; the one space set aside for frivolity in a house of otherwise impeccable rectitude. No theatre in the land can match its beauty.

May is summoned to rehearsal. At the sight of the rows and rows of gilt chairs being laid out, she wants to flee, but Liko has her arm firmly in his grip. The makeshift stage is buzzing with people. Painters with pots dab at scenery. Men on stepladders adjust the new electric lights. The players fuss and fret about exactly where they should stand for best advantage. Half the household gets roped into these theatricals, even poor Dr Reid, Aunt Queen's put-upon physician, who disapproves loudly about the waste of time and money.

'You could open a new ward in Newport Hospital for half the price of this,' he grumbles.

'Be quiet Reid, you miserable Scottish socialist,' shouts Liko.

'When the revolution comes, Prince Henry, you'll be in the first tumbril,' the doctor replies.

But Reid is smiling. Everyone is smiling. Everyone loves Liko.

May's own welcome is muted. Nobody cheers her appearance as their new leading lady. Nobody thanks her for stepping into the breach. Dumpy Beatrice is surprisingly good at this sort of thing; her Mary Queen of Scots on the block made strong men weep. As a stand-in, May Teck would never be anyone's first notion. She is not immediately thought of as a good sport. When they rehearse their positions, she is as awkward as they expect her to be. She sees Georgie's sisters muttering in a corner. Damn and blast it. Why did she agree to this? Because Liko asked her of course. Damn Liko too.

The following evening, after dinner, Aunt Queen takes the arm of her Indian servant and leads the guests into the Durbar Room. Everyone is here: Bertie and Alix, May's parents, all the aunts and uncles, their wives, their children, the ladies and gentlemen of the household. Even Cousin Willy, the German Emperor, is present; having sailed his yacht all the way across the Channel in the hope of thrashing his hated Uncle Bertie in the races.

'Oh May, it is almost like the old days,' Aunt Queen had said to her at breakfast. 'When this house was new-built and the children were young and on a summer night there were lights at every window. Oh May, what times.'

Behind the curtain, May hears the hum of conversation, the little bursts of laughter, the scraping of the gilded chairs. It is so hot, she can almost smell the audience. She can certainly smell her fellow thespians. Everyone is sweating quite dreadfully and worrying that their make-up might start to run. Dear God, she prays, don't let me faint or, worse, be sick. Her head was in the basin again that morning. Heavens, the very thought of it. The first *tableau* at which the leading actress not only moves but falls flat on her arse or vomits all over the scenery. They would talk about it for years.

Liko whispers to his players to adopt their positions. For once, he is subdued. The unlikely mantle of gravitas now descends upon him. This is his production after all and he wants a success. She can see it in his eyes. For the first time, she feels real pity for the puppy-dog. The smoking-room jokes about Liko's lost balls are not jokes any more. Now she sees how much this triviality matters to him and so it is not triviality at all. For this reason, it must not be so to her either. Suddenly this silliness matters.

Slowly, the curtain is wound back. Though her heart is pounding, she hears the click of every curtain ring. A merciful waft of slightly cooler air comes from the auditorium, bearing with it the perfumes of the ladies, fans fluttering like demented parakeets. For a second or two, there is utter silence, followed by a great intake of breath as if just one creature were lurking out there in the darkened room.

A painted backdrop depicts the ancient castle above the Thames, the standard flying on the fat round tower. In front of it is a beautiful summer garden. Dwarf trees, orange and lemon and bay, stand in pots; the containers hidden by artful banks of daisies and petunias. Box hedges are sculpted into the shapes of birds and animals. A musician sits on a bench strumming a lute, though of course his fingers do not move. A dog, a fine example of the taxidermist's art, sits at his feet. A group of richly caparisoned people, men and women, are strolling through the garden, though they do not move either. They are caught as if chattering to each other; a young man is whispering some wicked story into the ear of a young lady; she is laughing; her hand flying to her mouth, though the hand does not move. An old man in black is stroking his silver beard as he peruses some tome on Socrates or Plato, the next page of which will never be turned. An inattentive servant-boy is distracted by a stuffed hare that is running nowhere. The sky is blue. The sun shines down. All is well in this demi-paradise. The trials and tribulations of common humanity do not intrude.

But wait. But wait. This sylvan idyll has a stain upon it. A muddy patch of earth is centre stage; a disordered, soggy interloper upon the demi-paradise. Elizabeth Tudor, in all her finery, has frozen before it. The woman who has planned and plotted all her life, who has felled the Scottish queen and defeated the mighty Armada of imperial Spain, sees no way forward without ruining her slippers of golden velvet. But a handsome bearded courtier has saved the day, his fine satin cloak now spread across the impertinent excrescence; the soiled garment a tangible expression of Sir Walter Raleigh's fealty as he gazes up at her in blind devotion.

May Teck stands in a gown of scarlet silk trimmed with ermine. The dress is cut low, pushing up her fine breasts so they damn near tumble over the tightly-drawn bodice. Tiny pearls, twinkling like stars under the lights, are threaded through the flame-red wig. More pearls hang in gorgeous ropes right down to her waist. There are emeralds on her fingers and rubies in her ears. Her skin is lightly whitened against rouged lips. She has two ruffs; a little one to frame her face and neck, a larger fastened to her shoulders like angel wings. She is Gloriana to the teeth except of course that, unlike those of Elizabeth Tudor, May's teeth are perfect, white as the pearls in her hair.

But it is none of this that draws the gasp from the audience. It is the way May Teck stands there. She is known, even remarked upon, for her excellent carriage. As if she has a poker up her *derriere*, Toria often says. But this is different. This is something more. This is, and there is no other word for it, majesty. There is nobody on this hot summer night in the Durbar Room who does not see it. The fans stop fluttering and lie on laps like resting butterflies. The gentlemen look at May Teck as they have never bothered to look at her before.

And none more so than the man who now kneels before her. The *tableau* requires that Gloriana is looking down at Raleigh and he at her. Like everything else, their eyes are supposed to be motionless. In rehearsal, Liko has even urged them to restrict their blinking. But it is Liko himself who cannot now control his eyes. She sees them widen, his eyebrows rise despite himself. Nobody, she thinks, with the exception of Mr Thaddy, brush in hand, has ever looked at her like this. Yet in that distant Tuscan garden, there was no necessity to return the gaze. Now it is unavoidable. And she is powerless to prevent herself responding. Liko Battenberg is at May Teck's feet and it is no performance. As she stands there immobilised, the ground seems to tilt beneath her golden slippers.

At last, the applause breaks out. There are cheers and even vulgar whistles. Only Aunt Queen does not applaud. The old woman sits perfectly still, a *tableau* in her own right, her palms pressed together with the satisfaction of someone who has just been proved right.

After a minute or two, as is the custom, the curtain creaks shut. But it is the briefest of respites, no more than thirty seconds, in which the performers take quick gulps of air or shake a half-numbed leg. Only Gloriana and Raleigh scarcely move from their positions. The curtain parts again; more applause, more cheers, even a standing ovation. And then it is over.

Behind the curtain, the performers come alive again. They chatter and whoop and pat each other on the back. Oh how clever they are. What a triumph. The man with the lute now strums a few chords and sings 'Yankee Doodle'. One or two even bother to say, 'Well done May.'

At last, Liko gets up from the patch of earth and shakes the grubby cloak. He does not join the chatter and the whooping. He does not even smile. Instead, now that he is allowed to move, he simply takes her hot hand and plants a kiss upon it.

'My God,' he whispers. 'What a queen you make.'

XXIX

Summer, 1895

'Look at him,' says Aunt Queen as they climb into the pony trap. 'Look at the size of him these days. Like Humpty-Dumpty.'

In the afternoon sun, Bertie lies beached in a deckchair on the lawns below the terrace. His face is covered by a newspaper but, even at this distance, his outline is unmistakeable.

'One always tries one's best with a child,' she sighs. 'How unfair it seems when one's plans go so wrong.'

May does not know what to say. The afternoon after the *tableau*, she is the favoured choice to go out for a drive with Aunt Queen. The route rarely changes; a circuit of the grounds and perhaps down the track to the little beach.

'Dear Georgie is most devoted to his Papa,' she says feebly.

'I only wish that I could feel the same,' replies Aunt Queen. 'How sad it is to love your child, yet to not quite like him.'

As the pony trap passes close by him, Bertie manages to snore and break wind violently at the very same moment. His mother wrinkles her nose, adjusting the angle of her parasol as if to shut out the smell as well as the sound.

'You're a grown woman now, so I don't doubt that your mother has told you the tale,' says Aunt Queen.

'The tale, Grandmama?'

Nowadays, married to her grandson, May is entitled to address her thus, though it still feels like a gross impertinence.

'Of Bertie's first liaison. With the most unsuitable woman imaginable. An actress, little better than a woman of the streets. The stress of it pushed his Papa into an early grave and consigned me forever to an aimless life. I have tried to forgive, on my darling husband's own Bible I have tried, but I can never forget. Over thirty years on, when I look at Bertie, I still only see my own failure.'

'Oh Grandmama,' replies May. She wants to take the old woman's hand but dares not reach out.

'How could he fail so much in his duty to us and to his position? What was it that he sought that he had not already received? I've never understood it, never. I pray that no such calamity will ever befall you, May dear.'

'Perhaps Grandmama, it was just that he is a man,' says May. 'No more, no less. Aren't they so often of a weaker disposition than we are?'

Aunt Queen gives her shy, dimpling smile.

'My own Papa, much as I love him, is a fragile creature as anyone can see,' says May. 'And poor Eddy too was a wounded soul. Whereas you and my Mama are nothing less than titans. Even my tutor, Madame Bricka, once faced down a stag in Richmond Park until he ran away. All of you have the hearts of lions.'

'You have one too I think,' replies Aunt Queen. 'I knew I was not wrong to put my faith in you. And I was never more certain of it than last night.'

'I'm sure I looked quite ridiculous,' says May.

'On the contrary my dear, you were to the manner born. Everyone has remarked upon it. Even Cousin Willy and you know how hard it is to impress the German Emperor. And it had nothing to do with wigs and costumes. When one day you come into your position, you will be splendid. When Georgie's mother, sweet and lovely as she is, comes into hers before you, she will leave a little mark. But you May will be remembered. And I shall be looking down on you and cheering you on.'

May Teck's heart is in her mouth. Now she does reach out to take the tiny old hand inside its summer glove of white muslin.

'Dear Georgie is going to have to lean on you,' says Aunt Queen. 'He's a good boy but not, I think, over-blessed with imagination?'

It is a question so an answer is required and Aunt Queen will not be fooled by obfuscation.

'There are other virtues,' replies May. 'You can be sure that Georgie will always do his duty. And he is very afraid of it, which will surely make the doing even more admirable.'

'But perhaps *you* might have wished for a little more, my dear?'

'Grandmama?'

'The blessing which women are not supposed to expect, but for which most of us yearn in our secret heart. That which is not a duty, but a pleasure, a joy even. I was lucky. By a stroke of fortune, that miracle was bestowed on me, although snatched away too soon. But I suspect, May dear, that you have not found it?'

It is another question, but this time May Teck can no more answer than fly in the air. The old woman sees it and squeezes her hand. For a time, they ride in silence.

'But we needed you, don't you see?' Aunt Queen says at last. 'We simply couldn't let you get away. Even after poor Eddy died. We had to have you.'

'Since I was a child, I've always known that the good of the family must come first,' May replies. 'And I was never unwilling.'

'I had so wanted your strength and cleverness to bolster poor Eddy, but the good Lord moves in mysterious ways and now you must give that strength to Georgie. And give it heart and soul. Always remember that May, because it is God's choice for *you*.'

'You told me once Grandmama that I might do great things. Is that what you meant? To support Georgie? Nothing else?'

'Of course, my dear. Is that not enough?'

When the pony trap regains the upper terrace, the old woman

is handed down to the ground. She must go inside for her nap, she says. At the door, she turns and looks May Teck in the eye.

'If only poor Eddy had lived, he might have given you... that little more. I'm so sorry, my dear.'

It is the thought May has pushed away, locked in a box of possibilities and hidden on the highest shelf of an unvisited cupboard. For a moment, the yearning hangs between the two women in the doorway.

Then Aunt Queen says, 'And oh, wasn't he handsome? Eddy? Our beloved Liko, though not so tall, sometimes reminds me of our lost boy.'

May changes the angle of her parasol so her face is in the shadows.

'I really must lie down now,' says Aunt Queen. 'Heavens, when the children were young, I used to run from this terrace all the way down to the very edge of the sea. *Run!* Can you credit it? How awful to be old. I do so pray it doesn't last much longer.'

A lady-in-waiting, clucking like a mother hen, hurries out to take charge. Before disappearing into the cool gloom of the corridor, Aunt Queen turns with a smile.

'You're quite right my dear. We women are always the stronger, aren't we? How much it would please me if one day it could be written in the books, "Once Victoria sat on the ivory throne of Travancore and after her came May." Not consort but regnant. Oh well, *tant pis*.'

It is the greatest compliment May will ever hear in this life and she knows it. In the years to come, no other arrangement of words in a sentence, no speech of welcome, no panegyric in a newspaper, on the wireless or in a cinema newsreel will ever be its equal.

As the afternoon sun beats down on the palazzo on the island, May Teck makes her deepest curtsey to the small black figure in the doorway. When she raises her eyes again, the figure has gone and all she can hear is the song of the starlings among the towers.

*

While Aunt Queen dozes, May Teck goes to the dressing room she has been allocated and opens the wardrobes. For the rest of her days, she need never open a wardrobe again. Someone else will always do it for her, but that is not the point. Wardrobes are the repositories for things which it is possible to rearrange in a certain way, a way conducive to greater order and thus to peace of mind. The gowns, the cloaks, the hats, the shoes, the stockings, the nightdresses, even the undergarments all offer the prospect of an increase in serenity.

In London or in Norfolk, the sheer number of items means the rearrangement can easily consume one whole day or even two. Now, on the island for less than a week, the quantity is diminished but the principle holds true. On throwing open the wardrobe which shelters her evening gowns, she sees an immediate opportunity. Why on earth, she wonders, has her dresser here not noticed it? The gowns, currently hung in an aimless row, could so easily be grouped in a spectrum; ranging from whites, creams and silvers via pastels like lemon or blue and the middling shades of moss green and gold, right through to that one indispensable black dress in case some inconsiderate relative decides to die without warning. Or might it be better if the silks were placed together, then the satins, the organzas, the velvets and so forth? It is a quandary.

She bites her nails as she considers it. Such a dreadful habit. Something children do; something she herself never did before, yet now does. Of course she could try both options for the wardrobe and discover which brings the greater ease. And so she does just that. It swallows two whole hours as the afternoon sun begins to weaken and a kindly breeze skitters in from the sea, rustling the long net curtains that frame the open windows.

In her own houses, it is the same with her jewellery, her little *objets d'art* and, above all, her books. Not merely to arrange them perfectly, but to catalogue them also. How reassuring it is to write down in indisputable black and white exactly what one possesses. Not out of vulgar pride and certainly not of avarice, merely the quiet satisfaction of a well-ordered existence in a world half mad. She has done it since she was a little girl, when the corridors of White Lodge echoed to the tantrums of her father and the chatter of her mother.

'Why on earth do you do all that?' Georgie once asked when he discovered her making a list of which hats she has already worn at which country house weekend.

'For the same reason you collect stamps, Georgie dear,' she replied.

'Nonsense. That's a completely different thing. That's a serious occupation.'

'If you say so.'

'Good God, I hope you're not going a bit batty like your Papa.'

She had mustered so much fury in her eyes that, when she turned them on him, he had stared down at the carpet and shuffled his feet.

'Sorry Miss May. Out of order.'

Now, she closes the wardrobe doors as softly as she can, as if shutting away a secret between herself and the satinwood which nobody else must know. At the little click as the two doors meet, May Teck gives a gentle sigh. She could sleep now, she thinks.

Suddenly, from outside, the shouts of children knife into her solitude. It can only be Liko, bringing his brood back up from the Swiss Cottage. Hiding behind the net curtain, she looks out over the terraces. The older boy is throwing a ball for a dog, the girl clutches Liko's hand while the younger boy is enthroned on his father's shoulders, ruffling the brilliantined hair. How easy they look together, she thinks. How easy everything seems to be for Henry of Battenberg. It is not likely, she reflects, that he has ever felt the urge to rearrange the shirts and suits in his closet or to count the number of his cufflinks.

This morning she had woken in a flush of panic. She wondered if she could say she was unwell. It would not have been a complete falsehood for she had been sick yet again, damn it. As she lay there, she could not decide which thing she feared the most: facing Liko across the breakfast table, looking ashen and far from the goddess she had portrayed the previous night, or simply facing Liko at all. In the end it hadn't mattered because, when she went down, he had breakfasted already and gone out to play tennis.

'How strange,' said Cousin Willy, buttering his toast. 'Our precious Liko isn't usually an early riser. I sometimes wonder if he is really a German. What can ail him?'

Now, as Liko and the children pass beneath her window, May Teck too has a question. She would like to shout it out into the drowsy evening air and hear it echo around the terraces, but instead she just whispers it softly into the folds of the net curtain.

'Why have we not spoken today? Are you avoiding me? When will I see you again?'

XXX

Summer, 1895

Liko is smoking in the sunshine, his feet resting on the seat of an old rocking-horse. He has taken off his jacket and his collar, loosened his cravat and rolled up his shirtsleeves. It is a strange apparition; he is usually so dapper. When he sees her coming across the lawns, he does not stand up; odd too, for he is the most courteous of men. If she needed any signal that something had changed between them, she need look no further. He gives her no more than a lazy smile; a shyness in it which was not there before.

'Ah, Gloriana. Come and have a cucumber sandwich.'

Once again, Liko had not been at breakfast. Tennis again, it seemed. Nor at lunch. Aunt Queen complained that he had gone into Cowes to attend to some problem with his silly boat. It had never occurred to her that wood, canvas and rope could ever become her rival for his attentions. Later still, she moaned that he had now vanished to play with the children in the Swiss Cottage. Always gadding about, Aunt Queen said.

May summons the little prince's nurse, declaring that they will take a turn with the perambulator around the gardens. And why should she not find herself at the little wooden chalet? Here, for three generations now, the children, grandchildren and great-grandchildren of Aunt Queen have played in miniature at being the ordinary people they can never be. For the first and last time, they will scrub saucepans, sweep floors, make beds, bake cakes and brew tea. What fun ordinariness can be, they think, for a little while at least.

'Are you sure I'm not intruding?' May replies now to the offer of the cucumber sandwich.

Liko gives up his chair to her and himself straddles the rocking-horse. Aunt Queen is right. He does look a little like Eddy, even though the face is broader with higher cheekbones, its planes as smooth as skiing slopes. It is a beautiful face, made more so by the first tiny lines etched around the dark eyes. Above all, it is an open face. Nothing is dissembled on the features of Henry of Battenberg: joy, sadness, the frustration of his existence, the love for his children are writ large for anyone to see.

He coos over the little prince, scooping him up from the perambulator and bouncing him on his knee. The boy delivers the same gurgling smile given to Harry Thaddeus Jones on the day of the sketching. Again, May marvels how it is elicited so easily if one has the trick of it.

Georgie's son and heir is toddling by now. Liko tells May's nurse to take him into the kitchen to watch the tea being prepared by his own children. At the arrival of the little prince, a great shriek comes from inside the tiny house. The Battenberg siblings adore him, smothering him with kisses, licking him like a lollipop. May throws her hands over her ears.

'Dear God, the racket. Doesn't it bother you?' she asks.

'Of course not.' He smiles. 'Why, does it trouble you?'

'I'm not certain that I understand the mind of a child.'

'But you were a child yourself. Don't you remember?'

'I'm not sure that I do,' she replies. 'I remember being young of course, but not exactly being a child, whatever that means exactly. I don't believe I was given the time. I had to grow up rather fast, you see.'

'Then start being a child from now on,' he says. 'Do silly things. Annoy people. Stick your tongue out at Mr Gladstone. Take your shoes off and run barefoot through the cornfields. Show us your ankles.'

'I rather think it's a bit late for all that. Such things are no longer allowed to me.'

Liko watches her through the smoke of his cigarette.

'Well that's a shame. Harry Thaddeus Jones told me you've got very pretty ankles.'

'What?'

'Oh I heard all about May Teck long before I ever met you,' he grins. 'Ten years ago, more perhaps. He often talked of you then, scandalous old *roué* that he now is.'

'He spoke of me? To you?'

'When I still lived at our home in Heiligenberg, Jones was touring the small courts of Germany looking for commissions to build his reputation. Sadly we didn't have the money to pay him, so he didn't stay long.'

'But he spoke of *me*?'

'Oh yes,' replies Liko. 'The splendid young princess he had left behind in Florence. I do believe he was a little in love with you. His precious May Flower.'

'It's a long time ago,' she mutters. 'What else did he tell you?'

'That you were a girl of possibilities.'

'As what?'

'As a woman I should think,' he replies. 'Though to be honest, since I first met you, I could never quite see what he meant. But I did last night. And so does everyone else now. You should hear how catty Toria is being about you today. She knows you have something she and her stupid sisters will never have.'

She blushes now and asks for a cigarette.

'Why do you blush?' he asks. 'Don't be modest. In those who have nothing to be modest about, it might be regarded as an affectation.'

'Oh shut up, Liko dear and give me the damn cigarette.'

When he comes up close to light the match, she cannot look him in the eye. Her hand is trembling a little. For a moment, no more, he grasps it to steady the cigarette. If he wonders why the hand trembles, he does not ask.

He returns to the rocking-horse. Of course it is too small for him and his legs are spread wide across the seat. They are strong, broad legs and the position seems slightly indecent. She feels she should avert her eyes but she cannot. As the tumult from the kitchen continues, he asks her to tell him about her time in Italy. Though he is German, he was born and raised in Milan and knows Florence well.

So the conversation moves to safer ground: the view of the city from Bellosguardo, the frescoes of Santa Croce and Santo Spirito, the *baldacchino* in the Duomo. She has never imagined Liko any more of an aesthete than Georgie, but now she finds he has opinions on Titian, Raphael and Andrea del Sarto. Not the cool, academic opinions of Mr Thaddy, but opinions none the less; simplistic, inchoate but full of vigour and even spirituality. Liko has been to the monastery of La Certosa, climbed the tower of Castello Vincigliata and wandered the halls of the Uffizi and the Palazzo Pitti. He has even been to Lady Orford's weekly salon and joined her in smoking a cigar.

May tells him of the great flower *Corso* in the Cascine when the young bucks threw their blossoms into her carriage till she and her mother were half submerged in petals and stems.

'They shouted that they would die of love for me,' she smiles. 'Can you imagine it?'

'Oh yes,' says Liko.

Now it is her turn to hide behind a cloud of smoke.

Most of all though, she tells him of the Villa I Cedri. Of the garden unlike any other, the sound of the Arno crashing over the weir, the ruined mill on the opposite bank. The scent of the jasmine and the bougainvillea.

'The light and the warmth,' she says. 'If I close my eyes and think hard, I can still feel the glow of it on my skin. I seemed to have such freedom there. Or at least as much as the likes of you and me would be permitted. Did you feel that too?'

'Another world,' he replies. 'One with its corsets undone. England is such a tight little country, don't you think?'

They look at each other across three feet of grass. On the breeze, May catches the smell of the sea. And in Henry of Battenberg's dark eyes, usually so full of laughter and mischief, she sees, for a moment, a glimpse of misery.

She tells him too of the night of her seventeenth birthday, when her Mama and Papa gave a party and she danced among the fireflies.

'How different you are when you speak of these things,' Liko says.

'And Mr Thaddy presented me my portrait that night. He wasn't paid a penny for it; he'd asked if he might paint me. I think that's why I treasure it so much.'

'I'd like to see it. Where is it now?'

'In my room in Norfolk.'

'Your room? You only have the one?'

'Only one I can call my own,' she says. 'I keep it there because Georgie doesn't like it. He says it's not me.'

'I'm even keener to see it now.'

'Mr Thaddy said I would grow into something called a *maitresse femme*. Do you know the phrase?'

'Oh yes.'

'I've never been quite sure what it meant. I used to imagine it was slightly indelicate.'

'It simply means you're a strong woman.'

She takes a long slow draw on her cigarette.

'And am I?'

'If you'd asked me before you played Gloriana, I would have said you were quite the opposite. But now I know how wrong that was. Perhaps the role you've really been acting was that of the obedient little wife.'

The nurse comes out of the Swiss Cottage, the little prince stumbling beside her. The boy pulls towards Liko, his baby arms outstretched. Liko catches him just before he falls, lifting him high into the air, the sun circling the child's golden hair like a halo. For the first time, May sees her son as an object of beauty, as worthy of attention as an image of the Christ Child. But it is the vision of a moment. When Liko brings him back down to earth, the illusion is gone.

The little Battenbergs shout from the doorway that tea is all laid out on the kitchen table and they must come right this very minute. With his Walter Raleigh flourish, Liko picks up his jacket and spreads it on the grass before her.

'Idiot,' she says. As the word leaves her mouth, it strikes her how she could never use it to her husband. It is quite inconceivable. But then Georgie is a god; at least one in waiting.

'Tell me one thing before we go in,' says Liko. 'How many May Tecks are there?'

'How many?'

'Well, there's dull Georgie's spouse who walks behind him and wouldn't say boo to a goose. There's the Gloriana of the other evening. And there's the girl who dances among fireflies in an Italian garden. I should like to know which one is real.'

'Why?'

From inside the Swiss Cottage comes the crash of breaking crockery, shouts and screams. But May Teck scarcely hears it. She is waiting for an answer.

'Because I need to decide which one to fall in love with.'

Without another word, he goes rushing in through the doorway and out of her sight.

'What have you done now, you dreadful little devils?' he shouts. 'I'll swing for the lot of you, I really will.'

When finally she ventures into the tiny kitchen, spills have been mopped up and tears dried. The Battenberg brood are feeding the cake they have baked to their pet, the little prince. At the tiny table with the red-and-white chequered tablecloth she must squash herself in next to Liko. It is impossible to ignore his thigh resting against hers. At first, the pressure is light but, as the squealing rages on and tea is slurped, she feels it increase. One of his children remarks on how hot she looks. Is the lady going to faint? She asks the question of herself. How absurd. A leg is no more than flesh and muscle, tendon and bone. In the carriage, Georgie's leg brushes hers all the time. She scarcely notices that; certainly feels nothing. So why is this so different? Why is she so overwhelmingly aware of her own flesh and how it is responding now? Because there is no doubt that it is. And when he must stand up to separate two squabblers, the glimpse she gets of his lower body before he quickly hides it with a napkin is enough to tell her she really should get out of here at once.

Yet, as May Teck walks back across the lawns to the house, she remembers, as she often does, the cruel words of her uncle. That she would never inspire a passion in anyone. Well damn him. She stops for a minute and sits on the side of the fountain basin and listens to the gentle gurgling of the water. Half closing her eyes and turning her face to the sky, she feels again the sunlight of a Florentine garden.

XXXI

Summer, 1895

Until forty-eight hours ago, it would have lit up her day and carried her through a whole week at least. It would have been read again and again, trawled for meaning like some ancient piece of papyrus, before being folded and stored away with the others. Now though, she almost tosses it into the darkness of a drawer as if it hardly matters.

It is one of Georgie's little life rafts. The note was brought to her out in the garden, though it was no more than five minutes since she had seen him at breakfast, where he spoke scarce a word to her or to anyone else.

It occurs to me that I've not yet congratulated you on your excellent performance in the tableau vivant. *The real Virgin Queen could hardly have been more impressive, though we can't call you that any more can we, darling girl? Ha! Anyway, jolly proud of you. Your loving Georgie.*

But now the note can be banished to the darkness because May Teck no longer has need of its light.

*

A photograph has been arranged. Aunt Queen wishes a record of her house party. It is to be taken on the stone staircase leading from the upper to the lower terrace. Aunt Queen will sit in the centre of the front row, the family ranged on the steps behind her. It never changes; everyone could do this in their sleep.

May and Georgie stand several steps back. The photographer is still fussing with his tripod. Henry of Battenberg is on the step below them, telling Cousin Willy how much he needs a cigarette.

'Come on Georgie, how about a smile?' says Liko, glancing round to see who's behind him. 'It's not a firing-squad.'

'I prefer not to smile for formal photographs,' replies Georgie.

'Well then May, you'll have to give us a dazzler to make up for old flint-face.'

'May follows my lead in this matter,' says Georgie.

'That's a shame,' says Liko.

'Fool,' mutters Georgie.

The photographer is ready. May Teck pulls herself back a little so her husband is no longer exactly by her side. When the signal is given, she delivers a smile to light up a sepulchre.

The group begins to dissolve. The Battenberg children, released from best behaviour, charge up and down the staircase, in and out between the adult legs. One causes Georgie to miss his footing on the steps. He collapses with a yelp of pain. Helped to his feet, he yelps again, louder this time. Dr Reid is summoned from the house. The ankle is clearly twisted, swelling up already. Georgie's mother fusses and flaps. Two burly footmen cross their arms to make a cradle and Georgie is hoisted aloft, his face red and furious.

'Damn you Liko,' he shouts. 'Damn you and your ill-bred children.'

Liko draws himself to his full height and stands like the proud Prussian soldier he used to be.

'I apologise for my child, Georgie. I do not apologise for his breeding.'

'I'll make damn sure that every child of mine knows how to conduct himself.'

Georgie is carried back to his bedroom and dumped on his bed, a little too roughly. More yelps of pain, more curses against ill-bred children. Dr Reid declares the ankle will be like a balloon by teatime and so it proves. There is no answer apart from rest, a crepe bandage and a tot of whisky. Alix and the Wales girls fuss and flap some more. Poor darling Georgie-boy. In the morning, he still cannot put his weight on it.

'You'll have to go instead of me,' he says to May.

'What? But I hate the sea, Georgie. You know that quite well.'

'You must go as my representative,' he says. 'I lost my temper with him yesterday and your presence would show there are no hard feelings. And your parents are invited too, are they not?'

'But I really don't want to go out on Liko's yacht, Georgie,' she replies. 'Please don't force me.'

The lower lip juts forward, the mottled face grows red. But the usual explosion does not come. Perhaps, in his pain, it is too much effort. When he speaks, it is little above a whisper.

'You will do what I ask of you.'

And so Liko's cutter sails off from the jetty at Cowes. Under the sun, the sea is flat as a blue dinner plate. Liko is disappointed. The sails will be quite useless but, no matter, there is an engine too. We'll just chug as far as Yarmouth and back, he says. Again today, the jacket, collar and cravat have gone, the shirtsleeves rolled up; he looks like one of his own crew. May's parents are dressed as if for a ball at Blenheim.

'Goodness, you're all so smart,' says Liko as two sailors execute the tricky manoeuvre of helping Mary Adelaide aboard. 'Duchess, you must remove at least half your clothing.'

'Oh Liko, you're such a cheeky boy,' she replies. 'Wherever did dear Beatrice find you?'

Dear Beatrice, with her summer cold, is, like Georgie, still confined indoors. She has hardly been seen for days. That house is turning into a bloody infirmary says Liko. When it is May's turn to board, he reaches out for her himself. As he grips her, his thumb gently strokes the back of her hand. The tiniest intimacy, its impact beyond imagining.

'I'm a rotten sailor, Liko,' she mumbles. 'This is really not a good idea.'

'You will be a fine sailor today, May. I promise you that. The sun is shining, the sea is in excellent temper and you are so very welcome here.'

It is true. With his smile, broad as the horizon, resting upon her, she feels more wanted in this place than she has ever felt before. The little prince comes too, strapped into a harness, the leash held tightly by his nurse. He is dressed in a teeny sailor-suit. Liko bows and salutes him.

But it is Liko's kingdom they have entered; the only home he can truly call his own. They are shown around from prow to stern. They learn the names of the masts and the rolled-up sails. They explore inside the little saloon, the galley where a sailor is preparing their lunch, the bunk beds, even the heads. This last appals the Duchess.

'But I couldn't get in *there*,' she says. 'What on earth shall I do?'

'You'll just have to hold it in Duchess, or put your *derriere* over the side for the fish to gawp at.'

'Oh Liko Battenberg, you're the worst rascal in England,' Mary Adelaide replies, her jowls a-quiver.

But even the Duke, always alert for the slightest of slights, laughs too. Everyone loves Liko.

The Solent is dotted with sailing boats becalmed at their moorings, too sleepy to give more than half-hearted tugs on their ropes. Crews scrub decks, polish brass and buff up portholes. Their masters stretch out across banks of cushions, reading books, playing cards, sipping cordial.

Liko's boat putters in and out between the leviathans. They all wave up to Cousin Willy, standing at the rail of his gargantuan vessel.

'What a teeny-weeny craft, Liko,' he shouts down through a megaphone. 'Or perhaps it is just a lifeboat? Has your real ship sunk?'

'Cunt,' mutters Liko, waving cheerily back. 'Oh sorry, May.'

'I have three brothers and I'm married to a sailor,' she replies. 'It's not a word I'm unfamiliar with.'

'Well it should be,' he says. 'Forgive me.'

He looks at her as if he has just committed the worst of sins and must have that forgiveness or he will surely die. In that pleading look, May Teck is lost all over again.

It is hard to imagine a more idyllic day. The Duchess does indeed remove some of her clothing. So too does the Duke, usually a stickler in such matters. How kind Liko is to him, May notices again. Always deferring, always drawing him in, never abandoning him to a distant corner as so many have begun to do as his mind becomes less anchored, his unknown fears more oppressive. Perhaps, she thinks, it is because the narratives of their lives are so painfully similar. Two children of the Bavarian forests, both with blood tainted by the passion of their fathers for women deemed unsuitable. Wandering the courts of Europe, their prospects dim, trying to sell themselves on their good looks as blatantly as any tart in Leicester Square. Then, hallelujah, just before those prospects blow away completely, both finding an unexpected haven in the sturdy arms of two brides, whose luck is running out also. But, oh dear, the cost of it. A cost never to be spoken of, never admitted, except perhaps to themselves in the long dark hours of the night.

Today though the sea is balm to whatever troubled soul might embark upon it. The Duke looks out across the dappled water, his breathing slow and measured, the hand no longer drumming on the knee, but still and steady. Mary Adelaide's chatter slowly lessens then fades entirely. Under the blazing canopy of a midsummer sky and the seeming infinity of this blue-green pond, any sense of worldly importance dissolves like the spume in the wake of the yacht.

The four of them sit under the awning aft of the wheel, Liko with the little prince on his knee. Despite the sailor-suit, the child has not been on a boat before. He is mesmerised, his eyes saucer-wide. He has never seen such endless horizons, but he is not afraid. The small body twists this way and that to take it in, to grasp the beauty; his arms stretch skywards as if to touch the gaggle of attendant gulls that swoop and soar above the stern. As yet, the gurgles and squeals are incomprehensible, but Liko pretends that he understands every one. He nods his head in response, giving the child the words for which he struggles. Boat. Water. Bird. Island. Grandmama and Grandpapa. Mother. Friend.

'Are you feeling all right, May?' he asks suddenly, without looking at her.

She opens her mouth, but finds that her throat will not release an answer. Yes, she is all right. In fact, she has never been more all right in her entire life. Her parents loll half-asleep in the shade of the awning, her mother's head drooping on her breast. How rarely has May known such peace in their company. The little prince too, surfeited with excitement, is starting to doze, cradled in the strong arms of his new friend. This, she thinks, is how it might have been for her. A perfect family. A perfect life.

Liko stares out across the water, his feet up on the cushioned bench, stroking the head of the child. She wonders to where his mind is travelling. Perhaps to nowhere in particular, no destination necessary; the travelling all, as long as it takes Henry of Battenberg away from the life he must lead. But now he turns to her properly.

'May? Are you all right?' he asks again.

Still the words will not come. Perhaps her tongue refuses to interrupt the sudden contentment that has come to her. Only in its overwhelming presence does she become aware of how devastating its absence has been. She thinks for a moment that she might weep, though whether for the presence or the absence she is not sure. And how wonderful it would be to weep, without reticence or shame, till the decks of Liko's yacht were awash with the tears that she has restrained for most of her existence. They would all ask her what on earth was the matter with her and she would tell them. Only Liko Battenberg, she is quite sure, would not need to ask. There is nothing this man does not know about me, nothing he does not understand.

Instead, for now, she simply nods her head and smiles.

'Ah, that smile,' says Liko. 'If I were Georgie, I could never ban it. I'd want to see it a hundred times a day.'

When they reach the harbour at Yarmouth, the anchor is dropped and luncheon is served. Liko fusses around them like a butler. Is the food satisfactory? Would the Duchess like more chicken? Some more wine for the Duke? He allows the little prince to smear ice cream all over his beard. They are soon noticed by the other boats bobbing on the water. Sailing-caps are raised to salute them; some even applaud. For once, May Teck does not mind the ravenous eyes; indeed she almost welcomes them. Look at me if you like, she thinks. See how happy I am.

When they turn for home, they are suddenly chased by a wind. It comes from nowhere; the sleepy sea wakes up and takes notice.

'Yes!' cries Liko, delighted.

The engine is shut off. The crew races to unfurl the sails and raise them high. The wind can hardly wait to fill them, the sails becoming fat clouds of canvas. May is struck by the beauty of it. How much she usually hates the wind. She realises that she should feel afraid at this moment and wonders why she doesn't.

'You're going to be fine,' shouts Liko, as if reading her mind.

And she is. Her nervous stomach does not so much as flutter. The hated wind does not disturb her. The little prince, strapped tightly to his nurse, is unconcerned too. What a world this is. Why did nobody tell him? When a tired seagull, looking for a ride, alights on the rail, he is struck dumb with enchantment.

Liko, the master of his ship, has taken over the wheel. He shouts commands to his crew: a bit more sail, a bit less. The yacht is flying across the water now, cutting through the white-topped waves as if the Devil were at its stern. The Duke and Duchess are holding hands, smiles fixed bravely on their faces, their cheeks a little pale. But May Teck's cheeks are as pink as the little prince's bottom.

'May, come and take the wheel,' calls Liko above the wind.

'Don't be ridiculous,' she yells back.

Without taking his eyes off the sea, Liko stretches out one arm to her. She stares at his hand, the fingers splayed out ready to grasp her own. She could no more refuse him than walk upon the waves.

He slides her in front of him and places her hands on the great mahogany wheel. He stands right behind her, ready to grab it if he must. Despite the wind, she can feel his breath on her neck, the warmth of his skin and the sweat from his armpits. A little turn to port, he tells her, a little turn to starboard. No more than an inch. That's the girl. When a delinquent wave hits them side on, she stumbles for a moment. Liko's big hands cover her own against the mahogany; he pushes his body closer to hers. Surely he must feel it. Surely he must know what he is doing. Yet still she is not afraid, either of the sea or of this man. Perhaps, she thinks, I should be, but I am not.

'Freedom,' says Liko into her ear. 'Freedom, May.'

She wants to stand here forever and never reach harbour, but the wind hurries them homewards all too quickly. Soon Cousin Willy's floating palace is once more in view. They are just turning into the shelter of the mole when a second rogue wave thumps them mid-ships. Again May stumbles, even losing her grip on the wheel. She crashes back against Liko almost taking both of them down, but he wraps his strength around her and stops the fall. To do so, he does not worry where his hands may alight; they land squarely on her belly and he does not move them as swiftly as he should. Still his breath is against her neck, still his body against her own.

'Three cheers for Captain May,' he calls out to the crew at the prow and to her parents at the stern. The little prince giggles, opening and closing his fists.

The moment comes when they must move apart. Now, for the first time since she took the wheel, they look each other in the eye. Liko's glance moves from her face down to her belly and back again.

'Congratulations?' he whispers.

'Dear God, no. Condolences,' she murmurs.

May Teck's triumph over the waters does not long survive the sight of dry land. Though, in years to come, she will often reach for the golden memory of it, whatever joy has briefly come to her on a pleasure yacht on a hot summer's day is not destined to endure. The panic she has been banking down for weeks now rises up in her again. She throws herself against the rail and is spectacularly sick into the Solent, in full view of Cousin Willy.

'Oh May,' says Liko.

XXXII

Autumn, 1895

The fates are on her side. The package is brought to her when she is alone in her sanctuary.

Every day, she watches through the window as the trees around the little lake turn into russet, yellow and gold, a last few weeks of deceptive glory. The old rowing boat is tied firmly to its post and will not be used again this year, not even to satisfy the little prince's new-minted passion for excursions on the water. The sharpness of the morning air is a needling reminder of the coming of the endless evenings.

She begins to feel as if summer never happened, as if she had never stepped onto the island in the Solent, never indeed left this glum little villa. Again she sits in silence on the fan-backed chair. Only the muffled noise from the kitchens or an occasional yell from the nursery reminds her that she is not entirely alone, somewhere on the edge of the universe, on the very rim of an abyss. Georgie is out somewhere, talking to grooms or farmers or God knows whom. He rarely says where he goes; she has almost stopped asking.

When her shape made it necessary to admit her condition, he took the news with little more excitement than he did the first time.

'Two down then,' he joked again, before returning to the King's Lynn paper. 'So maybe just two more before we call it a day? Three at the most. That should be enough, don't you think?'

Now, on this moribund afternoon, May remembers those words for the umpteenth time. Three more? Above the fireplace, the girl in the straw hat still looks down. May turns away so the girl cannot see her swelling belly. When the soft knock comes to the door and a small parcel is placed upon the satinwood side table, the surprise comes not a moment too soon.

Nestled inside a little lacquer box, on a bed of sky-blue satin, sits a brooch of tiny diamonds in the shape of a starfish. A handwritten card is enclosed.

From Neptune, God of the Sea to Captain May, in memory of our wonderful voyage.

So he has not forgotten her. Oh thank you, Heaven. He has not forgotten her after all. He has thought of her as she has of him. Just as much? More even? Then the notion of some small present had come to him. Where? When? As he played with his beloved children? As he sat at the breakfast table with Beatrice and Aunt Queen, facing another day of servitude? Or, perhaps, in the middle of the night when, lying beside Beatrice, he could not sleep and may have thought of her? She blots that last image from her mind; she does not care to think of Beatrice and is ashamed of how easy it is to achieve that feat.

She goes to a mirror and holds the brooch against her. How beautiful it is. It must have cost a pretty penny and they say he has almost no money of his own. In the mirror now, she sees him standing close behind her, just as he had stood at the wheel of the yacht. Again she feels the warmth of his body and his breath on her neck. His arms reach round and pin it to her breast, his hands lingering there far longer than they need.

And now May Teck is transformed. The novel she is struggling to read is quite forgotten. The crinkling leaves on the trees beyond her window are now invisible. No longer does she hear the noises from the kitchen or the nursery. The swelling of her belly no longer defines her. As if there is music playing in her head, she lifts her skirts and twirls around the room. Breathless and giddy, she comes to a halt before the portrait above the fireplace.

'Look,' she says aloud to the face that gazes down. 'Oh just look.'

For an hour or more, she sits on the fan-backed chair watching the diamonds twinkle in the firelight. How good it is to have him with her, even in this feeble form. And she thinks now of that other picture by Harry Thaddeus Jones. The one she first saw in the sweaty studio behind Santa Croce; the one which refuses to loosen its hold on her heart. The wounded poacher and his wife; the seeking and the giving of comfort. How she wishes to give comfort to Liko Battenberg and to receive his in return.

It takes another crash from the kitchens to haul her back to her reality. Georgie will be back before too long. He never now trespasses here but she will be expected to appear in the drawing room well before dinner. Yet the starfish brooch cannot appear with her; that is quite certain. Her husband, for all his indifference to the accoutrements of fashion, never fails to notice a new possession. He will want to know whence it came and what its value might be. She could lie of course and say it came from her Mama or some other generous relation, but she will not. No falsehood or deception must ever tarnish the starfish brooch, it must remain pure and unblemished. And if that means it will live mostly in the darkness, then so be it.

She unpins it and, cradling it in the palm of her hand, retreats to her bedroom. Though she does not really feel like sleep, a languor overcomes her. She need not dress quite yet. She will just stretch out for half an hour.

As soon as she closes her eyes, she hears the voices from below. There is a small room directly beneath, which the maids use as a place for sewing. She keeps forgetting to tell the butler that the women's conversations can be clearly heard from above. She can place the voices: the young local girl who replaced Pilgrim and an older one who has just married one of the grooms. The newlyweds have moved into a cottage over by Wolferton, but chatter about the lovely view from the bedroom window soon moves on to the joys to be found within the bedroom itself. The new bride holds nothing back in her account of the wedding night. No kiss, caress or intrusion is missed out. No detail of the bridegroom's physical qualities is passed over either. Nor is any aspect of his bride's own responses considered too intimate to be related.

Above, on her bed, May Teck is at once shocked and riveted. But it is more than that. The words and pictures that float upwards from the sewing-room trigger in her own body a wave of feeling she has never experienced before. Her girlish fantasies of Harry Thaddeus Jones, vivid though they were at the time, are as nothing compared to this. Gingerly, she explores herself in line with the guidance coming up through the floorboards. The disgust she feels at her current condition quite melts away; the backache and the bladder all forgotten.

How tender her breasts feel, but how full they are too. And when she pulls the folds of her tea-gown high above her thighs, how wet she is between her legs. Again she feels his warmth against her, his breath on her neck. Now though, she yearns to shut out the coarse dialogue of the maids and hear only his gentle caring words in her ear. As she enters herself, she surrenders to the obvious pretence. In her other hand, she still clutches the starfish brooch. And when she feels her body impose its will upon her, stripping her of all control, when she shakes and shudders on her marital bed, she holds it against her heart and calls out his name.

There is a sudden silence from below. She lies shipwrecked on the quilt, gasping for air, her skin basted in sweat. Dear God, what happened? Her Mama never spoke of such a possibility, of such chaos and disorder. It must never happen again. Of that she is sure. But what is she to do with the memory of it? Of his head lying on her breast, telling her he loves her.

XXXIII

Autumn, 1895

When the train curves south towards Windsor, she looks through the window for that first glimpse. No matter how many times she sees it, it never fails to entrance her. Aunt Queen's castle high above the river. As the autumn sun creeps away to the west, washing the grey and ochre walls in a last patina of buttery gold, it stands defiant against the dying of the light as it has done for eight hundred years.

They are commanded to the birthday party of Prince Henry of Battenberg. Georgie comes moaning and groaning. For this nonsense, he complains, he must miss the chance of a damn good shoot at Bolsover? And all for bloody Liko? Now, in a corner of the carriage, he snores softly, all passion spent, for now at least. For the next three days, he will be the proverbial sore-headed bear. May's spirits sink at the thought of that, though they leap in every other way. She has hardly slept for nights. But she must be careful. Do not give them anything to see.

Liko is waiting at the door as their carriage rolls into the great quadrangle.

'She's ill again,' he cries, before he has hardly said hello. 'Would you believe it? For a woman who's built like a shire horse and given birth to three strapping children, she seems to have the constitution of a gnat. Georgie, I must borrow your wife tonight.'

Poor Beatrice, it seems, is due to take Liko to the theatre in town; a precursor to his formal dinner tomorrow. A new play, much talked about. He has so been looking forward to it. Might May go in her place? He knows how much she likes these things too. Her lady and his own equerry will of course come also. Dear May must be tired from her journey and going all the way back into town is so much to ask, but do say yes, dear May.

She looks to Georgie. He shrugs with that exasperated expression he has when he cannot comprehend the enthusiasms of others, but he does not refuse permission. May's heart races. She has less than an hour to change. An evening gown is snatched from her trunks and the creases stretched out. Her hair is rearranged and her jewels chosen. When all is done, her exhausted dresser near passes out in the servants' hall and has to be revived with a small brandy.

By eight-thirty, May is in a box at the Haymarket with Liko beside her, holding the bouquet intended for Beatrice, the applause and 'bravos' of their welcome ringing in her ears. She still blushes at this sort of thing, though less than she once did. But every blush she sees as a failure. Stop it at once, she tells herself. It is your due, your right no less. It is who you now are. And besides, when they were on the island, did Liko not chastise her for her blushes? Such an affectation, he had said. Would Gloriana ever have blushed?

'I'm so very pleased you've come,' he whispers. 'It is the making of my birthday.'

'Don't exaggerate,' she replies from behind her fan. 'You're such a terrible flirt Liko dear.'

The smile fades from the handsome face.

'I've never flirted with you in my life,' he says. 'Not once.'

The dashing cavalier dwindles into a little boy whose gift has been carelessly rejected.

When the house lights go down and the curtain goes up, it is quite dark in the box, lit only by two dimmed gas lamps on the rear wall. But even the grandest perch in the theatre is a cramped little nest. Her lady and his equerry are squeezed in behind them.

The gilded chairs are close together. Before long, through the folds of her gown, she senses the gentle pressure of his leg against hers. Just as it had at the kitchen table in the Swiss Cottage. Her breathing grows faster. The sweat breaks out on her neck and under her arms. She fans herself and when she lowers it again, lets the fan rest against her thigh.

Then it happens. His hand softly envelops her own. The spreading folds of her gown conceal the misdemeanour from the eyes of the pair sitting behind them. Now his hand squeezes hers. She feels something well up in her breast, like the call of some bird trapped and fluttering, yearning for release. Only with the greatest effort does she prevent its escape. Then, as quickly as the hand has come, it is gone again.

In the intermission, they withdraw to a small room behind the box where refreshments are laid out. The playwright is brought to be presented. She is glad of this diversion; she does not know how she could look directly at Liko and make vapid pleasantries, no idea at all. She sees him slip out of the room. A demand of nature no doubt. She is glad of that too. And yet, in the same second she sees him go, she longs for his return. The sight, the smell, the touch of him. Dear Lord, she asks herself, what are you thinking of? Does the instability of her father's nature course through her own veins too? She pictures dumpy Beatrice, marooned in the castle with a big red nose, sneezing into the soup.

Then he is back. But not alone. A man and woman follow him into the little room.

'I've brought an old friend to see you,' says Liko.

Harry Thaddeus Jones bows low before her.

'My dear Mr Thaddy! How pleased I am to see you.'

She cannot help the smile that lights up her face. But Mr Thaddy is not smiling. He is nervous, hesitant, the braggadocio of the Villa I Cedri quite absent. She has not seen him since the day he came to sketch her and the little prince. The sketches that never were. He kisses her hand.

'It's been far too long,' she says. 'Dear Mama was wondering about you just the other day. What *have* you been up to?'

He tells her something of his latest commissions. Yet another Pope, he says. But still no smile. He clears his throat.

'May I present my wife?' he asks.

Only now does May focus on the woman who hovers behind him. A flutter of panic comes to her throat. She glances at Liko, puffing on his cigar. A wisp of amusement floats among the smoke. She knows he is waiting to see what she will do. Poor Mr Thaddy is blinking rapidly; a muscle twitches below his eye.

But the woman herself is unperturbed. She bobs the slightest of curtseys and steps forward without hesitation. The scandalous Eva. The woman who has divorced her husband and left three daughters behind; banished by her own family and, it is said, well paid to keep her distance. She is plain-featured, flat-chested and her nose could be used to cut cheese. Yet her head is held high and there is something more. Anyone can see that at once. Indeed there must be, May thinks. How else did she attract the sybarite who once caroused in the back alleys of Florence and painted the prostitutes of Santa Croce? There is an impregnability about Eva Thaddeus Jones. Perhaps the attraction lies in the challenge of trying to find a way in.

As the woman comes closer, May feels Eva's gaze upon her. Like Liko, Mrs Thaddy is judging her in this moment. Testing her mettle. Instinctively, May knows that her rank will not figure in the evaluation.

'Mrs Jones,' she says.

She offers her hand. The woman takes it carelessly, as if it is of little value. May mentions Madame Bricka, their mutual friend, and the teas she and Eva take together at Fortnums.

'A clever lady,' replies Eva. 'So refreshing to come across one such. And so unusual too.'

The muscle below Mr Thaddy's eye is still twitching. May can see that he would prefer not to be here, not to be in her company and it hurts her. Then she wonders if his discomfort is more than that. Have the sacrifices he has made for this woman, his cavalier disregard for the world's view of them, perhaps even a sort of liberation from that same world, not led to the happiness which he had assumed these would bring? Had the hoped-for liberation even turned out to be precisely the opposite? Eva Thaddeus Jones slides her arm through that of her husband, embedding her sharp, painted fingernails into the black silk arm of his evening tailcoat.

May recalls the words of the note he had sent to her after the sketches that never were. He could not find her, he had said; she had gone from him. And now the roles are reversed. It is not her Mr Thaddy that stands before her, but someone who is somehow lesser.

The conversation in the little room behind the theatre box stumbles then falls. But they are saved by the bell; the intermission over.

'Might Mr and Mrs Jones not join us in our box for the next act?' asks Liko. 'What do you think May?'

May's panic rises again. What is he doing?

'Well it *is* rather cramped,' she says. 'I wouldn't wish them to be uncomfortable.'

'Nonsense. We can banish our people to another place. What do you say, Mrs Jones?'

'Most kind,' says Eva, looking at May with an eyebrow half raised.

Harry Thaddeus Jones stops being nervous. Suddenly he becomes himself again. He raises a hand, the palm flat out, like a policeman stopping a hansom cab from committing a misdemeanour.

'Thank you sir, but we'll not be putting you out.'

'It's no trouble at all, old friend,' says Liko.

'It might be fun, Harry dear; our own seats are not ideal,' says Eva, her eyes still fixed on May.

'No thank you, sir. It's very civil of you right enough, but we'll not be imposing upon you. We will return to where we're meant to be.'

Mr Thaddy slides out of his wife's grasp. He takes May's hand and raises it to his lips. Now at last she gets the smile she wanted. That big, broad Irish smile which, in another time, lit up her heart.

'I still have your portrait of me in the garden,' she says quietly. 'I see it nearly every day.'

'I often see it too,' he replies, tapping his forehead. 'I will always see it.'

May leans forward and kisses both his cheeks.

'Goodbye, Mr Thaddy.'

'Goodbye, May Flower.'

The exit to the corridor is closed on Harry and Eva Thaddeus Jones. The bells ring more insistently. The orchestra is tuning up again. Liko and May stand, several paces apart, looking at the doorway.

'Why didn't you back me up?' he asks.

'You know why,' she replies.

'Such a stupid world,' he says. 'Why does it condemn them?'

'I suppose for the pain they've caused to other people.'

'But think how brave they are,' he says. 'Don't you admire that?'

'Yes I do. And I wish them happiness, if they can find it.'

Liko stubs out his cigar.

'It looks to me that they have found it already. Her eyes sparkled when she looked at him. Didn't you notice?'

It was true. When husband and wife had left the room, her arm again through his, Eva had glanced over her shoulder at May Teck, with a smile which contained something like triumph.

'But his eyes did not,' replies May. 'Didn't you notice that too?'

'Stupid bloody world,' Liko says again.

'But the one in which we must live. Especially people like us.'

'Must we be so different?'

'Yes,' she says. 'It seems we must.'

The words leave her mouth like teeth reluctant to be pulled; each one a tiny agony. They look at each other. Her heart lurches. It is said.

Applause welcomes them back into the auditorium. They stand there, smiling and giving their little waves. How amazing, she thinks, that I can do this. Now. In this minute. But she knows quite well that she will be doing it for the rest of her life. And when, at the end, the doctor and the bishop arrive at her deathbed, will she still be doing it then? A smile and a little wave? To make them feel better, regardless of what she might be feeling herself.

In the box, they sit together side by side once more as the lights go down. After a little, the hand creeps through the folds of her gown and covers her own again. But this time, she does not return its gentle pressure and so it slips away.

And now, if anyone in the Haymarket Theatre is training their opera glasses on the royal box and not on the performance, their ravenous eyes will be rewarded by the sight of something quite remarkable. Illuminated for a moment by the stage lamps at their brightest, they will clearly see the face of May Teck. The good, sensible girl. The eminently suitable choice. Is that a tear spilling from the china-blue eyes, wending its way down a cheek as pale as alabaster. No surely not. It must just be a trick of the light.

XXXIV

Autumn, 1895

But there is a traitor in the Haymarket Theatre. Or at least a telltale tit. Some elderly countess who, as ill luck would have it, is due at the castle for luncheon the very next day. From behind her fan, she drops the poison into the ear of Aunt Queen, an old friend from the long-past days of Lord Melbourne. She herself, the countess claims, has never heard of Harry Thaddeus Jones or his scandalous spouse. It is her son, dutifully accompanying his desiccated mother to the play who, with his opera glasses, sees right through the royal box into the withdrawing room behind, recognises them at once and tells her all.

'Dear Raymond,' she explains, 'goes about much in artistic circles and is never mistaken in these matters.'

It is less than an hour before Beatrice knows and only slightly longer before Georgie does too.

'Where is Liko?' he asks, going from room to room like a bloodhound on a trail. But the quarry, alerted by some kind soul, is nowhere to be found. A servant reports a sighting of Prince Henry, cantering out through the southern gates onto the Long Walk.

'Heading for the hills, no doubt,' says Georgie to Aunt Queen. 'Well he can't stay out all night and I'll have him as soon as he's back.'

'Oh Georgie, do calm down,' snaps Aunt Queen, who has a toothache; the news of which has sent shudders down backs from the top of the Round Tower to the lowliest scullery.

'He may do what he likes with his own wife, but he has no right exposing mine to such a situation in public. It reflects very badly on me, Grandmama. As if I am not master in my own house.'

Aunt Queen is soaking a piece of gauze in a little Sevres bowl filled with oil of cloves.

'You're quite right of course, Georgie dear,' she sighs, 'but that's Liko. He can be such a wayward boy.'

'He's thirty-eight, for God's sake. Isn't it time he grew up? People here let him get away with far too much.'

It is an unwise sentence. Aunt Queen, toothache or not, pins him in her gaze like a butterfly to a wall.

'Well if *we* do, it's because he has charm. An attribute which goes a very long way in this miserable world. You could do worse than to study him.'

She opens her mouth to insert the gauze onto her gums.

'Now do toddle off, Georgie; there's a dear.'

For nearly an hour he stands at a southern window, peering down the Long Walk in the gathering dusk, drumming his fingers on the sill. Then, all at once, he knows what he will do. He orders a pony trap brought round to the quadrangle.

He finds her in their bedroom, writing letters. To her mother no doubt. Or that blasted Bricka woman. He tells her they are going out. She must put on her coat, and a scarf perhaps, for the evenings are chilly now.

'Where are we going?' she asks. 'My back is aching dreadfully today, Georgie. I'd really much rather stay here. Besides it's almost dark.'

'We're not going far,' he replies. 'A few minutes, no more. I've ordered the trap so you don't have to walk.'

They enter the great chapel of St George through the side door. Evensong is over. The organ has wheezed to a halt. The choirboys are already having their tea and toasted crumpets. Only a couple of minor canons are still there to receive them, their faces surprised and uncomfortable, anxious even. Most of the candelabra have been snuffed out, but a few are still lit in the choir and at the high altar. The anxious faces are told that all that is required of them is their absence. Right now. Go away.

There is bowing and fussing and scuttling. Somebody trips over a chair in his haste to get away; the clatter is enough to wake the dead beneath their feet. Georgie stands at the high doors between the nave and the choir and waits till not a sound can be heard beyond their own breathing.

'Why are we here, Georgie?' May asks.

He gives her no answer. He closes the high doors, takes her arm and marches her down the aisle between the stalls of the Garter Knights, across the tombs of the eighth Henry, sad Queen Jane, headless Charles and the poor mad king who was her own great-grandfather. This time, she has no chance to walk respectfully around it as she did on that childhood day, the second-best bridesmaid at the back of the queue. Now it is as if she herself is the bride again as her groom half drags her towards the altar. And in this impression she is not mistaken. When they reach the altar steps, Georgie falls to his knees and tries to pull her down alongside him.

'Kneel,' he says.

Kneeling is difficult for her now and she stifles a yelp as she sinks onto the hard stone steps. At first Georgie says nothing, simply stares ahead at the cloth of gold and the great crucifix shining in the flickering light of the candelabra. God, what now?

'Do you remember the vows we made?' he asks at last.

'Yes.'

'No, I mean do you remember them *exactly*?'

'Perhaps not word for word.'

'Well I do. I learned them by rote before the day. I was terrified of messing it up in front of all those people. I even learned your responses too, so I wouldn't mix them up with my own. Silly really, but I've still not forgotten them.'

He pauses now. May glances at him. The face is florid as usual, a vein pulsing in his forehead.

'I want you to repeat these vows now. Here before God.'

'What? But God has already heard them. I doubt He needs to do so again.'

'Perhaps, but does God not see all things too? If so, He will have seen that you may not have kept those vows you made.'

'That is nonsense, Georgie.'

'Is it? Well, I pray to Him fervently that you've kept at least some of them.'

He turns to look at her now. The red lips are quivering.

'Well have you?'

'I have kept every one of them,' she says.

'In your heart?'

'Not always in my heart perhaps. But I'm trying Georgie.'

'Then you must try harder,' he replies.

'Yes. I will.'

'So there is no impediment?' he asks. 'No impediment to the duty you must owe to me?'

The muscles of her back are screaming now. Inside her belly his second child kicks to remind her to give the right answer. She looks straight at the crucifix, takes a deep breath and begs God to forgive her.

'There is no impediment.'

'Then I will play the priest. Repeat the words after me.'

And so she does. For better or worse. For richer or poorer. In sickness and in health. To love, honour and obey. On that last, she is requested to repeat the line. When she does, he reaches over and takes her hand.

'If I were a strong man, I wouldn't care tuppence, you see. But I'm not. And I need to know that I can be always sure of you in everything I will be called upon to do, even if you do not agree with me. If not, God help me, for I will be quite lost.'

'Oh Georgie.'

He raises her gently to her feet.

'And I make a vow to you too,' he says. 'Here before God. I will never be like my father. I will never make you suffer like my poor mother has suffered. I'm not made like that. There will never be anyone else for me, Miss May. There will only ever be you.'

The candelabras are guttering now, the tiny flames dying one by one. The proud colours are fading from the golden altar cloth and the rainbow banners of the Garter Knights. On the great window above the reredos, the saints and the apostles silently retreat into the shadows.

'One day, when we have earned the right, you and I will rest here together,' says Georgie. 'Our parents will already be present and our children will come after us. All of us here. In this extraordinary place. Is that not wonderful?'

'Yes it is,' she replies.

'I always thought that was what you wanted.'

May Teck takes another deep breath.

'Yes Georgie,' she says. 'What I always wanted.'

He takes her arm and guides her back towards the high doors that lead to the nave. When he flings them open, it is to a dark and empty church. No well-wishers fill the pews, no joyous smiles or tear-filled eyes greet the appearance of the bride and groom. No rice will be thrown, no slippers tied to the back of the pony trap.

On a dank October night, this place no longer seems like the one she has held sacred since that distant morning when the sunlight thrust in through the high windows, like a dozen golden lances, onto her bridesmaid's dress and her wreath of jasmine and orange blossom. On that morning, May Teck had gazed up among the pillars into a vaulted infinity and believed that she saw the face of God. But tonight, as the last candles snuff out, it is chilly in here and not a little frightening. She pulls her coat more tightly around her and suppresses a shiver.

XXXV

Winter, 1896

The note is propped up against the salt and pepper. As is her reflex now, her brain flicks through what small crime she might have committed or, if nothing comes to mind, how she might have demonstrated commitment to her vows. Perhaps the shooting party yesterday. The rain was relentless and she was not yet quite over her cold but still she trudged out to meet the shooters for luncheon in that freezing tent. That must be it. That pleased him. Oh to hell, she will read it later. No papery life raft can rescue her from the lassitude she feels this morning.

The winter is almost as grim as that of four years ago which claimed poor Eddy. It cannot seem to make up its mind which form of misery to inflict upon them; alternating gales, downpours and squelching fields with fog, frost and the earth hard as marble, all good cheer buried deep beneath it. Ten days ago, on the awful anniversary, she went with Alix to lay some snowdrops on the little bed covered in the Union Jack. Already heaped with posies from the sisters, the household, the servants and the people on the estate, the bed looked like the very catafalque itself, dear Eddy buried somewhere underneath. Over time, she has trained herself not to think of him too often, but when she must, she is surprised how much she still mourns him.

At the breakfast table in the glum little villa, she wonders how she might pass one more sepulchral morning. Georgie has gone off to Holkham for another shoot. Dear Lord, the man is obsessed. When the time comes, she thinks, he will want his lifetime's bag inscribed upon his headstone.

The new baby's crying trickles down from the nursery. She sighs and spreads the butter on another slice of toast. She is grateful to God that this time was not quite as awful as the first. The birth not quite so dreadful, the feeling of her insides being torn apart not as terrifying, though, Christ knows, still bad enough. It is a second boy, so everyone is pleased with her. Is there anything more ridiculous in all humanity than the notion that the mother has some control over the gender of her child? Anyway, Aunt Queen is delighted. Never before, she writes to May, in the history of the kingdom has there been a monarch with three generations of male successors neatly lined up like a queue for an omnibus. And now a spare too, in case anything terrible might happen, as it did with poor Eddy. A diamond pendant is sent to the glum little villa from the castle above the Thames.

But, as before, dark intruders broke into May Teck's mind as soon as her body had done its duty. Again, she turned her face to the wall. Again the doctor was unable to explain to the new father why the new mother was not dancing with joy, hopelessly in love with the tiny thing in the bassinet. This time though, the process, for such she now recognised it to be, was an abyss of lesser depth. She could just about see the pinprick of blessed light somewhere high above her and, day by day, was able to pull herself up towards it. But, once more, she will reach it bruised and bleeding; the wounds will take time to scab over.

From the towering mountain of telegrams and letters, the private ones were excavated and brought to her. From a ship somewhere off the west coast of Africa, a message came.

'Keep sailing on,' it said. 'Whether the wind is with or against you, it always changes sooner or later.'

Liko Battenberg has gone to fight the Ashanti, who are causing trouble yet again. Making human sacrifices and being impertinent to their imperial masters who, after all, simply want the best for them, if only the stupid natives could see that. He begged Aunt Queen to let him go, to let him be a soldier like he used to be in Prussia, even just for a few weeks. He promised to be sensible and careful and not to end up being boiled in a pot. Goodness, he said, he would only be going as secretary to the British commander-in-chief. Besides it was hardly a war at all, just a spot of bother. He would likely encounter more danger on the streets of Cowes on a Saturday night. At first, Aunt Queen refused to allow such a thing. She couldn't possibly spare him. But dumpy Beatrice, wiser than she seemed, pleaded on his behalf. More than once, his wife has overheard the remarks about the removal of Liko's *cojones*. So permission was given. When the departure day came, poor Beatrice's eyes were sore with weeping, but Liko's blazed with excitement. Freedom. Even if only for a little while.

Still May Teck thinks of him every single day. The thing is in the past now, she tells herself. A bit of madness when, for just a while, she lost her compass, when she even wondered if chaos and disorder might sometimes be good things out of which some greater meaning might be found. Thankfully, on both sides, good sense soon prevailed. So that is that. Only of course it is not and never will be.

She sent a telegram back to the ship, aware that other eyes would see it.

I pray the wind will always be with you.

The windows of the dining room are still half-misted with early rain. The life she lives here is far quieter than the one she passed at White Lodge, the spinster daughter almost on the shelf. At least there she was needed, indispensable even, to the business of doing good works. Here, the good works are entirely the province of the big house. When in residence, Alix and the awful Wales girls guard them fiercely as if, in this far-flung sliver of England, they fear there is not enough adulation to go around. But it is here that Georgie is happiest, there is no doubt of that, quite fulfilled by his vacuum of an existence. What, she wonders, do I have to do to reach that sun-drenched plateau of contented pointlessness? Is that to be the great question of my life?

As if in answer, the mist on the window begins to evaporate beneath a beam of midwinter sun. She really must go out. Some air, some light, even for a little while, must surely help her spirits. Her maid wraps her up and sends her forth. She follows her usual route, past the little lake, along the twisting paths till she comes out on the far side of the park near the tiny church where they worship every Sunday and where Eddy lay four winters ago before they took him away to the great chapel above the Thames.

From here, she can spy across the lawns into the windows of the big house. There seem to be a lot of comings and goings for this time of day. Shadowy shapes are bustling about, moving from room to room. She wonders why, but gives the place a wide berth, as she always does unless it is unavoidable. As usual she heads for her retreat, the little Buddha at the far end of the avenue of pleached limes. She reaches for the cigarettes in her pocket.

Damn and blast. Two figures are already there, sitting at the feet of the Buddha. Dressed in black. How strange. It is the sisters, Toria and little Maudie. It is too late to turn back; they have spotted her and are already advancing. As they come closer, they hold handkerchiefs to their eyes.

'Isn't it just awful?' says Toria.

'What? Why are you in black?'

'Why do you think?' asks little Maudie. 'And why aren't *you*?'

'But who has died?' asks May.

'Didn't Georgie leave you a note?' asks Toria. 'He looked in on us all before he went off to Holkham. He shouldn't have gone shooting of course, not in these circumstances. Naughty Georgie.'

It is in her pocket. She takes it from its envelope and unfolds it. The sisters start to sob again.

A telegram has come from Africa. Liko Battenberg is dead. Malaria. Never cared for him much, but jolly bad luck all the same.

Somewhere, from a distant planet, May Teck hears the weeping of the sisters. It seems distant because her ears have started to ring and her legs to tremble. She must get back to her room while she still can, though God knows how she will manage it. She already knows that she cannot speak. How long might she have left before she cannot stand? Thirty seconds, a minute? She must get back to her room. Dear Lord, she prays, give me that comfort at least. She turns on her heel and walks away, as steadily as she is able, back along the avenue of pleached limes, their naked branches thrown up into the sky as if in lamentation. Despite the ringing in her ears, she hears a comment come from behind her.

'Cold-hearted bitch,' says Toria.

As May struggles to reach her sanctuary a fresh bank of filthy clouds rolls in from the German Ocean, defeats the feeble sunshine and parks itself over the two ugly houses on the dead fields of Norfolk.

XXXVI

Winter, 1896

'I'm coming home,' she telegraphs to her mother within minutes of stumbling back into the glum little villa.

A note is scribbled to Georgie. Her mother is distressed and needs her, she says. Within the hour, a bag is packed and the carriage brought round. In mourning weeds, she goes up to the nursery and kisses the boys goodbye. The little prince looks frightened by the spectre in the doorway. He clutches at the skirts of his nurse, giving her the strange look she has noticed lately, as if he knows her face but is not quite sure who she might be.

By luncheon, she and her lady-in-waiting are on the train to London. She is fond of this lady, but now she has to dissemble. She will be expected to show sadness of course, a degree of grief even, but there is a boundary she must observe and not cross. Yes, she says, how frightful it is for poor Beatrice and those dear children, fatherless so young. And yes, how happy Prince Henry had been at the prospect of serving his adopted land in its valiant struggle against the heathen and ungodly. The good Lord moves in mysterious ways, says the lady. To stifle the conversation, May closes her eyes in pretence of sleep. But then, God is merciful and allows her a little of the real thing; a blessed half hour of forgetting before she reawakens to face the truth of it. When she opens her eyes, her lady is watching her with a worried expression.

'Are you all right, Ma'am?'

'Yes my dear, thank you.'

Her lady is unconvinced.

'In your sleep, you spoke his name,' she says.

'Whose name, dear?'

'The late prince, Ma'am.'

May feels her stomach tighten. How careful she must be. Quickly, she arranges her features, an art at which she is becoming ever more adept. It will surely serve her well now. Even so, she cannot bring herself to dismiss his loss as if it is of no more than passing consequence.

'He was a kind friend to me,' she says.

'Of course, Ma'am. Everybody loved the prince.'

'They did,' May Teck replies, 'didn't they?'

Once in the city, she stops off at the old palace of St James's. Here, her lady is abandoned. She will go alone to Richmond Park, May says. No arguments, dear. Get yourself an early night, you must be tired.

It is long since evening by the time she reaches White Lodge. As the carriage rolls across the dripping park, she looks as always for the first sight of the friendly lights of its windows, but tonight there are none. The shutters are closed, the curtains drawn firmly against the night. Still, she has never been so glad to see the portico loom up out of the darkness. Tonight she would have crawled on her hands and knees to reach it.

Beneath the lamp in the porch, the black-clad figures wait to greet her. Her parents and Madame Bricka are pleased to see her as always. Their lives, since she left them, are the ghosts of what they once were. But they are surprised by her arrival too and do not hide it. They have prepared the large room in which she gave birth to the little prince, but she asks instead for her childhood room high above the park. In fact she insists upon it, she says. She will make up the bed herself if she has to.

At supper, she eats nothing beyond a little soup and bread.

She makes the excuse that her tummy is not yet recovered from the birth. The conversation is on one topic. The Duchess sheds many tears. Does May remember that wonderful day on his yacht? When darling Liko let her take the wheel? What fun it was. How they will all miss him. What a tragedy! Yet her mother's tears are unremarked upon because they are unremarkable. Mary Adelaide cries at the sight of a fallow deer with a limp. How May Teck yearns for that same release, except that hers would shake the old walls of White Lodge, loosen it from its foundations and set it adrift on a sea of scandal and sensation. She catches Madame Bricka watching her. Bricka knows her far better than the Duchess ever has. And Bricka, she is quite certain, is not fooled by dry eyes.

'It is wonderful to see you, *Princesse*,' she says, 'but why today? And in such sad circumstances.'

'Do I need a reason to return?' May replies. 'I just had a great ache to see you all and to sleep tonight in my old home, in my dear old bed.'

And so she does. And indeed it brings her comfort. When the house is stilled and silent, she stands in her nightgown at the window. The rain has cleared away now and the winter moon shines a pale wash of light over the park. She hears an owl in the big crumbling oak just beyond the garden gates. A little way down Queen's Ride, a shadowy shape moves from the cover of the bracken. It stops right in the middle of the bridle path and stares up at the house. Is it a man? A poacher? Then the moonlight catches the tips of the antlers as it shakes its great head. Does it see her at her window? Is that why it stops? It stands stock still for a minute, watching the house, then paws the ground a few times and canters off down the slope till it dissolves into the trees. She wonders why it is not asleep in the woods with the rest of its herd. Why is it pacing the night? Has something dreadful befallen it too? Does it hardly know which way to turn? Does it seem to it that all hope is gone and that nothing fine will ever happen again?

The fire in the grate is dying and a chill comes on the room. Without drawing the curtains, she melts into her little bed. Through the long hours, she lies and watches the light of the moon creep slowly across the dressing table, the wardrobe, the small bedroom chairs, the framed photographs on the shelf. She runs her fingertips over the dips and lumps of the mattress; every one familiar. The bed seems smaller now or perhaps she has simply outgrown it. How wonderful it would be to shrink down, like Alice, and feel the bed grow bigger and bigger until she is lost in the vast expanse of it, no bigger than a piece of fluff on the blanket which nobody will ever notice is there.

She aches to sleep but is afraid of it too. What pictures will come to her? The happy ones in which she herself will feature? Or the others, all the more awful for being imagined: the day he first shivers under a tropical sun, the tiny, fetid cabin on an unknown ship, the moment he knows he will never come home? In the event, when a brief oblivion does come, there are no pictures at all. Just an overwhelming, blessed darkness.

When Pilgrim brings her tea in the early morning, May wonders if the girl can tell, if she can see straight through even the most careful disguise. After all, Pilgrim already knows about death. May need not wonder long. The girl is nearly silent, but her eyes speak. When she passes May the tea cup, there is the slightest of pressures from her hand.

'I see you've not brought much with you Ma'am,' she says. 'Will more of your things be coming out from St James's?'

'I've not thought about it. I came in a hurry.'

'There are some of your old dresses still in the wardrobe here. Her Grace says she can't bear to part with them. Shall I choose one for you?'

'But it must be black. I shall just wear yesterday's again.'

After a clear night, the drizzle is speckling the window again. Her legs feel like an elephant has slept on them all night long.

When she tries to rise from the bed, she sags back down upon it. She drinks the tea and nibbles at the biscuit in the saucer, then puts on her robe and sits at the mirror. She looks ghastly; her eyes puffy, her skin pale but clammy to the touch. She must take a warm bath, throw cold water onto her face and then go down to breakfast. The thought of it is grim, but it will be done. And then what? The necessary letters must be written to Aunt Queen and, obviously, to Beatrice. My God, what will she write to Beatrice?

On her way to the bathroom, with little thought, she opens the door of the wardrobe to see which of her young dresses her sentimental Mama has kept. And then she sees it. The surprise takes her breath away. She grips a chair to steady herself. It is the scarlet dress from the *tableau vivant*. How in heaven's name did it get here? It seems like an intruder from another world, a time and place of blinding happiness. It is the dress before which Liko had bowed down and spread his cloak in the mud. The dress she had worn when, for a minute or two, she was Gloriana and she had been worshipped.

She lifts it down from the rail. The scent of the perfume she had used on that summer evening clings faintly to the fabric. She holds the gown against her body and stands before the long mirror. In doing so, she is ruined. All hope of containment is gone. May Teck, the good, sensible girl, is no more.

The scarlet dress falls from her grasp. She staggers from the room, down the servants' stairs and out into the feeble daylight of the garden. She does not see where she is heading. She merely runs, as fast as her leaden legs will allow. She unlocks the garden gates and stumbles out into the park. It is cold, but she does not feel it. It is wet, but she does not notice. All she wants is to run. The hems of her robe and the nightgown underneath are soon sodden from the grass and torn on the bracken. Her slippers turn to a velvety mush. Her hair, loose on her shoulders, is weaved by the hated wind into rats' tails. Yet still she runs, down the long grassy slope towards Pen Ponds, shouting curses at God. Only here does she stop, the water's edge a barrier around which she has no more energy to struggle. She is gasping for air, her breasts heaving against the drenched, thin fabric of her robe, her eyes no longer wet, but wide open as if in disbelief at what is happening to her.

Now she wonders if the water is truly a barrier? Might it not be a portal? The ponds are bordered all around by a jungle of reeds but, here and there, are small patches of sandy ground, where fishermen throw out their lines and her brothers once launched rowing boats in the summer to reach the tiny islands in the middle. On one of these patches, May Teck now finds herself. The water is dark, almost black; the breeze scalloping the surface, wavelets breaking against the banks. It is shallow, she knows that; yet it is deep enough. As the thought crosses her mind, she begins to weep again at the very horror of it. Then the shivers invade her. Just as he must have done when the illness first took him into its grip. Oh how cold she feels. Could the black water in front of her be that much worse?

Among the long grasses that fringe the water, the mandarin ducks take shelter from the weather. Now one or two begin to squawk and soon, like a chorus, it seems as if a hundred of them join in. The cacophony throbs in May's head as the tears spill down her face. At first, in the maelstrom of her mind, she does not notice the other noises trying to push their way in. Voices are calling her; distant at first, then ever closer. As she rocks backwards and forwards on her feet, she does not bother to turn and look. Then, suddenly, arms are round her; a thick cloak is draped across her shoulders, frightened eyes look into hers, wanting to comprehend. Madame Bricka and Pilgrim try to pull her back from the edge of the pond on to firmer ground, but she pushes them away. The gesture alarms them even more, because now they understand all too well.

Madame Bricka, stout and winded from running, takes a few steps back. She stands as still as she did on that day long gone when she had bearded the stag. Now she uses that stillness, not to repel but to embrace. She opens her arms wide.

'*Princesse, viens a moi.*'

At first, May Teck does not budge. Then, slowly, quivering like an aspen, she steps back from the water and falls into the strong, enfolding shelter.

Step by slow step, the tutor and the little maid half carry May Teck back up the grassy slope to the house. Her mother, pacing to and fro at the garden gates, hurries out to meet them. The first flush of relief on the nectarine cheeks pales at close sight of her child. The daughter who has given her everything of which she dreamed. Gloriana in waiting.

'Oh May,' she cries. 'What have we done to you?

XXXVII

Winter, 1896

It never happened. It never happened at all. By now, the wind and rain have obliterated the footprints in the sand at the water's edge and on the grassy slope. The garden gates are firmly locked again. If any servant caught a glimpse from an upper window or through a half-open door, he or she will never say. They will whisper of it among themselves of course. They will remember till their dying day the time the daughter of this noble house was smuggled back to her room like some broken doll. But they will never breathe a word beyond these walls.

In the room itself, the tutor and the maid dry and warm her and ease her gently into the little bed. There is much fussing and flapping. Her parents are almost hysterical. The local doctor must be sent for, cries the Duchess. Heavens above, it is less than six weeks since she gave birth. The Duke keeps rambling about poor Queen Jane. One motherless prince was bad enough back then, but might there now be two? And then he laughs, as he so often does these days, without reason and at the most inappropriate moments.

The doctor, a blunt old cove who has seen everything, tells them all to calm down. May Teck, he says, is of strong stock. You've only got to look at her. Strong, sweet tea and a few hours' sleep is the only medicine required. For everyone else, he prescribes a large brandy and gets back into his carriage. He too can be trusted;

his practice built on their patronage. When his wife asks tonight what took him to White Lodge, he will simply grunt that it was woman's trouble. That's all. Nothing of importance.

The old cove is right, though. In a few hours, May Teck finds herself again, or at least enough of herself to function. In truth, it is the fussing and the flapping of her parents that quietens her. She has been used to their melodramas all of her life, and if she is calm, they become so too. Such is the way of it. Thus the house in the park settles again. As usual, the rooms are dusted and swept. The dogs are walked and the horses exercised up and down Queen's Ride. Letters and invitations are answered and the demands of the Needlework Guild not entirely neglected. In the kitchens, the cook is chopping the heads off chickens. It must be a faultless meal tonight. Their princess's husband is coming to dine then take her back to the old palace. They know too well what a stickler he is. More than once, he has sent dishes back. A pain in the arse, says the cook under her breath.

A telegram arrived from Norfolk late last night after May had trudged up to bed. Her hand trembling a little, the Duchess opened it though it was addressed to her daughter. 'What on earth is going on?' the telegram asked gruffly. Was his wife there? Was somebody else dying? He would arrive tomorrow evening in time for an early dinner. Afterwards, they would both return to St James's.

While May Teck flits in and out of sleep, Madame Bricka slips into the room to watch over her. How good it is, when she opens her eyes, to see dear old Bricka sitting by the fire, book in hand. May reads less now than she did in the old days down in the white sitting room. It seems to her she does everything less now. Lives life less. Except of course in the losing of her heart.

Madame Bricka comes and sits on the bed and strokes May's cheek with her fingertip, in that strange way of hers.

'I wish you would stay here for a while,' says Madame Bricka. 'Until your spirits are a little better.'

'I must go back with him tonight. I have no choice.'

'Well. I warned you, remember? In the great chapel at Windsor, before you were married. Be careful what you wish for.'

'I told you there was something else I wished for too,' replies May. 'That I wanted the chance to feel love? Well I got that after all. It just wasn't where I expected it to be.'

'And I wanted it too, remember?' says Madame Bricka. 'At least you found it. Even for a while. At least you know what it's like.'

'And I know too that it is in me. The ability to love. I'd been so afraid that it wasn't.'

'Then do you think you can learn to re-direct it? To the place it is supposed to go?'

May turns her head away, gazes into the flames of the fire.

'I don't know. Not yet, I think. In time perhaps.'

Madame Bricka flares her nostrils like an angry horse.

'How feeble they are, these men,' she snorts. 'Yet husbands expect wives to see them as gods, do they not? Your problem, *ma pauvre*, is that you've married a man whom half the world will one day believe to actually be one. And what pray, is the solution to that dilemma?'

'Oh shut up, Bricka dear, and give me a cigarette.'

For a while, they sit smoking quietly together as they have done so many times, their breathing almost as one.

'I could never bow down to any man,' says Madame Bricka. 'Never accept that he is intrinsically better than me. Just couldn't do it and that's that. Which is why I'm a spinster lady working as a secretary in somebody else's house, instead of having my own.'

'And was that the right decision?'

'For me, yes,' replies Madame Bricka. 'Except for the children of course. I've come to realise what I have missed. The little prince has taught me that. I was quite wrong about the children.'

May Teck feels the familiar pulse of guilt. She turns away again and looks out through the window at the tops of the old oaks, each one as familiar as the fingers of her hand.

But Bricka is right about men, she thinks. All May's life, she has been surrounded by fragile men and valiant women.

But Liko did not conform to the pattern. He whom the other men looked down upon. The puppy-dog clinging to his wife's skirts. The master of the revels. Liko, suffocated by the life he led, was still stronger than any of them. Because, despite it all, he managed to do what Georgie had once told her none of their kind could ever achieve. To stay themselves. To hold on to whatever was their essence. Liko had managed it through his love for his children, his affection for his uninspiring wife, through the joy he found in guiding his boat across the wildest waves and safely into harbour. And had he, May wondered, in the crumbs of time they had spent together, also found fragments of himself in what he had felt for her? Had she given him that at least?

Again she pictures, as she so often does, the box at the theatre. When his hand had enclosed hers, when she did not return the pressure and so it slipped away. In the long procession of years to come, she will not forget the slipping away of the hand. The nothingness that it left behind in her. It will come back to her at the oddest moments when she believes herself contented enough; on a day when the sun is shining, when the newspapers have said something nice about her or she has been given some pretty new trinket to add to her countless collections of objects. Like a sickness once believed cured, it will strike again with double its force.

Now, in her old bedroom, she turns her face back into the pillow. Madame Bricka kisses the top of her head.

'Hush now, *Princesse*,' she whispers. 'You will survive this. I know you will. I've told you before, you are the best of all my precious girls, of all my half-children. Always the best of them.'

Madame Bricka throws on a few more coals on the fire. The rain is coming down again.

'Would you like me to read to you a little? Shall we journey into Barsetshire for a while?'

'No, not now. I don't think the books will work today.'

When May wakes again, the January afternoon is giving way to dusk and the room has darkened. A figure still sits by the fire, but it is her mother now, half asleep, the embroidery drooping from her fingers.

Not for the first time, May thinks how old and tired Mary Adelaide has become. Twice or thrice now, and without warning, she has fainted clean away. She has even lost some weight. Like a slow puncture on a bicycle, the ebullience seems to be leaving Fat Mary. The thing she wanted most from this life was given to her. Is the price to be paid that there is no longer any point to it?

May uncurls herself from the little bed and kneels down by the fire. She takes the embroidery from the wrinkled fingers and gently rests her cheek against her mother's knee. A hand stirs and softly strokes May's head.

'I'm sorry chick. I didn't realise how much you would feel the loss.'

'I rather think you *did*, Mama,' she replies, looking up now into her mother's face.

Mary Adelaide avoids her eyes, glancing nervously at the door, as if the entire household might have its ear to the keyhole. She leans close in towards the child in her lap.

'Dear God May, you will hold the highest position there is,' she whispers. 'I pray that nothing…'

'No Mama. Nothing,' she replies. 'Nothing at all. Yet, at the same time, everything.'

The Duchess leans back in her chair, closes her eyes and exhales a quiet sigh of relief.

'So the baby…? The baby isn't…?'

'Oh good heavens, Mama. Don't be ridiculous. Don't you know me at all?'

'Maybe I don't. Maybe I never have,' replies Mary Adelaide. 'I so wanted you to want what your Papa and I desired for you. What we desired for us all of course. To be right up there, near the head of the table. But perhaps we've committed a terrible cruelty.'

Whatever the truth of that, May cannot, will not, give her mother comfort. For a while, they sit in silence by the fire in the little room high above the park.

'Though when I really think about it, I can't be sorry that he touched your heart,' says Mary Adelaide at last. 'I was beginning to wonder if anyone ever would.'

'Mama, what a thing to say.'

'I'd prayed it would be Georgie of course, but I see now that is a fragile hope. So I cannot bring myself to regret that those feelings have come to you.'

'And nor do I. But oh, the ache now Mama.'

Again, May sinks her head into her mother's lap. Again, the Duchess strokes her daughter's hair. Despite the fire, there is a chill in the room now.

'It will all be fine, Mama,' she whispers. 'I know what I have to do now and I will never deviate from it. You may rest easy.'

After a while, the Duchess shoehorns herself out of the chair.

'I'd best take a proper nap now,' she says. 'Before Georgie comes to take you home.'

'This is home, Mama.'

'No May dear, it is not. It can never be that again.'

Mary Adelaide pauses in the doorway.

'You will find a way through this, May. Whatever it is, I pray it is one which will allow you to find some happiness.'

When her mother goes, May sits and thinks about what that way must be. But no debate is really required. She already knows the answer. She knew it on that night in the big house in Norfolk when she had found Georgie, drunk as a skunk, weeping on Eddy's bed. She remembers the terror in his eyes that night and the fright she had felt too, when the realisation of what she might have to do had first come to her with a merciless certainty. To lose herself in this little, ordinary man whom God had called. To be sacrificed on the altar of monarchy as the expression of God's will for the good of a wider humanity. Since that night, she had resisted, rebelled even, to keep hold of May Teck. For surely, if she lost herself, if she let the light within her flicker and fade, she would offend against God in a different way. Which is the greater and which the lesser sin? But that struggle must now be over. There is little doubt of the answer God wants and now she must give it without the slightest tremor of doubt or hesitation.

But not quite yet, she thinks. Not tonight anyway. She lights every lamp in the room. She rings for Pilgrim to run her a bath and help her to dress. She feels a little stronger now. Not quite yet, she says to herself again.

XXXVIII

Winter, 1896

As evening draws in, the winter chill wraps itself tighter around the old house in Richmond Park. Freezing rain hardens into snow.

An hour later, Madame Bricka taps on the door. Georgie has come and is taking sherry with her parents in the drawing room. The journey in vile weather has put him out of sorts, though he has made it clear he does not wish to linger long under this roof. If she does not hurry, May will be late for dinner. But though bathed, powdered and coiffured, she has not yet put on her gown.

'For once, they'll have to wait for me. They've never had to do so in my life, but tonight they will.'

A quarter-hour later, down in the inner hall, Georgie and her parents are still waiting. In mourning black, they stand in virtual silence, even Mary Adelaide, all conversation spent; though Georgie tries a remark about a potted plant which needs water. Then, with some sixth sense, they all look up.

May Teck comes down the staircase wearing the scarlet dress. Gloriana's ruffs and red wig are gone, but a choker of rubies circles her neck and pearls twinkle in her hair and hang from her ears. Liko's brooch is pinned just above her heart. She walks slowly down, never looking at the steps, but always straight ahead to some place both in the near distance, yet as remote as a star. It is as if she does not even notice they are there.

Georgie and her mother are frozen to the floor. The Duke

gives a wild laugh. Mary Adelaide takes a step forward, her hands clasped together in supplication.

'Good heavens May, what are you wearing? We are in mourning. You cannot possibly wear that. What about the servants? What are you thinking of?'

'I am thinking of the one we have lost,' she replies. 'Tonight, I wear this in remembrance of him.'

'But the dress is scarlet, dear. It will never do.'

'I wear this in remembrance of him,' she says again.

'You must go back upstairs and change at once,' says Georgie, finding his voice. 'It's a shocking misjudgement. Most unlike you.'

'Are you going to rip it from my back?' she asks. 'I think not.'

'Then go and change into something decent, instead of this... this abomination,' he says.

'I wear this in remembrance of him.'

May sweeps past them and into the dining room. She takes her usual place at the table and waits. Georgie and the Tecks walk slowly to their chairs. Not a single word is said. The servants come and go. Now and again, there is another peal of rogue laughter from her Papa. Each time, Mary Adelaide near jumps out of her skin. May sees her mother's great jowls quivering, the tired eyes filling up. She leans across to her father and strokes the back of his hand. Little is eaten; yet again, the cook's best efforts will be sent back to the kitchen.

When her wine glass is full, May raises it.

'To the dear departed,' she says. 'May God grant him the freedom in heaven he was denied in this life.'

As if the crystal goblets suddenly weigh a ton, the others slowly raise their glasses but do not repeat the toast.

'Did you all not hear me?' she asks. 'I say again, to the dear departed.'

The words are mumbled around the long table, then silence falls once more. She catches Georgie's eye for a moment, but he quickly turns away. How unattractive he looks. His skin is getting even worse; for the thousandth time, a piece of food is trapped in his beard. And is it her imagination or does he smell faintly of gunshot? She shudders.

At the end of the half-eaten supper, May rises and walks from the room without a word. In the scarlet dress, she climbs back up the staircase as slowly as she had descended it. Madame Bricka is waiting on a chair on the landing. In the little bedroom, Pilgrim waits too. The mourning dress is already spread out across the bed.

May stands stock still before the long mirror. Pilgrim removes the rubies and the pearls and the starfish brooch, then her fingers reach for the first hooks on the back of the dress.

'Stop. Wait a moment.'

May looks at herself in the glass. In the long life ahead of her, there will never be any shortage of rubies and pearls or robes of silk, satin and velvet, but she will never look quite like this again, not even with a crown upon her head. Never quite as magnificent as she does in this moment, this moment in remembrance of him. She stares into the glass for one long minute, then holds out her bare, swan-white arms.

'You may take it off now.'

Gloriana's gown is lowered to the floor, like a standard from a flagpole. Now she puts first one leg then the other into the dark chasm of black silk. Pilgrim lifts it smoothly up to the neck and begins to envelope her in hooks and eyes. Her hips and her breasts disappear, flattened out into propriety; the naked arms swallowed up by the leg-of-mutton sleeves.

'Goodness, how pale you've gone, Ma'am,' says Pilgrim. 'Are you quite all right?'

Her reflection tells her it is true. Somehow the scarlet dress had brought a little colour to her cheeks, but now it has vanished; her face as swan-white as her arms. But it is something more than that. Now she can see the skull beneath the skin. It is as if her face has been drawn in like her corsets; the features tighter, the bones more pronounced. For a moment, she glimpses what she may look like when she is old.

Pilgrim puts the final hook into the final eye and stands back. May goes on gazing at herself in the long glass. Now she thinks, I am immured. Suddenly, from the deepest well of memory, she remembers a tale Harry Thaddeus Jones had told her when they strolled past a crumbling convent in a shady backstreet of Florence. This is where, he said, nuns had once allowed themselves to be walled up inside tiny cells, to better devote themselves to the service of their Lord. Through a small slit in the brickwork, they were given just enough food and water to stay alive. Some went swiftly mad but many lived on for years, never seeing the sun or speaking to another human being until the day when the scraps of food would remain untouched, the wall would be broken through and a withered, stinking corpse at last pulled back into the light.

'Let that be a lesson to you, May Flower.' Mr Thaddy had laughed. 'No man is worth it.'

Now, as she recalls it, a wild terror invades May Teck in the bedroom high above the park. Her heart hammers in her breast and a sweat breaks out inside the mourning dress.

'*Princesse? Mon Dieu, que est que c'est?*' asks Madame Bricka.

In the mirror, May sees her terror reflected on the face of her friend.

'Nothing, Bricka dear. Really, it's nothing.'

To cool herself, she walks to the window and pushes up the sash. The lamps flicker in the rush of freezing air. May breathes in the winter's night, the smell of the blanketed ground and the bare, frigid woods. She breathes slowly, deliberately, imbibing the solace she only seems to find in this one tiny corner of the earth. She closes the window and looks around the little room. The scarlet dress hangs limp against the wardrobe door. She reaches out her hand as if to touch it. Her fingers hover an inch above the fabric, then the hand drops away.

Now her fingers gently brush the cheek of the little maid whom May saved from desolation, even when she could not save herself. Then she turns to her friend and places the lightest of kisses on Madame Bricka's lips; the first acknowledgement of what can never again be acknowledged.

When May Teck comes down the staircase for the second time, the trio awaits her once again. Georgie already has his coat and scarf on. He does not bother with the usual courtesies, does not kiss Mary Adelaide on the cheek nor shake the hand of the Duke. Instead he merely walks to the foot of the stairs and reaches out his arm.

'Good,' he says. 'That is much more appropriate in which to mourn Liko.'

'Oh no,' she replies. 'The scarlet dress was in mourning for Liko. This dress is in mourning for myself.'

She glances up to the landing where Madame Bricka stands, gripping onto the balustrade as if her life depended on it. May raises her black-gloved hand. A smile and a wave. She crosses to her mother, wrapping her in a tight embrace. The big body shakes against her own.

'I'm so sorry, chick,' her mother whispers.

'I told you, Mama. It will all be fine. Rest easy.'

May pulls back and cups her mother's tired face in her hands.

'But just one thing, Mama. From time to time, I should like you to think of me as I was.'

'Oh May.'

A loud cough behind her. She turns. The arm is still outstretched. They must leave at once, he says, or the road through the park will be impassable. On the very spot where she tore around on a tricycle and played hide and seek with her little brothers, May Teck sweeps down into her deepest curtsey, bows her head and does not rise.

Across the floor, the shoes of shiny crocodile creak towards her. Again, the hand reaches out for her to take. And when she does, it is a vice around her heart. Her Papa laughs once more and this time does not stop.

Georgie does not remove his arm from her until she is deposited inside the carriage. The snow has carpeted the ground. Apart from the whinny of the horses, there is no sound. The lamp in the porch casts a wan, jaundiced glow on the faces of the couple in the carriage. She leans her head back against the velvet seat and closes her eyes. Again, she longs for sleep.

'Please look at me, Miss May,' he says.

Her eyelids are as heavy as lead but she does it.

'I believe you've lately been in some other place,' he says. 'Somewhere very far from me. I don't need to know where. But I'm grateful that you're here again with me now.'

Once more, he stretches out his arm to her, yet this time it is quite different. Even in this light, she can see that his hand is trembling. In her heart, something shifts a little. Not much perhaps, but it is something nonetheless. She thinks of another hand that had reached out to her, in the shadows of a theatre. A hand she had not taken, a hand now cold as ice. And somehow, it is in memory of that dead hand that, in the shadows of a carriage on a cruel winter's night, she reaches out to take the one now offered.

As the carriage rolls away into the skeletal trees, the lamp in the porch is turned off and the doors of May Teck's home are locked behind her. She watches as the house curves from sight, now as deathly white as its name beneath the falling snow, a ghost from a time now barred to her.

From its hiding place beneath an ancient oak, a solitary, sleepless stag watches them go and bellows a farewell into the darkness.

*

It comes a few weeks later. After the ship has brought him safely home and he is already buried in the church on the island where he had been married and his beloved children christened. A letter from the ship's doctor arrives at the glum little villa; a letter which encloses a second letter. He knew he was dying, the doctor says, and used the very last of his strength to write to those for whom he had cared.

I am not coming home and will not see you again. My only comfort is the gallery of loving faces which I carry with me into the unknown. Yours is one of those, dear friend. Make me proud one day.

May Teck stands by the fire in her little boudoir, already dressed for dinner. She reads the words over and over until each of them is safe in her memory. She bows her head to the piece of paper in her hand then gently kisses it. For a moment, she holds it high above the flames before she lets it fall.

The gong sounds from below. She checks her appearance in the mirror. Her hair is in place, her jewels carefully chosen. The dress is one that is approved. Her back straight as always, she goes down the narrow staircase and walks towards the dining room. Her features show no trace of what has just happened to her heart.

An old dog must be put down, he tells her. So sad. An invitation has come for a shoot at Chatsworth. Always fine sport there, so they really must go. Poor Aunt Queen is having more trouble with her teeth. Speaking of teeth, that damn baby woke him up with its crying last night. What does the nurse think she's about? An auction is to be held for a coveted stamp; a rare Bermuda 1848. A small fortune of course, but he would die happy if he got it.

May Teck sips her glass of hock and lets her lips curve upwards into what can pass for a smile. Do not give them anything to see.

XXXIX

Winter, 1953

When the message comes, he is in America. He tells himself now that he should have gone sooner, though he is well aware of why he did not. In part, the belief that, like the Rock of Gibraltar, she would never sink. In part, the resentment still festering inside him, like the cancer which will one day claim him, just as it claimed his brother and is claiming her now.

In the glittering tower above Park Avenue, his wife is surprised by what she sees written on his face. Over the years, the face has become bland and unanimated, trapped in the aspic of boredom. But feelings so long submerged have woken again. His eyes dart to and fro, the muscles in his jaw twitch, he cannot sit still. Orders to minions are rapped out: a flustered valet packs suitcases, a secretary commandeers a seat on the evening flight from Idlewild, a car is ordered with a chauffeur not afraid to drive like hell over Manhattan Bridge in the rush hour.

They pad together across silent Waldorf carpets to the elevator. This evening, they are scheduled to dine with Cole Porter at Sardi's, but now she will go alone. She is dressed as he likes to see her; shimmering in his grandmother Alix's jewels, every inch the duchess he has made her, though of course that has never been enough for him. She deserves so much more, he thinks, which is why he gives her every ounce of the love inside him, the love for which he had never before found much use. Not once, not for a single second in the darkest pit of the night, has he ever regretted the giving of it. It is for this blessing, this absence of regret, that he thanks Providence, even more than he thanks it for the woman herself.

On the heaving sidewalk, separate limousines wait side by side, his and hers, the doors held open. She allows him to kiss her on both cheeks, then fixes him with those eyes of hers, hard as his grandmother's emeralds draped around her neck. There are nothing like emeralds, she likes to say, to hide the rings on a girl's bark.

'I know how difficult this is for you,' she repeats for the fifth time today. 'But remember that it's also an opportunity. A new era. You must get what you can.'

He waves till her car is swallowed up by the snaking traffic. Instantly, he feels the chasm open up inside him, as it always does when they are separated, even for an hour or two when she goes to the hairdresser or to the lunches with the women in large hats at which men are not wanted, not even him.

His chauffeur says they must leave urgently. What an odd word that seems to him now. Urgency has been a stranger for so long. Nothing in his life need ever be done at more than a languid pace. Nothing in fact really need be done at all. As the car slides out into the swell of Park Avenue, he glances up at the tower of the Waldorf Astoria. A thousand pinpricks of light. Electric diamonds against the smoky grey-black velvet of the sky. And all around, on the broad avenues and boulevards, millions more. It is the city of diamonds and dazzle, of sharp edges and sharp elbows. It is the perfect setting for her. In Park Avenue, in the penthouses of Central Park West and the Upper East Side, in Sardi's and the Stork Club, they are both treated as monarchs of their little kingdom. Here, they are equally enthroned. That is why she loves it here. That is why they come.

At thirty thousand feet above the ocean, the display put on by the stars seems feeble after the diamond city. And soon, heavy cumulus bustles past the plane and rain splatters the window beside him. The wind is from the east and is against them all the way. He wonders if his mother has arranged it. One last rebuff. Pushing him from her, even now. He prays the plane will not hit a storm; ever since he can remember he has been petrified of thunder and lightning.

He orders a martini and tries not to think of what awaits him in London. Instead he rifles his recollection for any memory that does not pain him. But they are few and far between, fragments of another age. That hour before dinner in the glum little villa when she would receive him and his siblings in her boudoir. While they wound the wool for the mittens she knitted for the poor, she would read to them; some book she thought might improve their minds and so make them more interesting. With the intuition of a child, he had realised early that children bored her and he had willed himself to grow up as fast as he could. But the pencil marks on the door frame of the nursery made slow, painful progress. He would always be the 'little prince' and then, behind his back at least, the 'little man'. And he had never come to like books very much, though he had really tried, just as she had tried to be interested in him but never quite managed it.

Neither he nor his brothers and sister had ever really captured her heart. That seemed to lie elsewhere in a realm of which he knew nothing and, as the years passed, he began to wonder if such a place even existed. If it did, it was locked and shuttered, the key long since lost.

But still he remembers the cooking smells wafting up from the kitchen as he sat at her feet and wound the wool while she read, in her soft, low voice, of heroes and heroines, of noble deeds and selfless sacrifice. Yet often she would smile, and sometimes even laugh; that strange deep laugh that seemed to come from some other creature entirely. For a little while, she would raise the curtain on herself and let them peep inside. As if, when his Papa was not in the room, she had a different soul.

But then the heavy footsteps would be heard along the corridor and the curtain would fall again. The gentle voice would go silent and be replaced by the intruding one that boomed, hectored and criticised. And she would sit there, looking down at the book now closed and never defend them, never protect them from the onslaught of his words or of his hand. How the 'little prince' had longed for her to do that. Just once. But she never did. Why not, Mama?

As the plane battles the east wind and he sinks into a second martini, he can still see the light from the fire flickering in her hair and hear that voice. He is amazed how clear the picture remains. What a fragile wisp of memory, he thinks, weighing so lightly on the scale against all the other stuff. Yet somehow it survives, unscathed and unblemished. Something salvaged from the wreckage, not just of his childhood but of his whole bloody life.

The wind wins the battle. The plane is late and so is he. No courtier is there to meet him, no escort to speed his way. The old wound nips again. The cunts never let him forget he is nobody to them now. The traffic is thick on the Great West Road, there are pipe-laying works on Constitution Hill. He shouts at the driver and at once feels ashamed. Never ever be rude to the servants, she had always taught him and, as a rule, he never is. Princes must always be better than the rest, she had said, wagging her finger. Are they not chosen by God? Do you really want to let Him down?

When he reaches Marlborough House, the lamp outside is lit, but otherwise no light can be seen at any window. His stomach flips over. He strides in, through the lobby, into the Saloon, past small knots of people standing in darkened corners. Some drop their eyes at the sight of him, others bow or curtsey. One or two approach him, hands outstretched.

'Sir.'

He sweeps past them all, past the little lift with the seat of rose-red brocade and half runs up the staircase and along the upper landing. He sees her doctor, whose face he knows, outside her door, smoking a cigarette. The man flounders for somewhere to stub it out, but fails and must speak to him through a haze of smoke.

'Sir, I'm so sorry...'

'What?'

'About twenty minutes ago, sir.'

He walks into the dimly lit sitting room. It is so many years since he was last admitted to her private apartments that, even now, it feels like an intrusion. He passes the vast desk crammed with all her things. His eyes fall on the litter of framed photographs. There he is, an angel in a sailor-suit. She must have looked at it every day, right up to the end. How he wishes he knew what she was thinking as the shadows gathered round her.

The people in the room melt back against the walls and cede him his proper place. The eldest son. The first child of her body. The king across the water. For once, they accept him as the man he used to be.

The double doors to the bedroom are closed. He stares at them as if they are a barrier he can never cross. He wants to reach for the door handles, but his arms are frozen at his sides. The doctor, a kindly man, does it for him. Does he wish to be accompanied into the room? No, he will enter alone. Oh Christ.

Whatever distress has been witnessed in this chamber, whatever agonies or indignities, they are all gone now. She lies in the middle of the big bed, beneath the quilt of moss-green satin, all majesty intact. Her hands are folded across her breast, the nails manicured and varnished pale pink. She wears one of her pretty lawn nightgowns; the golden wig fixed firmly in place. Is it his imagination or does the wrinkled face look smoother now? Is that what happens? Does death wipe away the evidence of your troubles and woes and allow you a last brief moment of earthly beauty before it takes you into the darkness?

She must be still warm, he thinks suddenly. An urge floods through him, to scoop her up in his arms before that warmth fades forever, to hold her close to him in a way never permitted in life. To hell with majesty. Fuck dignity. Let the golden wig fall off. Let the lawn nightgown be crumpled and sodden with his tears.

But the urge of the heart passes quickly, when the brain reminds him how she would hate any such thing. With this thought, rage fills him and drives him, for a minute or two, just a little mad. She will not be warm he decides; the ice in her veins will have chilled her in no time. Christ, the old bitch had *rigor mortis* half her life. Why, even near the end, could her spirit not have bent just a little, in imitation of her aged body? It would only have taken a few words to have bridged those sixteen years. Not the detached politeness of their occasional letters and even rarer meetings, but a few words of respect and acceptance for the woman he loved and for the choice he had made in refusing to settle for a life without her. A few words of compassion from a mother to a son. Everything would have been all right again; the past forgiven, the future, however short, richer than it had ever been before.

But oh no, duty had always come first. By the time he was old enough to vaguely grasp its meaning, she was chanting the mantra of duty. But when he had grown from boy to man, he had seen the price she herself had paid. Instead of the little word meaning everything to him, as she had hoped, it had come to mean absolutely nothing. A word as empty as the husk that now lies under the quilt of moss-green satin. So when the chance of some kind of love had finally come his way, he had not hesitated to grasp it, terrified that if he did not, he might suffer the same fate.

He sits down in a chair beside the bed and tries to still the pounding in his chest. He lights a cigarette; her people can say what they like, he doesn't give a fuck. She would have understood that impulse at least, he thinks. The cigarette calms him. But the rage ebbs only for the sadness to flow back. Now nothing can ever be resolved. The story of mother and son is set forever. There will be no happy ending.

As he smokes and watches over the body in the bed, he remembers the ankles. Such fine ankles she always had. Her best feature she used to say. On those distant evenings when he and his siblings sat at her feet winding the wool, she had sometimes displayed them, turning them this way and that for their perusal. Aren't they pretty, don't you think my dears?

Now, though it feels bizarre, indecent even, he lifts the edge of the quilt, the blankets and the sheets of fine linen. Hidden so much from the sunlight, there is not a mark on them. They might be the ankles of a seventeen-year-old girl. Incapable of kissing her face, he kisses them instead. The little prince had only ever wanted to be loved. And she had, after all, been the first woman whose love he had craved. Mama, he says out loud. And at last he weeps.

When he is able to leave, he strides past the people in the sitting room without a word. And then he sees it. The picture above the chimney piece. The girl in an Italian garden in a dress of creamy muslin and a straw hat with red ribbons. It stops him in his tracks. He knows it at once. It used to hang in the boudoir in Norfolk. He stands and stares at it for a long minute.

'I want this picture,' he says to nobody in particular.

'I'm sure that may be possible,' says some silken voice from a darkened corner.

'I want it now,' he says.

The silken voice protests politely that the correct procedures must be gone through, so he crosses to the fireplace and lifts it down from the wall. Seeing a shawl draped across an armchair, he snatches it up and wraps it around the canvas. It strikes him how the colour of the shawl matches the violets in the young girl's lap.

'Try to get what you can,' his wife said. But this, for now at least, is all he wants.

With the picture under his arm, he goes slowly down the stairs on which he and his brothers used to slide on tea trays whenever their Papa was safely elsewhere. In the Saloon, he pauses and looks about him. He will not return to this place. For all he cares, the earth can open up and consume it like the House of Usher. He climbs into the waiting car and does not look back.

Soon the girl in the straw hat will find a new home. She will live with her son on the wall of his bedroom in a mansion in the Bois de Boulogne. The place which, after the years of wandering, after all hope of some meaningful existence is gone, he finally manages to call a sort of home. His wife rarely comes into this room, so it is just the two of them. His bed is positioned so that she is the last face he sees at night and the first in the morning. And when, nearly twenty years later, he lies dying in this bed, it comforts him to know that she is there.

But now, in the harsh new century, decades after they have all been turned to dust, in the golden chapel of his forefathers, a quite different image rests beside that of his Papa. On a mattress of marble, they are sculpted in flowing folds of stone; she in gown and tiara, he in the uniform of an admiral. It is a representation each might have found a shade indelicate, vaguely redolent of the marriage bed. Yet in every other way, it is the image both had fought and died for. At their feet, they are guarded by the lion and the unicorn. Above their heads, infant angels now support the weight of both their crowns, the burden lifted at last. Their palms clasped in supplication, May and Georgie pray for a kindly judgement from their God, the appreciation of one deity for another. Frozen together in Valhalla, they lie forever.

But in the dark hours, when all the people are gone, when the candles are snuffed out, when the choristers are tucked up and the last notes of the organ are long lost in the vaulted roof, does something stir in Valhalla? Does a young spirit float defiantly up from the cold heart of the marble? A spirit in a straw hat with red ribbons down her back, spot-lit by moonbeams from the high windows, dancing in and out of the pillars and among the choir stalls, lifting her skirts to show her pretty ankles. Then, by some kindly magic, the moonbeams become shards of sunlight, so dazzling that the ancient walls seem to dissolve beneath their rays, and a landscape of infinite possibility stretches out before the dancing spirit. But it is the illusion of a moment. The sunlight fades as swiftly as it came, the walls rise up again. The spirit sinks back into the marble and Valhalla returns to sleep.

It is the waste that breaks the heart.

Afterword

May and Georgie remained Duke and Duchess of York until the death of Queen Victoria in 1901, then became Prince and Princess of Wales upon the accession of Georgie's parents as King Edward VII and Queen Alexandra. In 1910, they succeeded to the throne as King George V and Queen Mary.

They had six children: the future kings Edward VIII and George VI, the Dukes of Kent and Gloucester, the Princess Mary and the epileptic 'lost' Prince John. In 1919, John died aged only thirteen. In 1942, the Duke of Kent was killed in an air crash. King George VI died in 1952, just over a year before his mother.

King George V died in 1936, aged seventy. His death removed the most restrictive component of Queen Mary's life and World War Two accelerated that liberation. Evacuated to the countryside, she enjoyed more freedom, and much greater connection with 'ordinary' people, than she had known since her youth. Despite the ongoing trauma of the Abdication Crisis, the enthusiasms of her early life, particularly for the arts, reasserted themselves in her final years. She also took a keen interest in the upbringing of her eldest granddaughter, the future Queen Elizabeth II, who so strongly resembles her, not just physically but in her lifelong devotion to duty.

When returning to the capital after the war, an unusually tearful Queen Mary had said, 'Oh I have been happy here. Here

I've been anybody to everybody and back in London I shall have to begin being Queen Mary all over again.'

Perhaps, in that one sentence, May Teck summed up the dilemma of her life.

*

Mary Adelaide, Duchess of Teck, the people's beloved 'Fat Mary', lived just long enough to be cheered by the crowds one last time at the Diamond Jubilee of 1897. She died a few months later at White Lodge of heart failure following an emergency operation. She was granted her heart's desire of being interred in the royal vault at Windsor.

*

Franz, Duke of Teck, deteriorated rapidly after his wife's death. Ultimately, his mental state confined him to White Lodge in the care of male nurses. Even visits from his children distressed him and, when he mercifully died in 1900, none of them had seen him for several months. He was buried beside his wife.

*

Madame Bricka eventually became a tutor to some of Georgie and May's children. Still a close friend of her adored princess, she retired to a flat in Pimlico and died in 1914.

*

Harry Thaddeus Jones, 'Mr Thaddy', eventually rearranged his names to become Harry Jones Thaddeus, a title he felt to be more memorable and by which he is remembered by art scholars today. After his controversial marriage, he was never invited to paint any member of the royal family again, though he continued to be a notable artist. He and his wife emigrated to America for some years before returning to England after World War One, by which time his celebrity had greatly dimmed. Taking to alcohol, he was found dead in 1929 with a bottle of port beside him. Family relations having become strained, neither his wife nor his two sons attended his funeral.

*

Liko, Prince Henry of Battenberg, was buried in Whippingham Church on the Isle of Wight, where he had been married to Princess Beatrice. She lived on until 1944, a widow for even longer than her mother, and was buried beside him. After King George V ordered the anglicisation of the British royal family's Germanic titles during World War One, the name Battenberg was changed to Mountbatten. Liko and Beatrice's daughter Ena became Queen of Spain and is the great-grandmother of the present monarch Felipe VI.

*

The Little Prince, May and Georgie's eldest son, known in the family as David, became King Edward VIII on his father's death in 1936. He abdicated ten months later in order to marry the twice-divorced Wallis Simpson, thereafter becoming the Duke of Windsor. After his mother's funeral in 1953, a lunch was held for family members. He was not invited. He died of throat cancer in Paris in 1972. His wife lingered on till 1986, bedridden and befuddled in her final years. They now lie together at Windsor, though not among the monarchs in St George's Chapel, but merely in the burial ground for lesser royalty at Frogmore. A measure of forgiveness at last, but Valhalla still firmly denied.

Author's Note

First and foremost, this book is simply about one young woman and how she eventually became one of the most famous figures of the twentieth century. However, the figure of May of Teck still holds striking relevance today; although she eventually had a crown on her head and an existence of spectacular privilege, her tale is a memorable example of the crushing dominance of patriarchy.

As with my earlier novel *The Prince of Mirrors*, this book is a work of both fiction and fact and while dramatic licence has obviously been taken, the characters, events, dates and places presented are, as closely as possible, based on historical and biographical records.

Acknowledgements

Much of the research for my previous book *The Prince Of Mirrors* has also been utilised in this 'companion' novel, so I thank again here the individuals, libraries and other archival sources who advised and assisted me back then. For *Valhalla* specifically, I'm indebted to the following:

To the author Hugo Vickers for his generosity in allowing me to use the information about a possible attachment between May and Liko, first revealed in his book *The Quest for Queen Mary*.

To Anna Meadmore of The Royal Ballet School at White Lodge, Richmond Park for her time and trouble in giving me an exhaustive tour of Princess May's family home – and to Lady Anya Sainsbury for making it possible.

To my wise and wonderful agent Peter Buckman who first suggested I should pick up the tale of Prince Eddy's dramatically bereaved fiancée.

Again last, but certainly not least, to the team at my publisher Fairlight Books with whom it has once more been a great pleasure to work: Louise Boland, Urška Vidoni, Lindsey Woollard, Mo Fillmore, Laura Shanahan and Bradley Thomas. Also to the editor Saxon Bullock for his invaluable and painstaking contribution and to Emma Rogers for designing a beautiful cover.

Select Bibliography

For any reader interested in knowing more about Princess May of Teck, two volumes stand out. Firstly, *Queen Mary* (George Allen & Unwin 1959), the authorised biography by James Pope-Hennessy and as yet unsurpassed. Secondly, *The Quest for Queen Mary* (Zuleika 2018), Hugo Vickers' riveting and often highly amusing disclosure of the material that Pope-Hennessy was unable to publish sixty years ago.

Other excellent books which feature the principal characters in *Valhalla* include:

A Memoir Of Princess Mary Adelaide, Duchess of Teck (two volumes), Clement Kinloch Cooke (re-published by Forgotten Books 2012)

The Life and Work of Harry Jones Thaddeus, Brendan Rooney (Four Courts Press 2003)

King George V, Harold Nicolson (Constable 1952)

Bertie, a Life of Edward VII, Jane Ridley (Chatto & Windus 2012)

Life With Queen Victoria: Marie Mallet's letters from Court (John Murray 1968)

Prince Eddy, Andrew Cook (History Press 2008)

King Edward VIII, Philip Ziegler (William Collins 1990)

The Last Princess, Matthew Dennison. Biography of Princess Beatrice. (Weidenfeld & Nicolson 2007, re-published 2019)

Fairlight Books

ALAN ROBERT CLARK

The Prince of Mirrors

Two young men with expectations.
One predicted to succeed, the other to fail...

Prince Albert Victor, heir presumptive to the British throne, is seen as disastrously inadequate to be king. The grandson of Queen Victoria, he is good-hearted but intensely shy and, some whisper, even slow-witted.

By contrast, Jem Stephen is a renowned intellectual, poet and golden boy worshipped by all. But a looming curse of mental instability is threatening to take it all away.

Appointed as the prince's personal tutor, Jem works to prepare him for the duty to come. A friendship grows between them – one that will allow them to understand and finally accept who they really are and change both of their lives forever.

'Touching and compelling – a beautifully written re-imagining of the story of Prince Eddy, perhaps Britain's most mysterious and intriguing 'lost' king.'
— Gyles Brandreth, author and TV personality